HILO
RISE OF THE CAT

BY JUDD WINICK

COLOR BY MAARTA LAIHO

RANDOM HOUSE 🏠 NEW YORK

Published in the United States by Random House Children's Books, a division of Penguin Random House LLC, New York.

Random House and the colophon are registered trademarks of Penguin Random House LLC.

RH Graphic with the book design is a trademark of Penguin Random House LLC.

Visit us on the Web! rhcbooks.com

Educators and librarians, for a variety of teaching tools, visit us at RHTeachersLibrarians.com

Library of Congress Cataloging-in-Publication Data
Names: Winick, Judd, author. | Laiho, Maarta, colorist.
Title: Hilo. Book 10, Rise of the cat / by Judd Winick; color by Maarta Laiho.
Description: First edition. | New York: Random House Children's Books, [2024] | Series: Hilo; book 10 | Audience: Ages 8–12. | Summary: "Hilo's friends Polly the warrior cat and her brother Pip are sent to a magical boarding school for bad kids"—Provided by publisher.
Identifiers: LCCN 2022050851 (print) | LCCN 2022050852 (ebook) | ISBN 978-0-593-48814-0 (library binding) | ISBN 978-0-593-48812-6 (hardcover) | ISBN 978-0-593-48813-3 (ebook)
Subjects: CYAC: Graphic novels. | Magic—Fiction. | Boarding schools—Fiction. | Schools—Fiction. | Cats—Fiction. | Fantasy. | LCGFT: Fantasy comics. | Graphic novels.
Classification: LCC PZ7.7.W57 Hr 2022 (print) | LCC PZ7.7.W57 (ebook) | DDC 741.5/973—dc23/eng/20230227

The artist used digital medium to create the illustrations for this book.
The text of this book is set in 11-point ImaginaryFriend BB.

Editor: Shana Corey
Designer: Juliet Goodman
Copy Editor: Melinda Ackell
Managing Editor: Katy Miller
Production Manager: Jen Jie Li

MANUFACTURED IN CHINA

10 9 8 7 6 5 4 3 2 1

First Edition

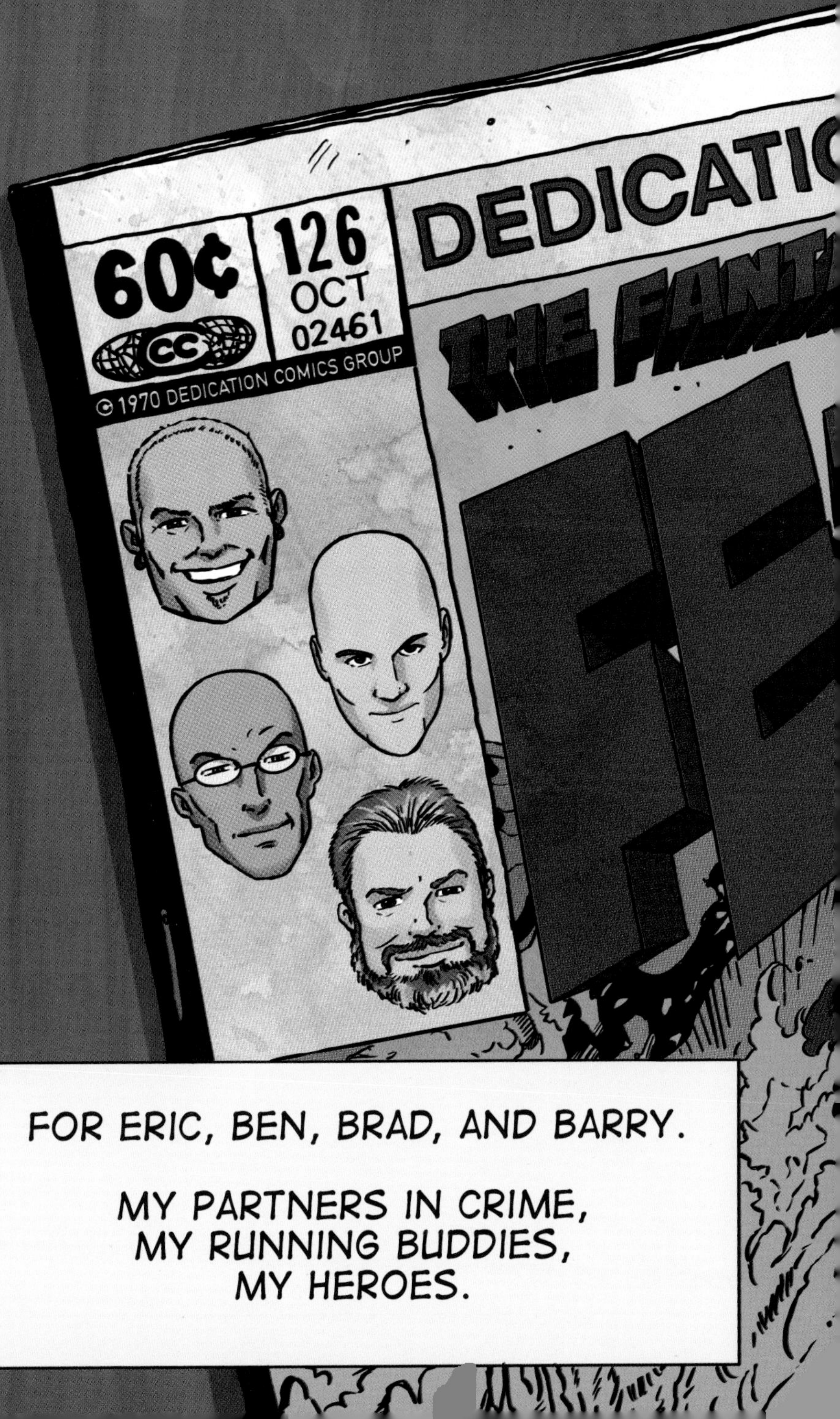
60¢
126
OCT
02461
CC
© 1970 DEDICATION COMICS GROUP

FOR ERIC, BEN, BRAD, AND BARRY.

MY PARTNERS IN CRIME,
MY RUNNING BUDDIES,
MY HEROES.

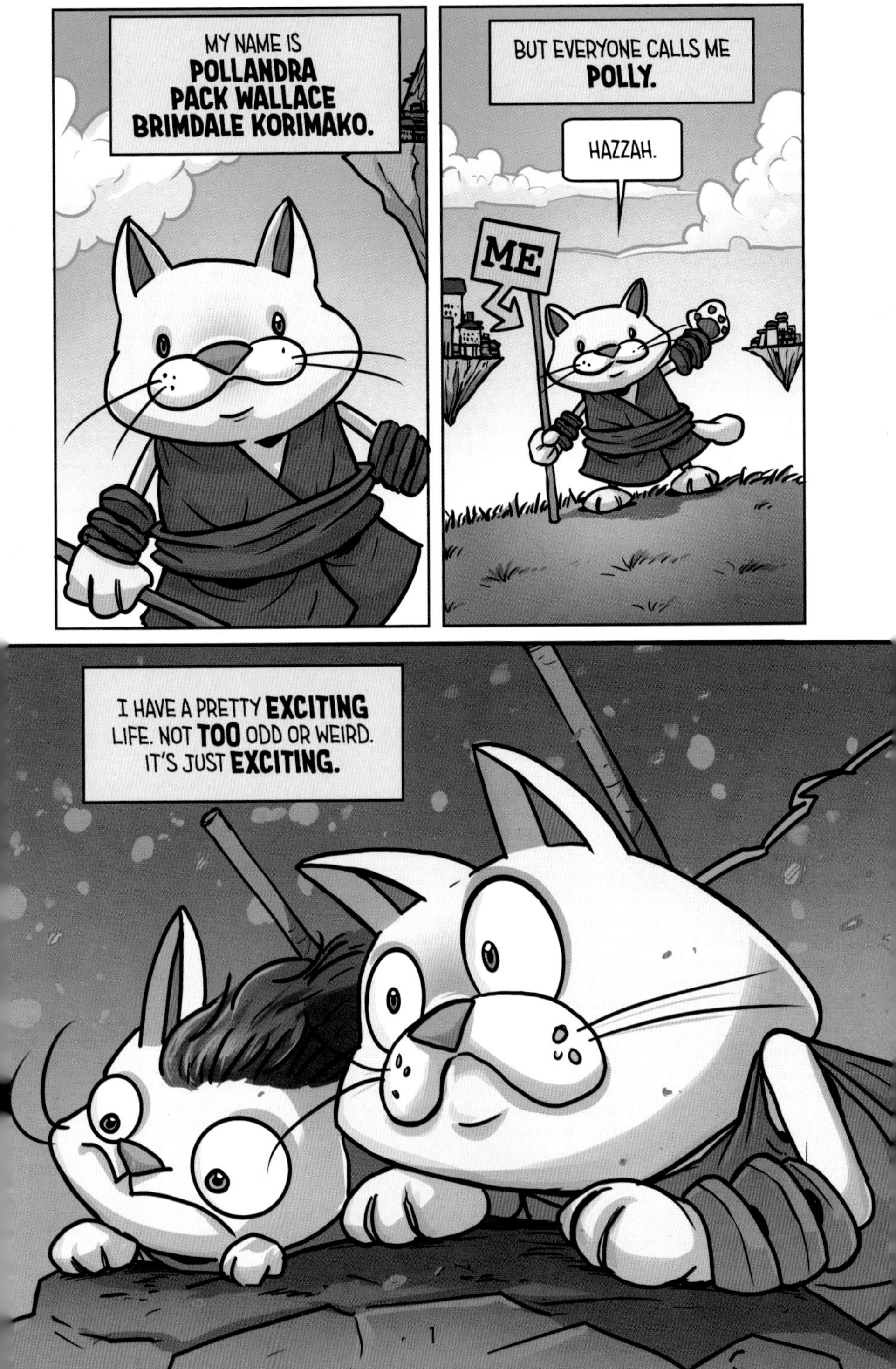
MY NAME IS **POLLANDRA PACK WALLACE BRIMDALE KORIMAKO.**
BUT EVERYONE CALLS ME **POLLY.**
ME
HAZZAH.
I HAVE A PRETTY **EXCITING** LIFE. NOT **TOO** ODD OR WEIRD. IT'S JUST **EXCITING.**

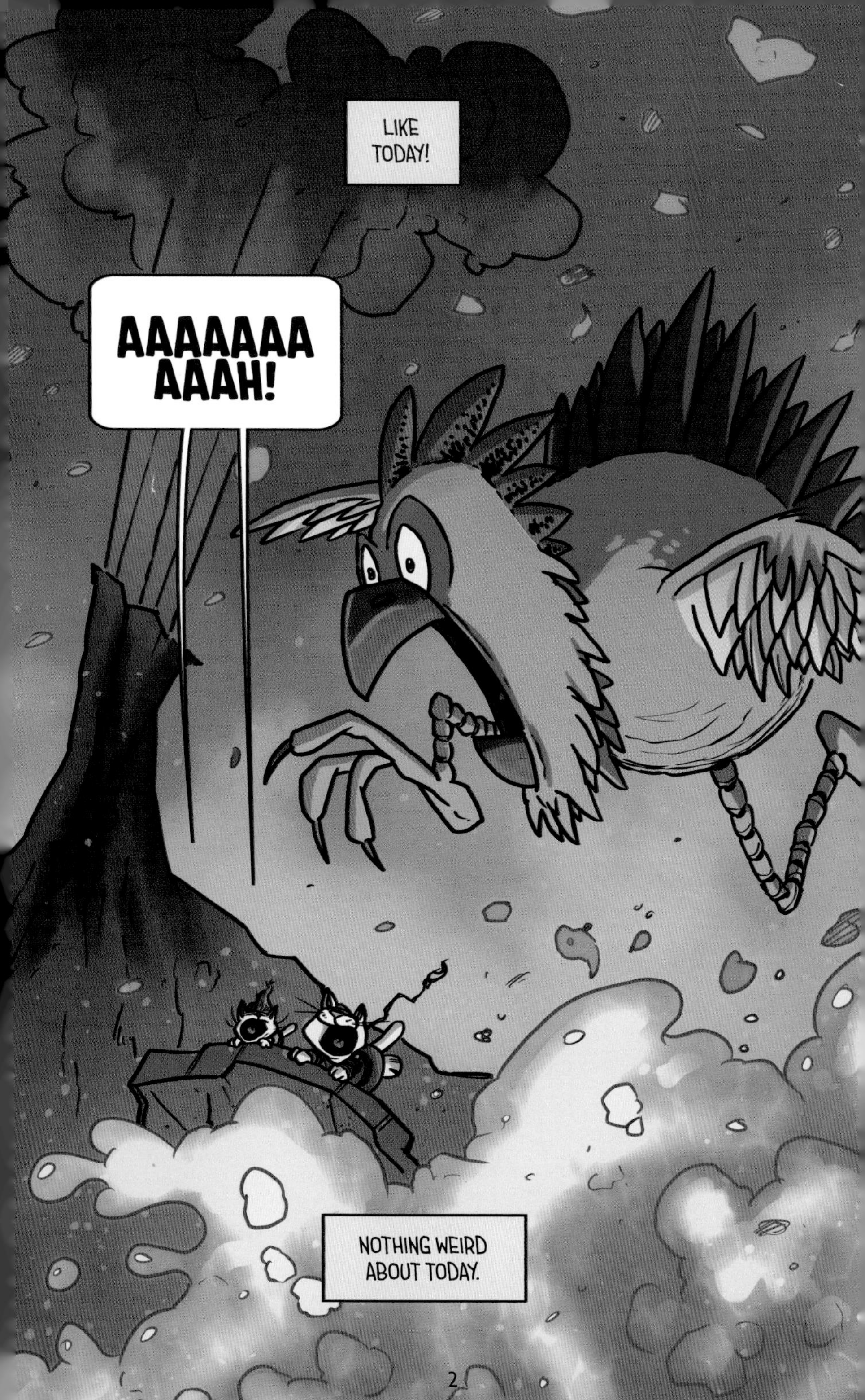
LIKE TODAY!
AAAAAAA AAAH!
NOTHING WEIRD ABOUT TODAY.

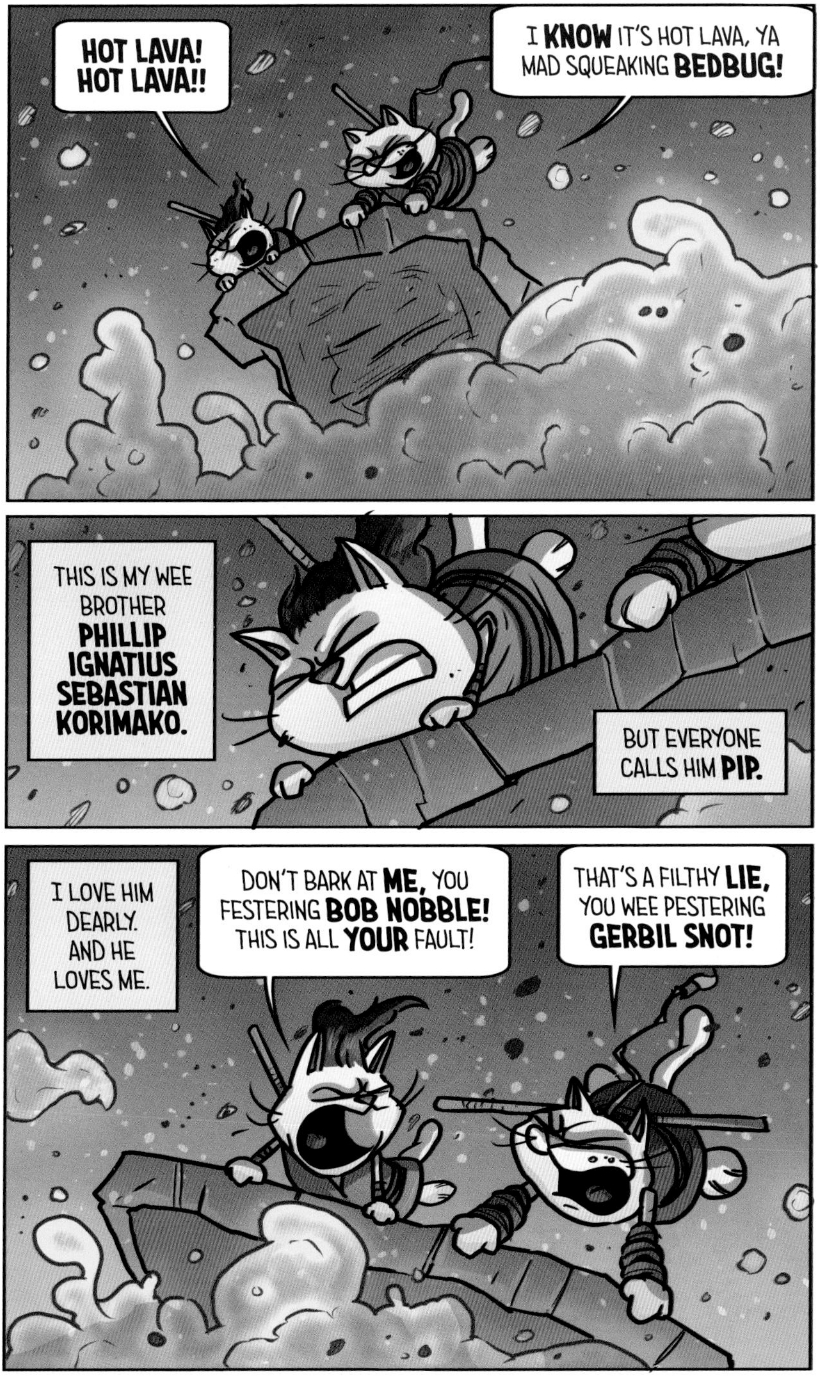
HOT LAVA! HOT LAVA!!
I KNOW IT'S HOT LAVA, YA MAD SQUEAKING BEDBUG!
THIS IS MY WEE BROTHER PHILLIP IGNATIUS SEBASTIAN KORIMAKO.
BUT EVERYONE CALLS HIM PIP.
I LOVE HIM DEARLY. AND HE LOVES ME.
DON'T BARK AT ME, YOU FESTERING BOB NOBBLE! THIS IS ALL YOUR FAULT!
THAT'S A FILTHY LIE, YOU WEE PESTERING GERBIL SNOT!

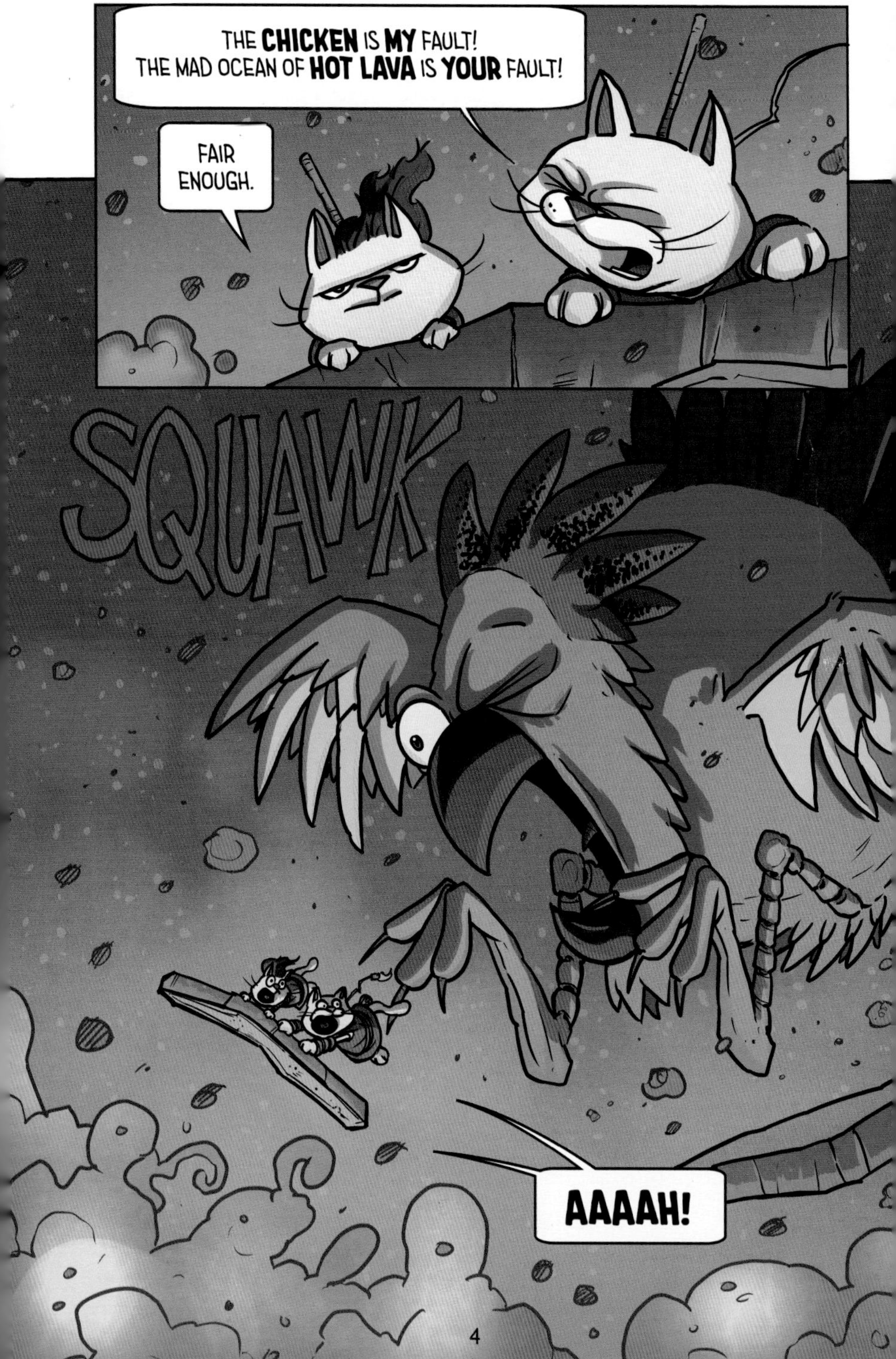

THE CHICKEN IS MY FAULT! THE MAD OCEAN OF HOT LAVA IS YOUR FAULT!
FAIR ENOUGH.
SQUAWK
AAAAH!

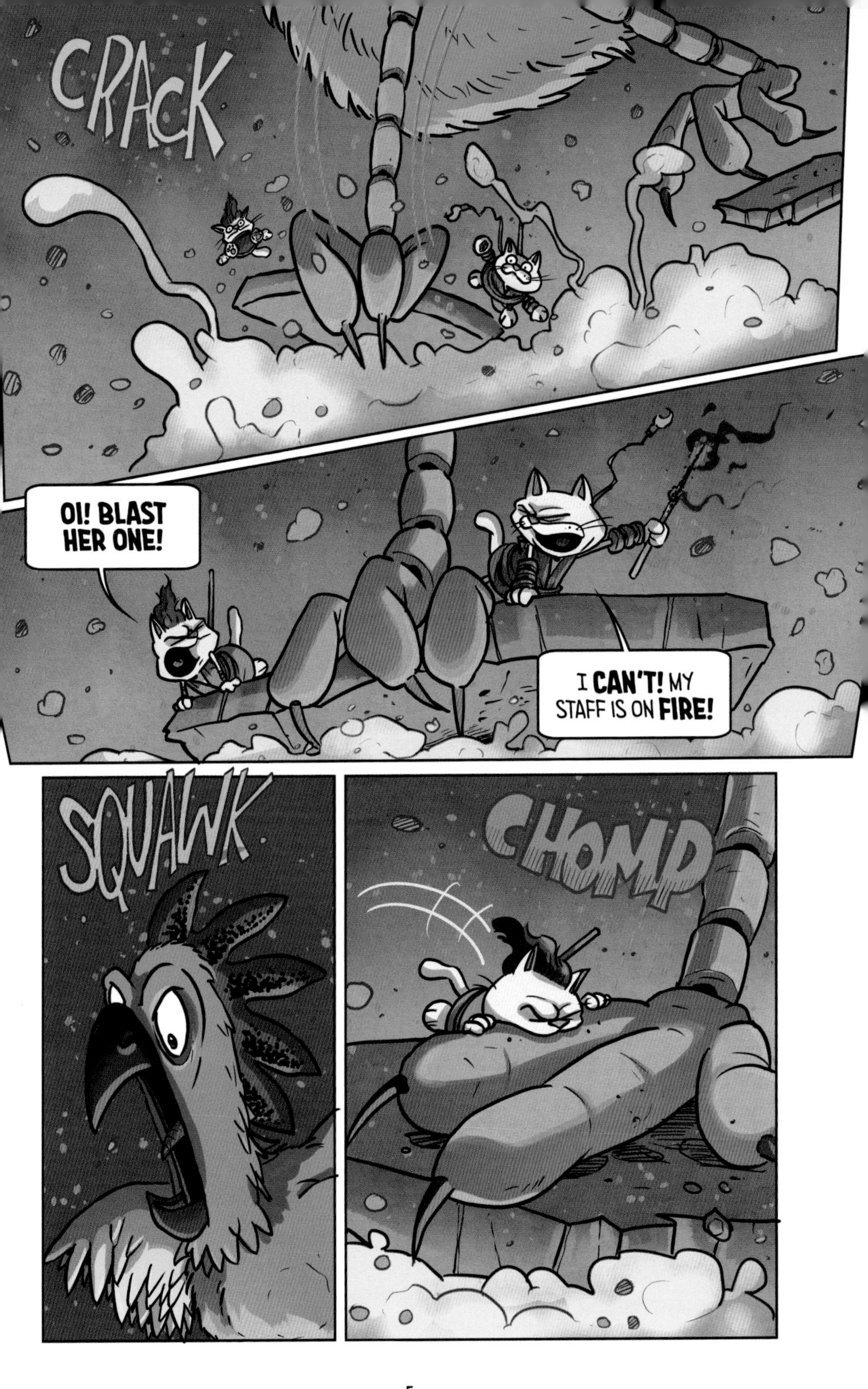
CRACK
OI! BLAST HER ONE!
I CAN'T! MY STAFF IS ON FIRE!
SQUAWK
CHOMP

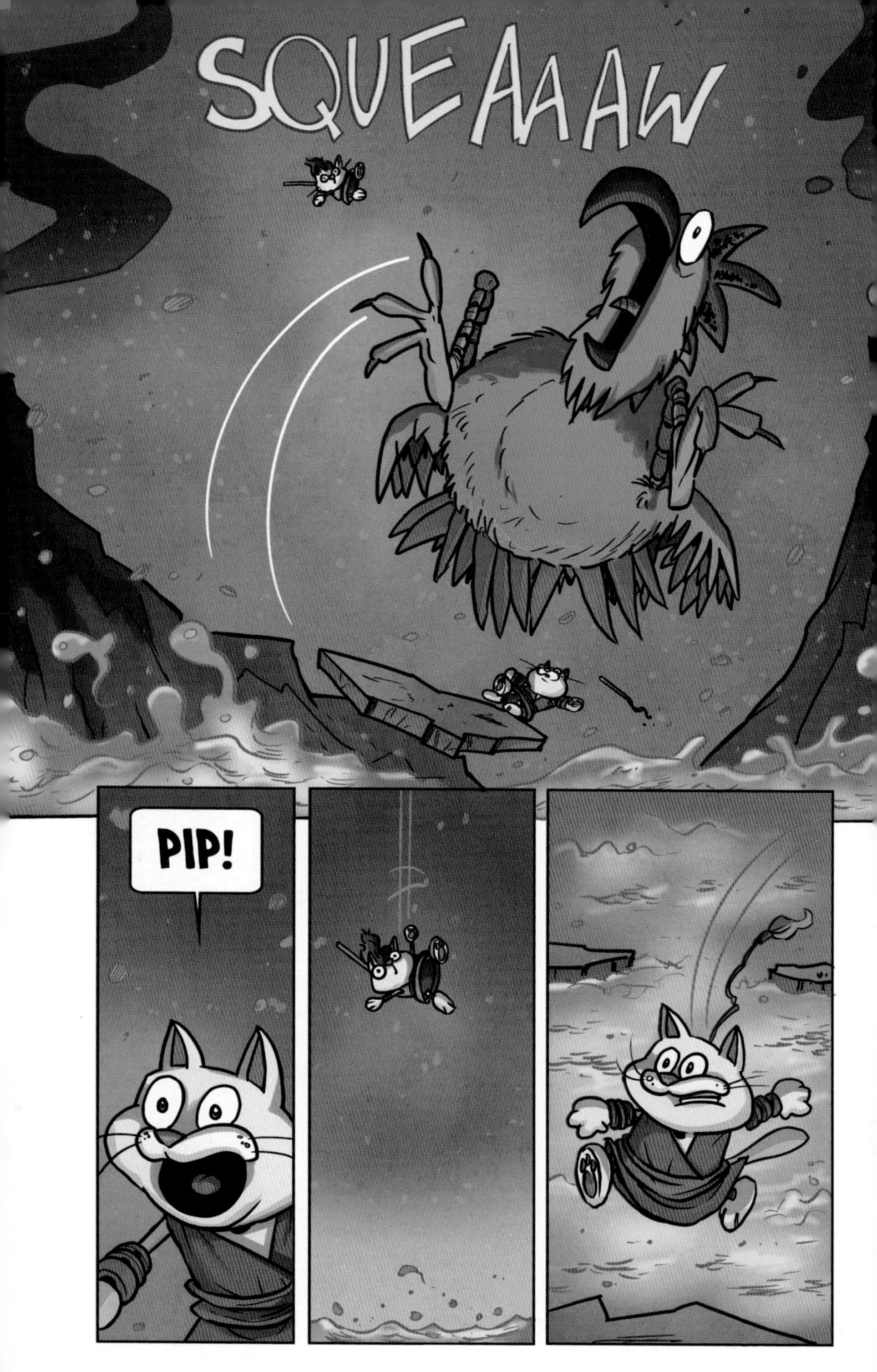
SQUEAAAW
PIP!

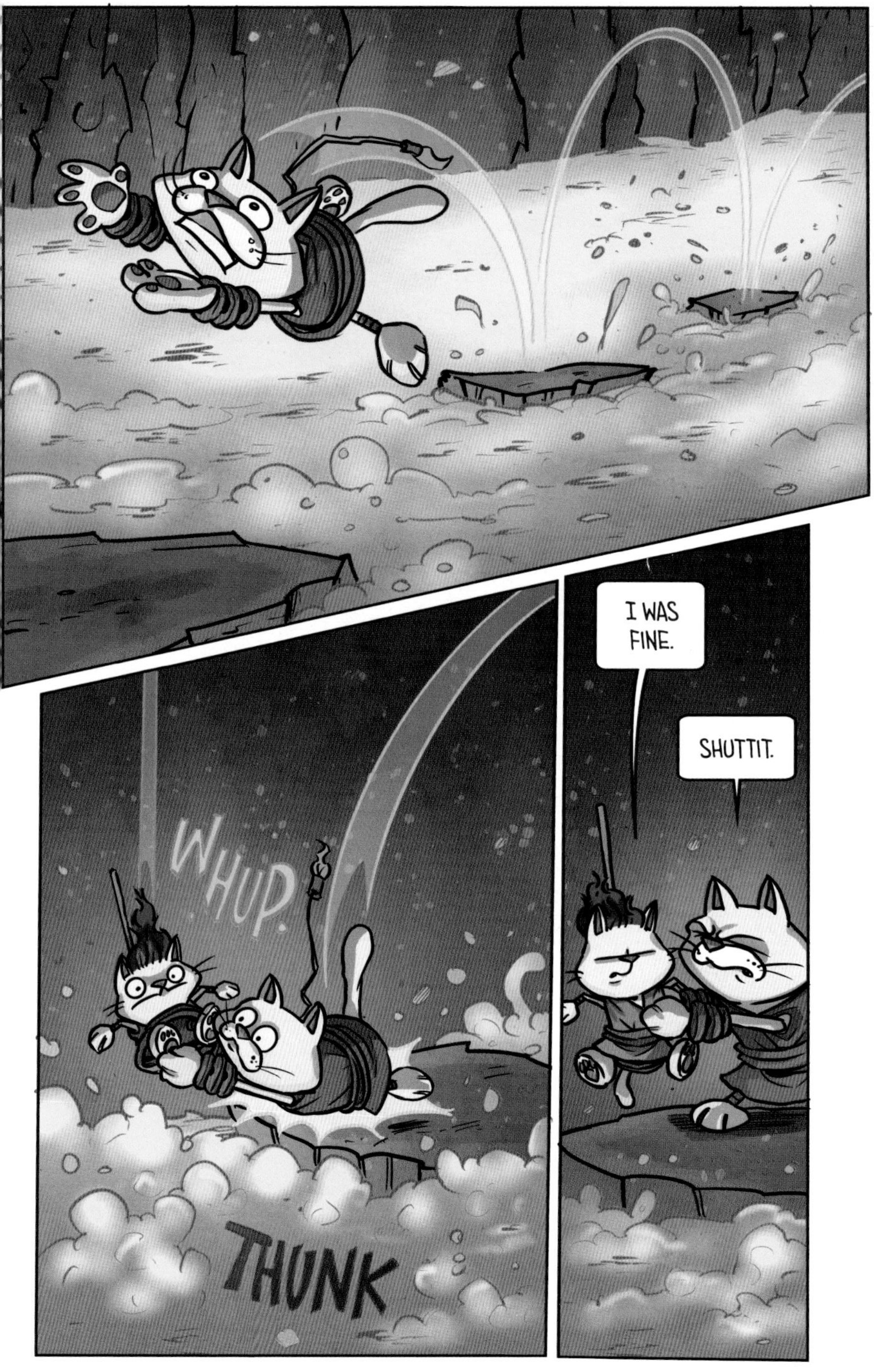
WHUP
THUNK
I WAS FINE.
SHUTTIT.

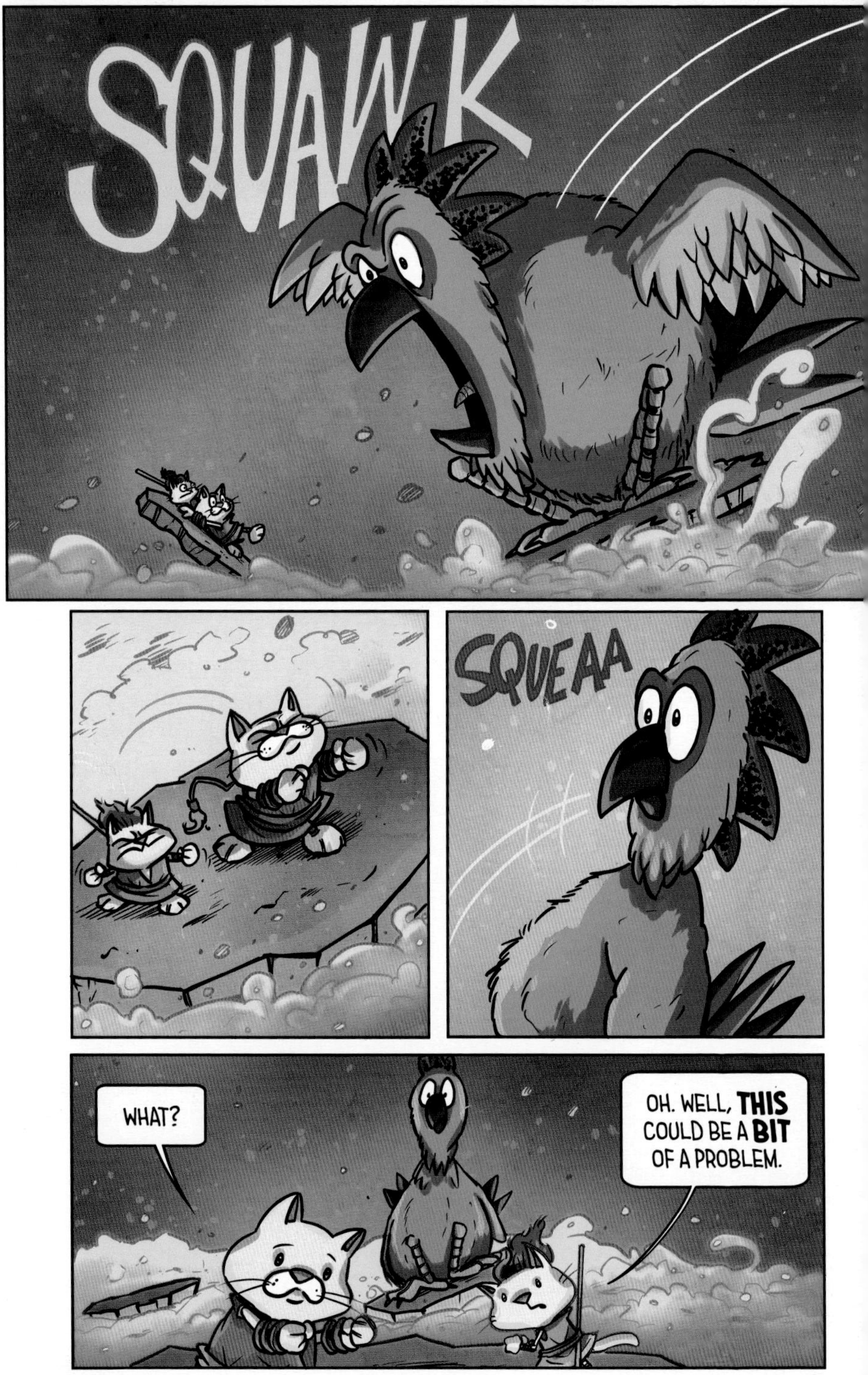
SQUAWK
SQUEAA
WHAT?
OH. WELL, **THIS** COULD BE A **BIT** OF A PROBLEM.

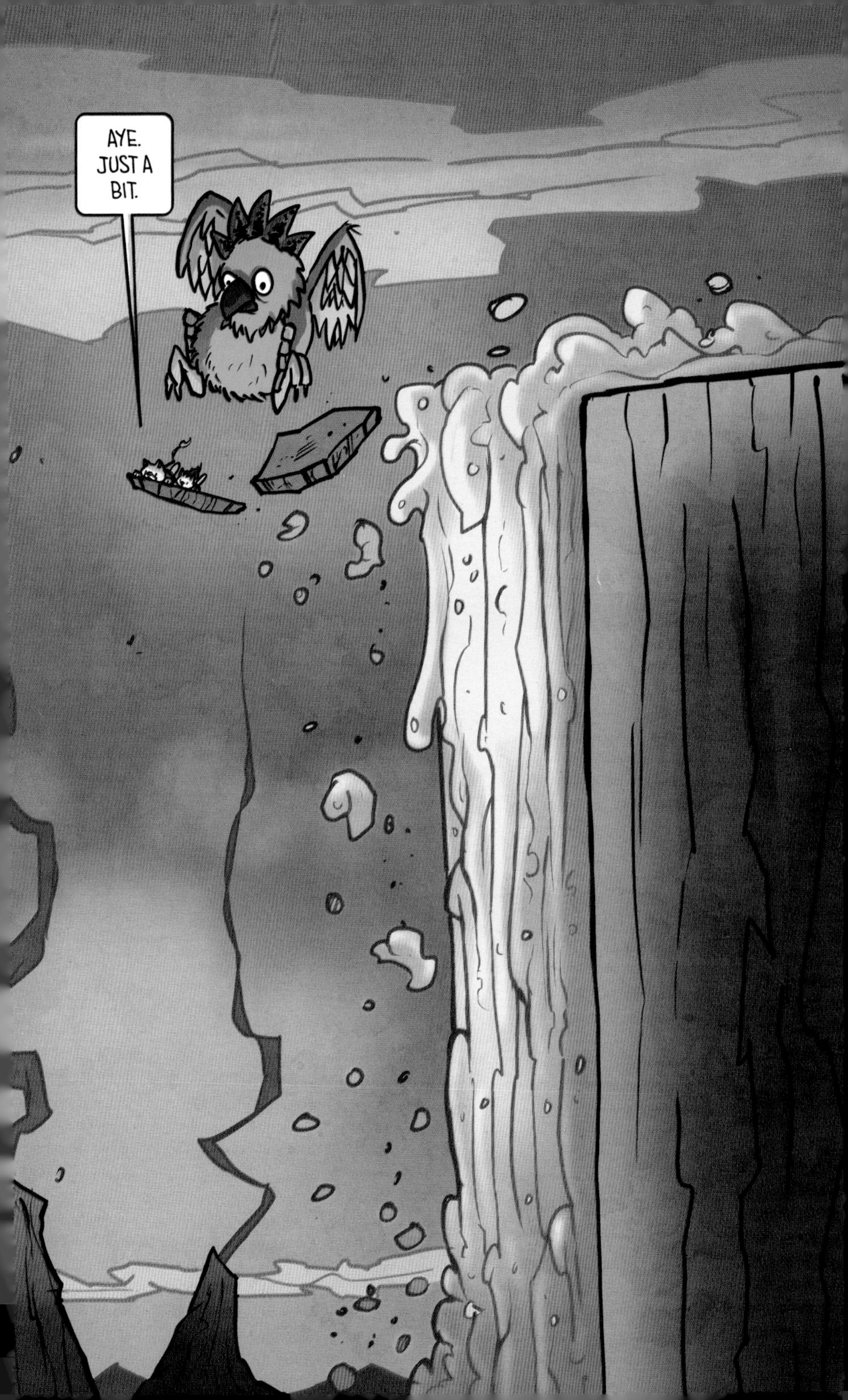
AYE. JUST A BIT.

CHAPTER

THE BEST

THREE WEEKS EARLIER.

THE PLANET OF **OSHUN.** A WORLD OF MAGIC.

THE VILLAGE OF **THE FURBACK CLAN.**

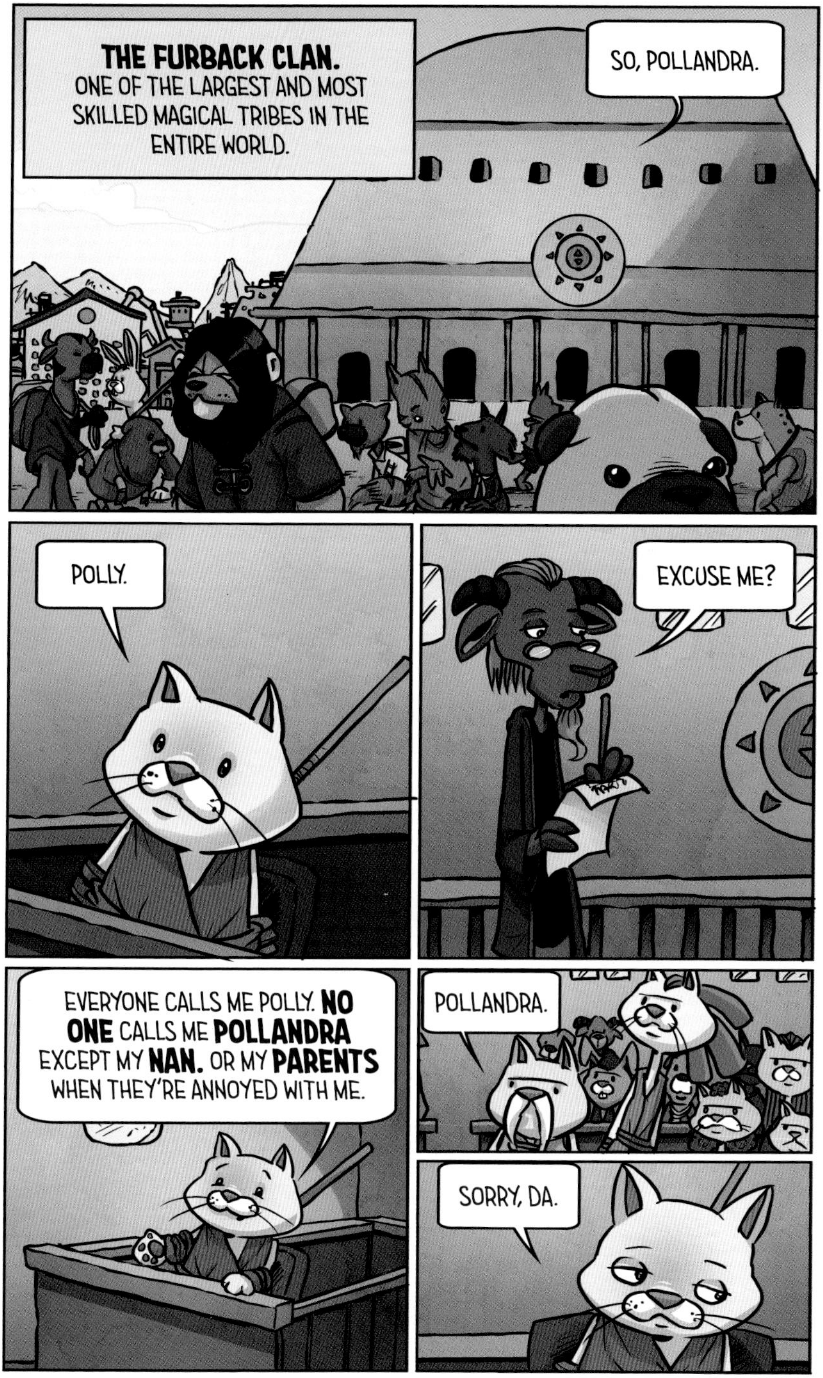
THE FURBACK CLAN.
ONE OF THE LARGEST AND MOST SKILLED MAGICAL TRIBES IN THE ENTIRE WORLD.
SO, POLLANDRA.
POLLY.
EXCUSE ME?
EVERYONE CALLS ME POLLY. **NO ONE** CALLS ME **POLLANDRA** EXCEPT MY **NAN.** OR MY **PARENTS** WHEN THEY'RE ANNOYED WITH ME.
POLLANDRA.
SORRY, DA.

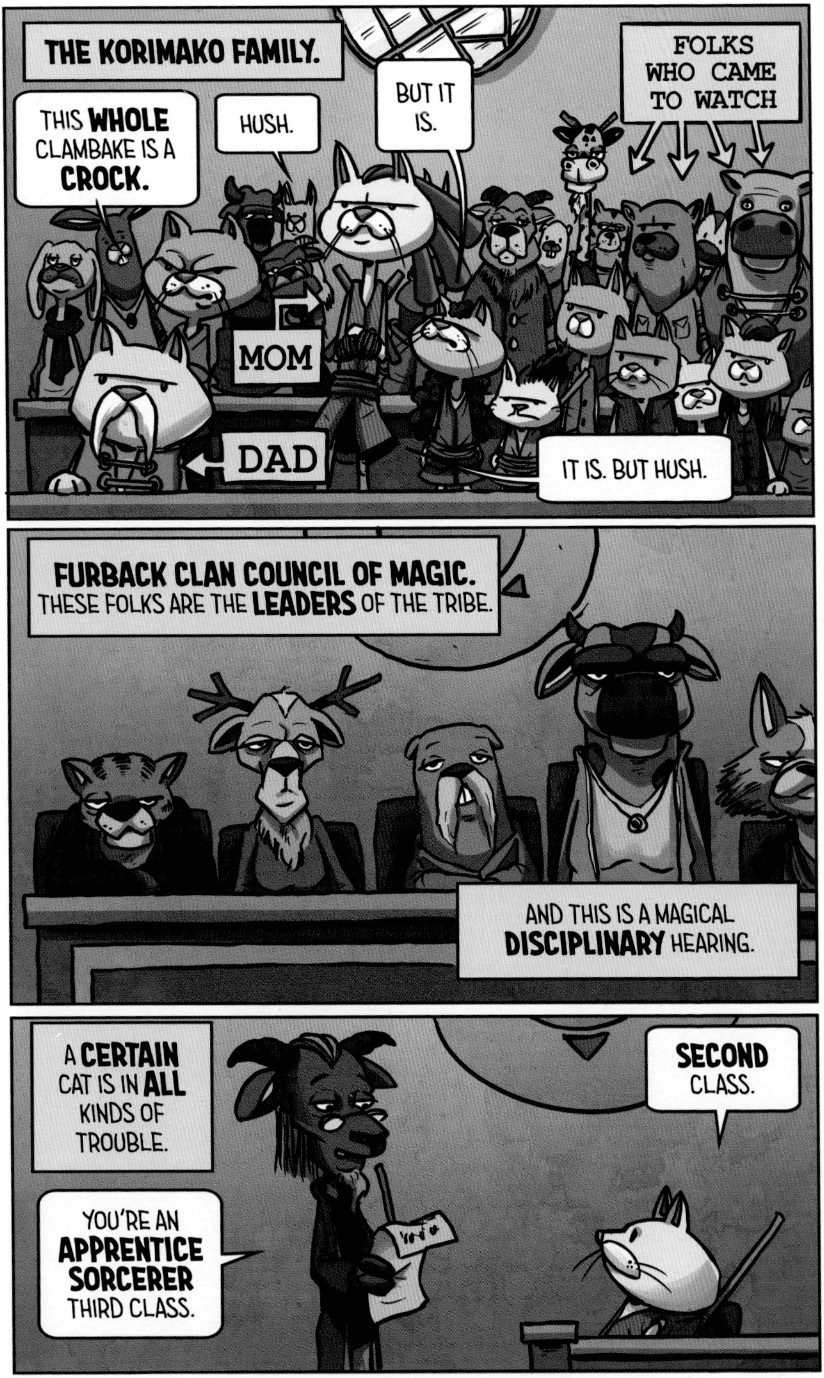
THE KORIMAKO FAMILY.
THIS WHOLE CLAMBAKE IS A CROCK.
HUSH.
BUT IT IS.
FOLKS WHO CAME TO WATCH
MOM
DAD
IT IS. BUT HUSH.
FURBACK CLAN COUNCIL OF MAGIC. THESE FOLKS ARE THE LEADERS OF THE TRIBE.
AND THIS IS A MAGICAL DISCIPLINARY HEARING.
A CERTAIN CAT IS IN ALL KINDS OF TROUBLE.
SECOND CLASS.
YOU'RE AN APPRENTICE SORCERER THIRD CLASS.

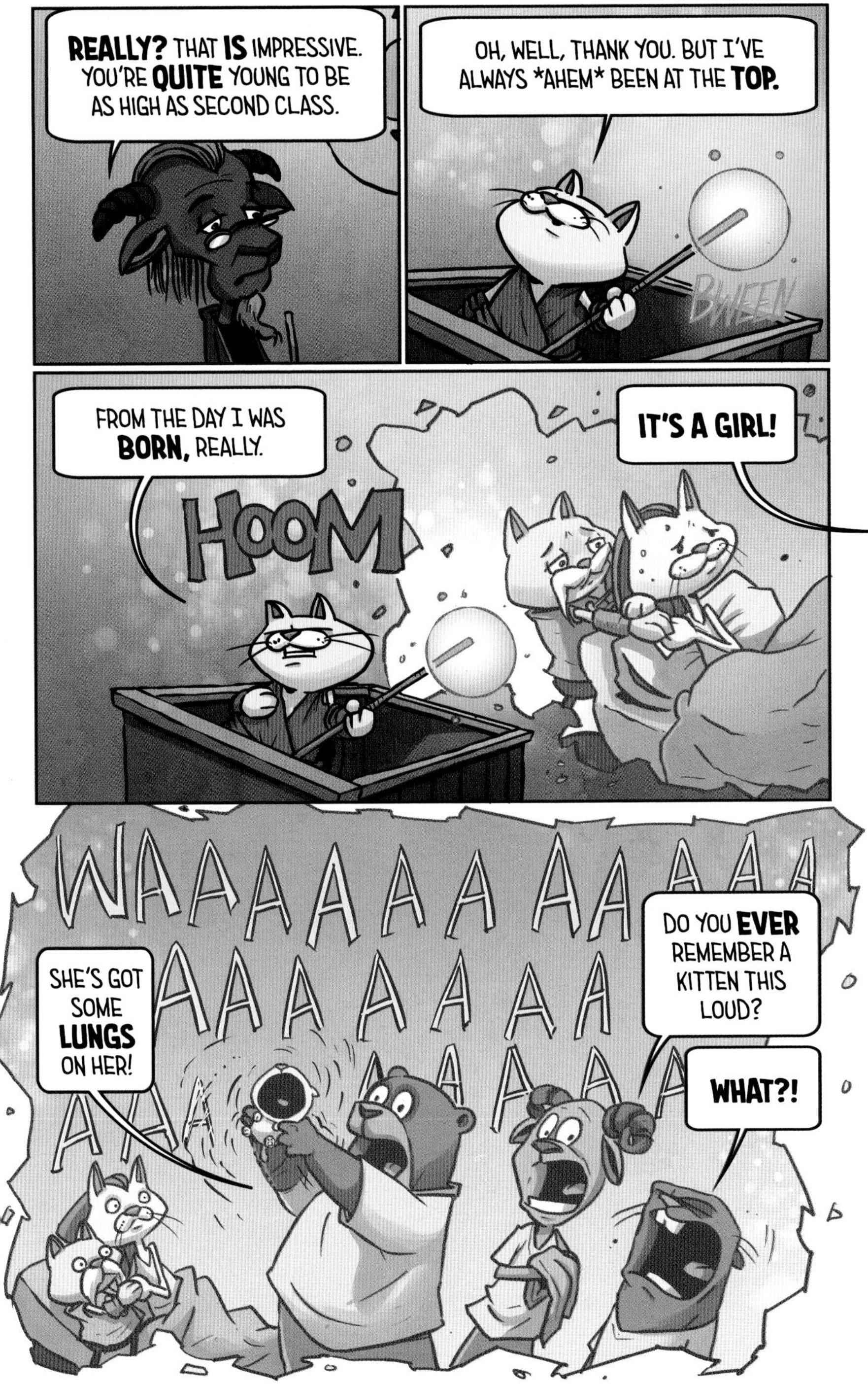
REALLY? THAT IS IMPRESSIVE. YOU'RE QUITE YOUNG TO BE AS HIGH AS SECOND CLASS.
OH, WELL, THANK YOU. BUT I'VE ALWAYS *AHEM* BEEN AT THE TOP.
BWEEN
FROM THE DAY I WAS BORN, REALLY.
HOOM
IT'S A GIRL!
WAAAAAAAAAAAAAAAAAAAAAAAAAAA
SHE'S GOT SOME LUNGS ON HER!
DO YOU EVER REMEMBER A KITTEN THIS LOUD?
WHAT?!

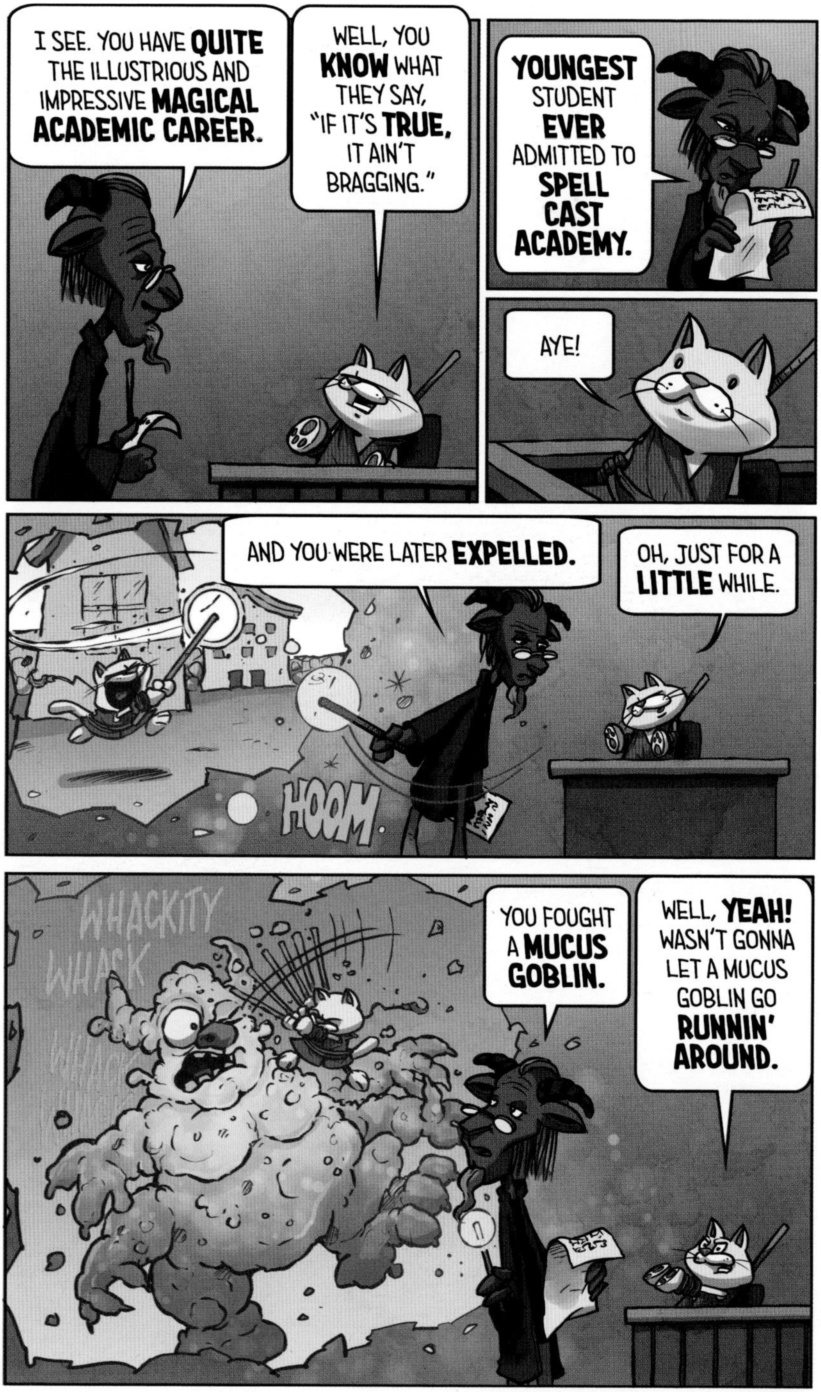
I SEE. YOU HAVE QUITE THE ILLUSTRIOUS AND IMPRESSIVE MAGICAL ACADEMIC CAREER.
WELL, YOU KNOW WHAT THEY SAY, "IF IT'S TRUE, IT AIN'T BRAGGING."
YOUNGEST STUDENT EVER ADMITTED TO SPELL CAST ACADEMY.
AYE!
AND YOU WERE LATER EXPELLED.
OH, JUST FOR A LITTLE WHILE.
HOOM
WHACKITY
YOU FOUGHT A MUCUS GOBLIN.
WELL, YEAH! WASN'T GONNA LET A MUCUS GOBLIN GO RUNNIN' AROUND.

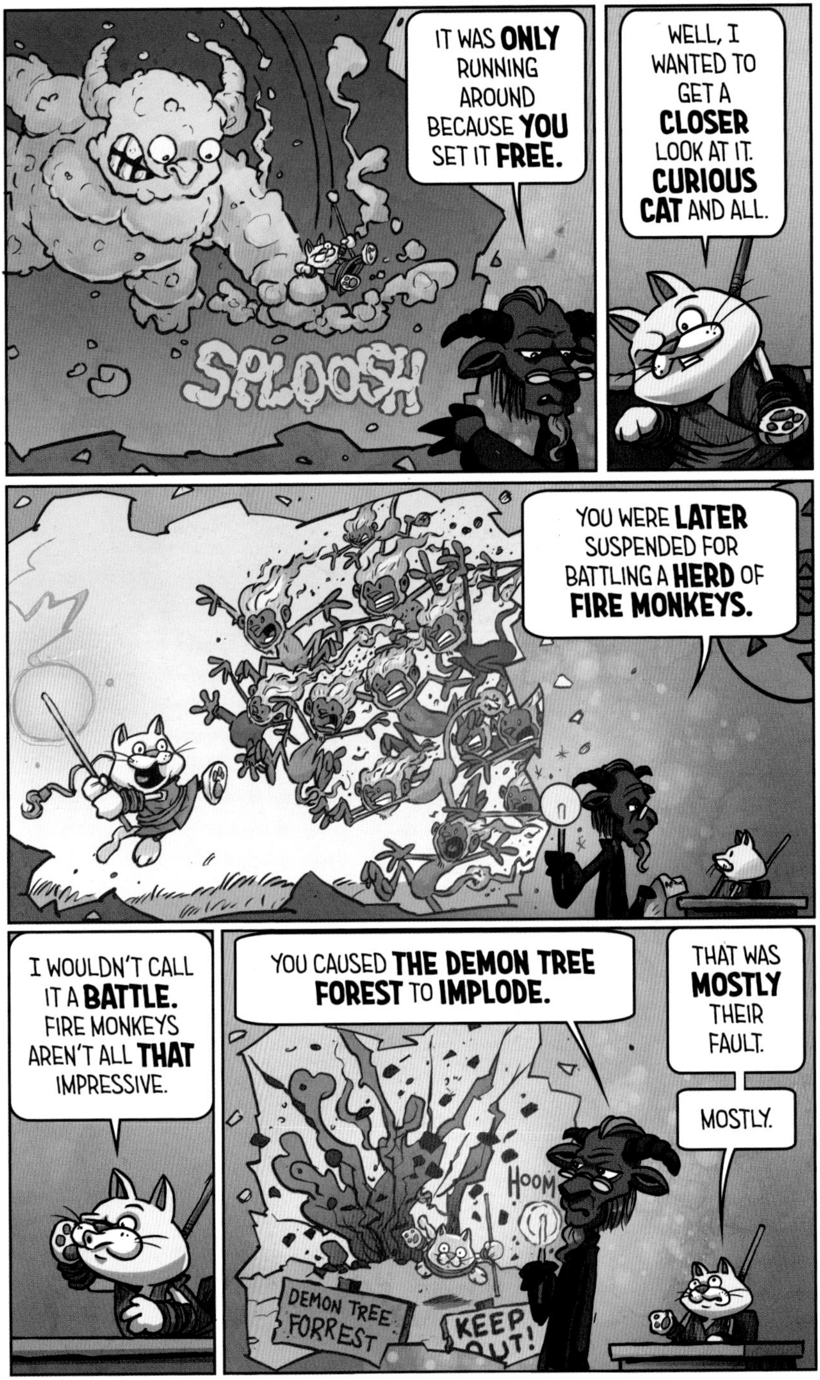
SPLOOSH
IT WAS ONLY RUNNING AROUND BECAUSE YOU SET IT FREE.
WELL, I WANTED TO GET A CLOSER LOOK AT IT. CURIOUS CAT AND ALL.
YOU WERE LATER SUSPENDED FOR BATTLING A HERD OF FIRE MONKEYS.
I WOULDN'T CALL IT A BATTLE. FIRE MONKEYS AREN'T ALL THAT IMPRESSIVE.
YOU CAUSED THE DEMON TREE FOREST TO IMPLODE.
HOOM
DEMON TREE FORREST
KEEP
THAT WAS MOSTLY THEIR FAULT.
MOSTLY.

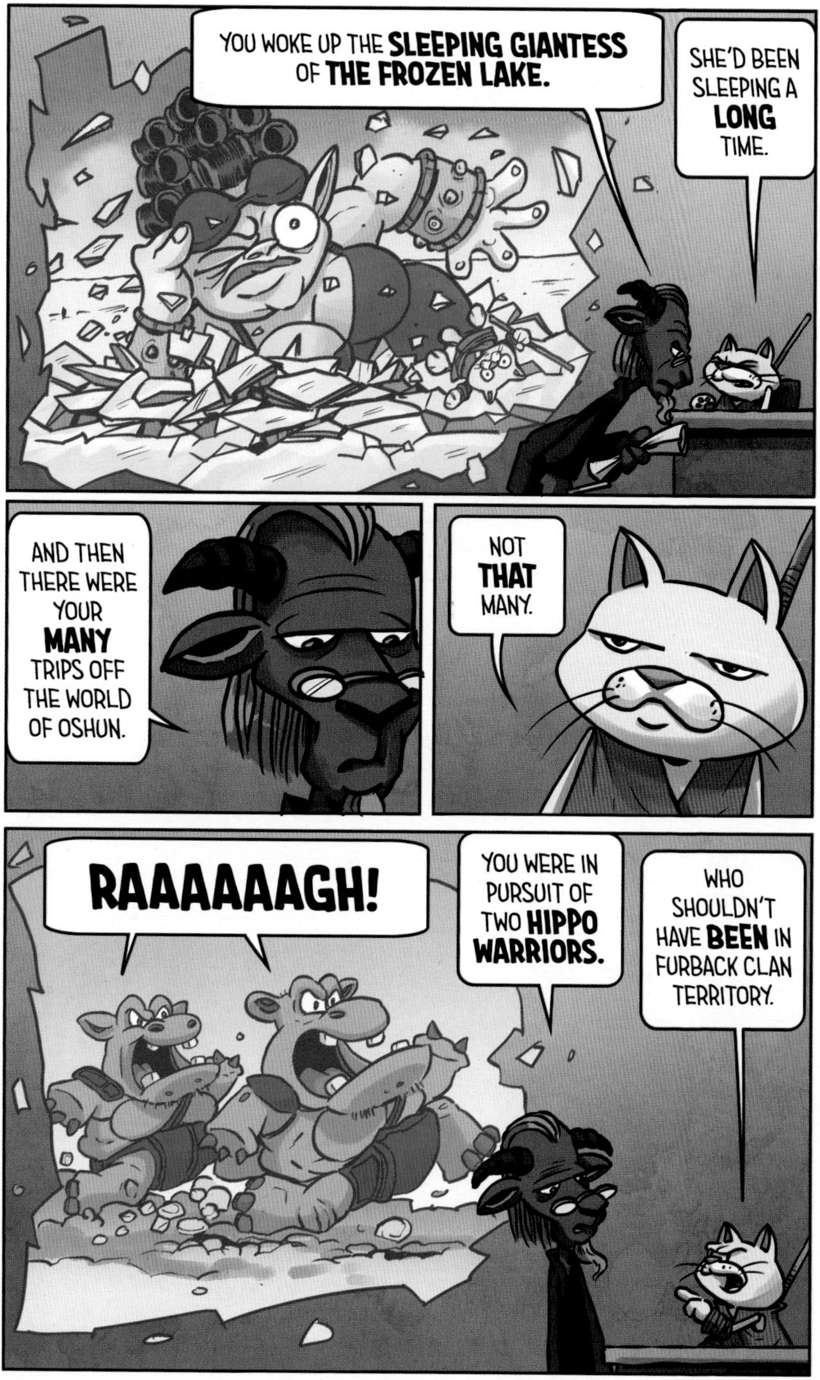
YOU WOKE UP THE **SLEEPING GIANTESS** OF **THE FROZEN LAKE.**
SHE'D BEEN SLEEPING A **LONG** TIME.
AND THEN THERE WERE YOUR **MANY** TRIPS OFF THE WORLD OF OSHUN.
NOT **THAT** MANY.
RAAAAAAAGH!
YOU WERE IN PURSUIT OF TWO **HIPPO WARRIORS.**
WHO SHOULDN'T HAVE **BEEN** IN FURBACK CLAN TERRITORY.

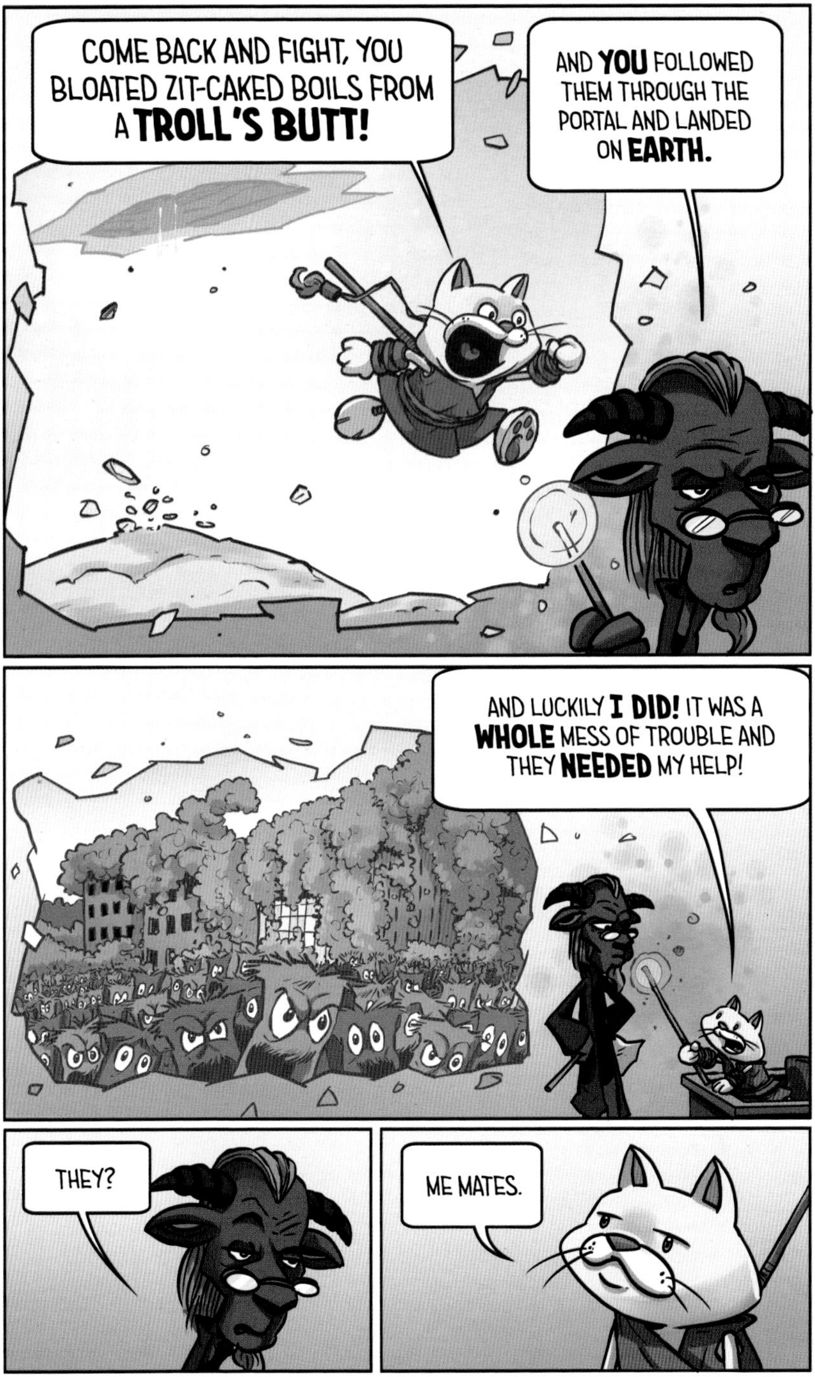
COME BACK AND FIGHT, YOU BLOATED ZIT-CAKED BOILS FROM A TROLL'S BUTT!
AND YOU FOLLOWED THEM THROUGH THE PORTAL AND LANDED ON EARTH.
AND LUCKILY I DID! IT WAS A WHOLE MESS OF TROUBLE AND THEY NEEDED MY HELP!
THEY?
ME MATES.

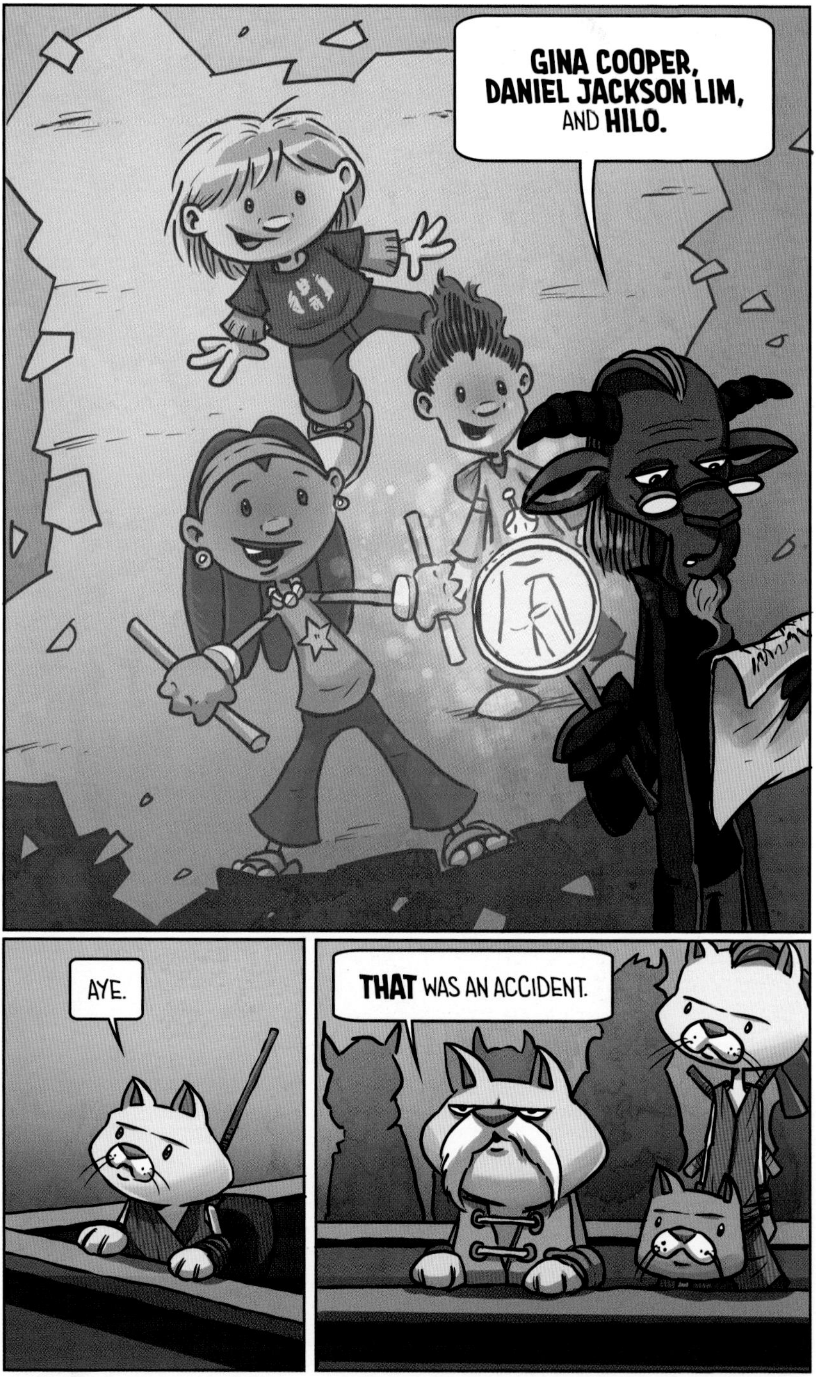
GINA COOPER,
DANIEL JACKSON LIM,
AND HILO.
AYE.
THAT WAS AN ACCIDENT.

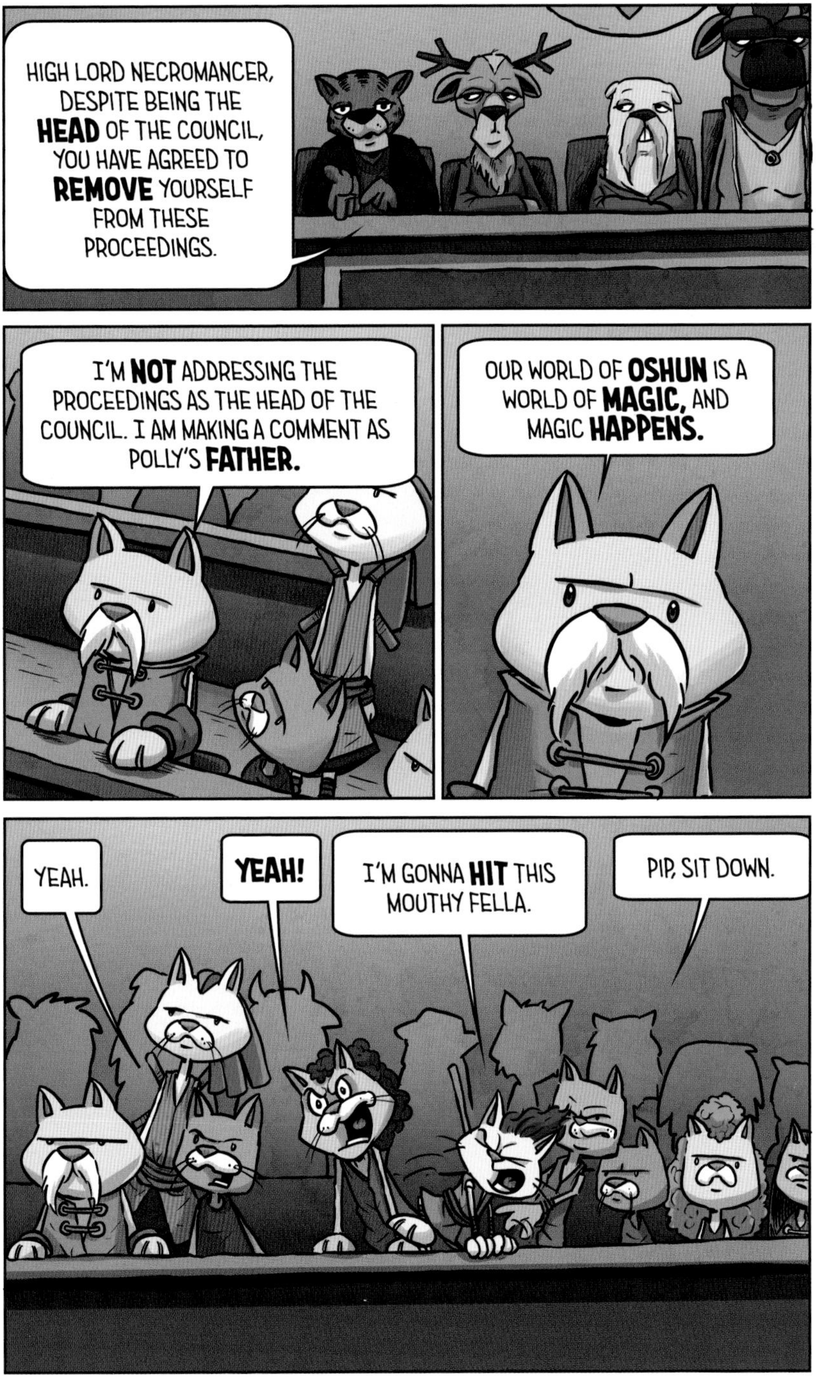

HIGH LORD NECROMANCER, DESPITE BEING THE **HEAD** OF THE COUNCIL, YOU HAVE AGREED TO **REMOVE** YOURSELF FROM THESE PROCEEDINGS.
I'M **NOT** ADDRESSING THE PROCEEDINGS AS THE HEAD OF THE COUNCIL. I AM MAKING A COMMENT AS POLLY'S **FATHER.**
OUR WORLD OF **OSHUN** IS A WORLD OF **MAGIC,** AND MAGIC **HAPPENS.**
YEAH.
YEAH!
I'M GONNA **HIT** THIS MOUTHY FELLA.
PIP, SIT DOWN.

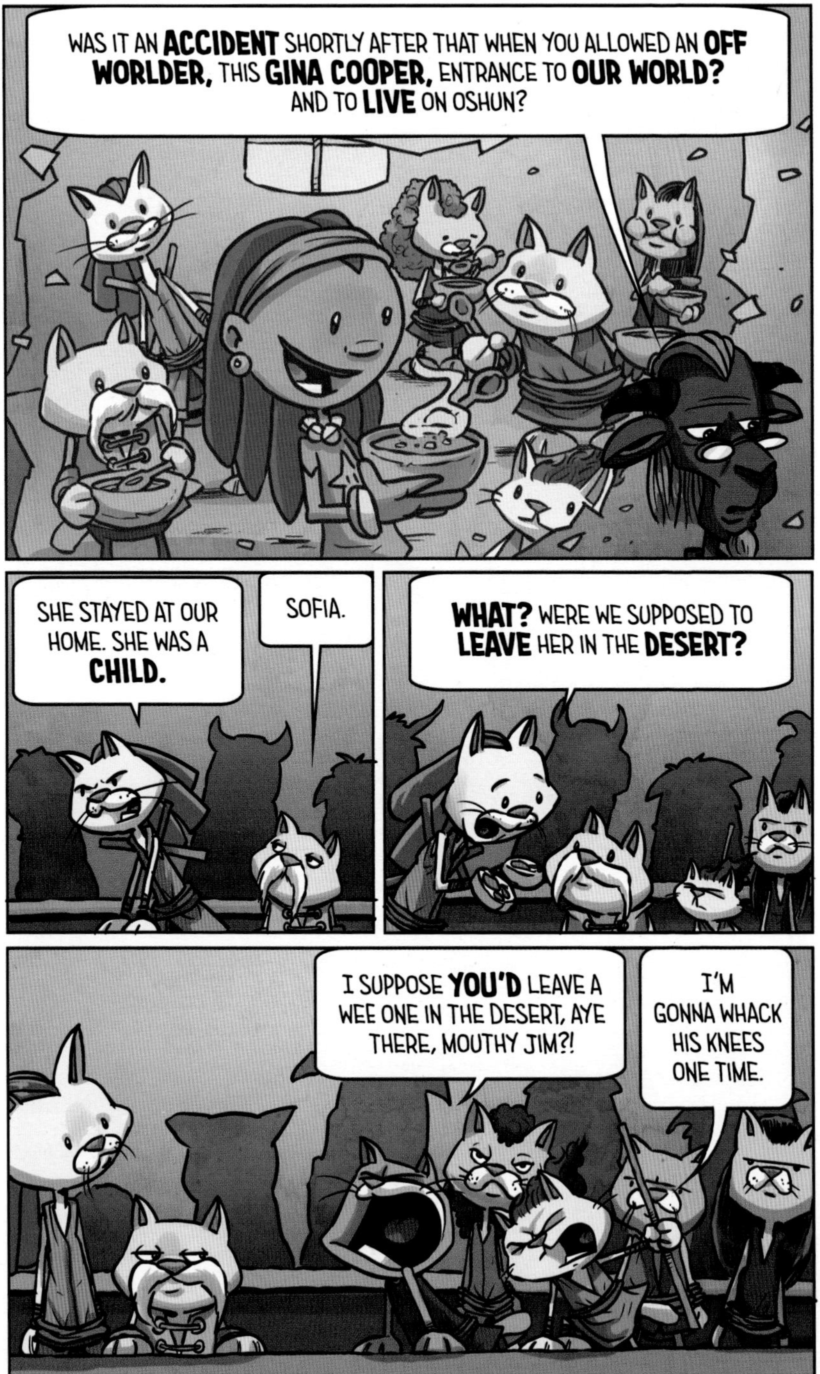
WAS IT AN ACCIDENT SHORTLY AFTER THAT WHEN YOU ALLOWED AN OFF WORLDER, THIS GINA COOPER, ENTRANCE TO OUR WORLD? AND TO LIVE ON OSHUN?
SHE STAYED AT OUR HOME. SHE WAS A CHILD.
SOFIA.
WHAT? WERE WE SUPPOSED TO LEAVE HER IN THE DESERT?
I SUPPOSE YOU'D LEAVE A WEE ONE IN THE DESERT, AYE THERE, MOUTHY JIM?!
I'M GONNA WHACK HIS KNEES ONE TIME.

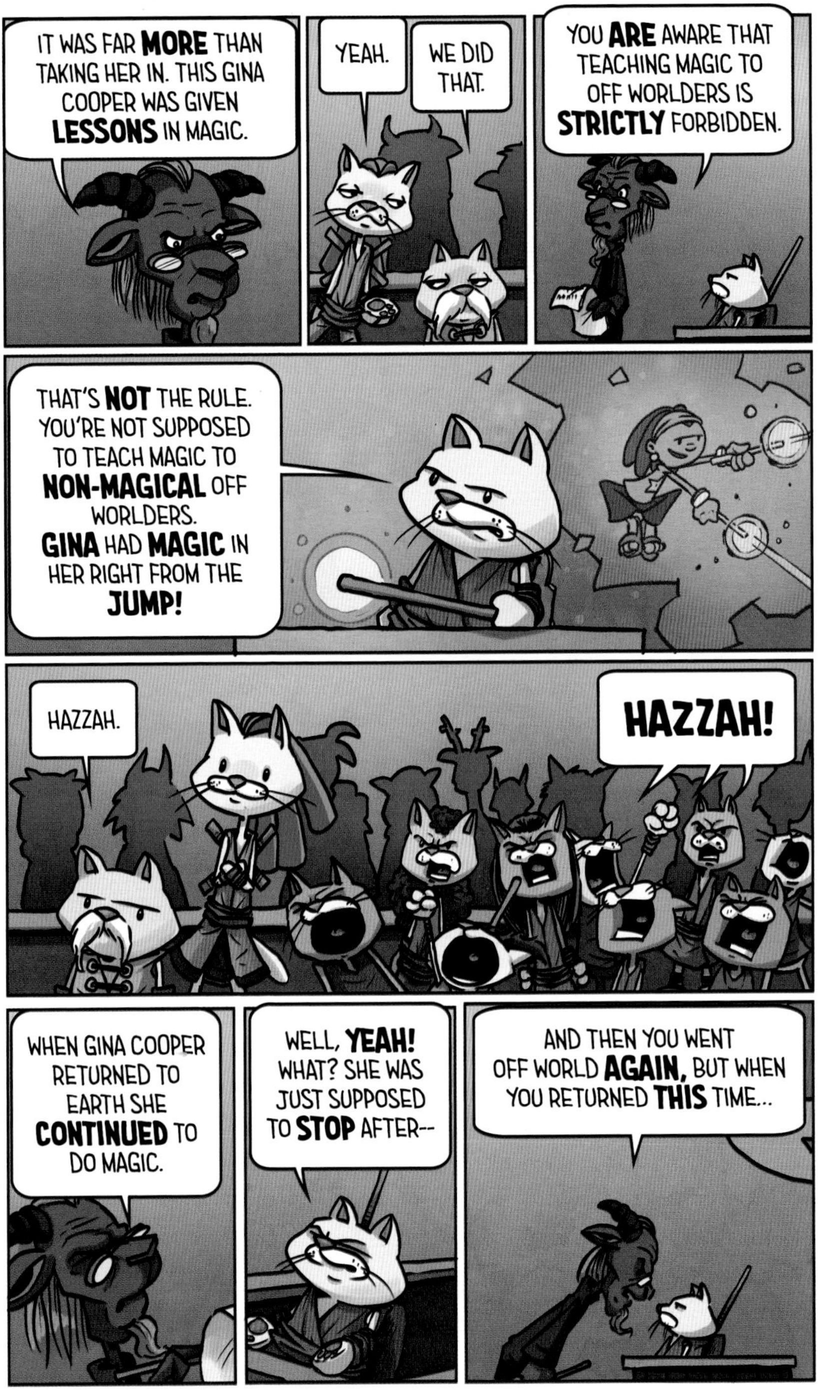
IT WAS FAR **MORE** THAN TAKING HER IN. THIS GINA COOPER WAS GIVEN **LESSONS** IN MAGIC.
YEAH.
WE DID THAT.
YOU **ARE** AWARE THAT TEACHING MAGIC TO OFF WORLDERS IS **STRICTLY** FORBIDDEN.
THAT'S **NOT** THE RULE. YOU'RE NOT SUPPOSED TO TEACH MAGIC TO **NON-MAGICAL** OFF WORLDERS. **GINA** HAD **MAGIC** IN HER RIGHT FROM THE **JUMP!**
HAZZAH.
HAZZAH!
WHEN GINA COOPER RETURNED TO EARTH SHE **CONTINUED** TO DO MAGIC.
WELL, **YEAH!** WHAT? SHE WAS JUST SUPPOSED TO **STOP** AFTER--
AND THEN YOU WENT OFF WORLD **AGAIN,** BUT WHEN YOU RETURNED **THIS** TIME...

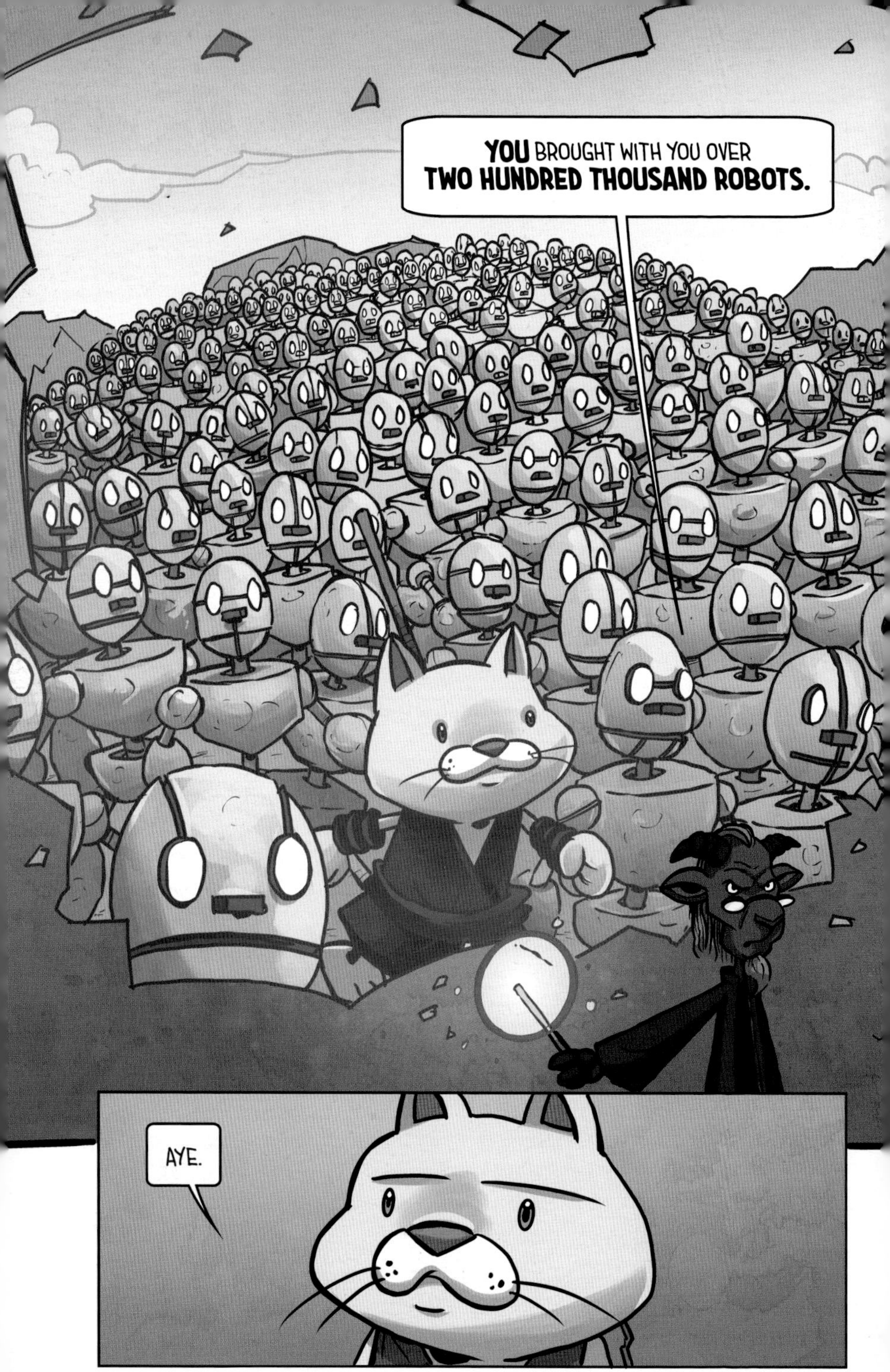
YOU BROUGHT WITH YOU OVER
TWO HUNDRED THOUSAND ROBOTS.
AYE.

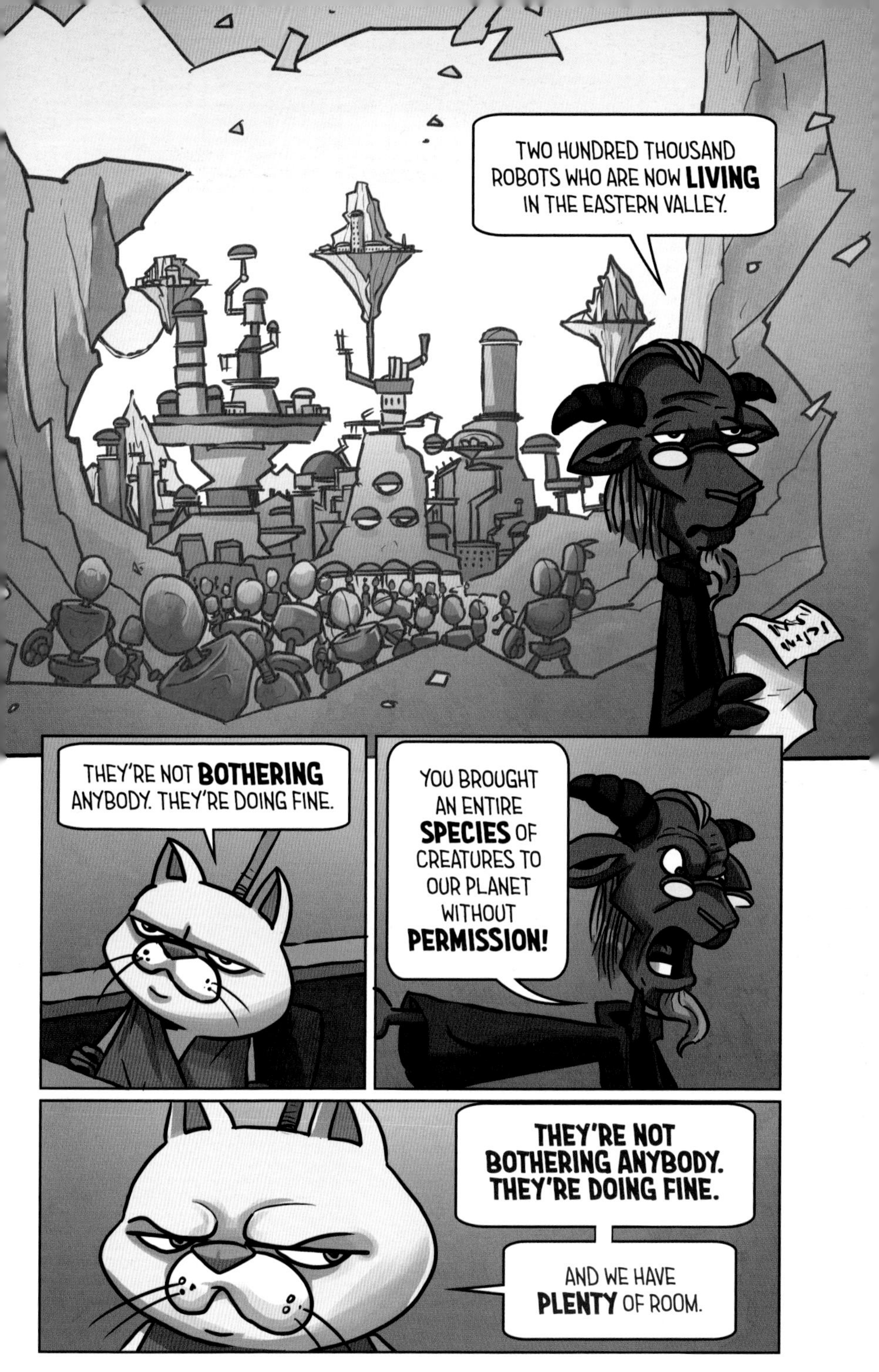

TWO HUNDRED THOUSAND ROBOTS WHO ARE NOW **LIVING** IN THE EASTERN VALLEY.
THEY'RE NOT **BOTHERING** ANYBODY. THEY'RE DOING FINE.
YOU BROUGHT AN ENTIRE **SPECIES** OF CREATURES TO OUR PLANET WITHOUT **PERMISSION!**
THEY'RE NOT BOTHERING ANYBODY. THEY'RE DOING FINE.
AND WE HAVE **PLENTY** OF ROOM.

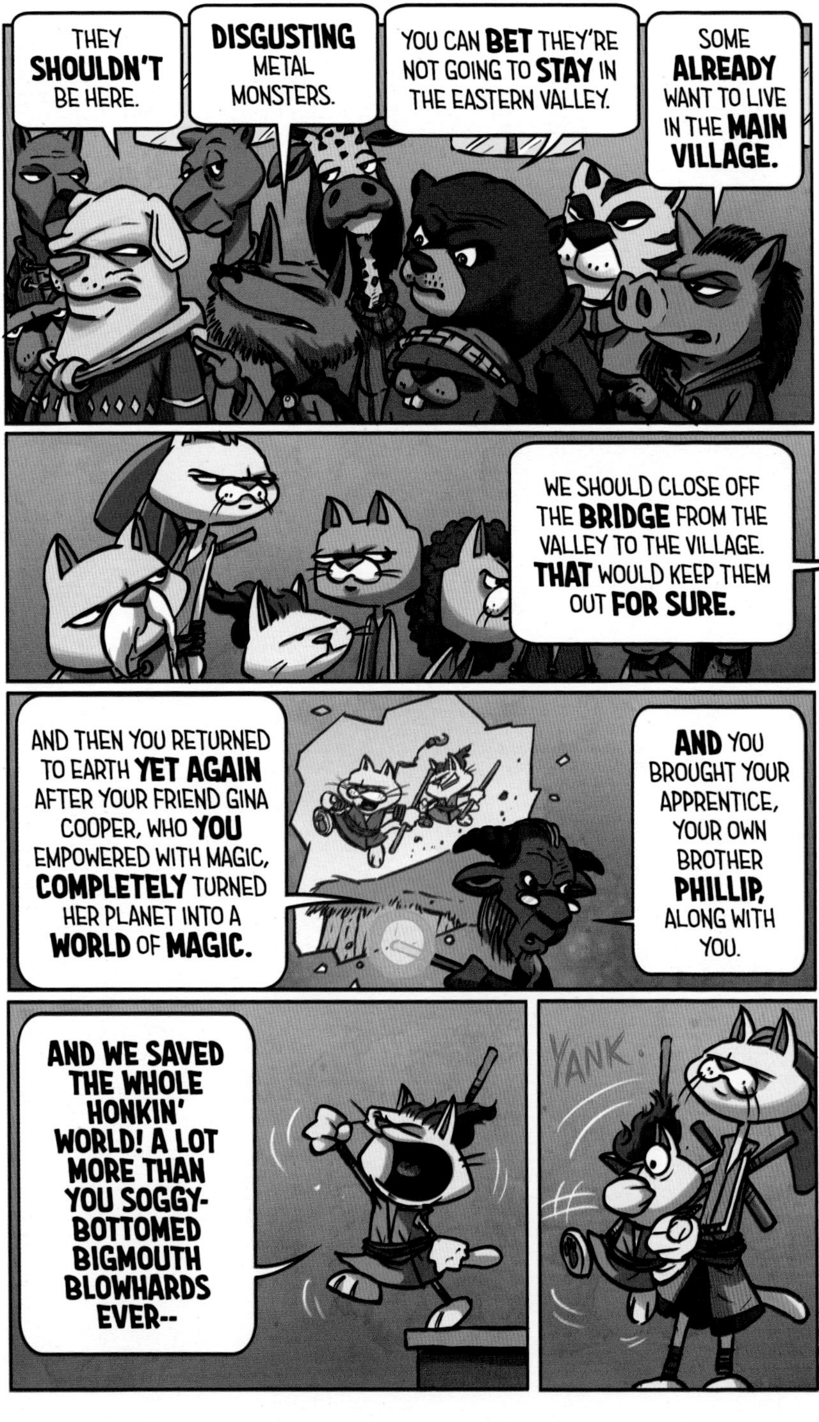
THEY SHOULDN'T BE HERE.
DISGUSTING METAL MONSTERS.
YOU CAN BET THEY'RE NOT GOING TO STAY IN THE EASTERN VALLEY.
SOME ALREADY WANT TO LIVE IN THE MAIN VILLAGE.
WE SHOULD CLOSE OFF THE BRIDGE FROM THE VALLEY TO THE VILLAGE. THAT WOULD KEEP THEM OUT FOR SURE.
AND THEN YOU RETURNED TO EARTH YET AGAIN AFTER YOUR FRIEND GINA COOPER, WHO YOU EMPOWERED WITH MAGIC, COMPLETELY TURNED HER PLANET INTO A WORLD OF MAGIC.
AND YOU BROUGHT YOUR APPRENTICE, YOUR OWN BROTHER PHILLIP, ALONG WITH YOU.
AND WE SAVED THE WHOLE HONKIN' WORLD! A LOT MORE THAN YOU SOGGY-BOTTOMED BIGMOUTH BLOWHARDS EVER--
YANK

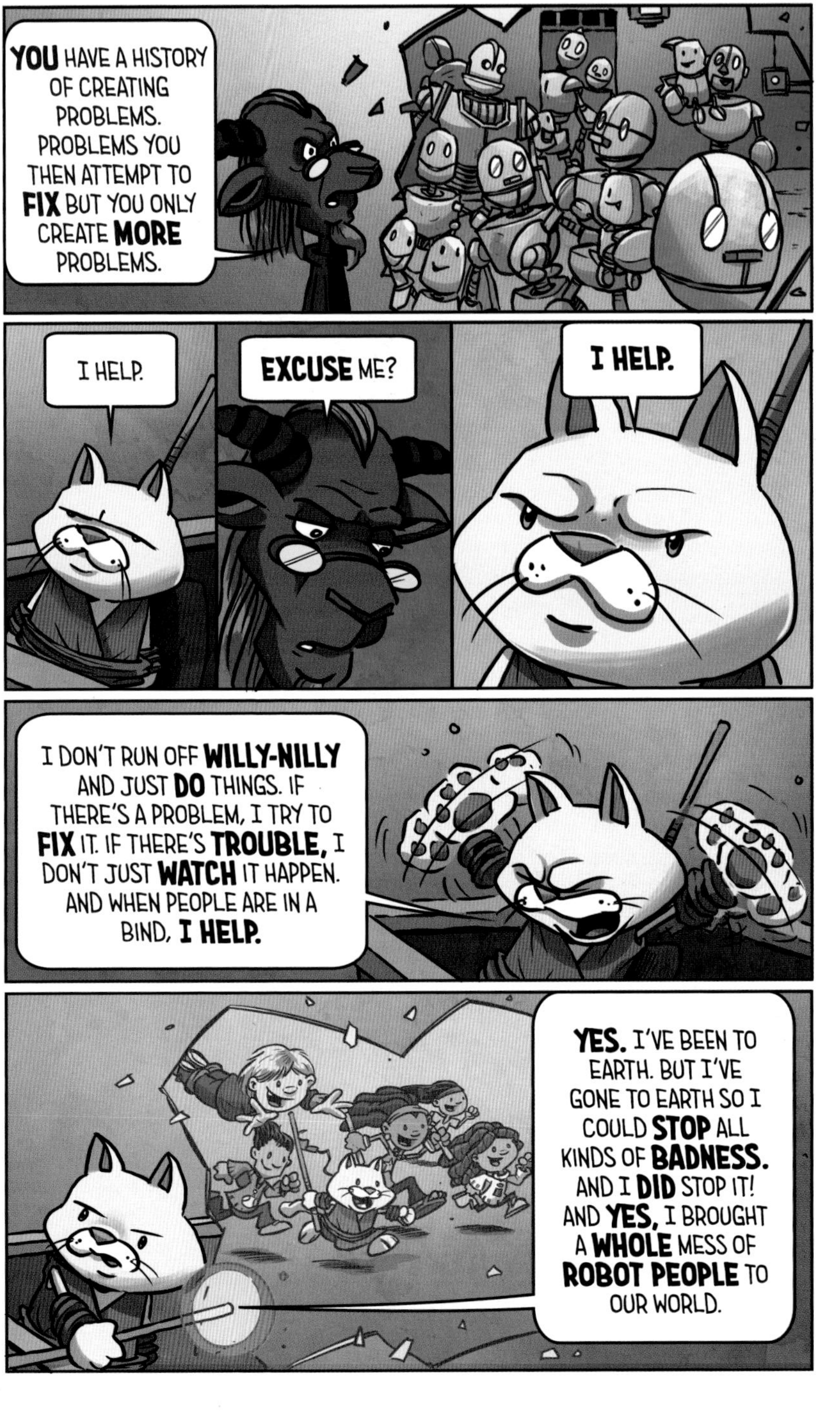
YOU HAVE A HISTORY OF CREATING PROBLEMS. PROBLEMS YOU THEN ATTEMPT TO FIX BUT YOU ONLY CREATE MORE PROBLEMS.
I HELP.
EXCUSE ME?
I HELP.
I DON'T RUN OFF WILLY-NILLY AND JUST DO THINGS. IF THERE'S A PROBLEM, I TRY TO FIX IT. IF THERE'S TROUBLE, I DON'T JUST WATCH IT HAPPEN. AND WHEN PEOPLE ARE IN A BIND, I HELP.
YES. I'VE BEEN TO EARTH. BUT I'VE GONE TO EARTH SO I COULD STOP ALL KINDS OF BADNESS. AND I DID STOP IT! AND YES, I BROUGHT A WHOLE MESS OF ROBOT PEOPLE TO OUR WORLD.

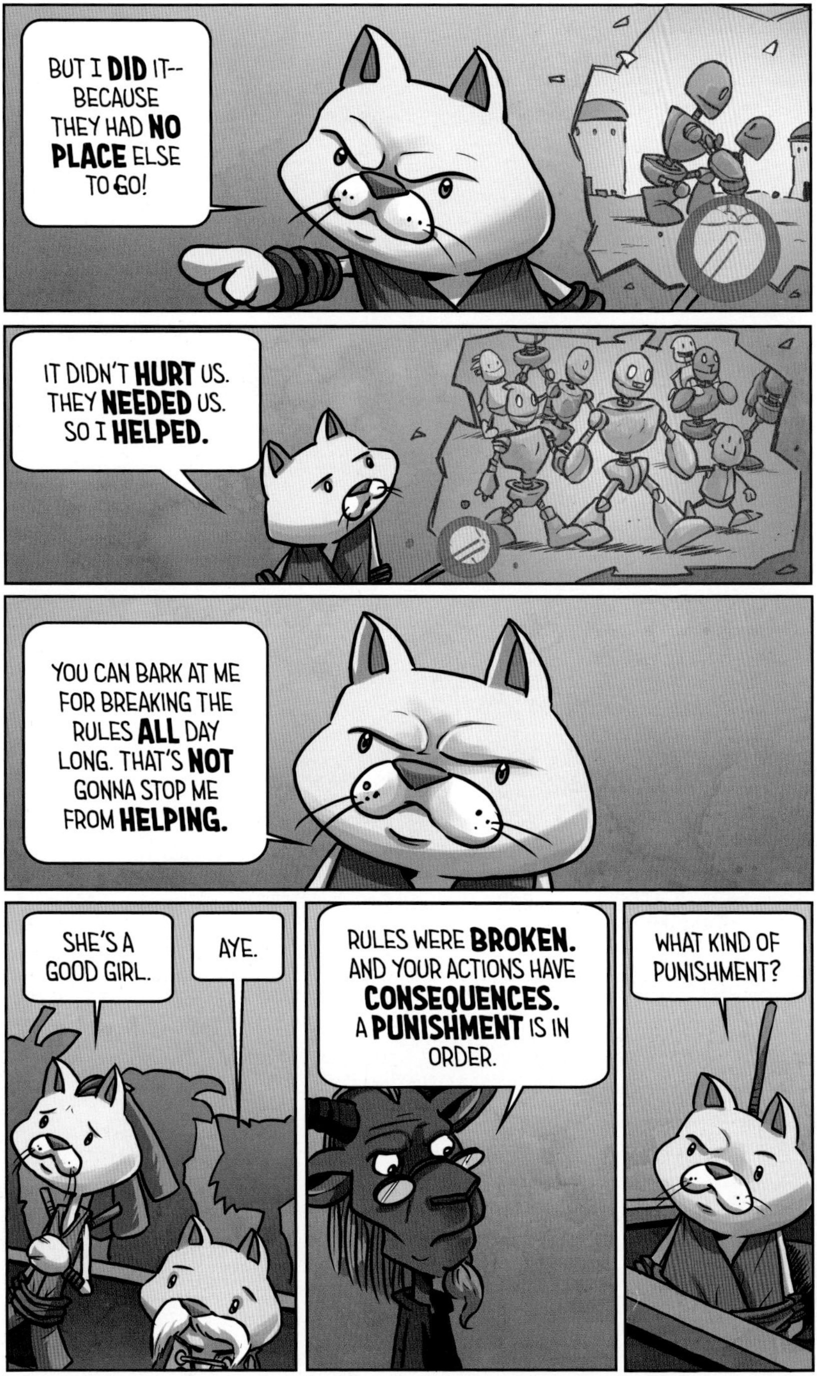
BUT I DID IT-- BECAUSE THEY HAD NO PLACE ELSE TO GO!
IT DIDN'T HURT US. THEY NEEDED US. SO I HELPED.
YOU CAN BARK AT ME FOR BREAKING THE RULES ALL DAY LONG. THAT'S NOT GONNA STOP ME FROM HELPING.
SHE'S A GOOD GIRL.
AYE.
RULES WERE BROKEN. AND YOUR ACTIONS HAVE CONSEQUENCES. A PUNISHMENT IS IN ORDER.
WHAT KIND OF PUNISHMENT?

CHAPTER

GETTING SCHOOLED

THE HOME OF THE KORIMAKOS.

WOMBATTON!

WOMBATTON! THEY'RE SENDING ME TO WOMBATTON!

IT'S A GOOD SCHOOL.

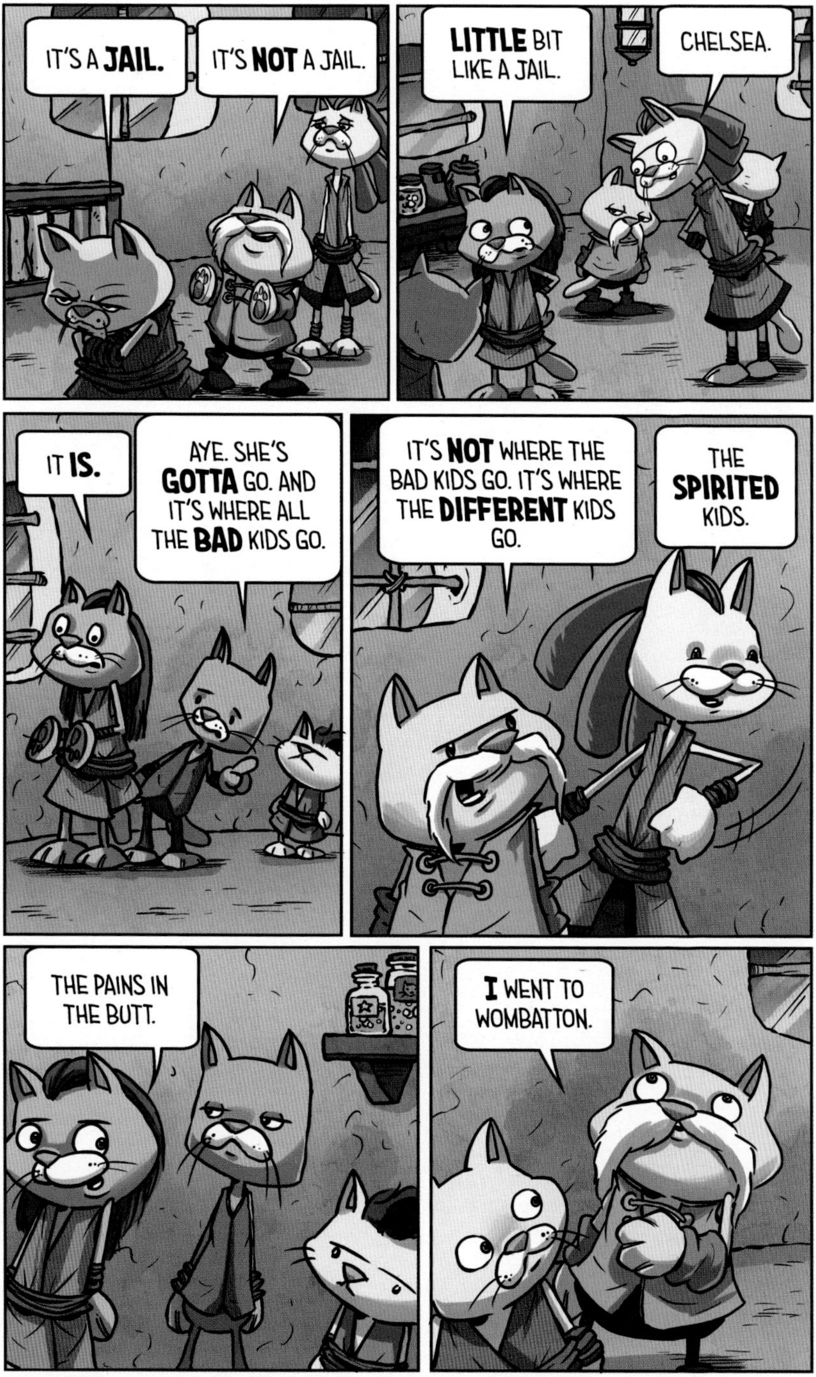
IT'S A **JAIL.**
IT'S **NOT** A JAIL.
LITTLE BIT LIKE A JAIL.
CHELSEA.
IT **IS.**
AYE. SHE'S **GOTTA** GO. AND IT'S WHERE ALL THE **BAD** KIDS GO.
IT'S **NOT** WHERE THE BAD KIDS GO. IT'S WHERE THE **DIFFERENT** KIDS GO.
THE **SPIRITED** KIDS.
THE PAINS IN THE BUTT.
I WENT TO WOMBATTON.

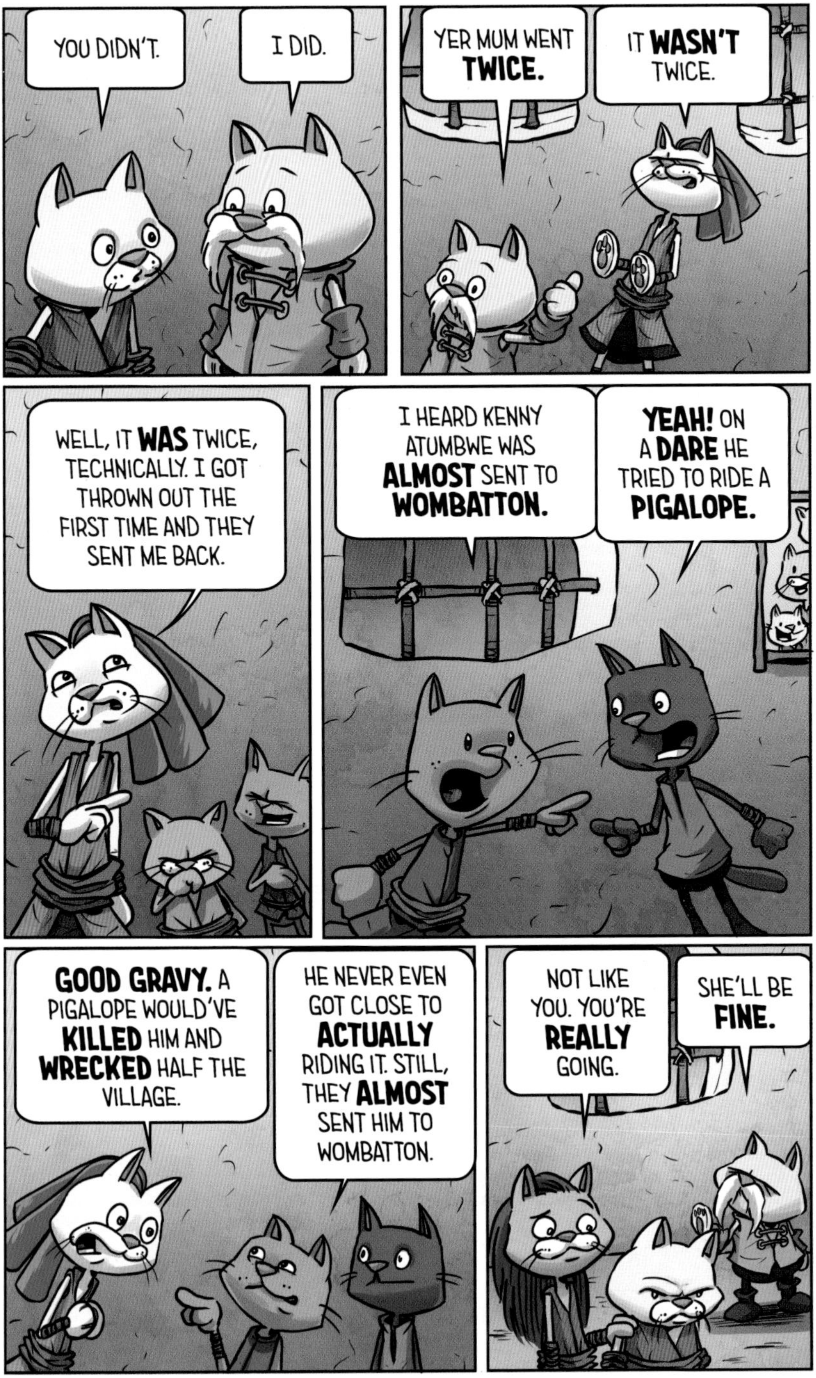
YOU DIDN'T.
I DID.
YER MUM WENT **TWICE.**
IT **WASN'T** TWICE.
WELL, IT **WAS** TWICE, TECHNICALLY. I GOT THROWN OUT THE FIRST TIME AND THEY SENT ME BACK.
I HEARD KENNY ATUMBWE WAS **ALMOST** SENT TO **WOMBATTON.**
YEAH! ON A **DARE** HE TRIED TO RIDE A **PIGALOPE.**
GOOD GRAVY. A PIGALOPE WOULD'VE **KILLED** HIM AND **WRECKED** HALF THE VILLAGE.
HE NEVER EVEN GOT CLOSE TO **ACTUALLY** RIDING IT. STILL, THEY **ALMOST** SENT HIM TO WOMBATTON.
NOT LIKE YOU. YOU'RE **REALLY** GOING.
SHE'LL BE **FINE.**

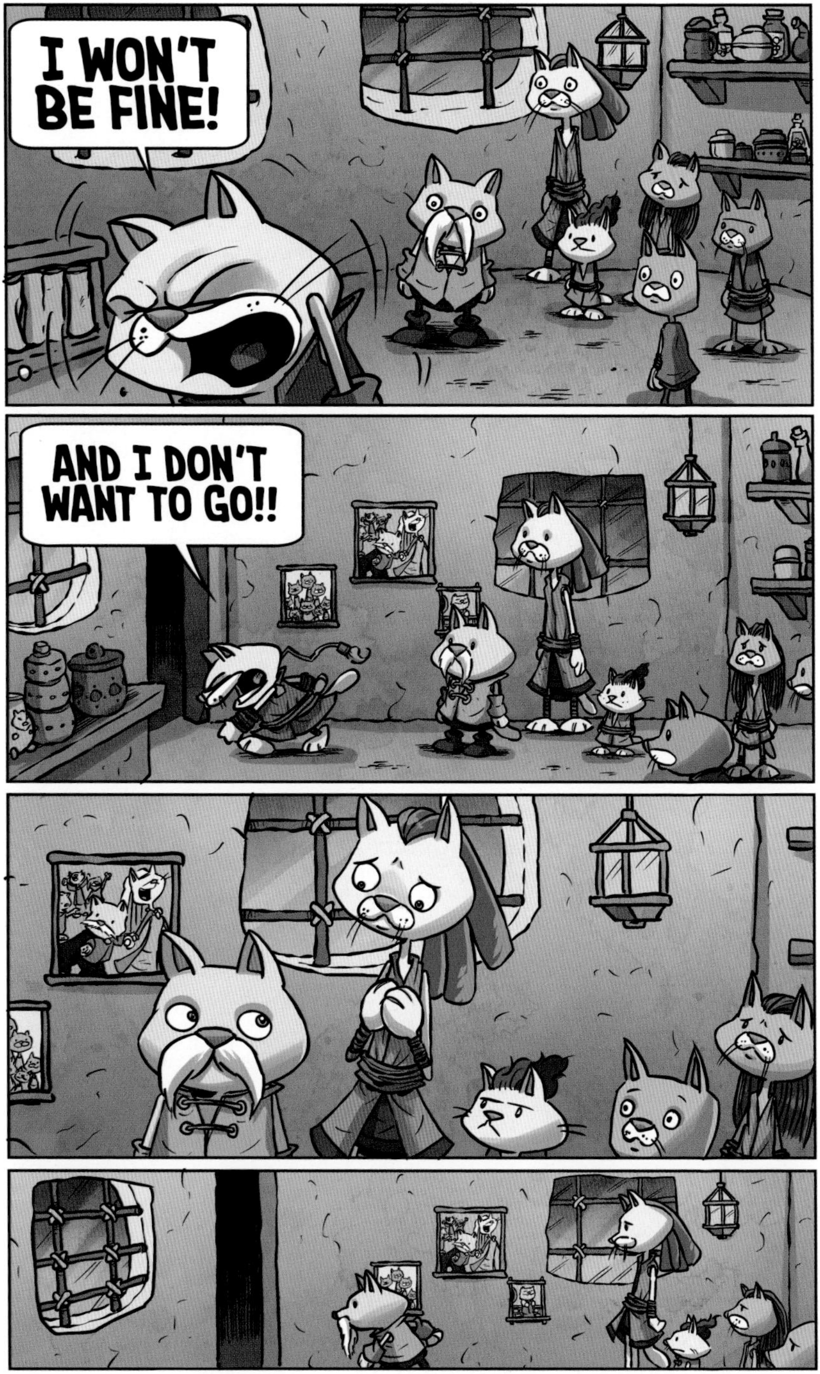
I WON'T BE FINE!
AND I DON'T WANT TO GO!!

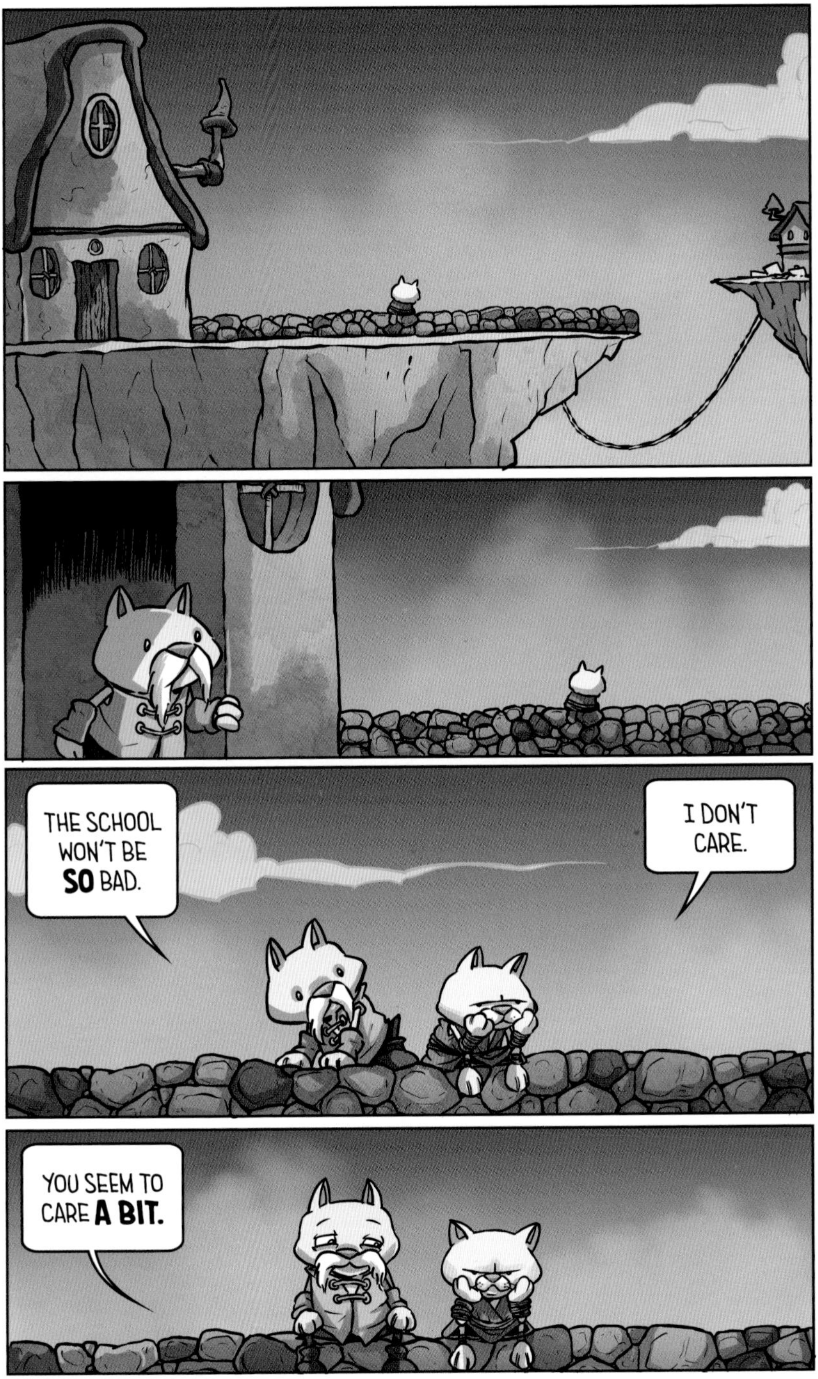
THE SCHOOL WON'T BE **SO** BAD.
I DON'T CARE.
YOU SEEM TO CARE **A BIT.**

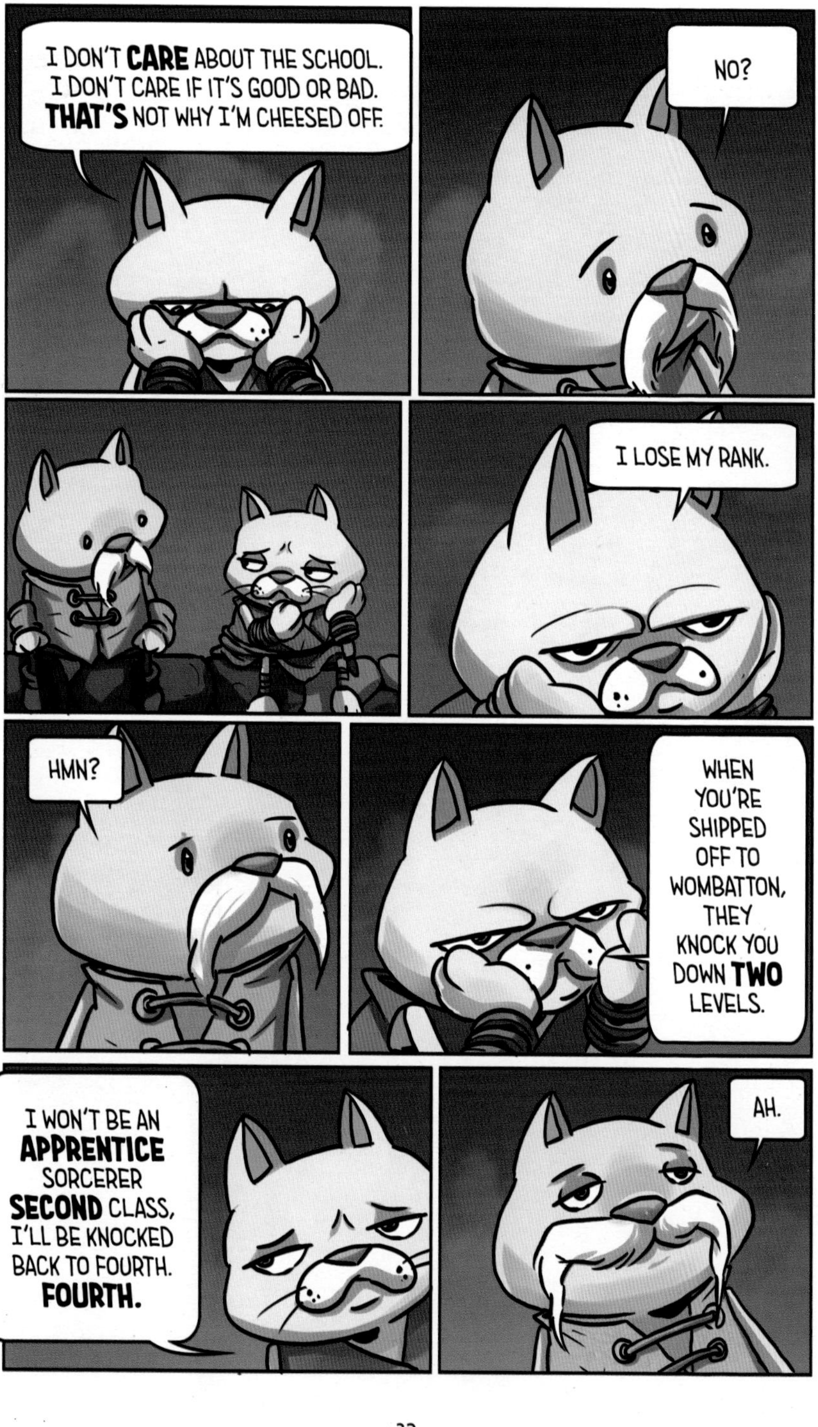
I DON'T **CARE** ABOUT THE SCHOOL. I DON'T CARE IF IT'S GOOD OR BAD. **THAT'S** NOT WHY I'M CHEESED OFF.
NO?
I LOSE MY RANK.
HMN?
WHEN YOU'RE SHIPPED OFF TO WOMBATTON, THEY KNOCK YOU DOWN **TWO** LEVELS.
I WON'T BE AN **APPRENTICE** SORCERER **SECOND** CLASS, I'LL BE KNOCKED BACK TO FOURTH. **FOURTH.**
AH.

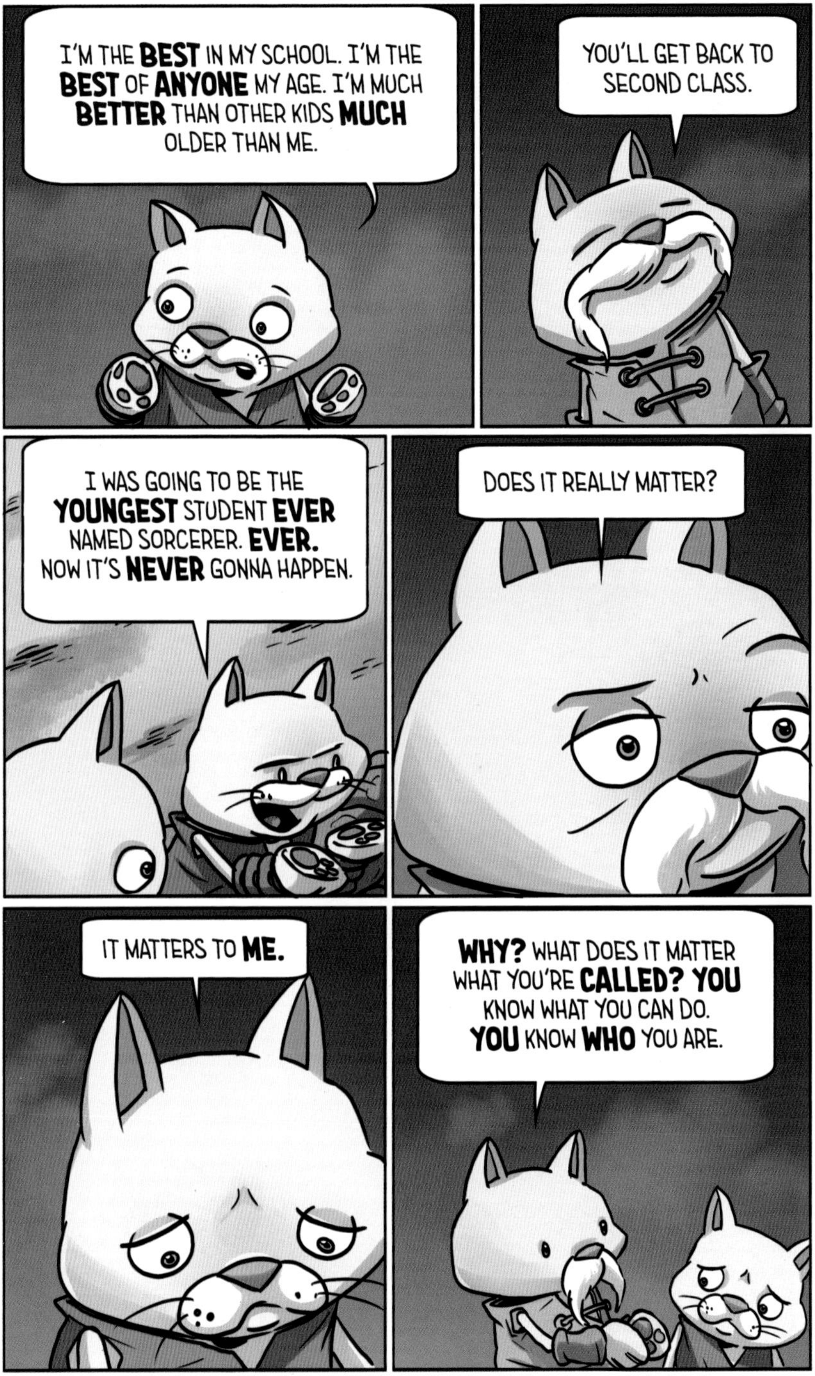
I'M THE BEST IN MY SCHOOL. I'M THE BEST OF ANYONE MY AGE. I'M MUCH BETTER THAN OTHER KIDS MUCH OLDER THAN ME.
YOU'LL GET BACK TO SECOND CLASS.
I WAS GOING TO BE THE YOUNGEST STUDENT EVER NAMED SORCERER. EVER. NOW IT'S NEVER GONNA HAPPEN.
DOES IT REALLY MATTER?
IT MATTERS TO ME.
WHY? WHAT DOES IT MATTER WHAT YOU'RE CALLED? YOU KNOW WHAT YOU CAN DO. YOU KNOW WHO YOU ARE.

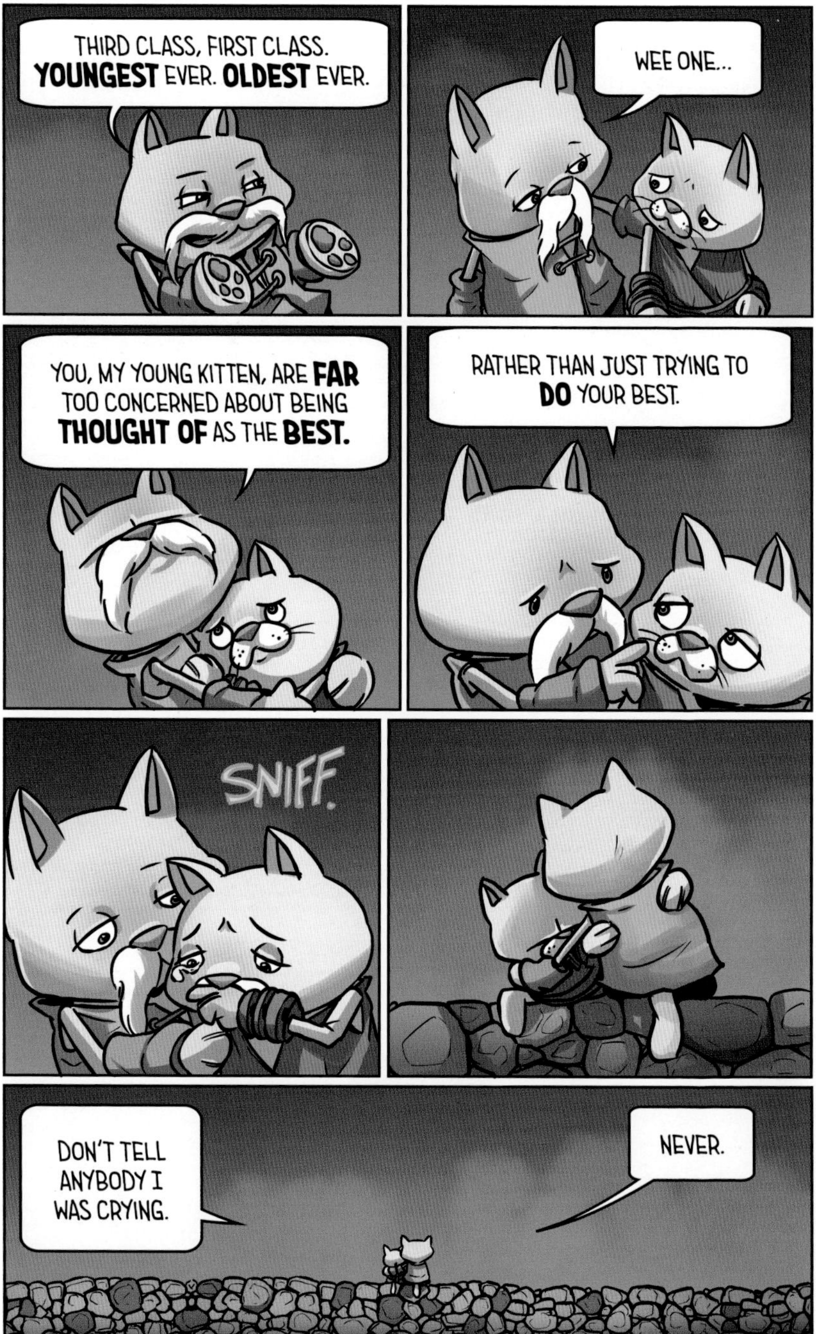
THIRD CLASS, FIRST CLASS. YOUNGEST EVER. OLDEST EVER.
WEE ONE...
YOU, MY YOUNG KITTEN, ARE FAR TOO CONCERNED ABOUT BEING THOUGHT OF AS THE BEST.
RATHER THAN JUST TRYING TO DO YOUR BEST.
SNIFF.
DON'T TELL ANYBODY I WAS CRYING.
NEVER.

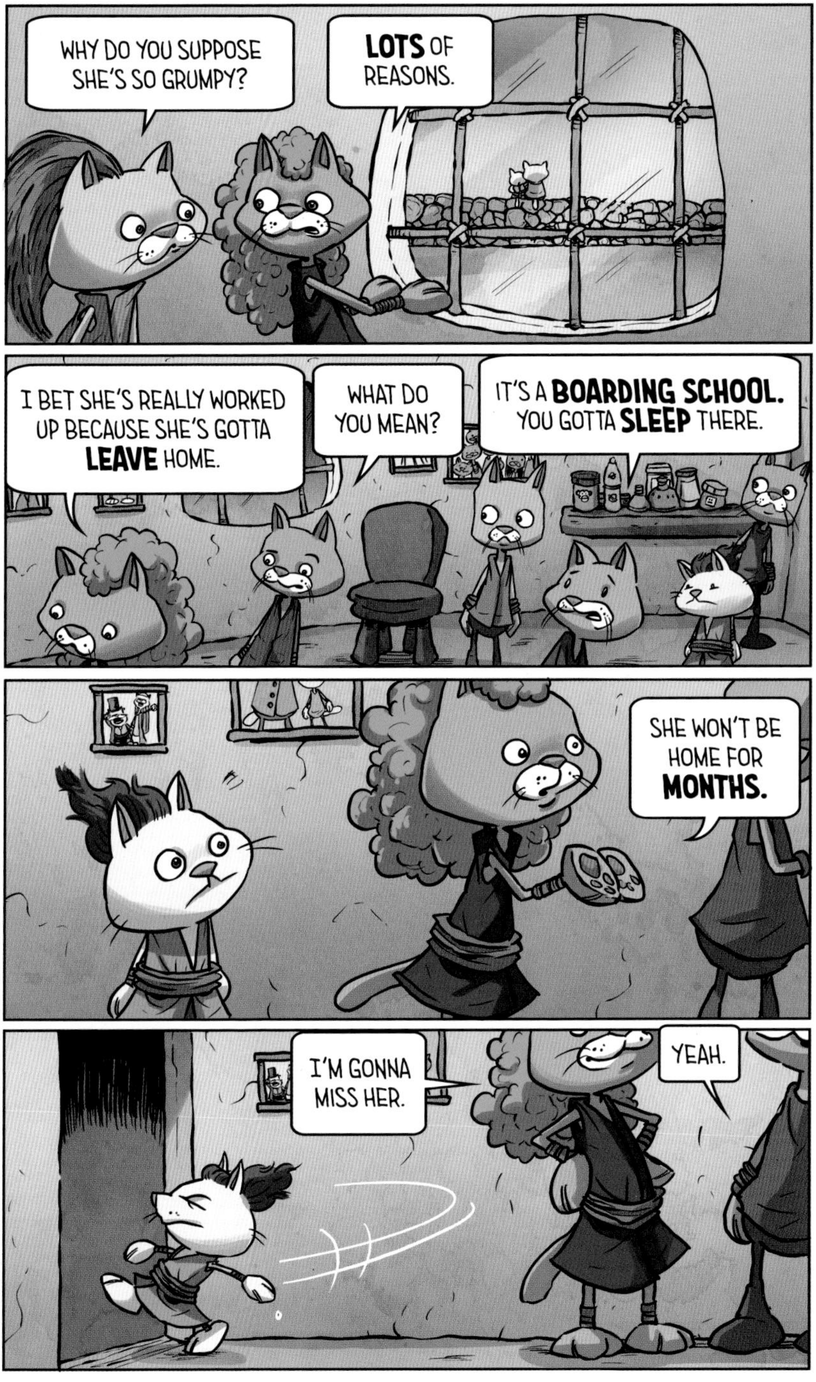
WHY DO YOU SUPPOSE SHE'S SO GRUMPY?
LOTS OF REASONS.
I BET SHE'S REALLY WORKED UP BECAUSE SHE'S GOTTA **LEAVE** HOME.
WHAT DO YOU MEAN?
IT'S A **BOARDING SCHOOL.** YOU GOTTA **SLEEP** THERE.
SHE WON'T BE HOME FOR **MONTHS.**
I'M GONNA MISS HER.
YEAH.

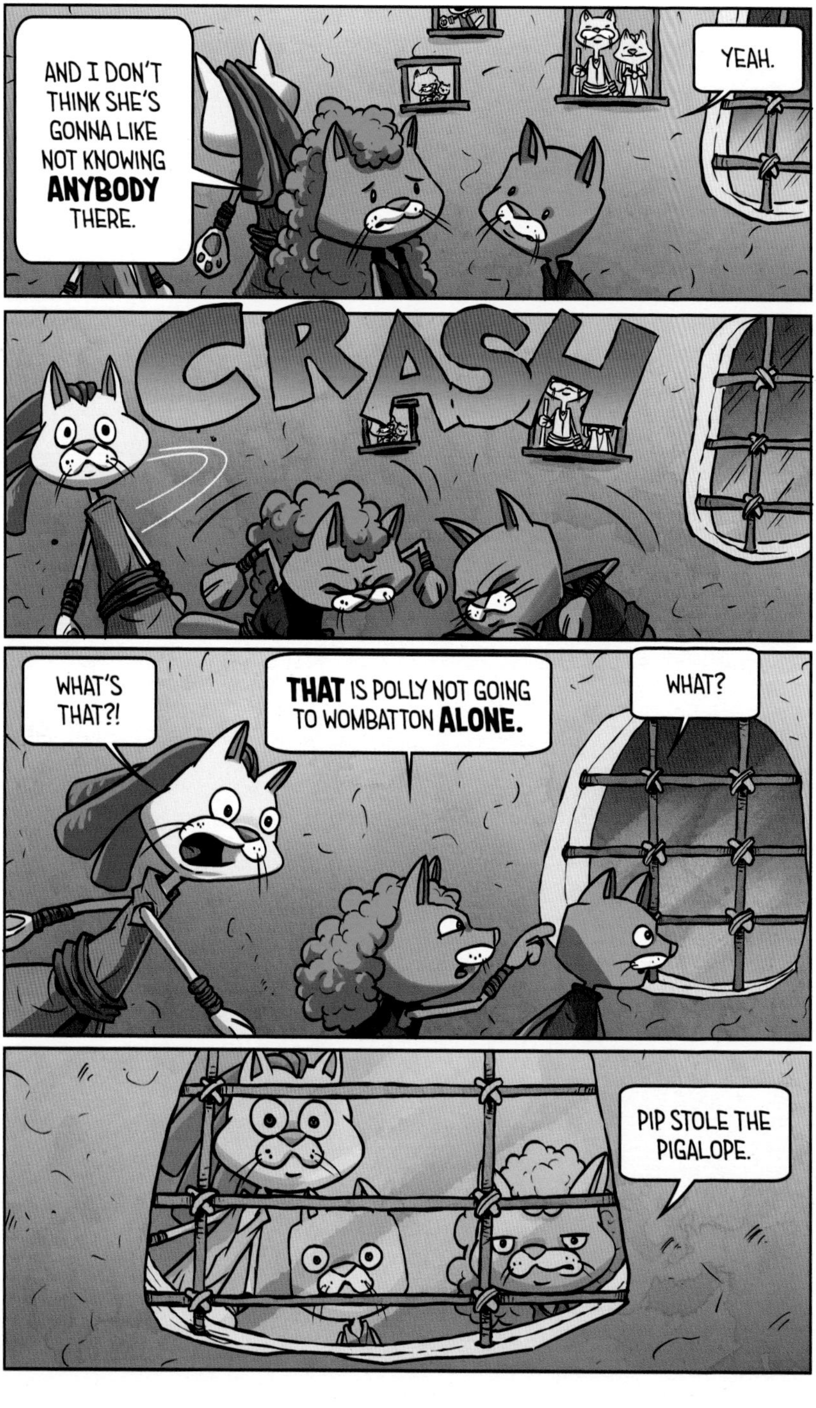
AND I DON'T THINK SHE'S GONNA LIKE NOT KNOWING **ANYBODY** THERE.
YEAH.
CRASH
WHAT'S THAT?!
THAT IS POLLY NOT GOING TO WOMBATTON **ALONE.**
WHAT?
PIP STOLE THE PIGALOPE.

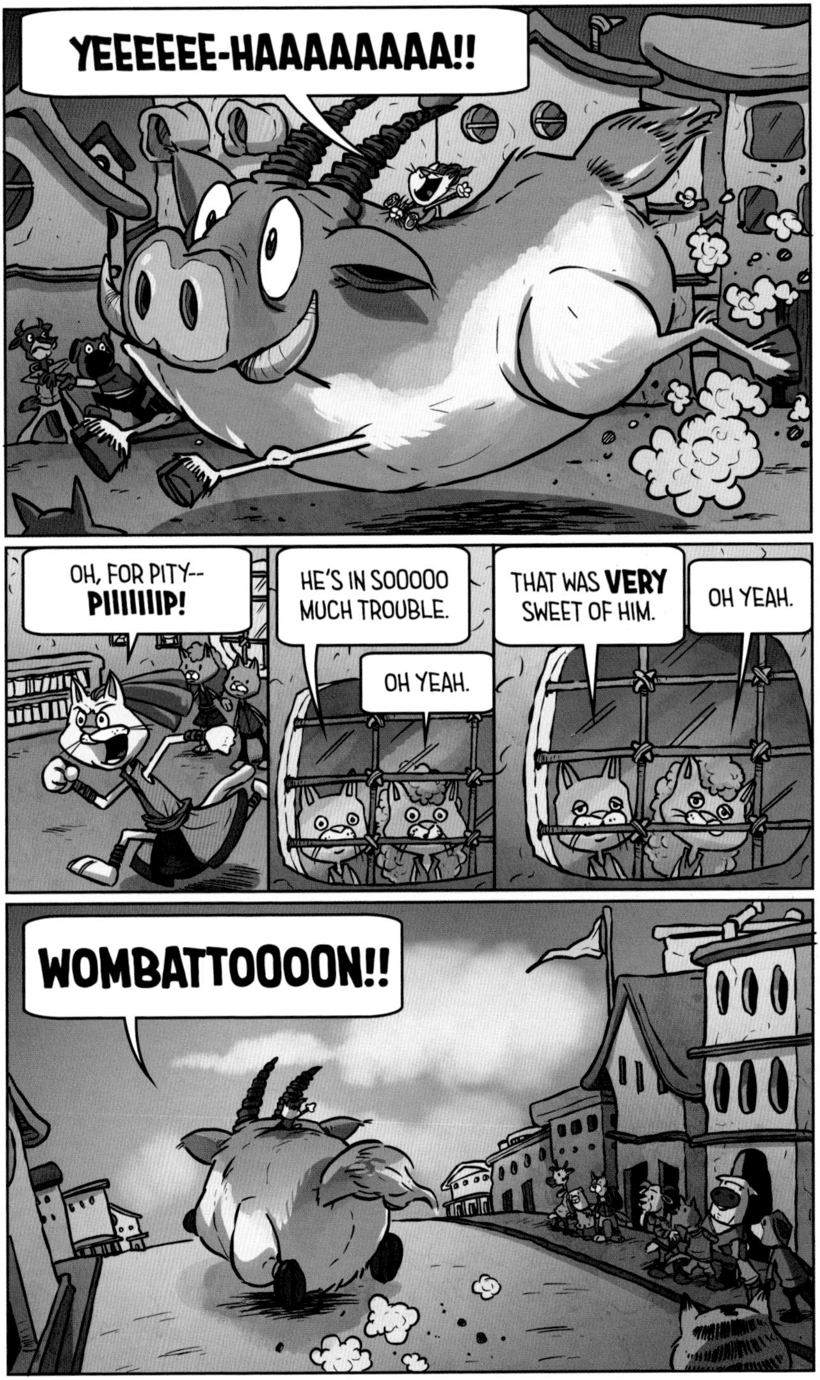
YEEEEEE-HAAAAAAAA!!
OH, FOR PITY--
PIIIIIIIP!
HE'S IN SOOOOO MUCH TROUBLE.
OH YEAH.
THAT WAS **VERY** SWEET OF HIM.
OH YEAH.
WOMBATTOOOON!!

CHAPTER 3

THE FIRST OF HER KIND

SPELL CAST ACADEMY.
THE KORIMAKOS ARE GOING TO JAIL!
THE HOOSEGOW! THE PEN! THE COOLER! THE JOINT! THE CAN! THE POKEY!
IT'S A SCHOOL.
YEAH, FOR THE KIDS WHO ARE TROUBLE.

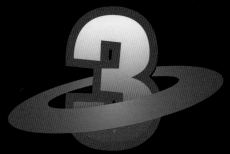

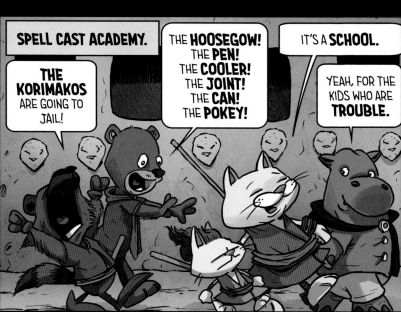

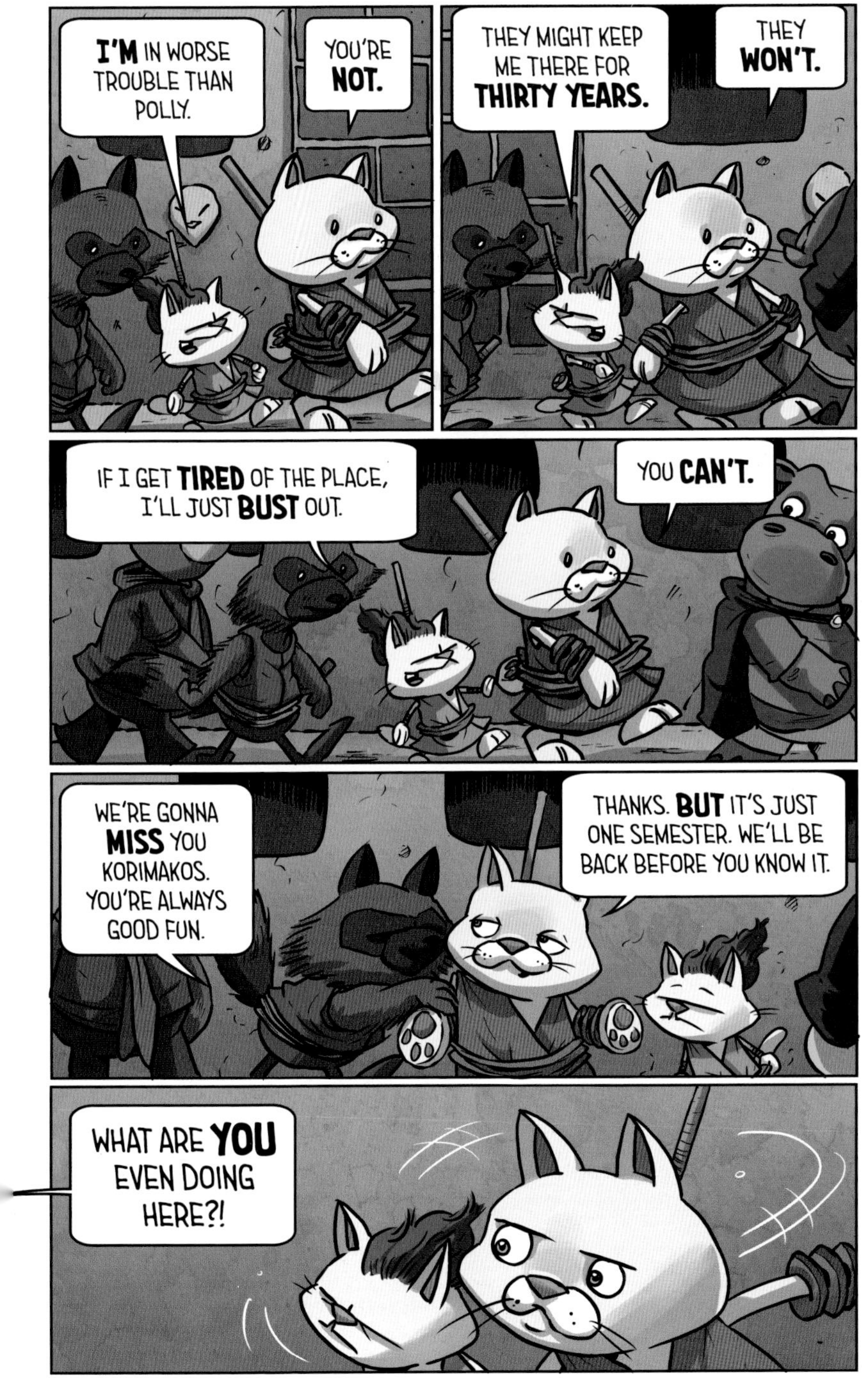
I'M IN WORSE TROUBLE THAN POLLY.
YOU'RE NOT.
THEY MIGHT KEEP ME THERE FOR THIRTY YEARS.
THEY WON'T.
IF I GET TIRED OF THE PLACE, I'LL JUST BUST OUT.
YOU CAN'T.
WE'RE GONNA MISS YOU KORIMAKOS. YOU'RE ALWAYS GOOD FUN.
THANKS. BUT IT'S JUST ONE SEMESTER. WE'LL BE BACK BEFORE YOU KNOW IT.
WHAT ARE YOU EVEN DOING HERE?!

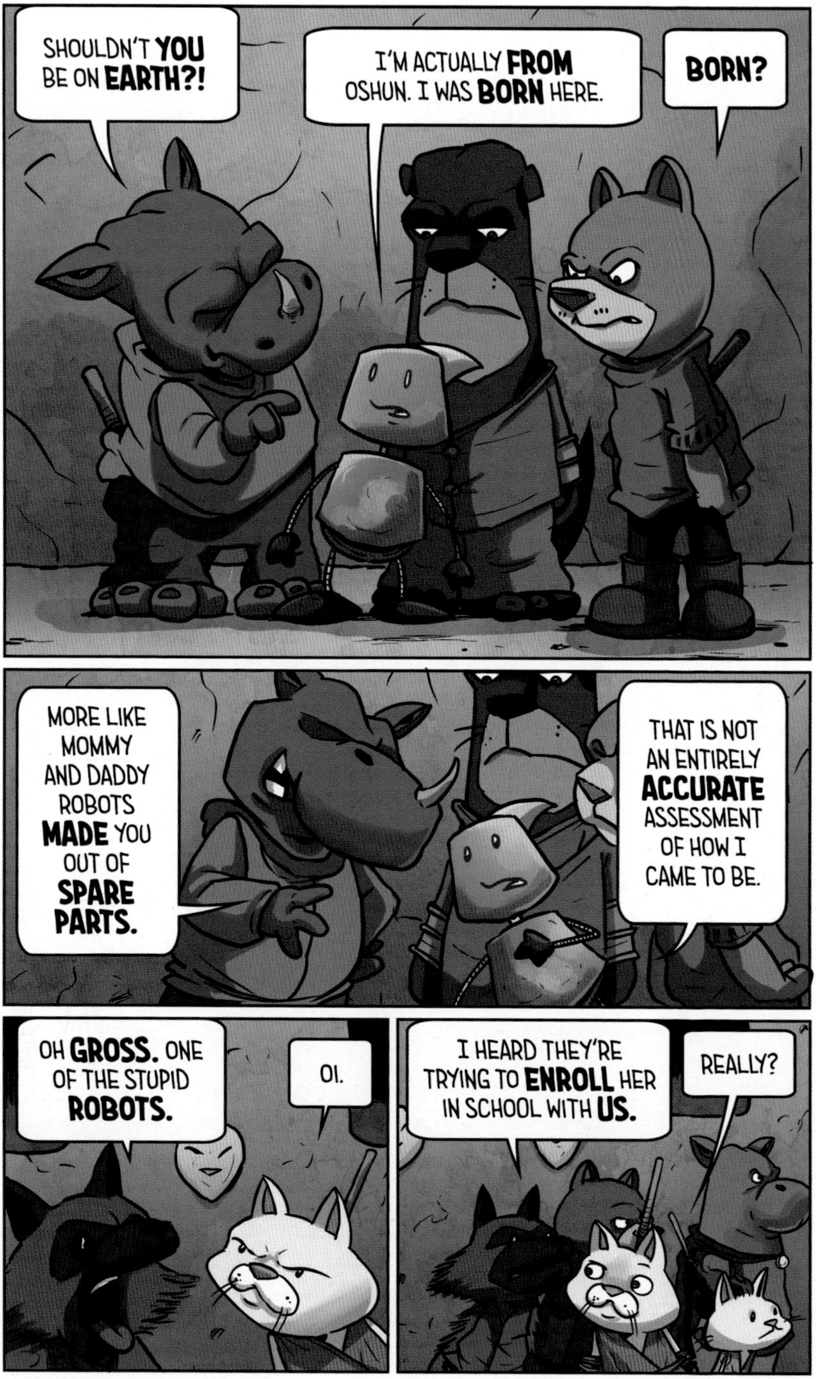
SHOULDN'T **YOU** BE ON **EARTH?!**
I'M ACTUALLY **FROM** OSHUN. I WAS **BORN** HERE.
BORN?
MORE LIKE MOMMY AND DADDY ROBOTS **MADE** YOU OUT OF **SPARE PARTS.**
THAT IS NOT AN ENTIRELY **ACCURATE** ASSESSMENT OF HOW I CAME TO BE.
OH **GROSS.** ONE OF THE STUPID **ROBOTS.**
OI.
I HEARD THEY'RE TRYING TO **ENROLL** HER IN SCHOOL WITH **US.**
REALLY?

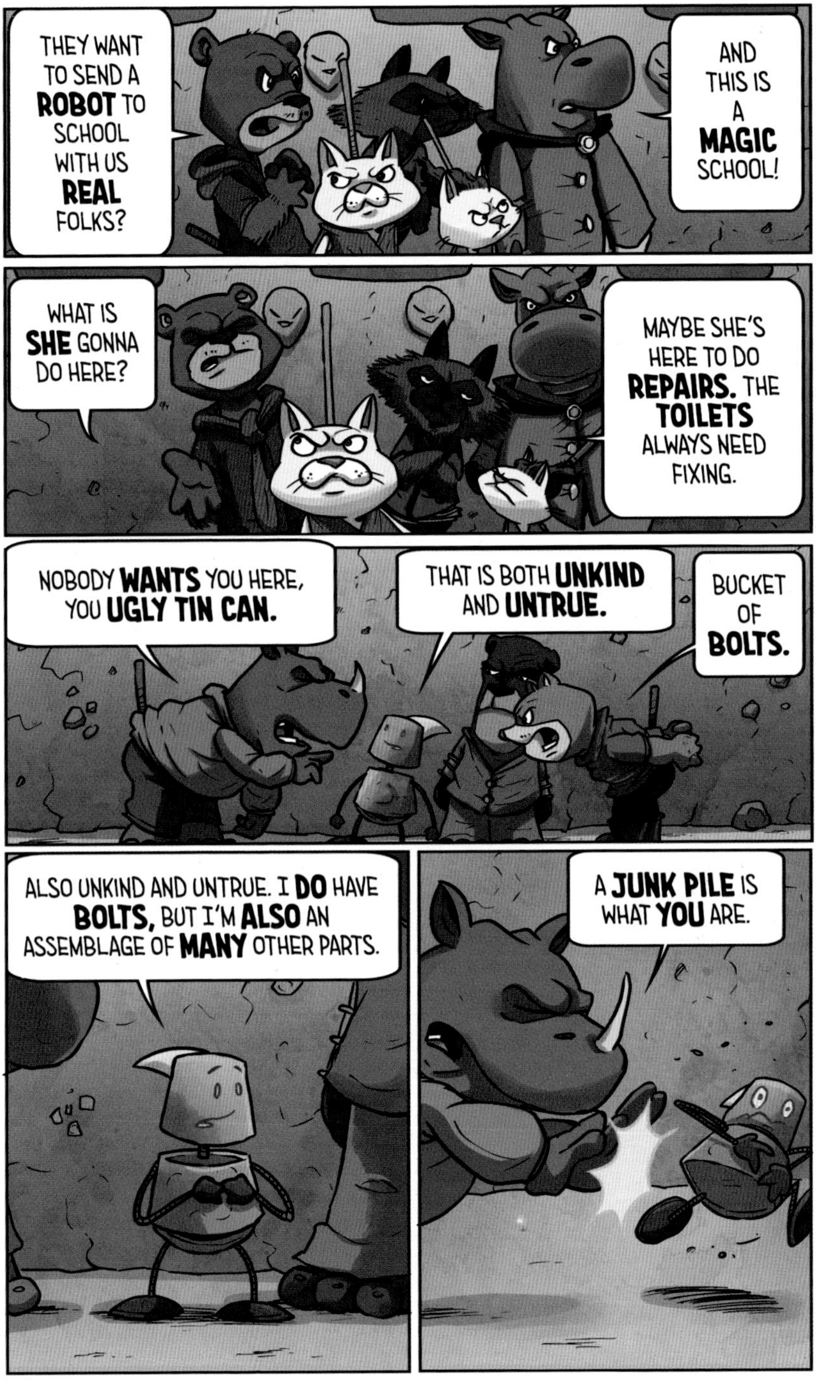
THEY WANT TO SEND A **ROBOT** TO SCHOOL WITH US **REAL** FOLKS?
AND THIS IS A **MAGIC** SCHOOL!
WHAT IS **SHE** GONNA DO HERE?
MAYBE SHE'S HERE TO DO **REPAIRS.** THE **TOILETS** ALWAYS NEED FIXING.
NOBODY **WANTS** YOU HERE, YOU **UGLY TIN CAN.**
THAT IS BOTH **UNKIND** AND **UNTRUE.**
BUCKET OF **BOLTS.**
ALSO UNKIND AND UNTRUE. I **DO** HAVE **BOLTS,** BUT I'M **ALSO** AN ASSEMBLAGE OF **MANY** OTHER PARTS.
A **JUNK PILE** IS WHAT **YOU** ARE.

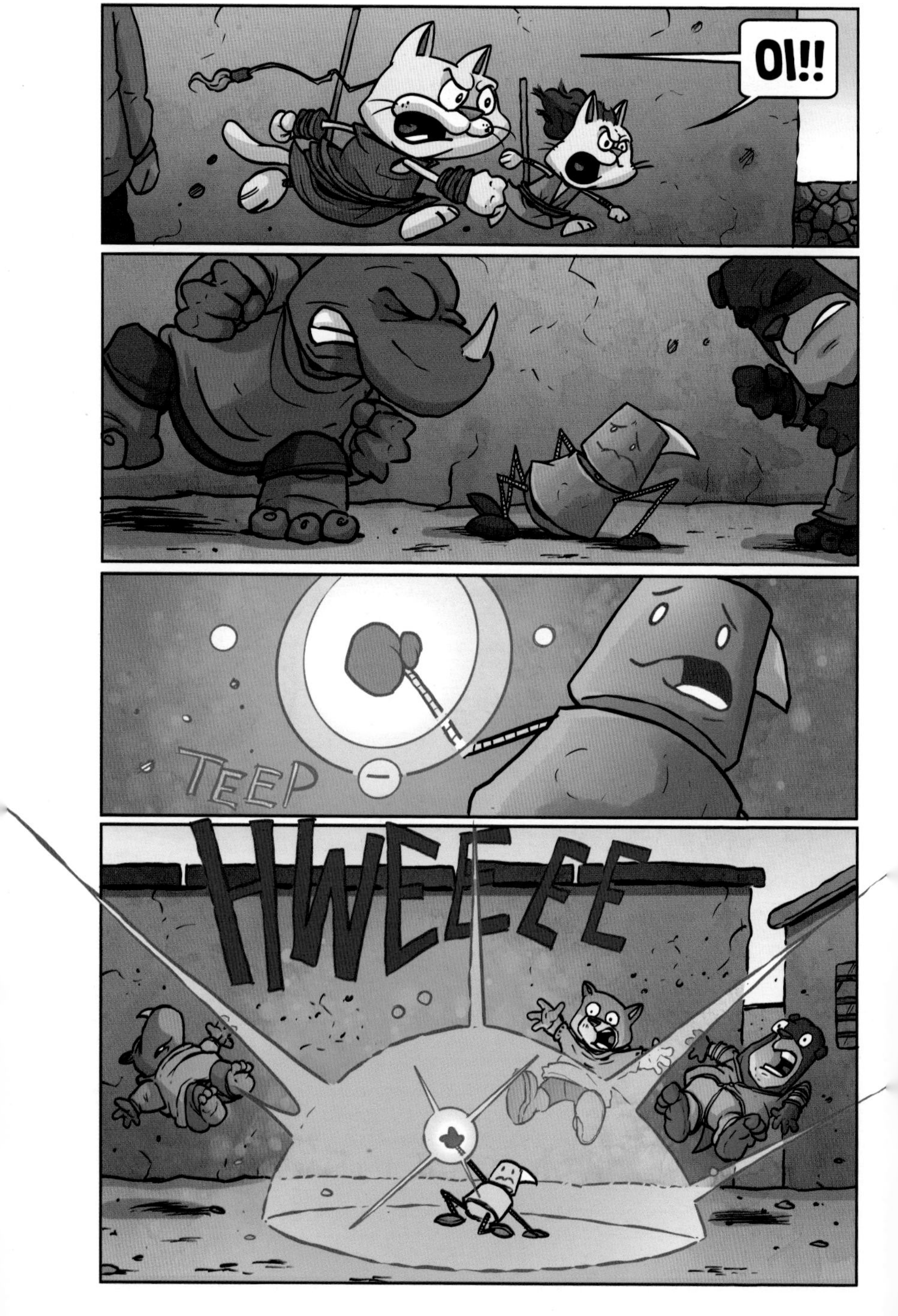
OI!!
TEEP
HWEEEE

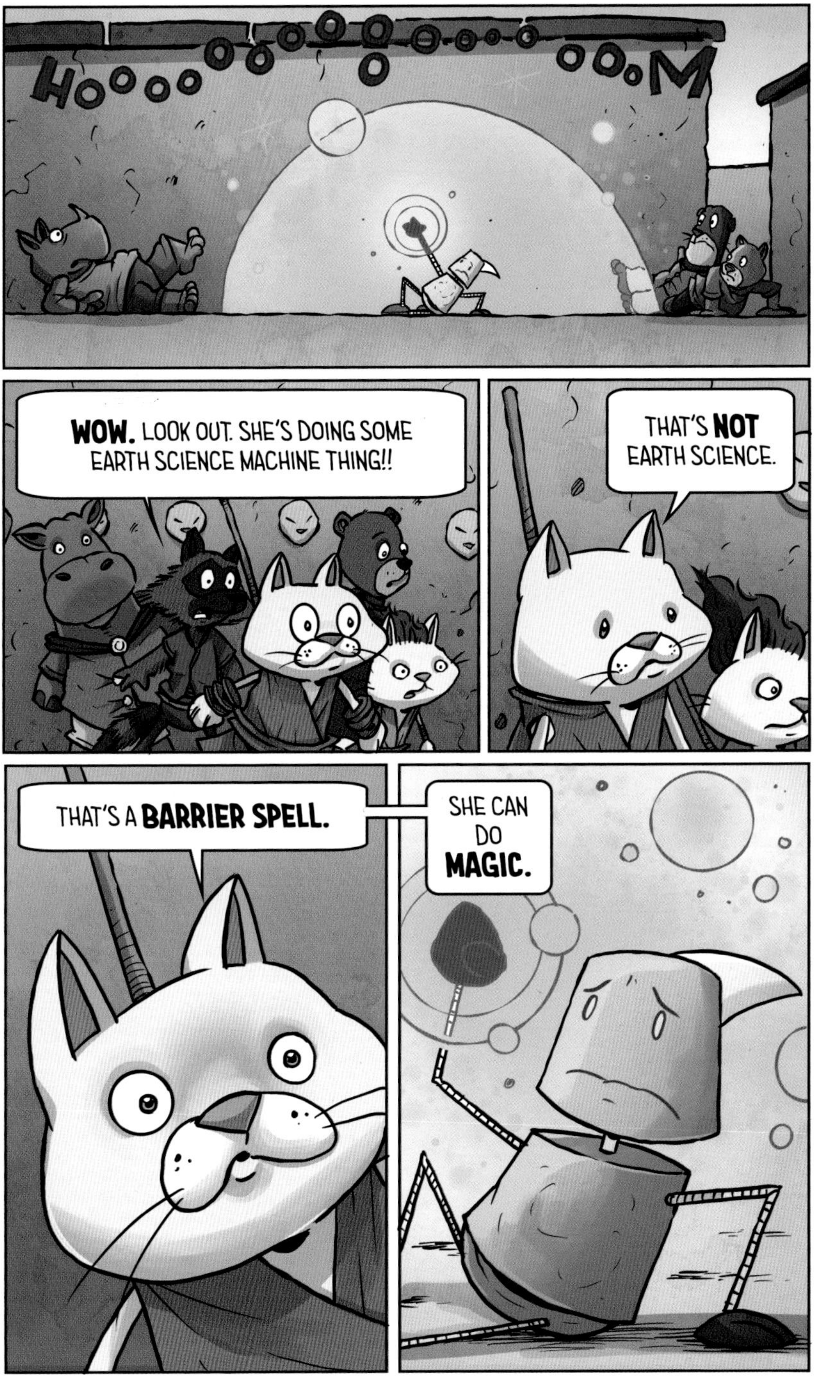
HOOOOOOOOOOOOOOOOOOOM
WOW. LOOK OUT. SHE'S DOING SOME EARTH SCIENCE MACHINE THING!!
THAT'S **NOT** EARTH SCIENCE.
THAT'S A **BARRIER SPELL.**
SHE CAN DO **MAGIC.**

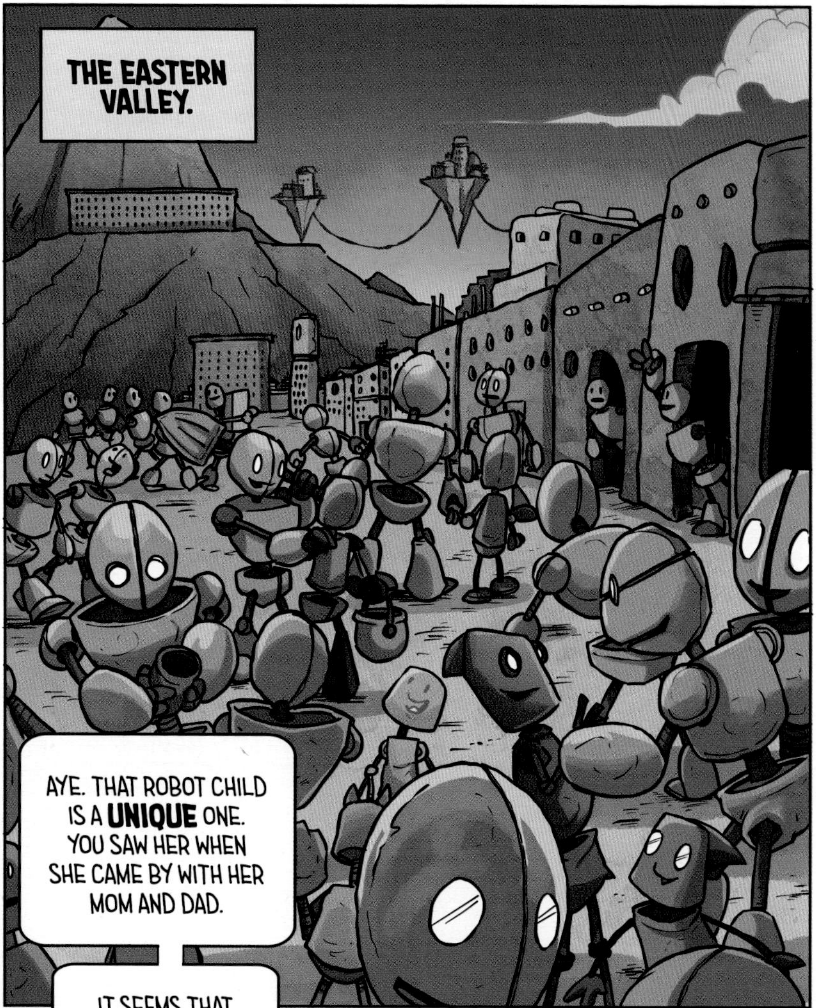
THE EASTERN VALLEY.
AYE. THAT ROBOT CHILD IS A **UNIQUE** ONE. YOU SAW HER WHEN SHE CAME BY WITH HER MOM AND DAD.

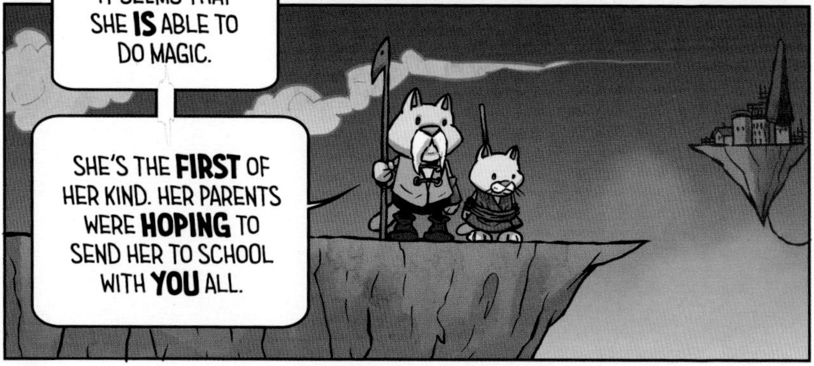
IT SEEMS THAT SHE **IS** ABLE TO DO MAGIC.
SHE'S THE **FIRST** OF HER KIND. HER PARENTS WERE **HOPING** TO SEND HER TO SCHOOL WITH **YOU** ALL.

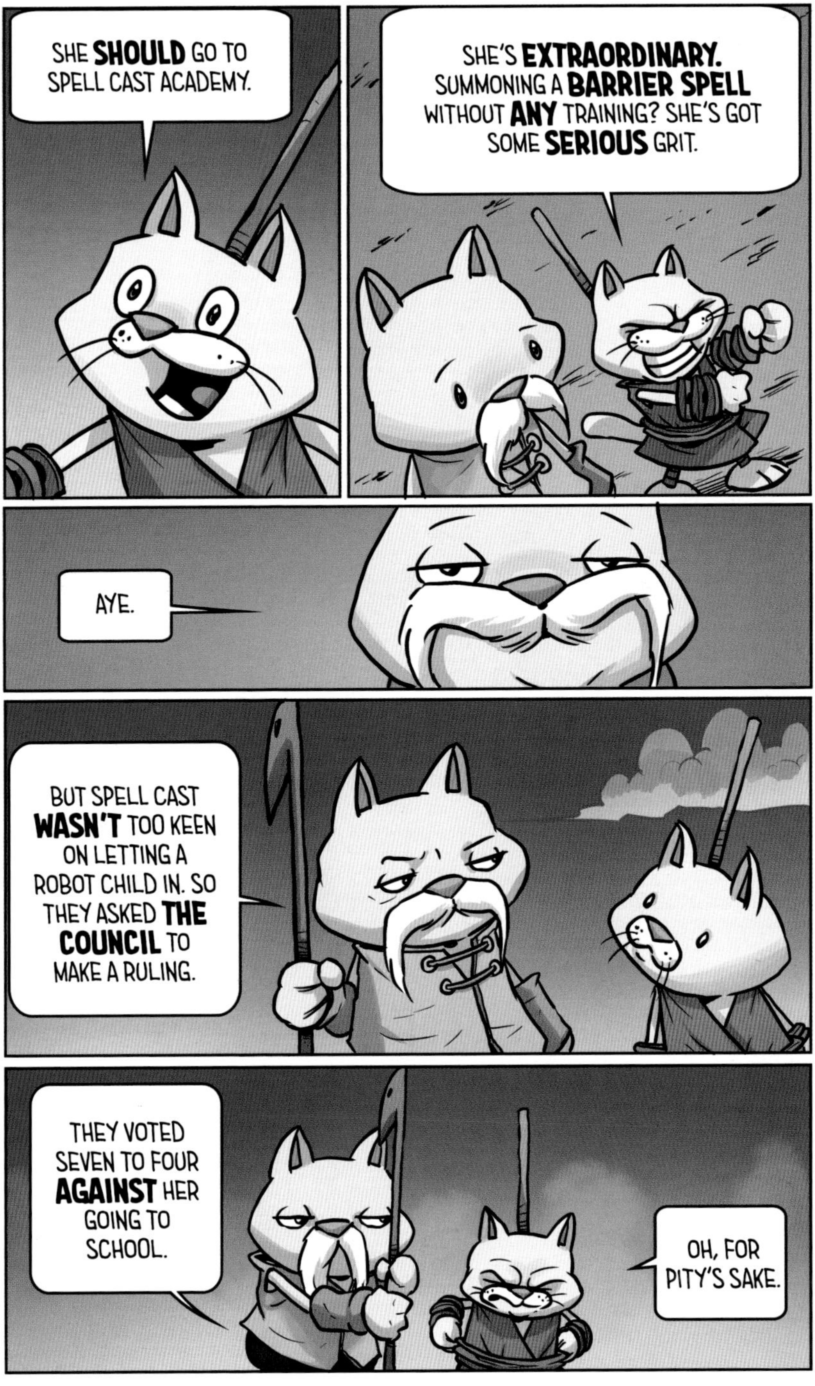
SHE **SHOULD** GO TO SPELL CAST ACADEMY.
SHE'S **EXTRAORDINARY.** SUMMONING A **BARRIER SPELL** WITHOUT **ANY** TRAINING? SHE'S GOT SOME **SERIOUS** GRIT.
AYE.
BUT SPELL CAST **WASN'T** TOO KEEN ON LETTING A ROBOT CHILD IN. SO THEY ASKED **THE COUNCIL** TO MAKE A RULING.
THEY VOTED SEVEN TO FOUR **AGAINST** HER GOING TO SCHOOL.
OH, FOR PITY'S SAKE.

YEAH. THE COUNCIL MIGHT BE A **WISE** BUNCH, BUT THEY **ALSO** CAN MANAGE TO BE A SCARED IGNORANT BUNCH OF **HOLYILLIAS.**

BUT **I'M** GOING TO WORK ON THEM. IT'S **NOT** OVER FOR HER.

THEY'RE **NOT** BEING FAIR, DAD.

NO.

PEOPLE DON'T LIKE **CHANGE.** AND PEOPLE **REALLY** DON'T LIKE IT WHEN **PEOPLE** CHANGE.

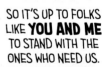

SO IT'S UP TO FOLKS LIKE **YOU AND ME** TO STAND WITH THE ONES WHO NEED US.

CHAPTER 4

REALLY GETTING SCHOOLED

WELCOME TO WOMBATTON ACADEMY OF BETTER MAGIC.

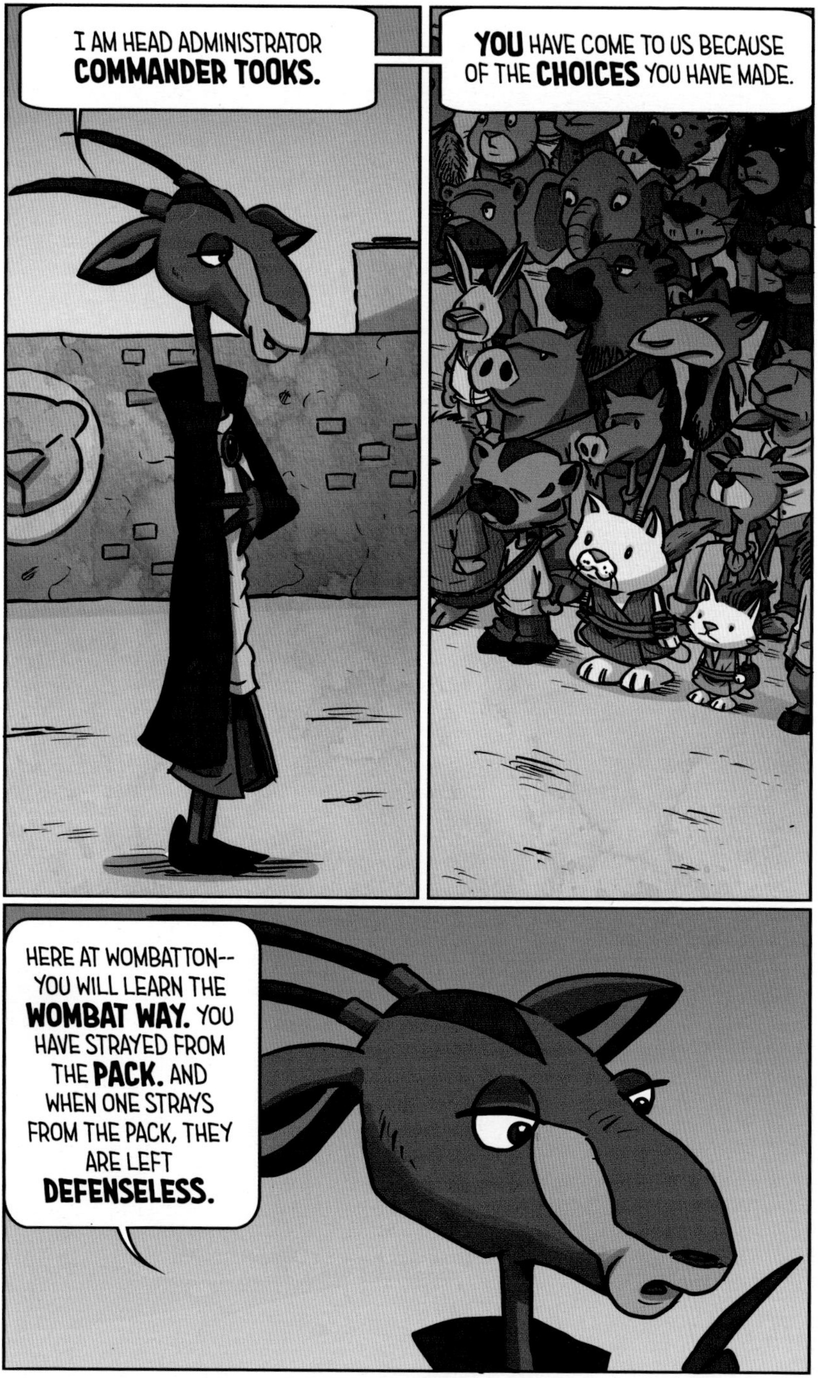
I AM HEAD ADMINISTRATOR COMMANDER TOOKS.
YOU HAVE COME TO US BECAUSE OF THE CHOICES YOU HAVE MADE.
HERE AT WOMBATTON-- YOU WILL LEARN THE WOMBAT WAY. YOU HAVE STRAYED FROM THE PACK. AND WHEN ONE STRAYS FROM THE PACK, THEY ARE LEFT DEFENSELESS.

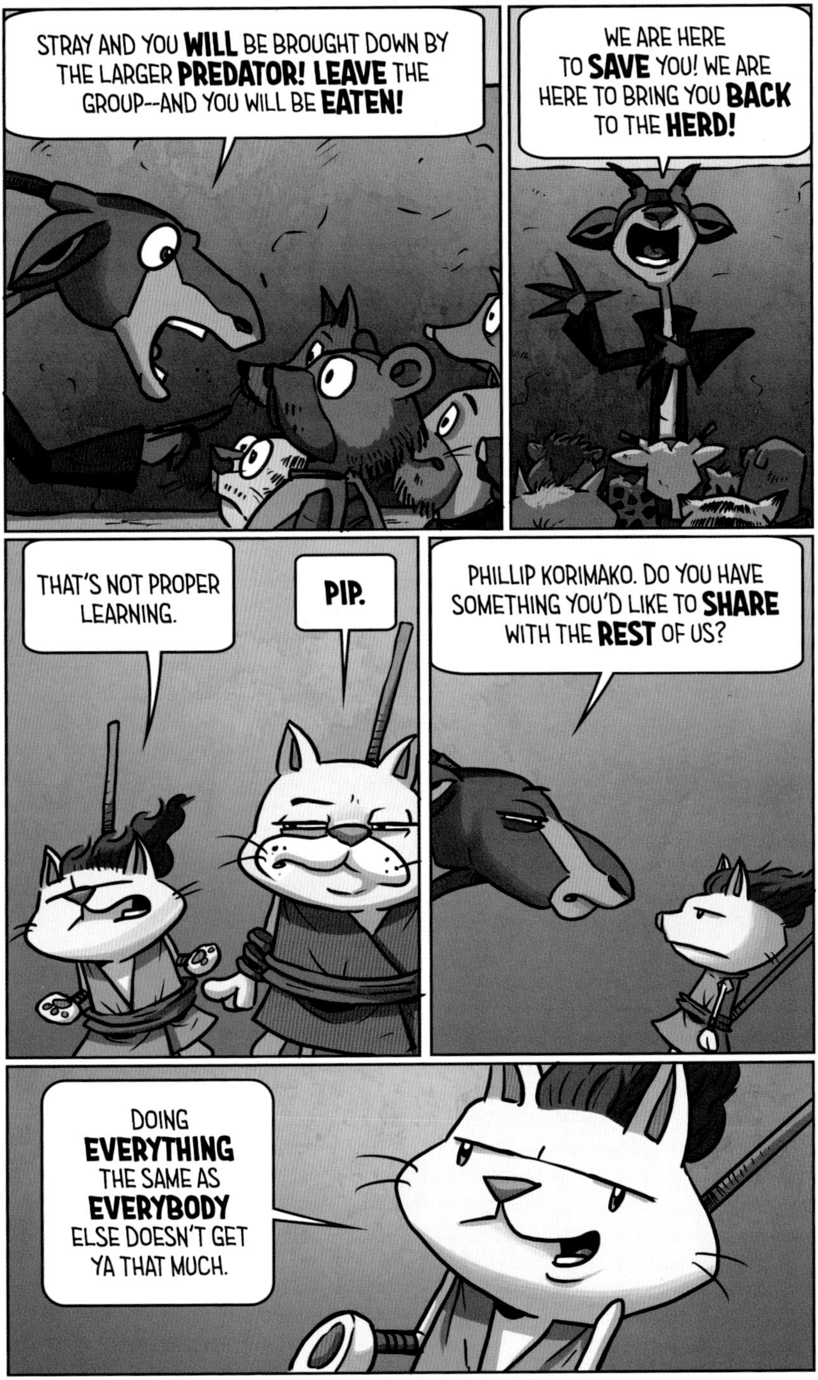
STRAY AND YOU WILL BE BROUGHT DOWN BY THE LARGER PREDATOR! LEAVE THE GROUP--AND YOU WILL BE EATEN!
WE ARE HERE TO SAVE YOU! WE ARE HERE TO BRING YOU BACK TO THE HERD!
THAT'S NOT PROPER LEARNING.
PIP.
PHILLIP KORIMAKO. DO YOU HAVE SOMETHING YOU'D LIKE TO SHARE WITH THE REST OF US?
DOING EVERYTHING THE SAME AS EVERYBODY ELSE DOESN'T GET YA THAT MUCH.

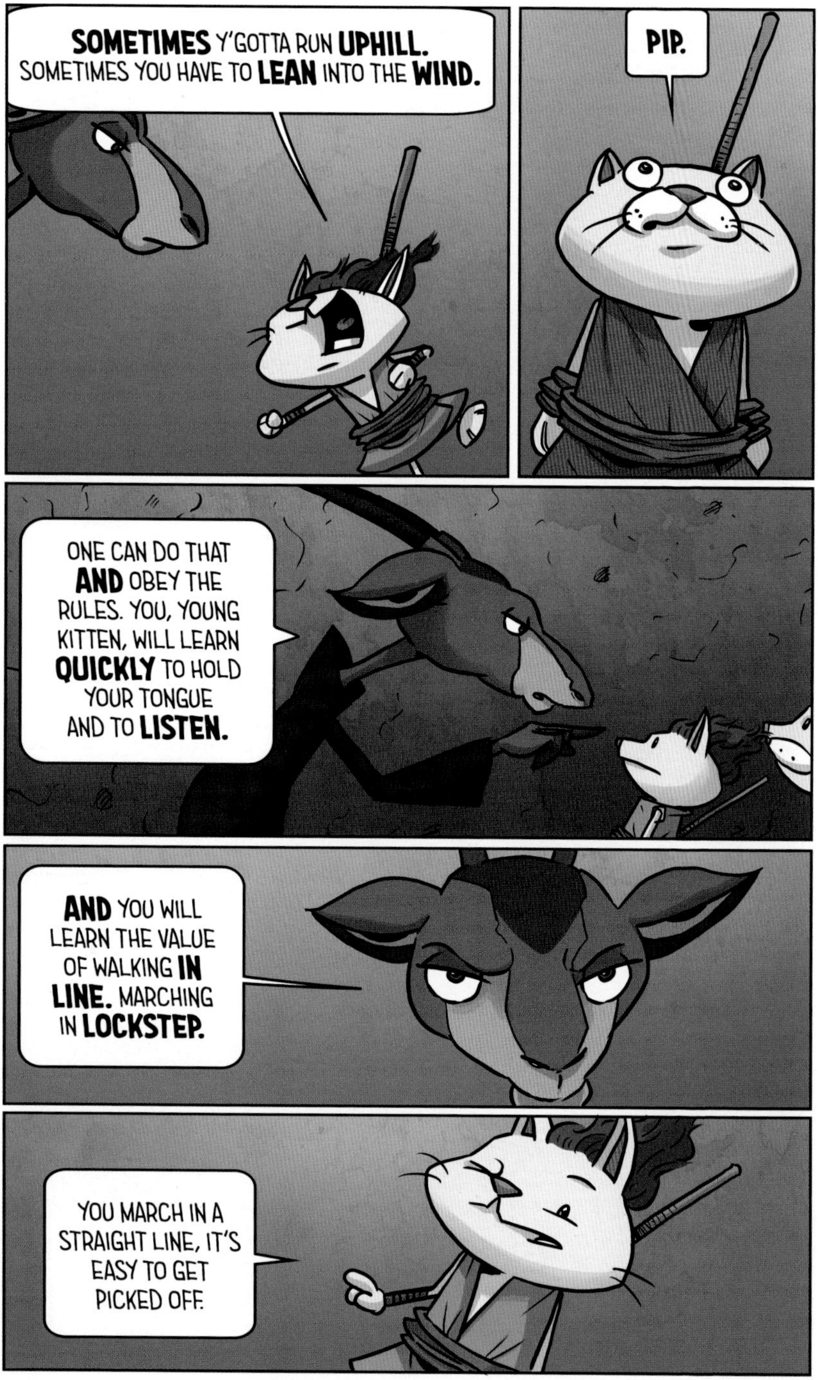
SOMETIMES Y'GOTTA RUN UPHILL. SOMETIMES YOU HAVE TO LEAN INTO THE WIND.
PIP.
ONE CAN DO THAT AND OBEY THE RULES. YOU, YOUNG KITTEN, WILL LEARN QUICKLY TO HOLD YOUR TONGUE AND TO LISTEN.
AND YOU WILL LEARN THE VALUE OF WALKING IN LINE. MARCHING IN LOCKSTEP.
YOU MARCH IN A STRAIGHT LINE, IT'S EASY TO GET PICKED OFF.

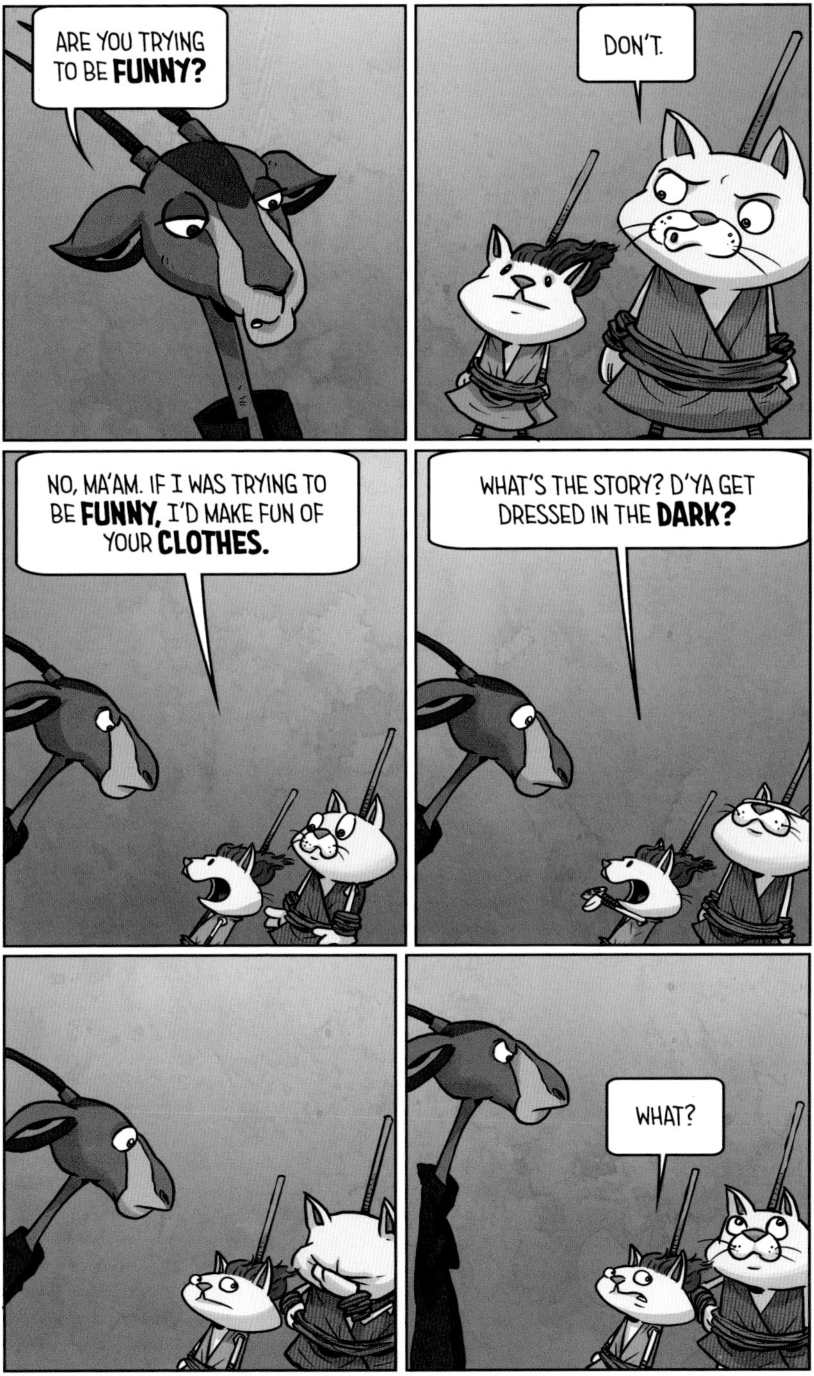
ARE YOU TRYING TO BE FUNNY?
DON'T.
NO, MA'AM. IF I WAS TRYING TO BE FUNNY, I'D MAKE FUN OF YOUR CLOTHES.
WHAT'S THE STORY? D'YA GET DRESSED IN THE DARK?
WHAT?

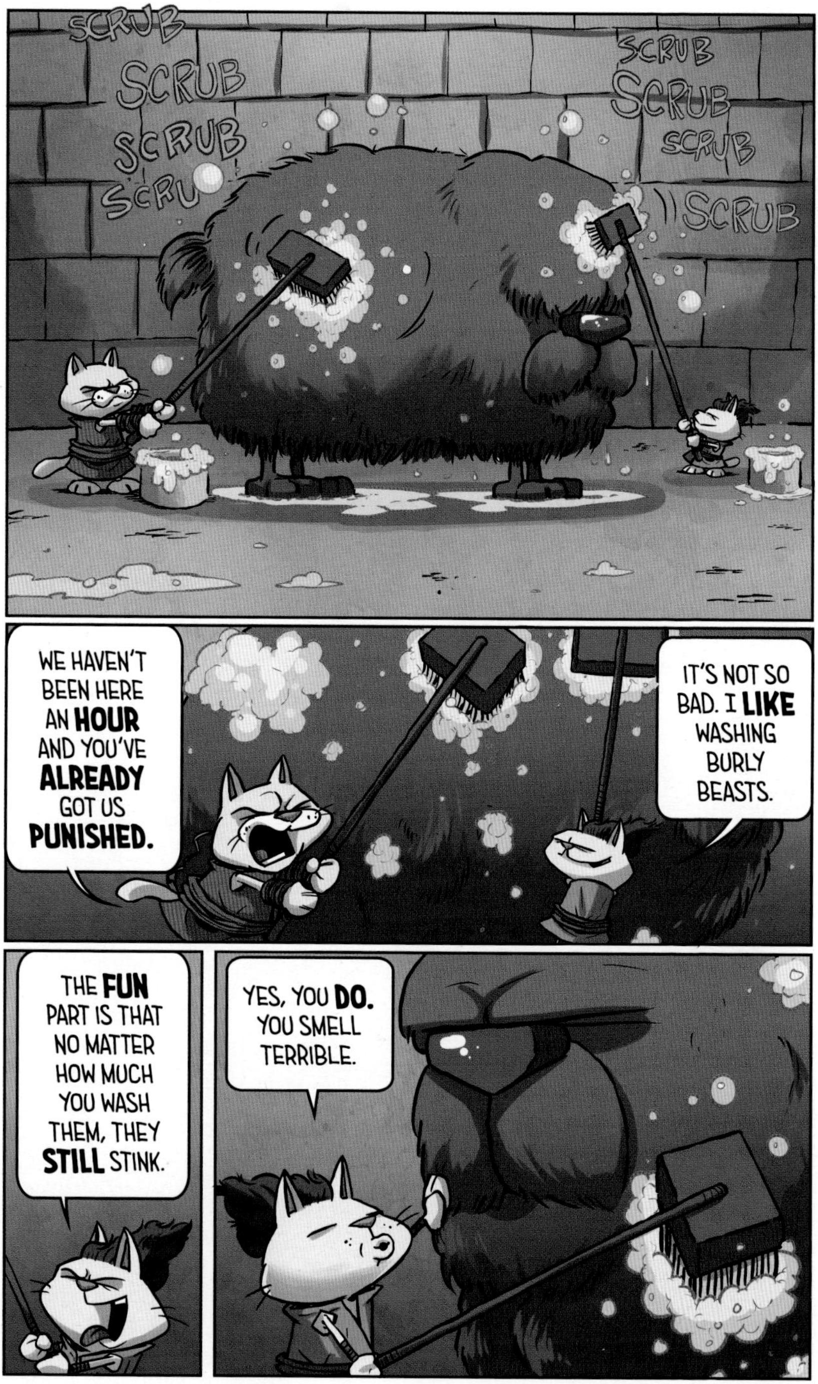
SCRUB
SCRUB
SCRUB
SCRU
SCRUB
SCRUB
SCRUB
SCRUB
WE HAVEN'T BEEN HERE AN **HOUR** AND YOU'VE **ALREADY** GOT US **PUNISHED.**
IT'S NOT SO BAD. I **LIKE** WASHING BURLY BEASTS.
THE **FUN** PART IS THAT NO MATTER HOW MUCH YOU WASH THEM, THEY **STILL** STINK.
YES, YOU **DO.** YOU SMELL TERRIBLE.

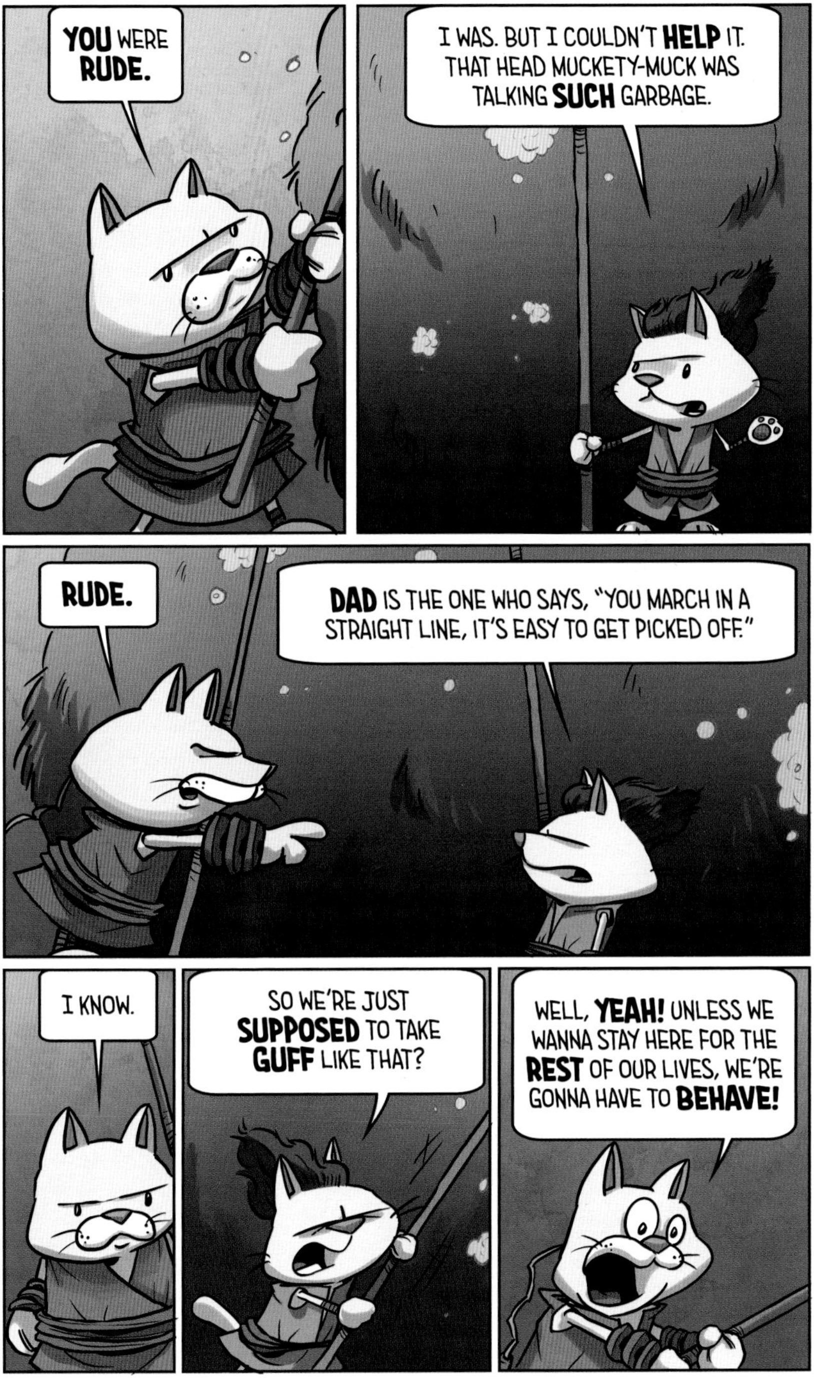

YOU WERE RUDE.
I WAS. BUT I COULDN'T HELP IT. THAT HEAD MUCKETY-MUCK WAS TALKING SUCH GARBAGE.
RUDE.
DAD IS THE ONE WHO SAYS, "YOU MARCH IN A STRAIGHT LINE, IT'S EASY TO GET PICKED OFF."
I KNOW.
SO WE'RE JUST SUPPOSED TO TAKE GUFF LIKE THAT?
WELL, YEAH! UNLESS WE WANNA STAY HERE FOR THE REST OF OUR LIVES, WE'RE GONNA HAVE TO BEHAVE!

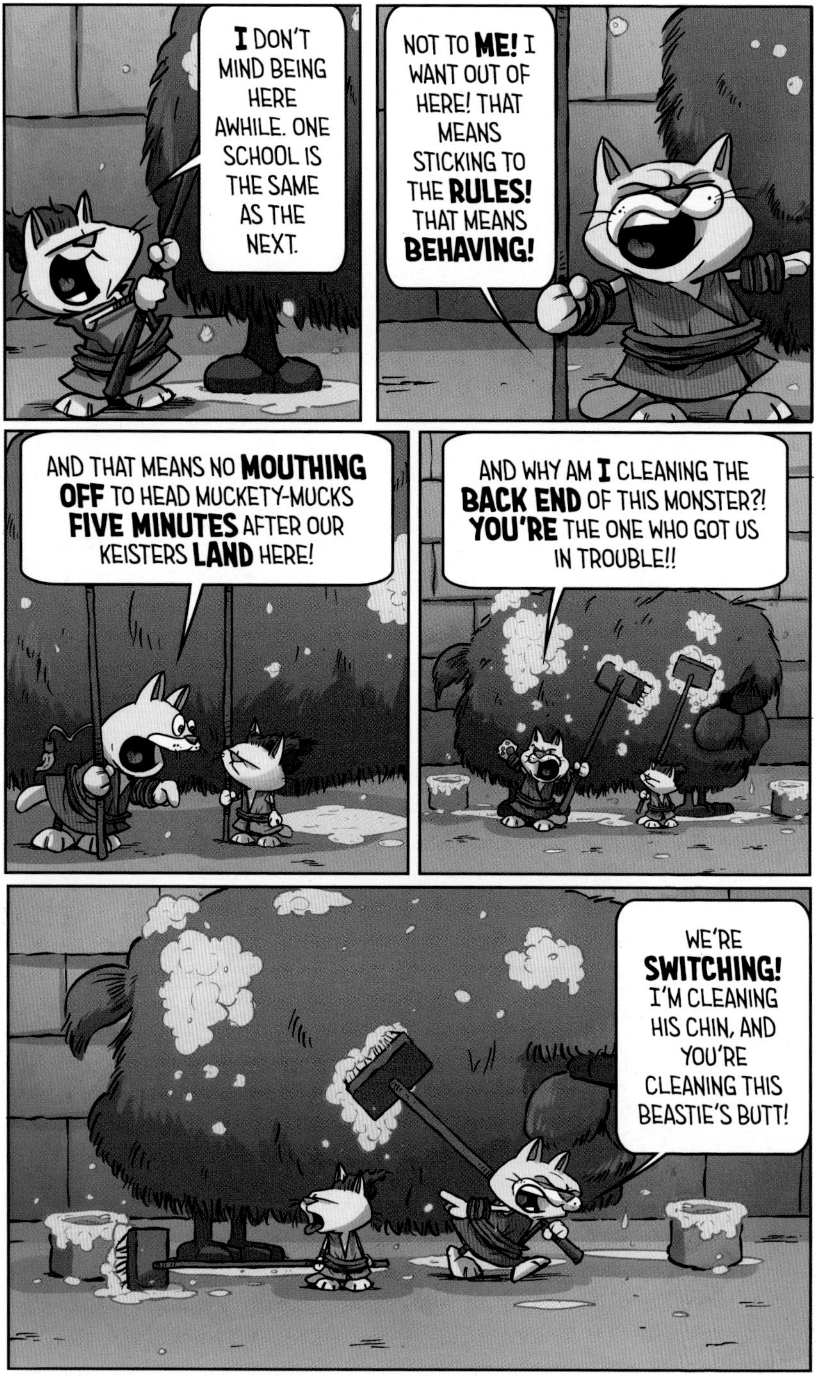
I DON'T MIND BEING HERE AWHILE. ONE SCHOOL IS THE SAME AS THE NEXT.
NOT TO ME! I WANT OUT OF HERE! THAT MEANS STICKING TO THE RULES! THAT MEANS BEHAVING!
AND THAT MEANS NO MOUTHING OFF TO HEAD MUCKETY-MUCKS FIVE MINUTES AFTER OUR KEISTERS LAND HERE!
AND WHY AM I CLEANING THE BACK END OF THIS MONSTER?! YOU'RE THE ONE WHO GOT US IN TROUBLE!!
WE'RE SWITCHING! I'M CLEANING HIS CHIN, AND YOU'RE CLEANING THIS BEASTIE'S BUTT!

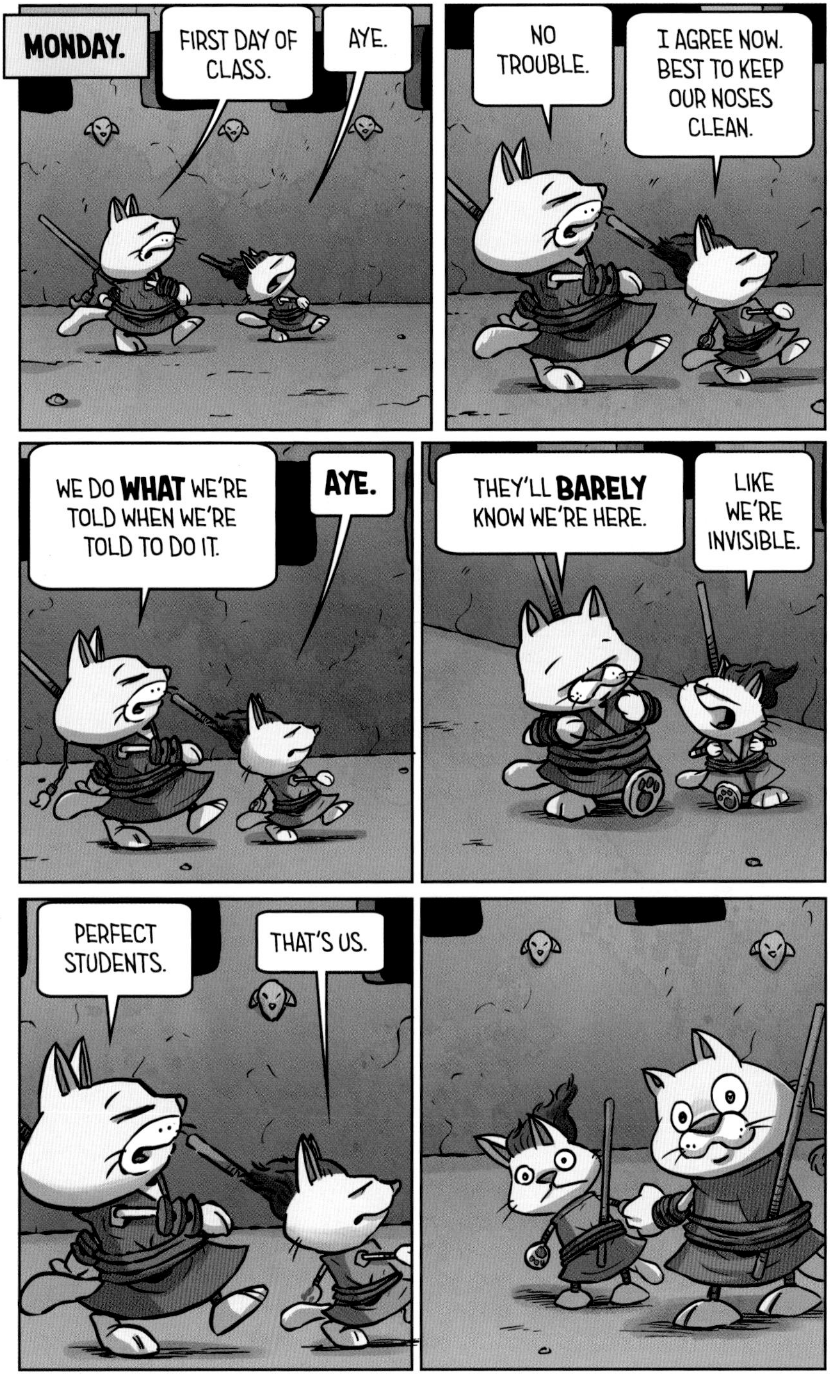
MONDAY.
FIRST DAY OF CLASS.
AYE.
NO TROUBLE.
I AGREE NOW. BEST TO KEEP OUR NOSES CLEAN.
WE DO **WHAT** WE'RE TOLD WHEN WE'RE TOLD TO DO IT.
AYE.
THEY'LL **BARELY** KNOW WE'RE HERE.
LIKE WE'RE INVISIBLE.
PERFECT STUDENTS.
THAT'S US.

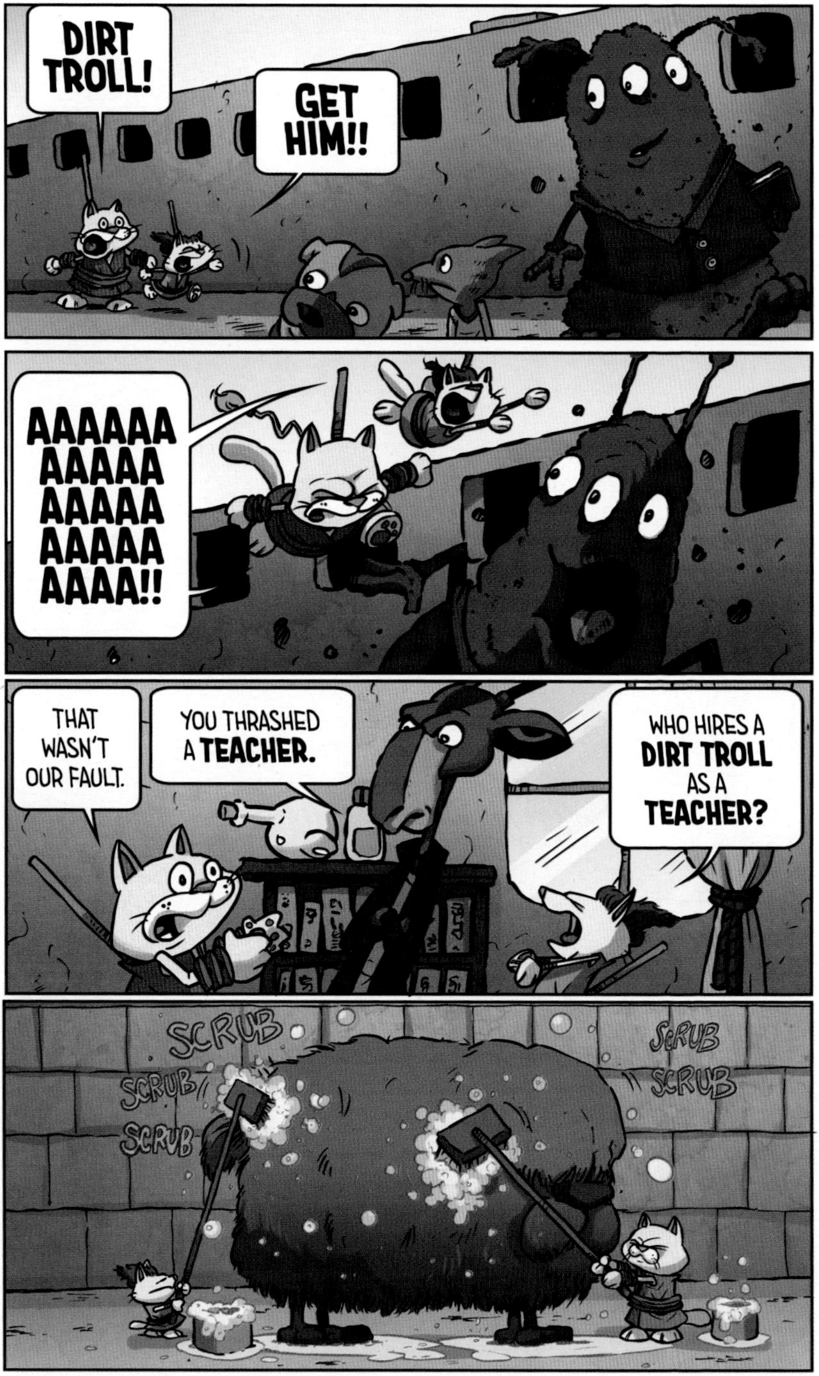
DIRT TROLL!
GET HIM!!
AAAAAA AAAAA AAAAA AAAAA AAAA!!
THAT WASN'T OUR FAULT.
YOU THRASHED A TEACHER.
WHO HIRES A DIRT TROLL AS A TEACHER?
SCRUB
SCRUB
SCRUB
SCRUB
SCRUB

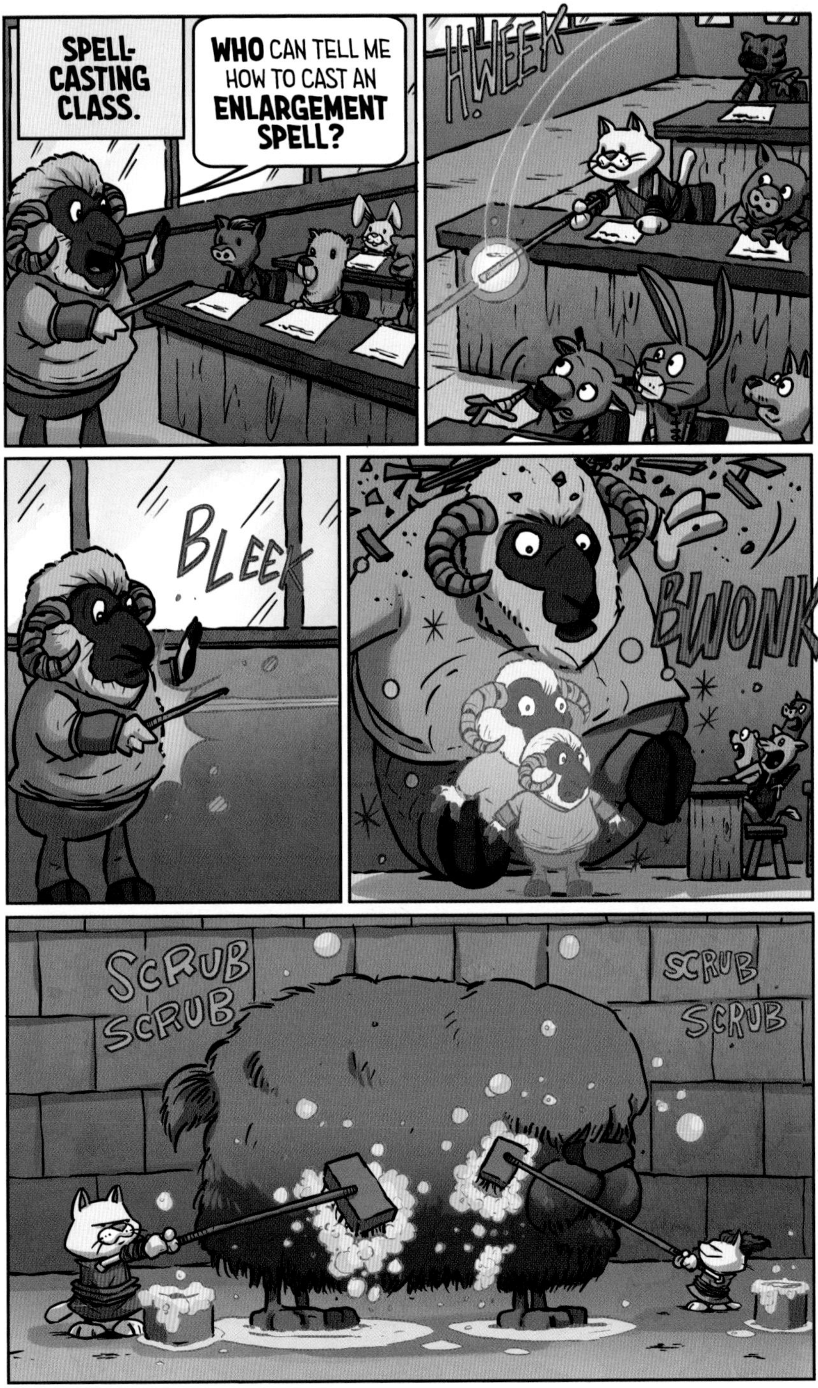
SPELL-
CASTING
CLASS.
WHO CAN TELL ME HOW TO CAST AN ENLARGEMENT SPELL?
HWEEK
BLEEK
BWONK
SCRUB
SCRUB
SCRUB
SCRUB

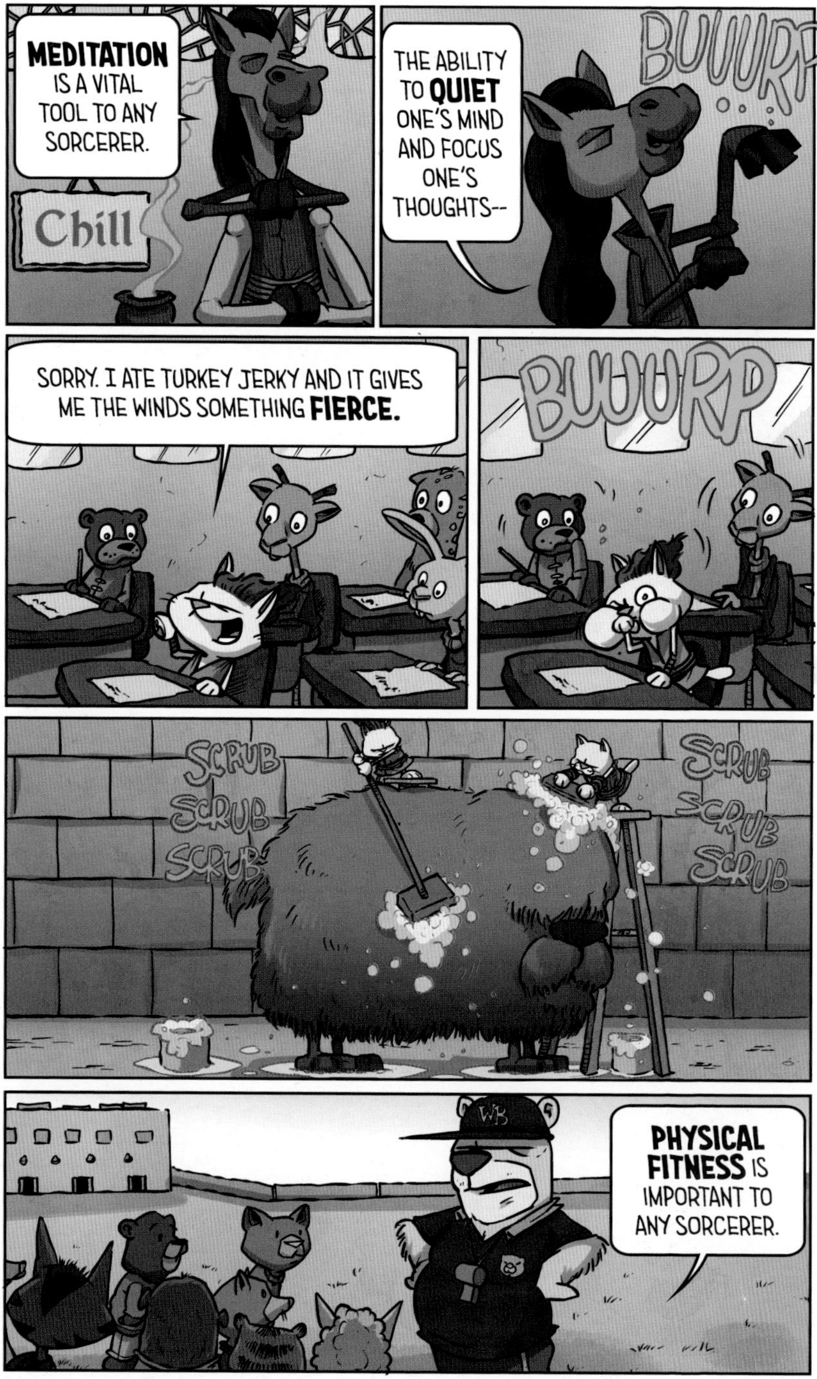
MEDITATION IS A VITAL TOOL TO ANY SORCERER.
Chill
THE ABILITY TO QUIET ONE'S MIND AND FOCUS ONE'S THOUGHTS--
BUUURP
SORRY. I ATE TURKEY JERKY AND IT GIVES ME THE WINDS SOMETHING FIERCE.
BUUURP
SCRUB
SCRUB
SCRUB
SCRUB
SCRUB
SCRUB
WB
PHYSICAL FITNESS IS IMPORTANT TO ANY SORCERER.

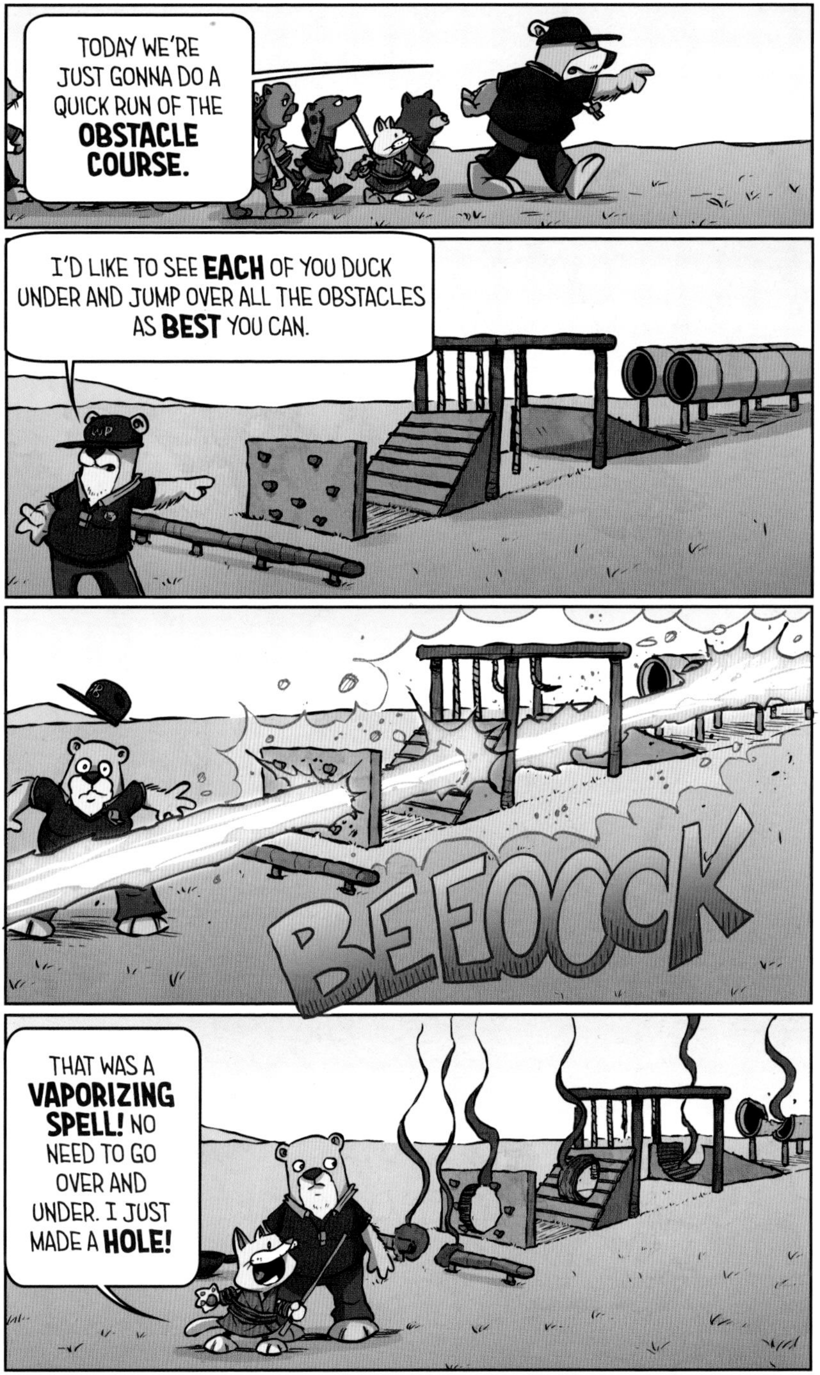
TODAY WE'RE JUST GONNA DO A QUICK RUN OF THE OBSTACLE COURSE.
I'D LIKE TO SEE EACH OF YOU DUCK UNDER AND JUMP OVER ALL THE OBSTACLES AS BEST YOU CAN.
BEEOOCK
THAT WAS A VAPORIZING SPELL! NO NEED TO GO OVER AND UNDER. I JUST MADE A HOLE!

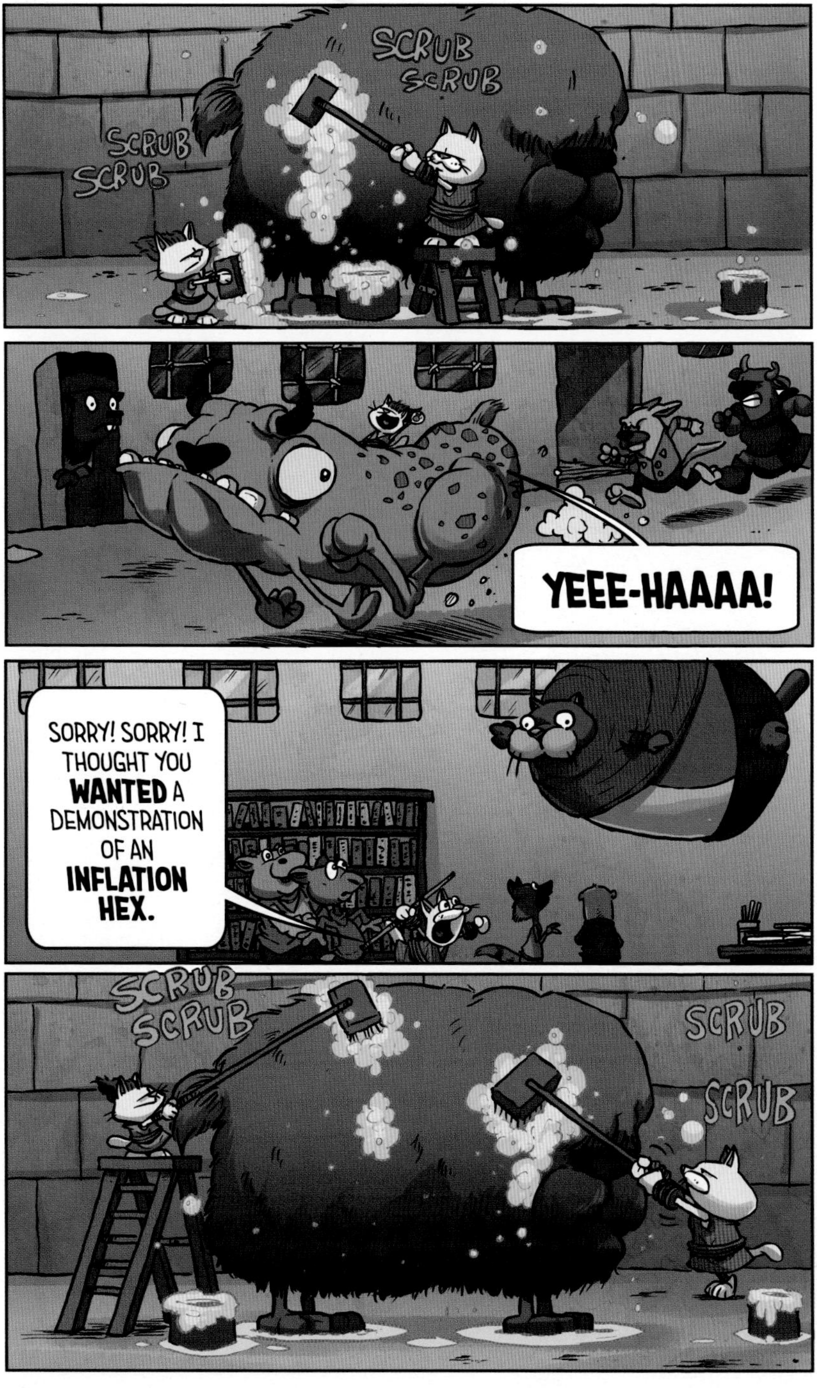
SCRUB
SCRUB
SCRUB
SCRUB
YEEE-HAAAA!
SORRY! SORRY! I THOUGHT YOU **WANTED** A DEMONSTRATION OF AN **INFLATION HEX.**
SCRUB
SCRUB
SCRUB
SCRUB

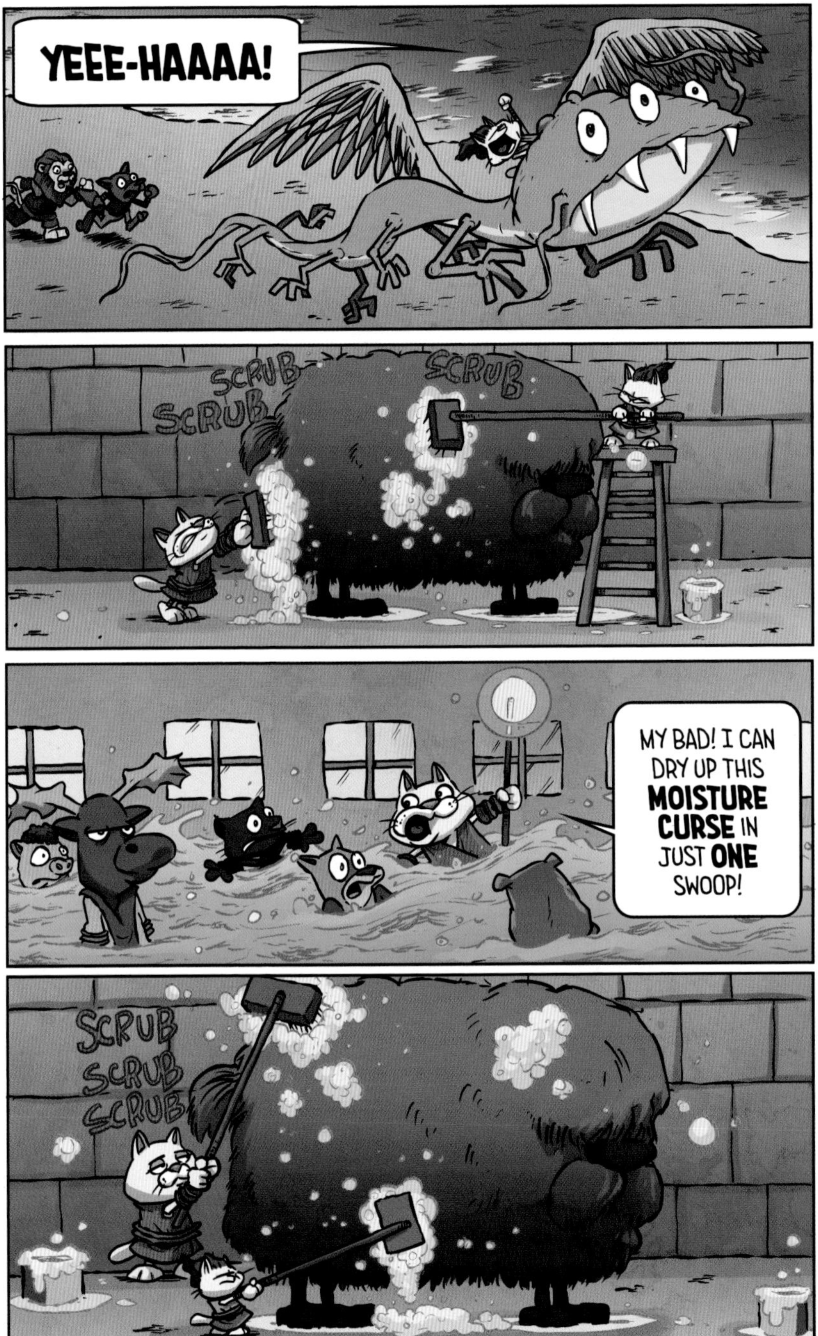
YEEE-HAAAA!
SCRUB SCRUB SCRUB
MY BAD! I CAN DRY UP THIS MOISTURE CURSE IN JUST ONE SWOOP!
SCRUB SCRUB SCRUB

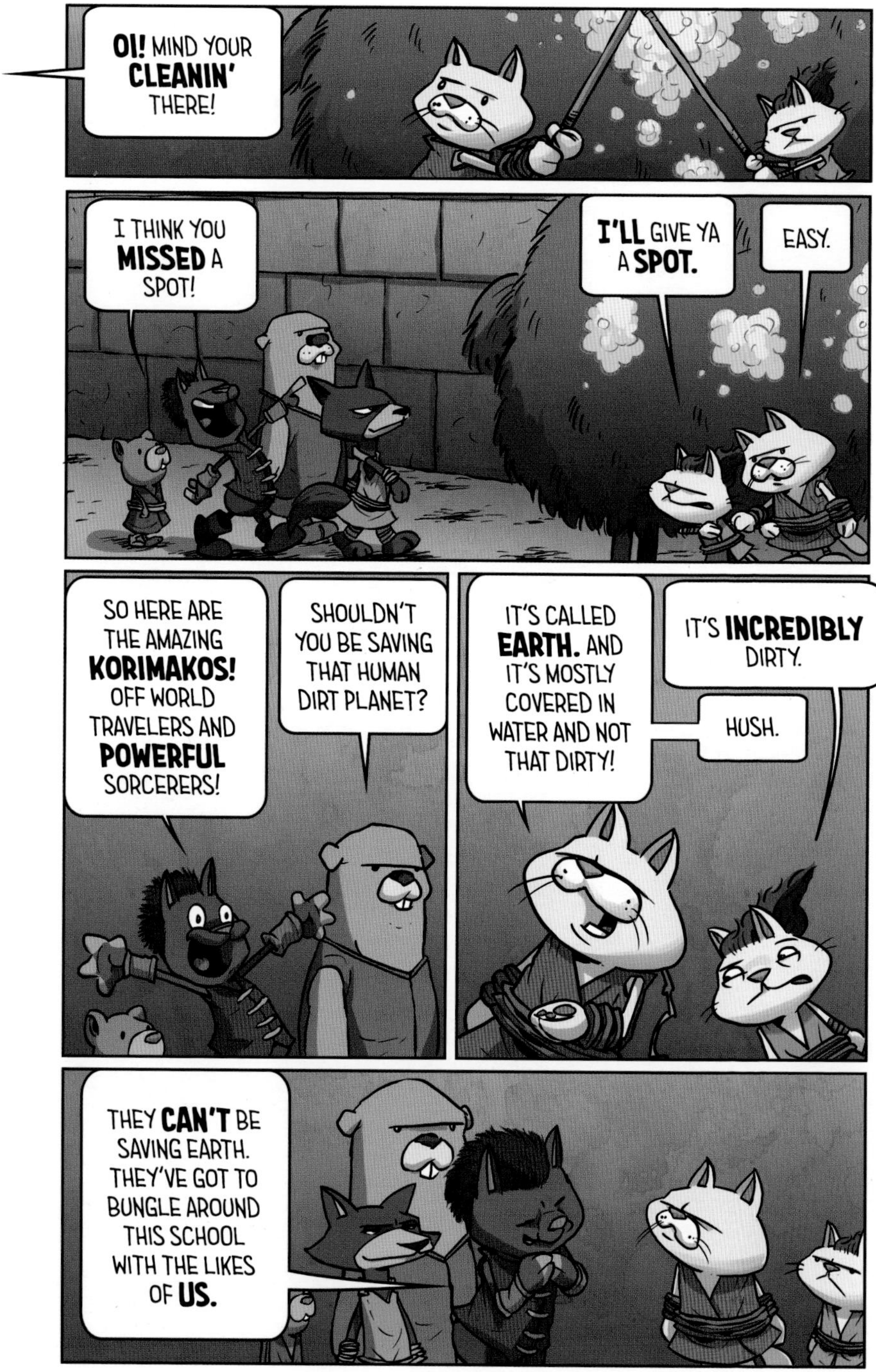
OI! MIND YOUR CLEANIN' THERE!
I THINK YOU MISSED A SPOT!
I'LL GIVE YA A SPOT.
EASY.
SO HERE ARE THE AMAZING KORIMAKOS! OFF WORLD TRAVELERS AND POWERFUL SORCERERS!
SHOULDN'T YOU BE SAVING THAT HUMAN DIRT PLANET?
IT'S CALLED EARTH. AND IT'S MOSTLY COVERED IN WATER AND NOT THAT DIRTY!
IT'S INCREDIBLY DIRTY.
HUSH.
THEY CAN'T BE SAVING EARTH. THEY'VE GOT TO BUNGLE AROUND THIS SCHOOL WITH THE LIKES OF US.

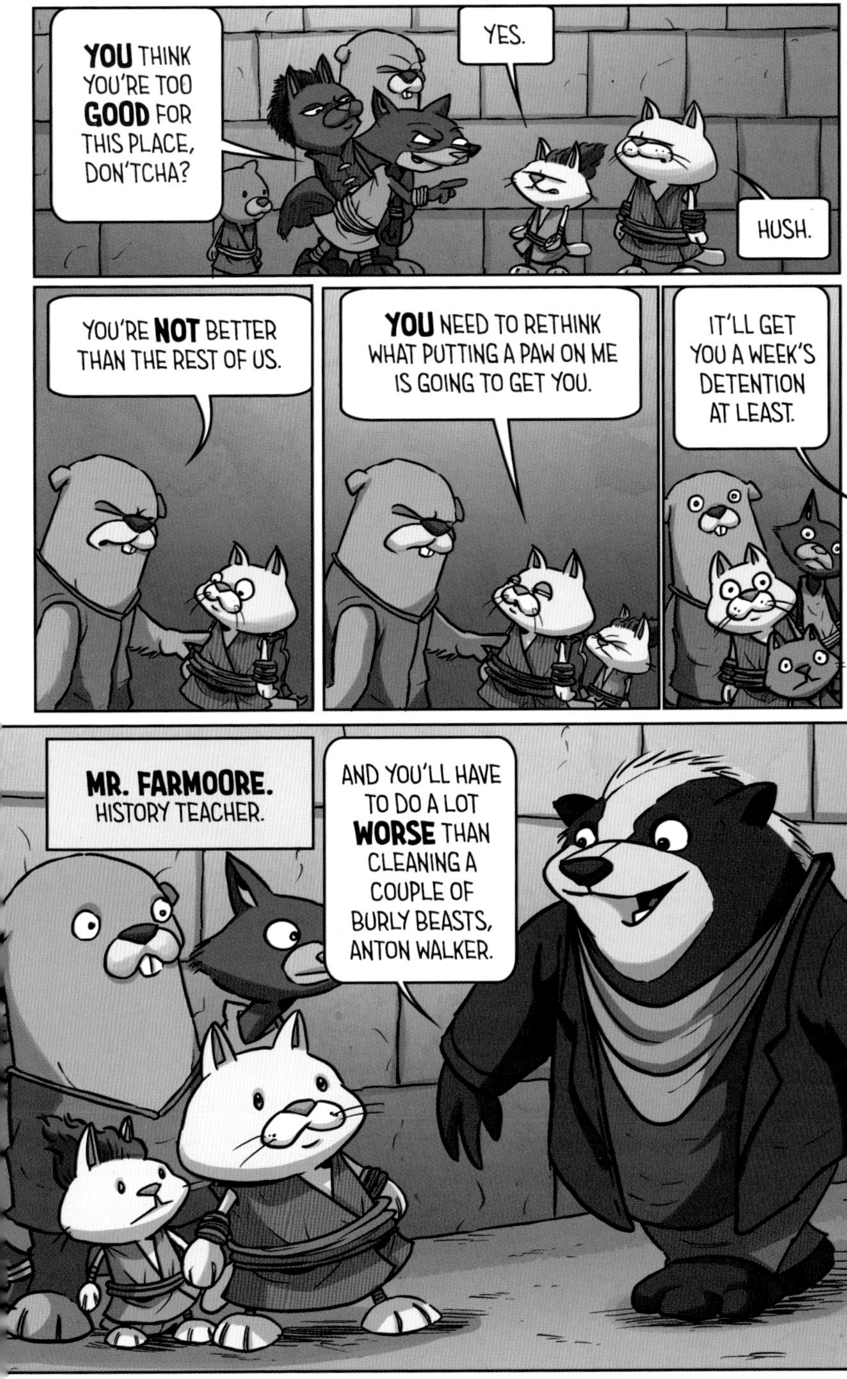

YOU THINK YOU'RE TOO GOOD FOR THIS PLACE, DON'TCHA?
YES.
HUSH.
YOU'RE NOT BETTER THAN THE REST OF US.
YOU NEED TO RETHINK WHAT PUTTING A PAW ON ME IS GOING TO GET YOU.
IT'LL GET YOU A WEEK'S DETENTION AT LEAST.
MR. FARMOORE. HISTORY TEACHER.
AND YOU'LL HAVE TO DO A LOT WORSE THAN CLEANING A COUPLE OF BURLY BEASTS, ANTON WALKER.

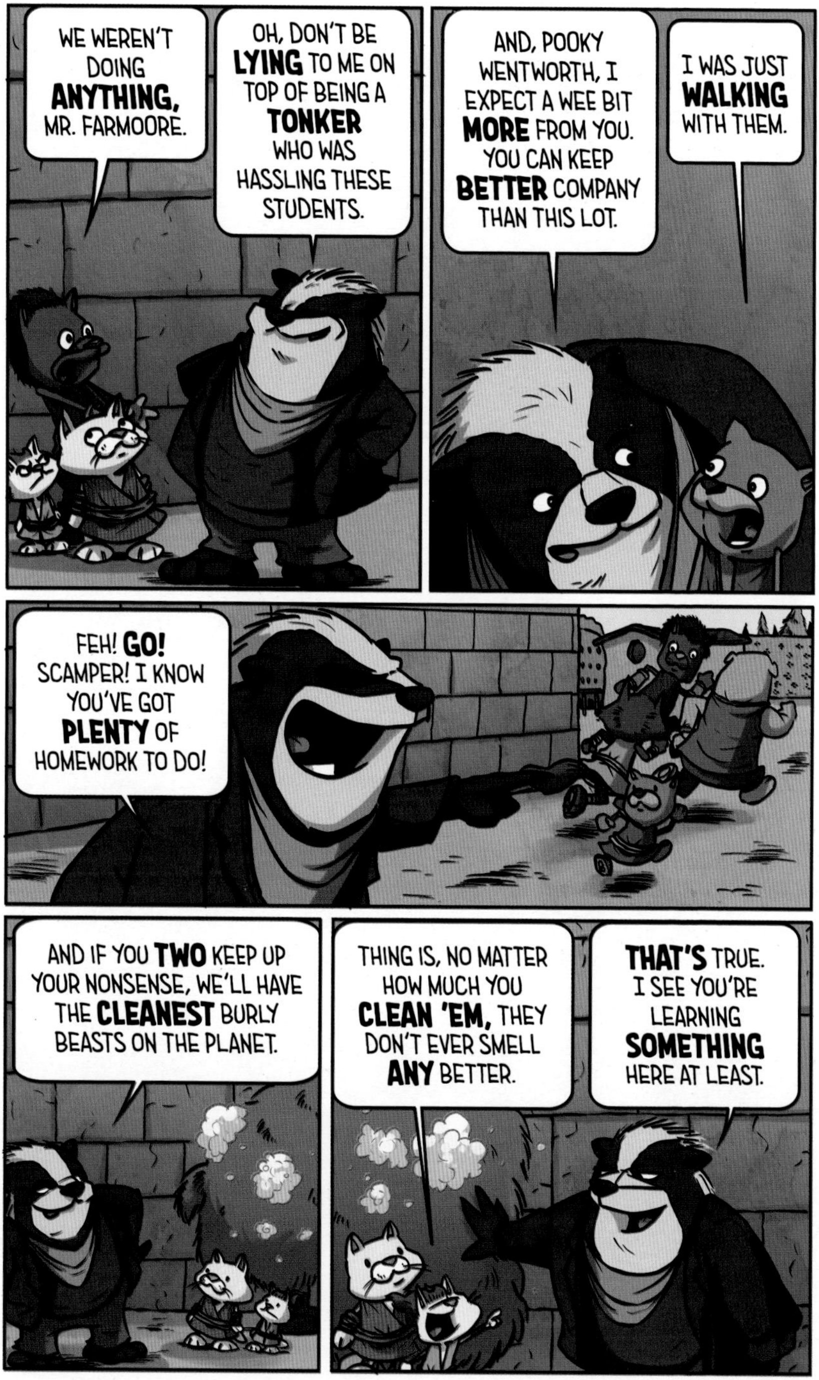
WE WEREN'T DOING ANYTHING, MR. FARMOORE.
OH, DON'T BE LYING TO ME ON TOP OF BEING A TONKER WHO WAS HASSLING THESE STUDENTS.
AND, POOKY WENTWORTH, I EXPECT A WEE BIT MORE FROM YOU. YOU CAN KEEP BETTER COMPANY THAN THIS LOT.
I WAS JUST WALKING WITH THEM.
FEH! GO! SCAMPER! I KNOW YOU'VE GOT PLENTY OF HOMEWORK TO DO!
AND IF YOU TWO KEEP UP YOUR NONSENSE, WE'LL HAVE THE CLEANEST BURLY BEASTS ON THE PLANET.
THING IS, NO MATTER HOW MUCH YOU CLEAN 'EM, THEY DON'T EVER SMELL ANY BETTER.
THAT'S TRUE. I SEE YOU'RE LEARNING SOMETHING HERE AT LEAST.

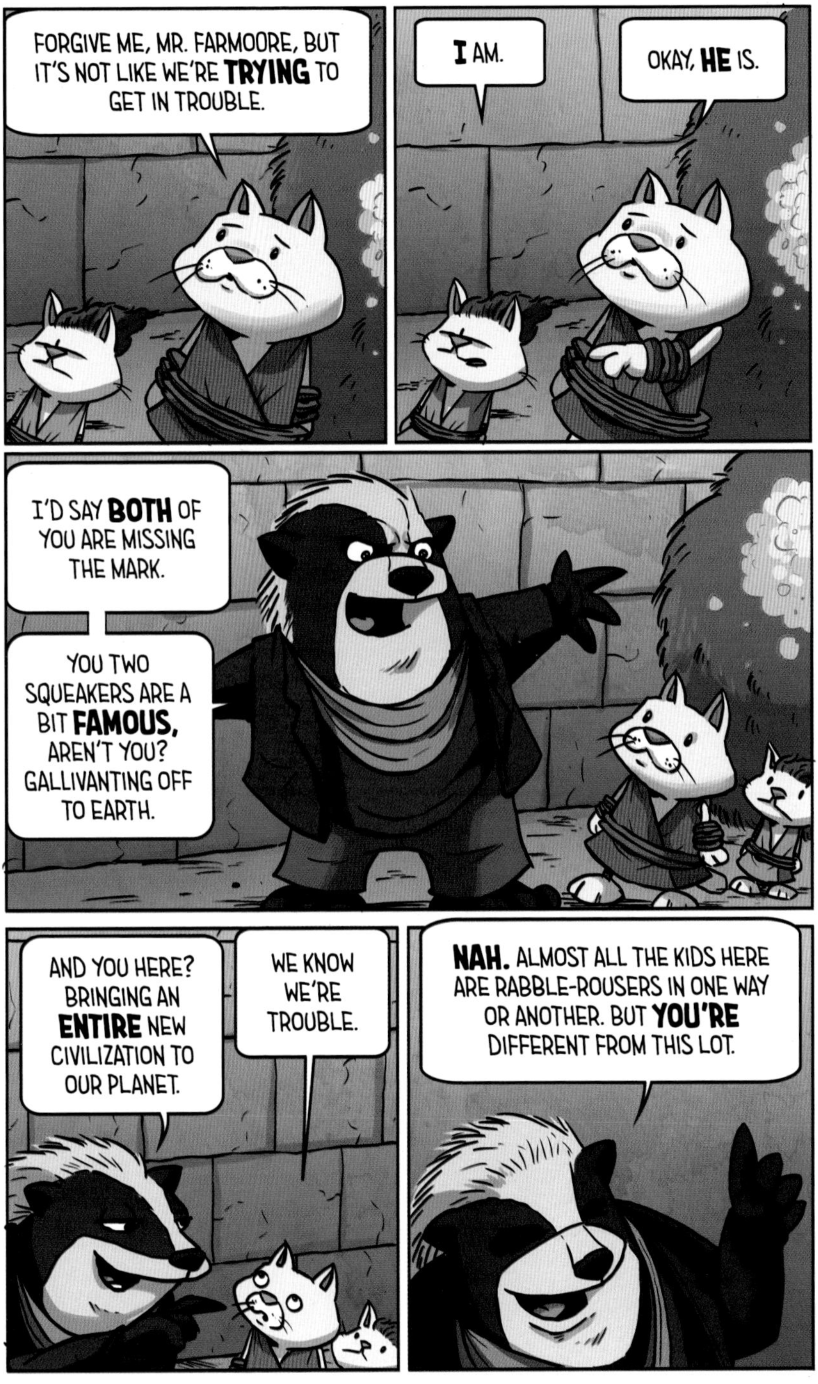
FORGIVE ME, MR. FARMOORE, BUT IT'S NOT LIKE WE'RE **TRYING** TO GET IN TROUBLE.
I AM.
OKAY, **HE** IS.
I'D SAY **BOTH** OF YOU ARE MISSING THE MARK.
YOU TWO SQUEAKERS ARE A BIT **FAMOUS,** AREN'T YOU? GALLIVANTING OFF TO EARTH.
AND YOU HERE? BRINGING AN **ENTIRE** NEW CIVILIZATION TO OUR PLANET.
WE KNOW WE'RE TROUBLE.
NAH. ALMOST ALL THE KIDS HERE ARE RABBLE-ROUSERS IN ONE WAY OR ANOTHER. BUT **YOU'RE** DIFFERENT FROM THIS LOT.

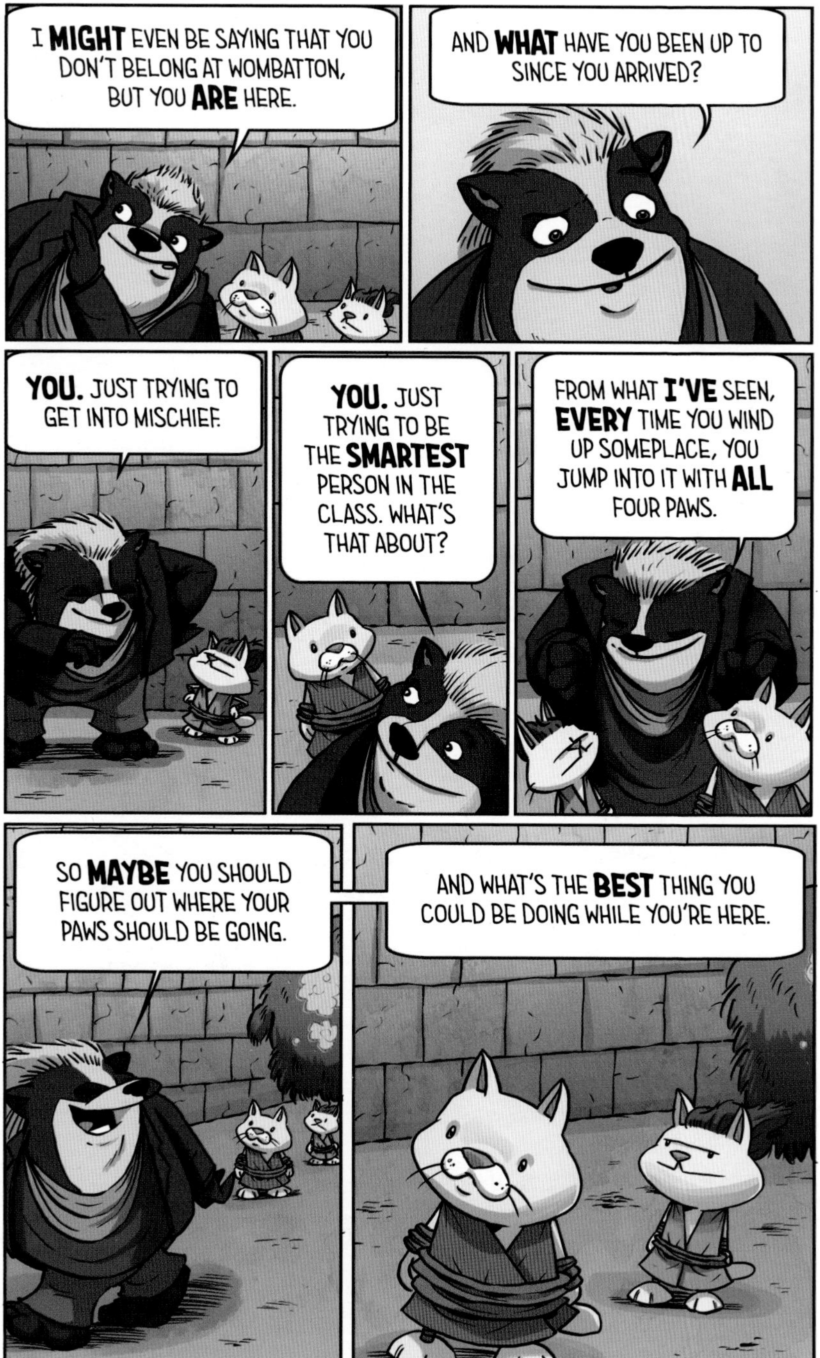
I MIGHT EVEN BE SAYING THAT YOU DON'T BELONG AT WOMBATTON, BUT YOU ARE HERE.
AND WHAT HAVE YOU BEEN UP TO SINCE YOU ARRIVED?
YOU. JUST TRYING TO GET INTO MISCHIEF.
YOU. JUST TRYING TO BE THE SMARTEST PERSON IN THE CLASS. WHAT'S THAT ABOUT?
FROM WHAT I'VE SEEN, EVERY TIME YOU WIND UP SOMEPLACE, YOU JUMP INTO IT WITH ALL FOUR PAWS.
SO MAYBE YOU SHOULD FIGURE OUT WHERE YOUR PAWS SHOULD BE GOING.
AND WHAT'S THE BEST THING YOU COULD BE DOING WHILE YOU'RE HERE.

CHAPTER 5

EXTRACURRICULAR ACTIVITY

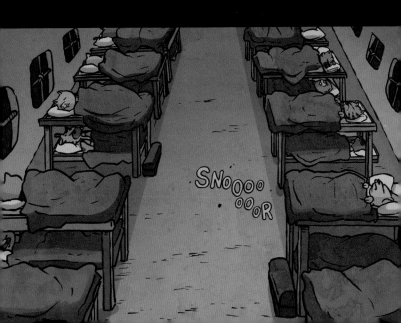

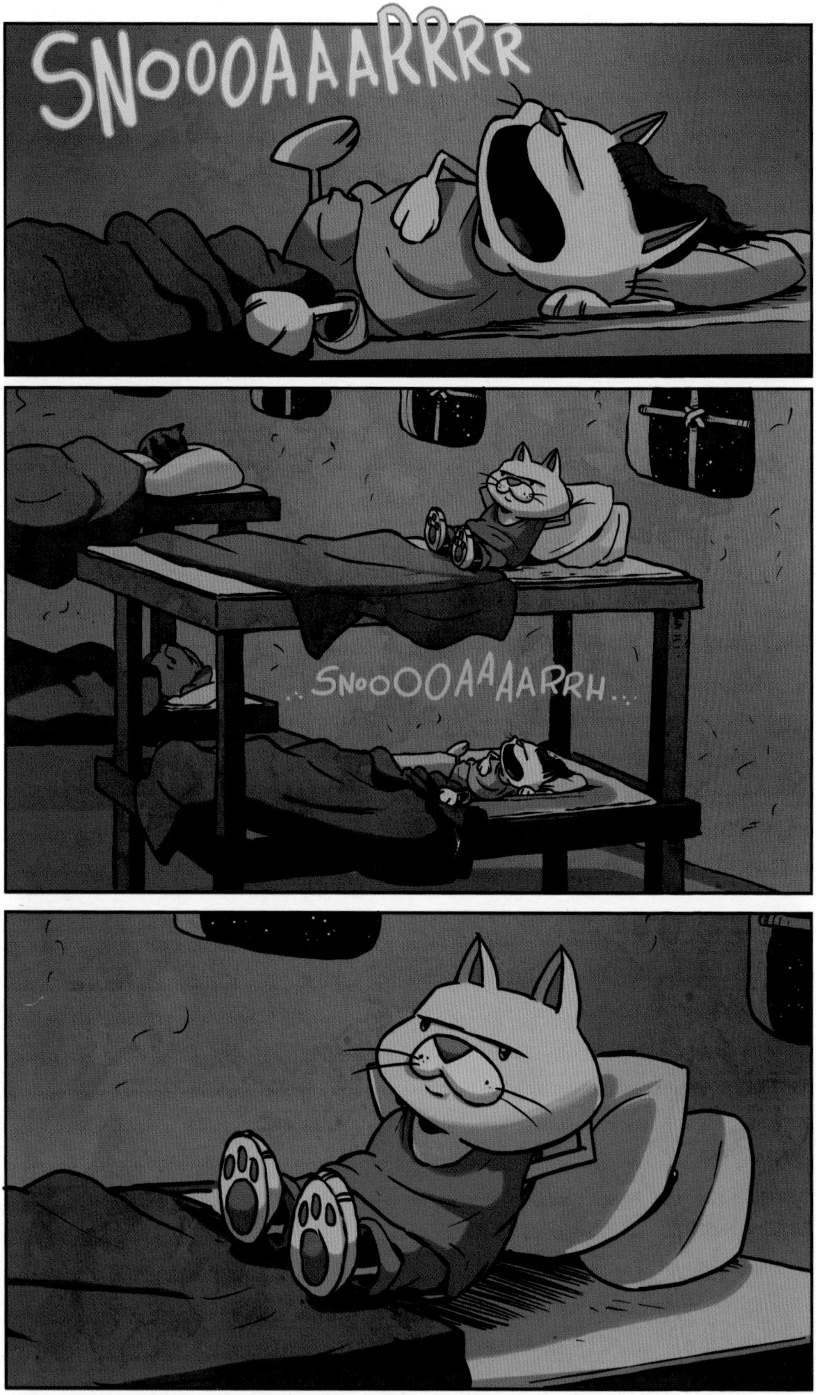
SNOOOAAARRRR
..SNoOOOAAAARRH...

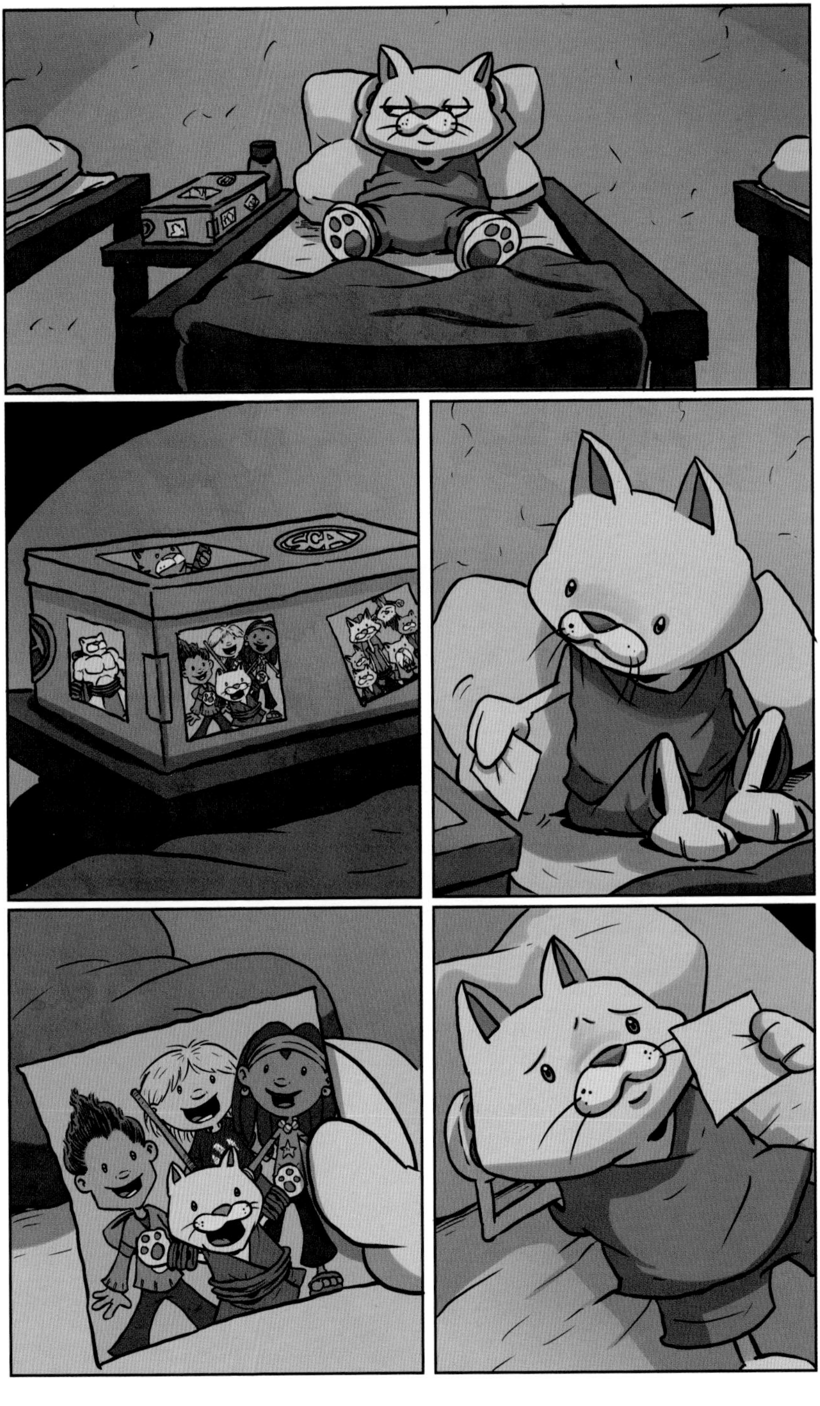

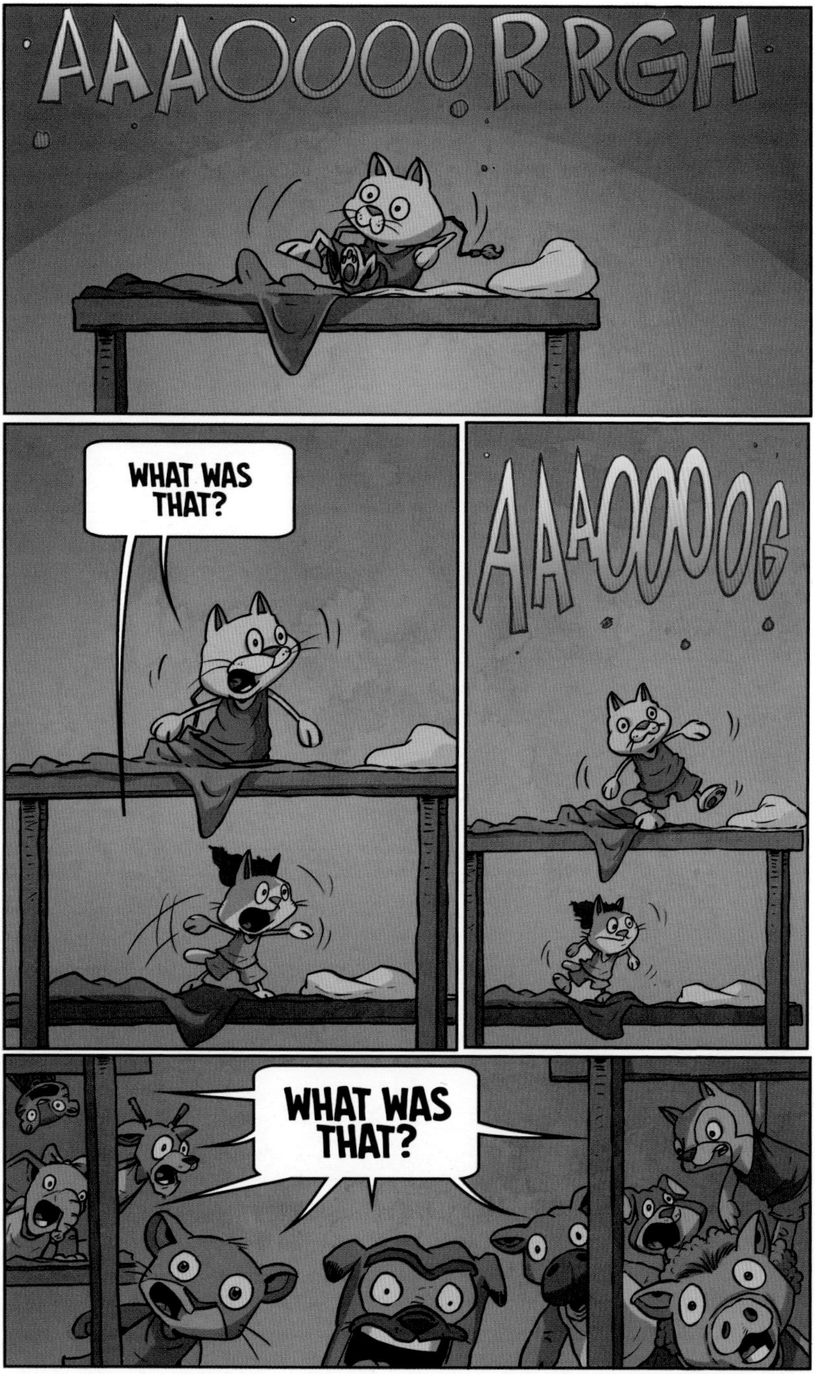
AAAOOOORRGH
WHAT WAS THAT?
AAAOOOOG
WHAT WAS THAT?

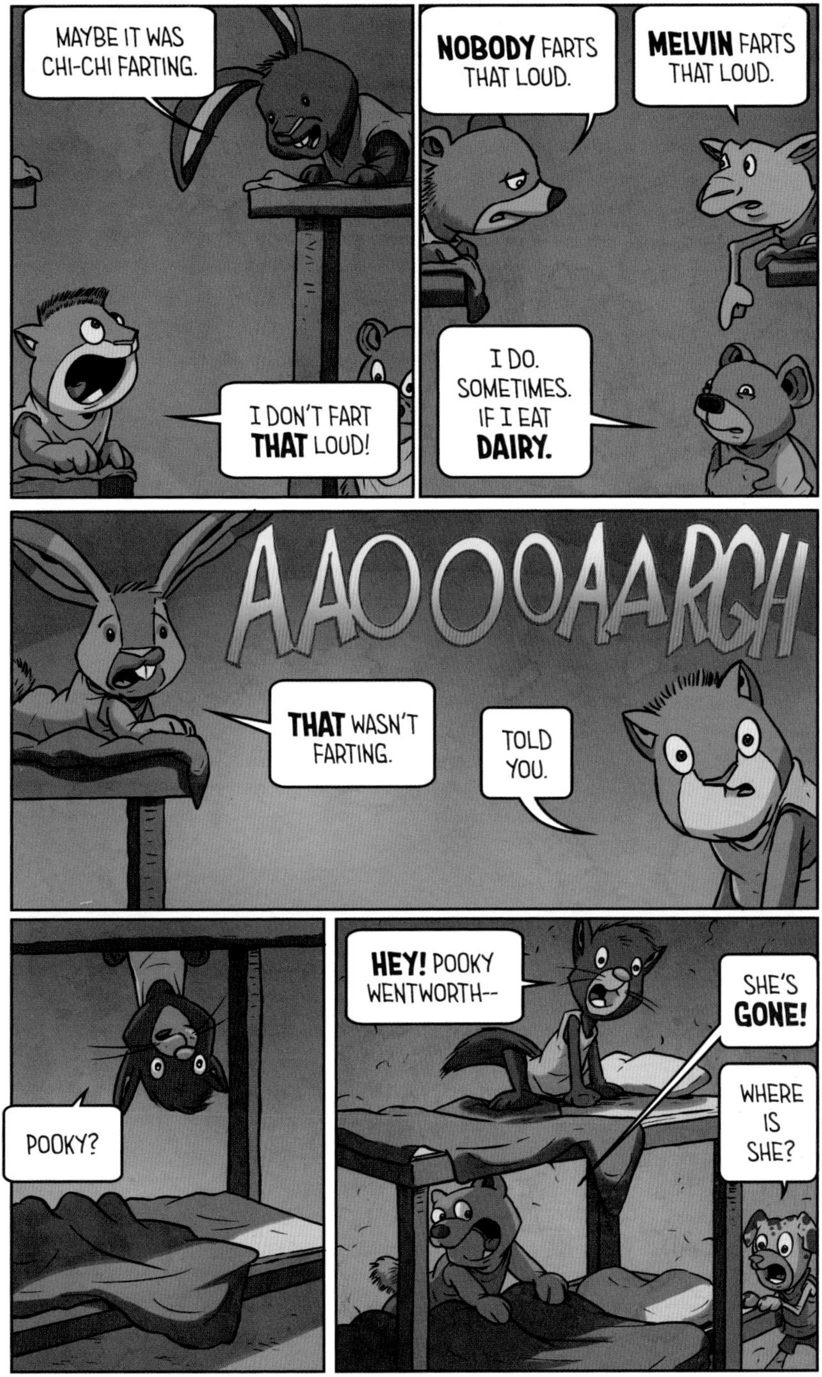
MAYBE IT WAS CHI-CHI FARTING.
I DON'T FART THAT LOUD!
NOBODY FARTS THAT LOUD.
MELVIN FARTS THAT LOUD.
I DO. SOMETIMES. IF I EAT DAIRY.
AAOOOAARGH
THAT WASN'T FARTING.
TOLD YOU.
POOKY?
HEY! POOKY WENTWORTH--
SHE'S GONE!
WHERE IS SHE?

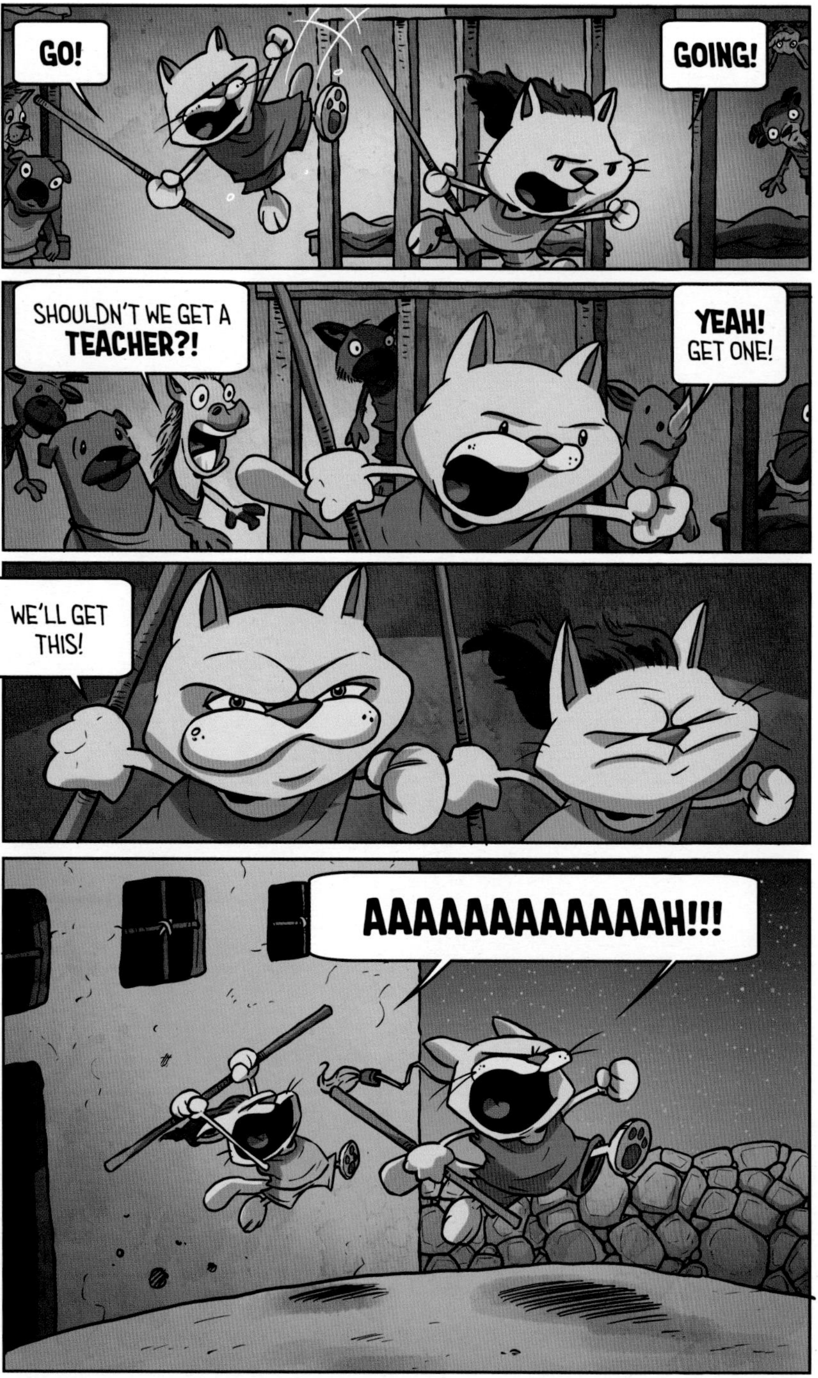
GO!
GOING!
SHOULDN'T WE GET A TEACHER?!
YEAH! GET ONE!
WE'LL GET THIS!
AAAAAAAAAAAAAH!!!

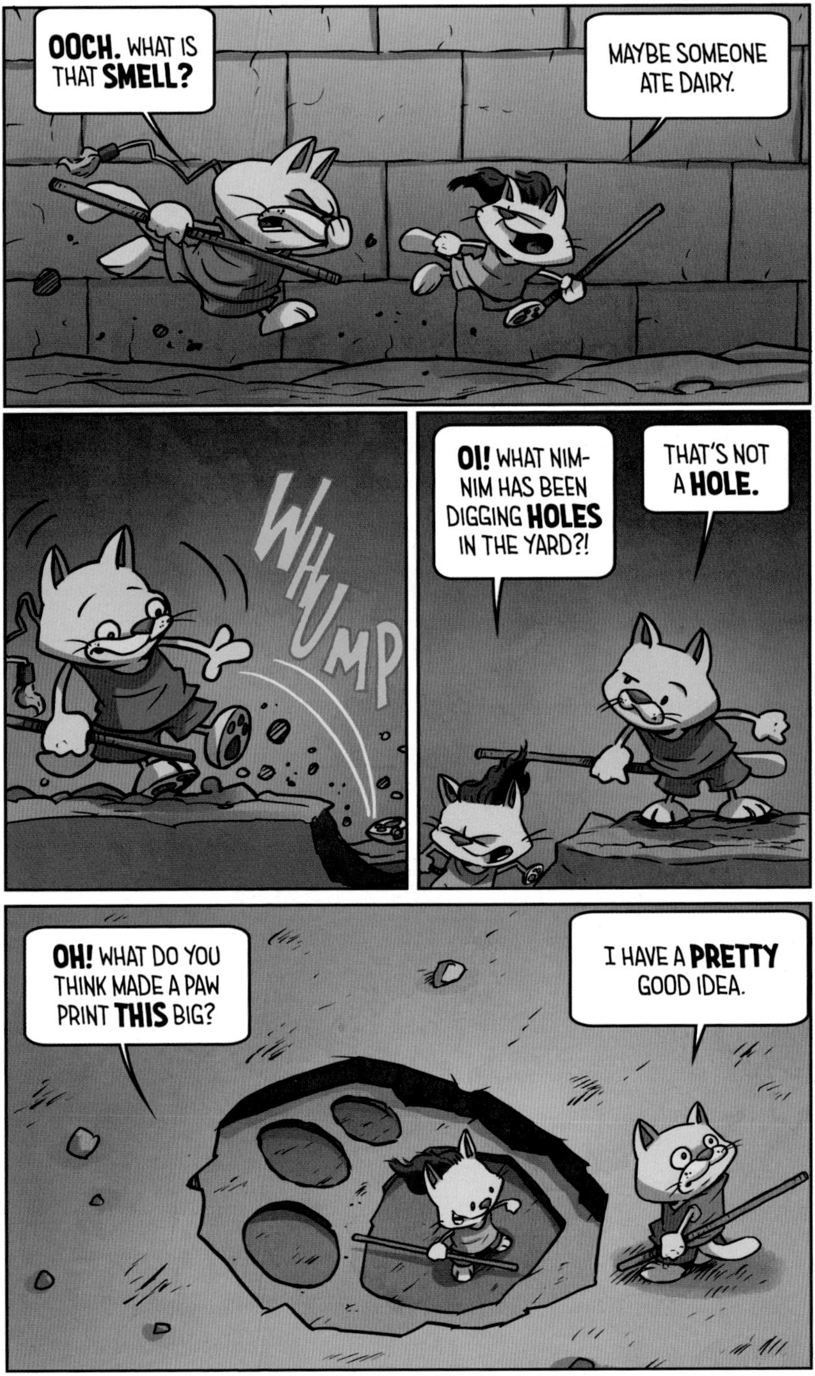
OOCH. WHAT IS THAT SMELL?
MAYBE SOMEONE ATE DAIRY.
WHUMP
OI! WHAT NIM-NIM HAS BEEN DIGGING HOLES IN THE YARD?!
THAT'S NOT A HOLE.
OH! WHAT DO YOU THINK MADE A PAW PRINT THIS BIG?
I HAVE A PRETTY GOOD IDEA.

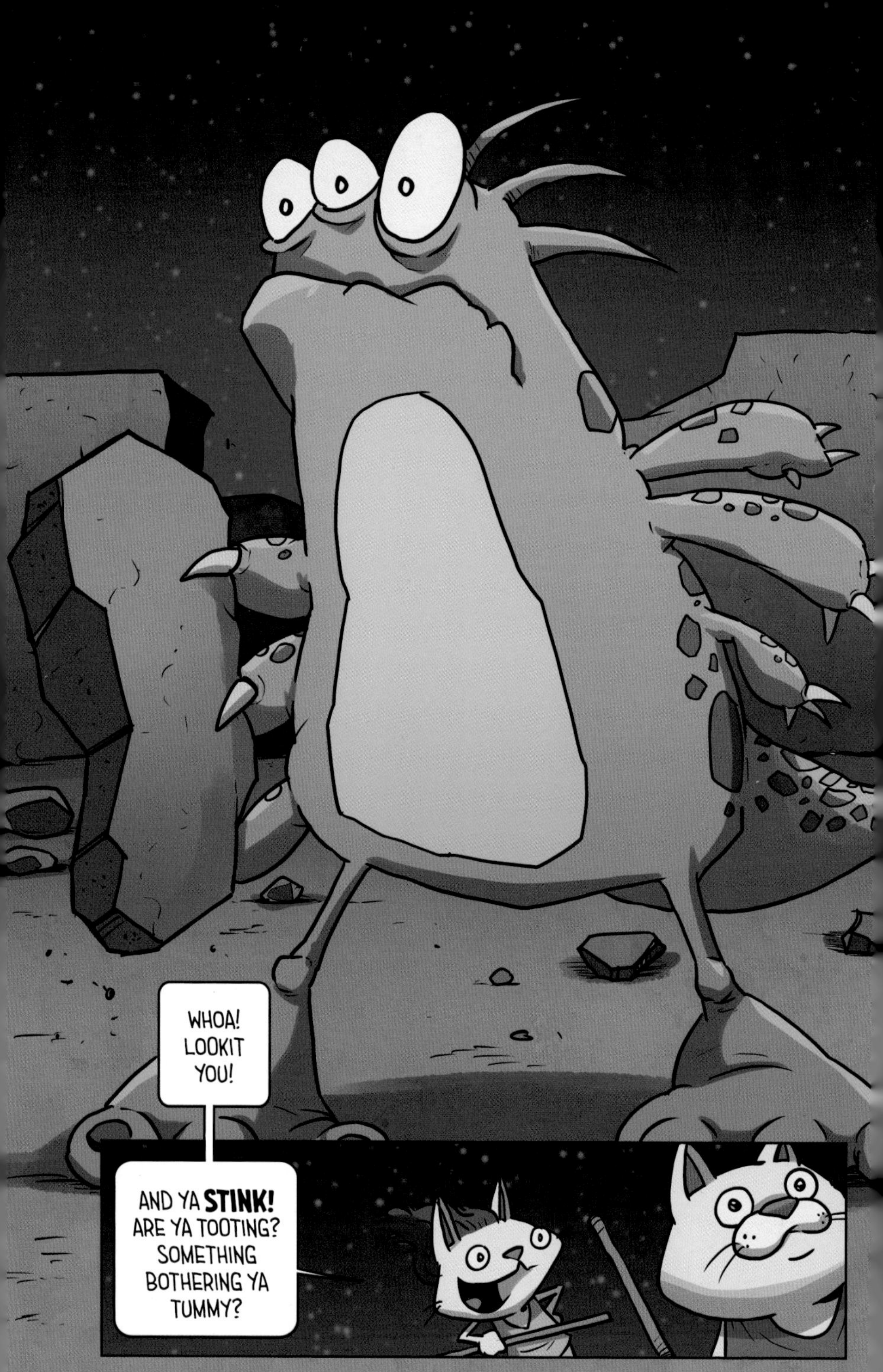
WHOA! LOOKIT YOU!
AND YA **STINK!** ARE YA TOOTING? SOMETHING BOTHERING YA TUMMY?

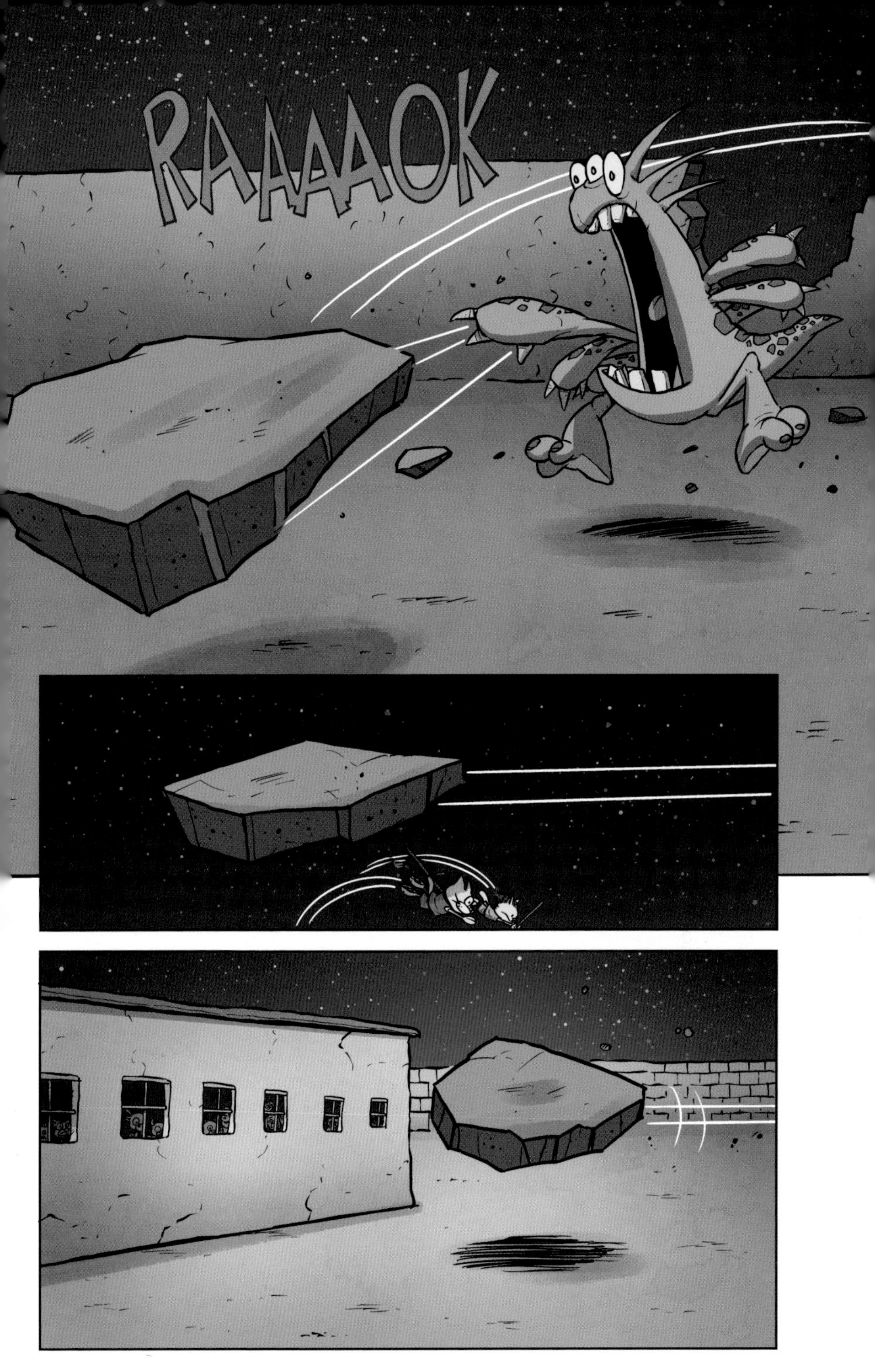
RAAAAOK

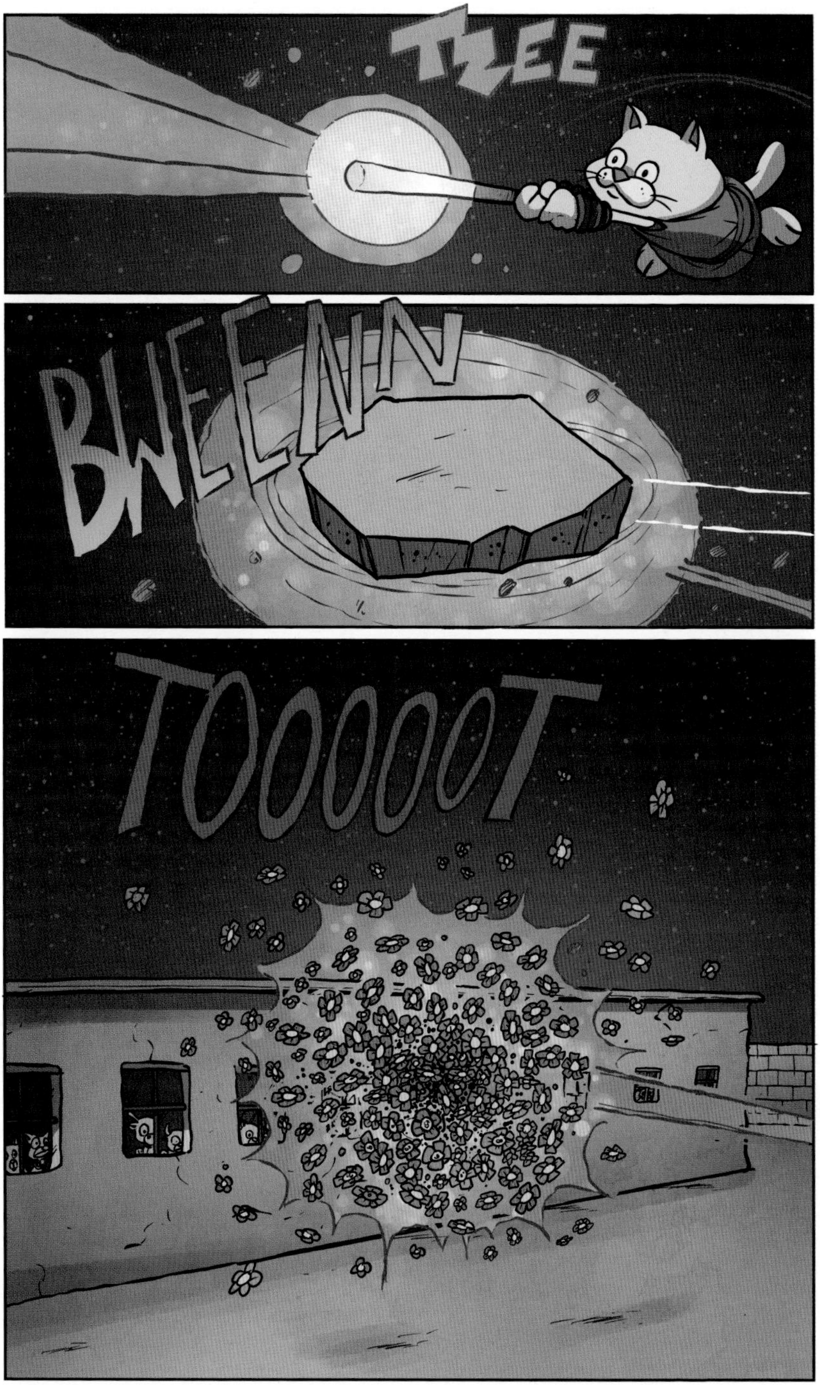
TZEE
BWEENN
TOOOOOT

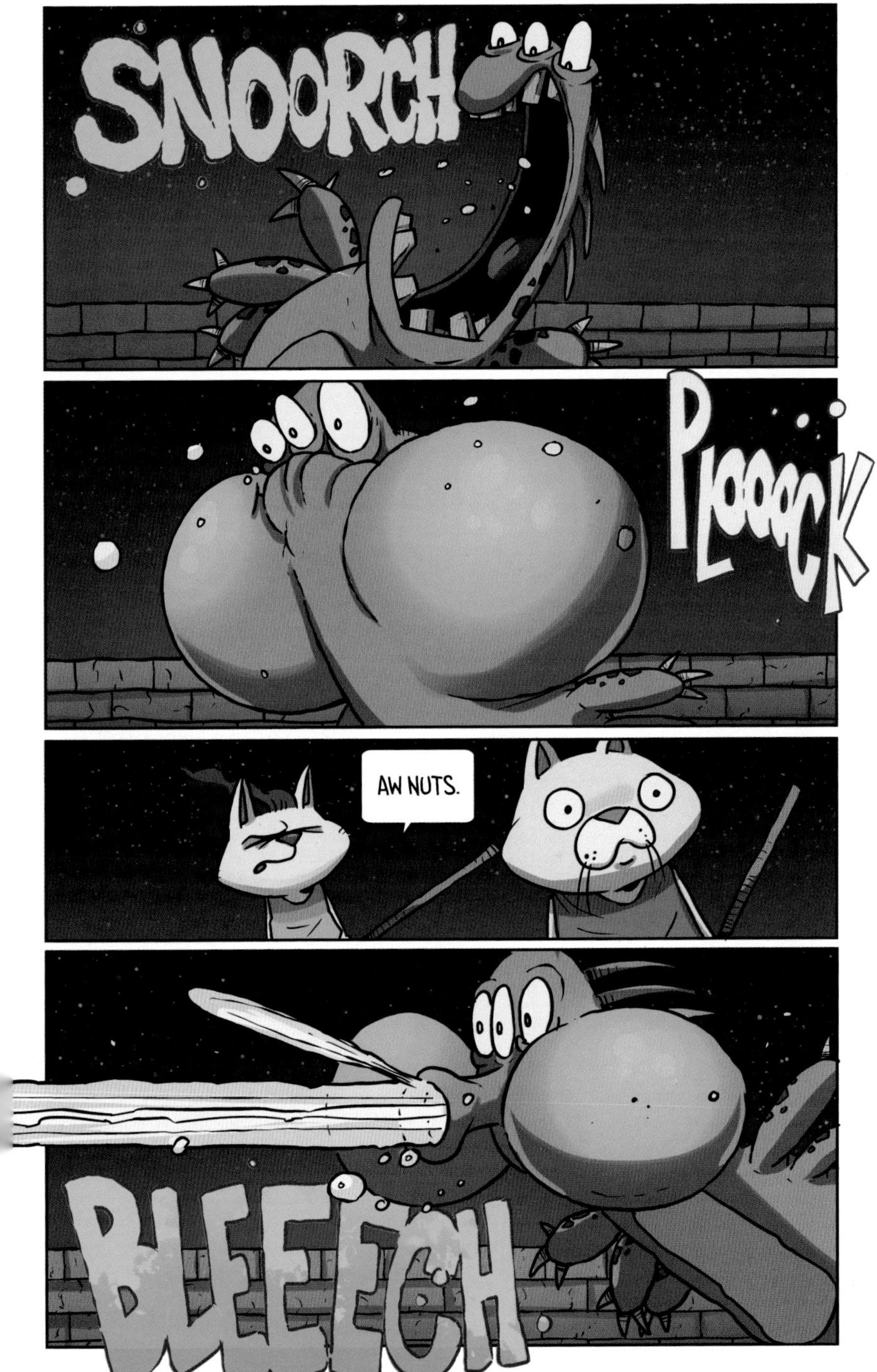
SNOORCH
PLOOOCK
AW NUTS.
BLEECH

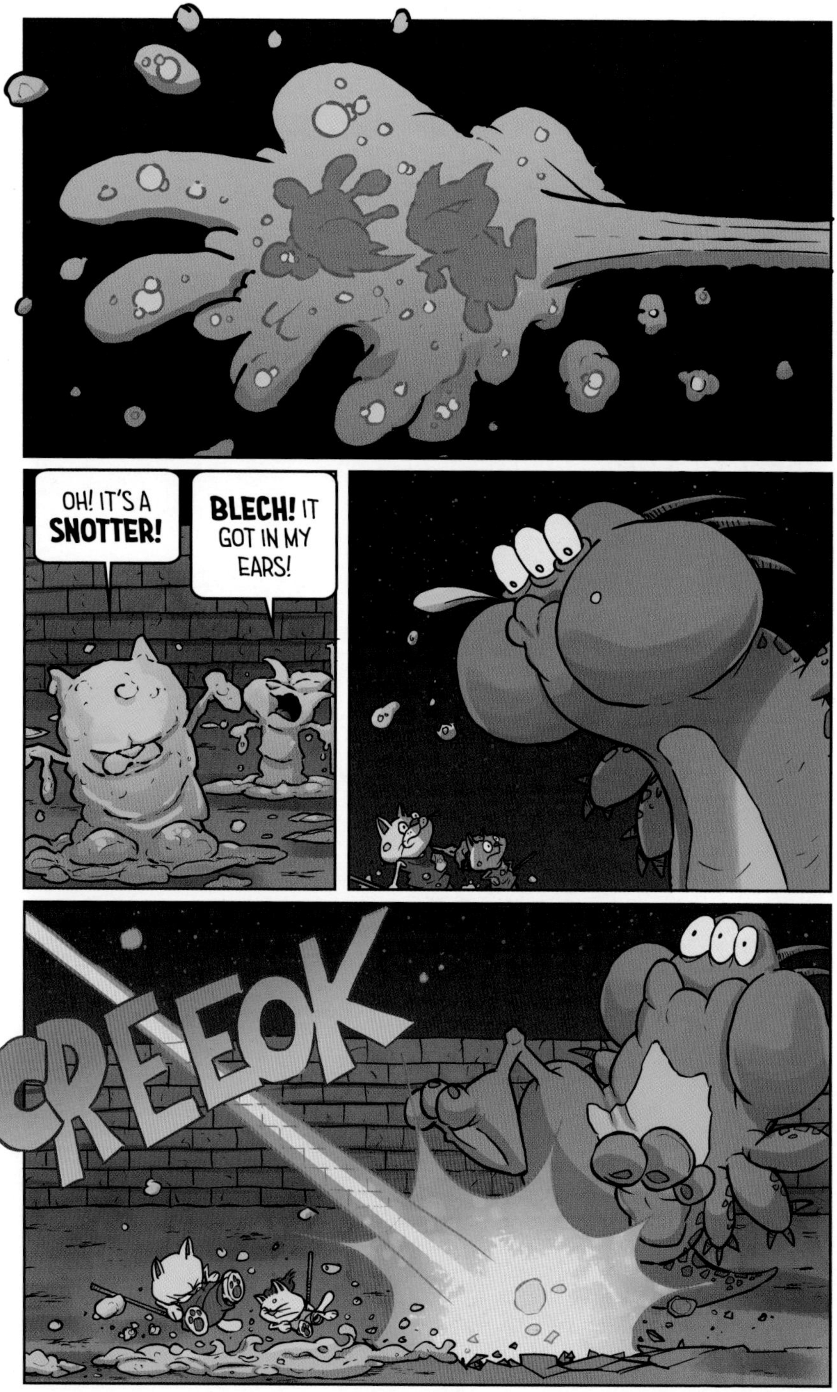
OH! IT'S A **SNOTTER!**
BLECH! IT GOT IN MY EARS!
CREEOK

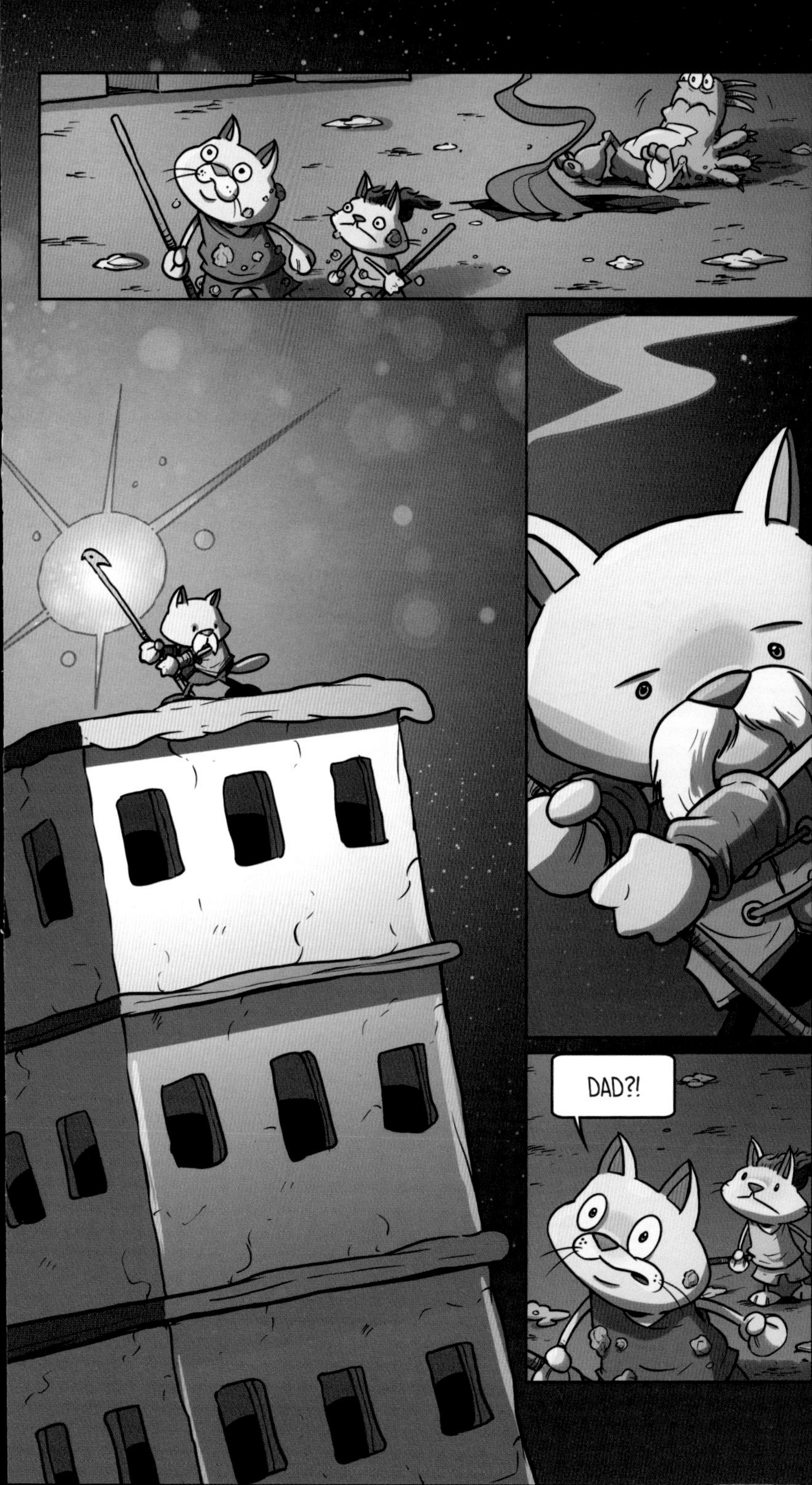
DAD?!

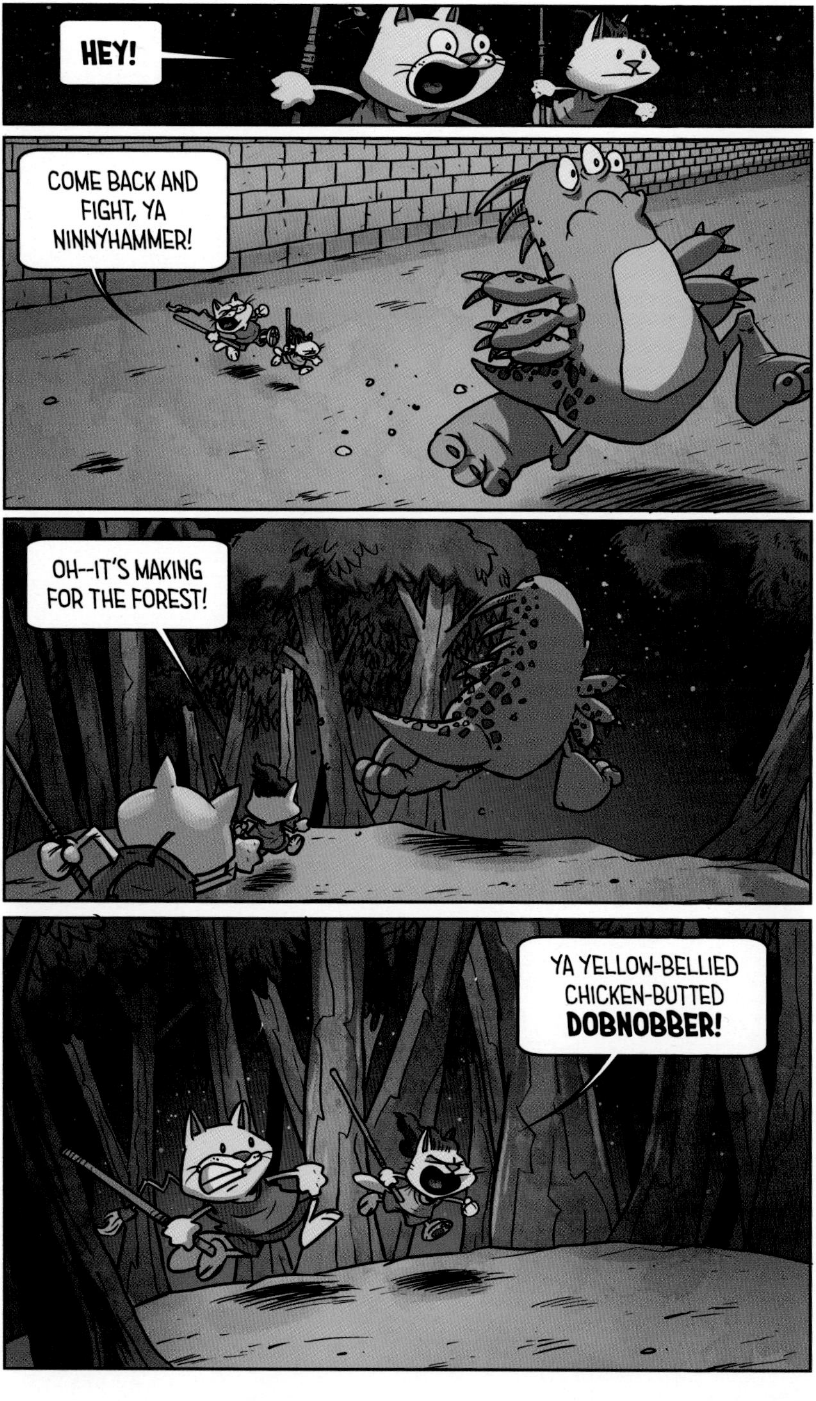
HEY!
COME BACK AND FIGHT, YA NINNYHAMMER!
OH--IT'S MAKING FOR THE FOREST!
YA YELLOW-BELLIED CHICKEN-BUTTED DOBNOBBER!

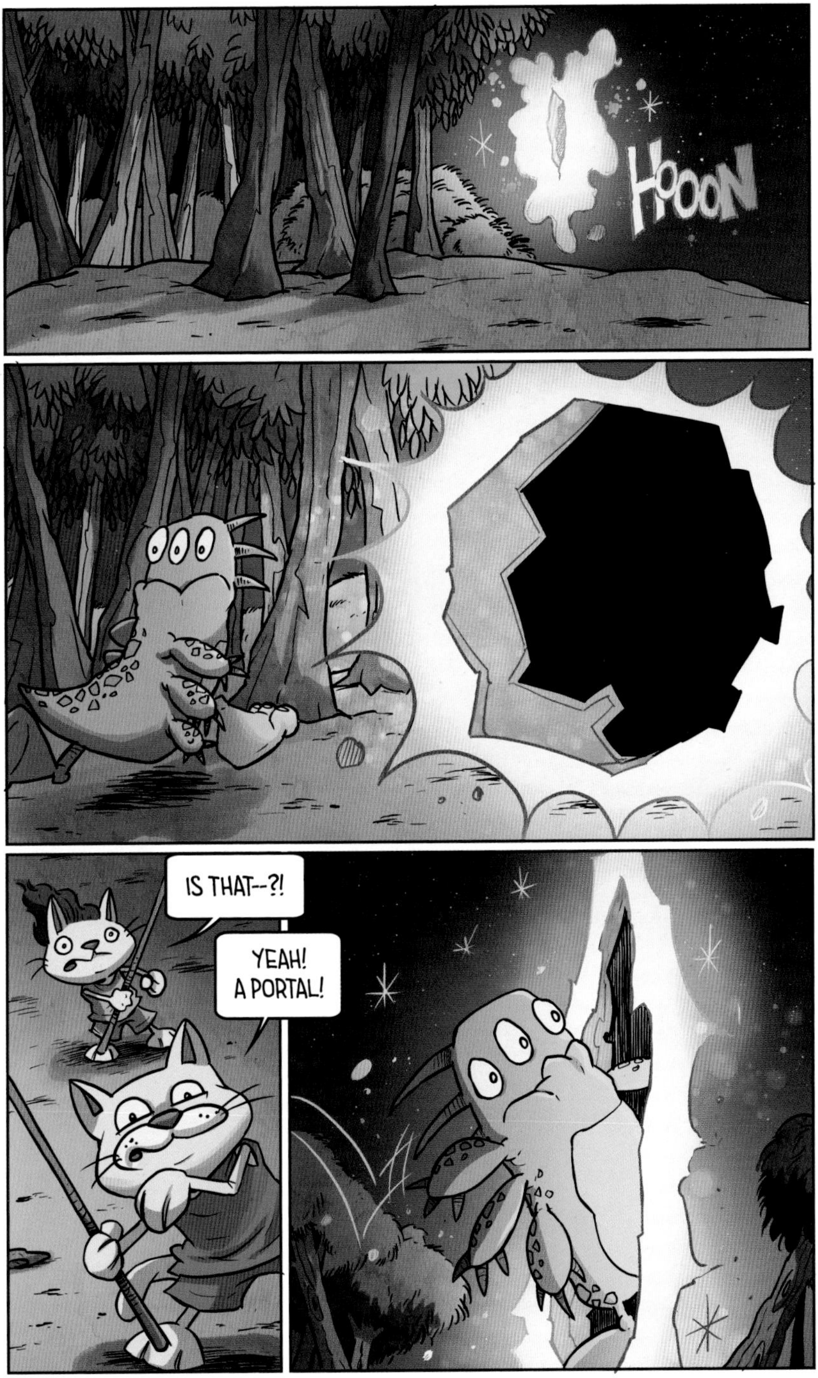
HOOON
IS THAT--?!
YEAH! A PORTAL!

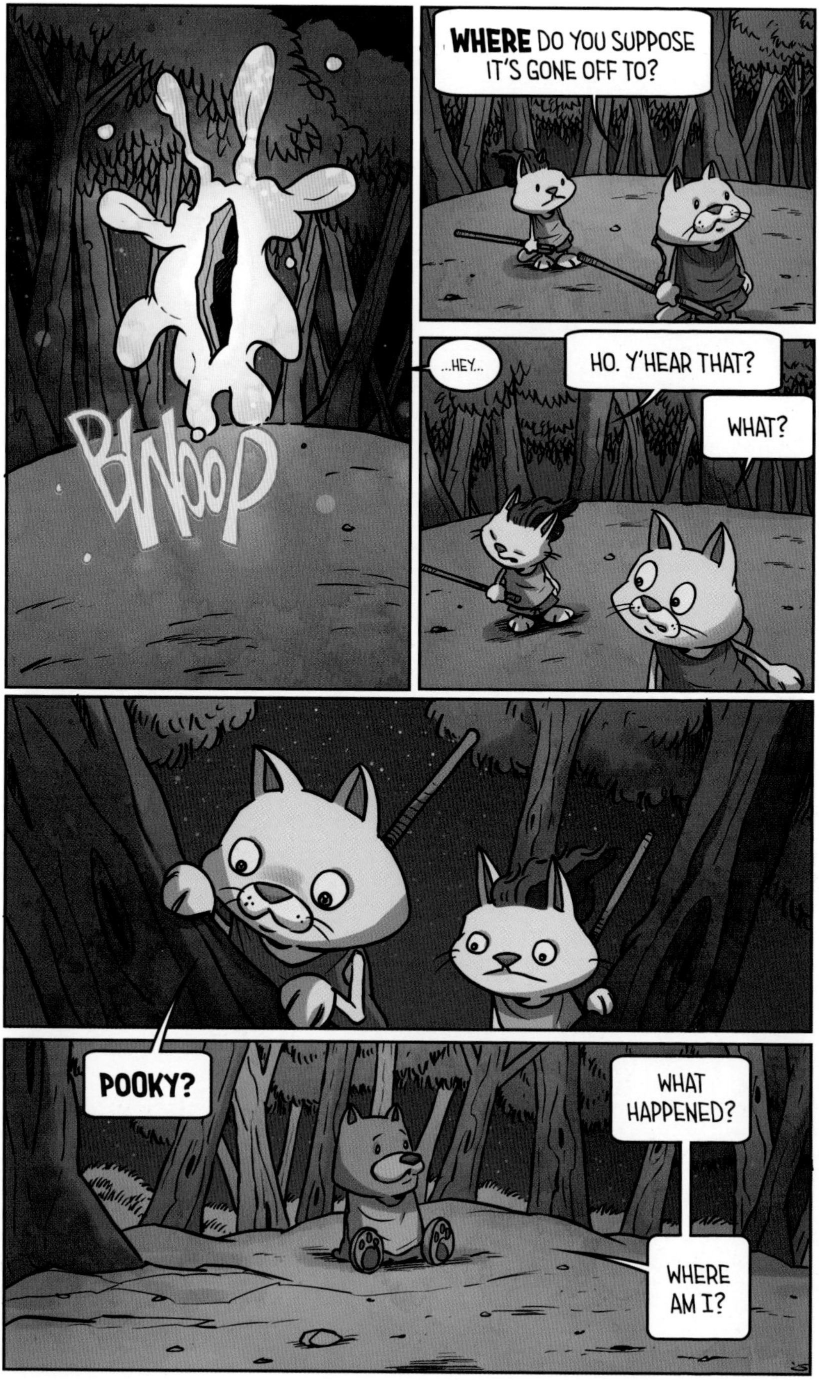
BWOOP
WHERE DO YOU SUPPOSE IT'S GONE OFF TO?
...HEY...
HO. Y'HEAR THAT?
WHAT?
POOKY?
WHAT HAPPENED?
WHERE AM I?

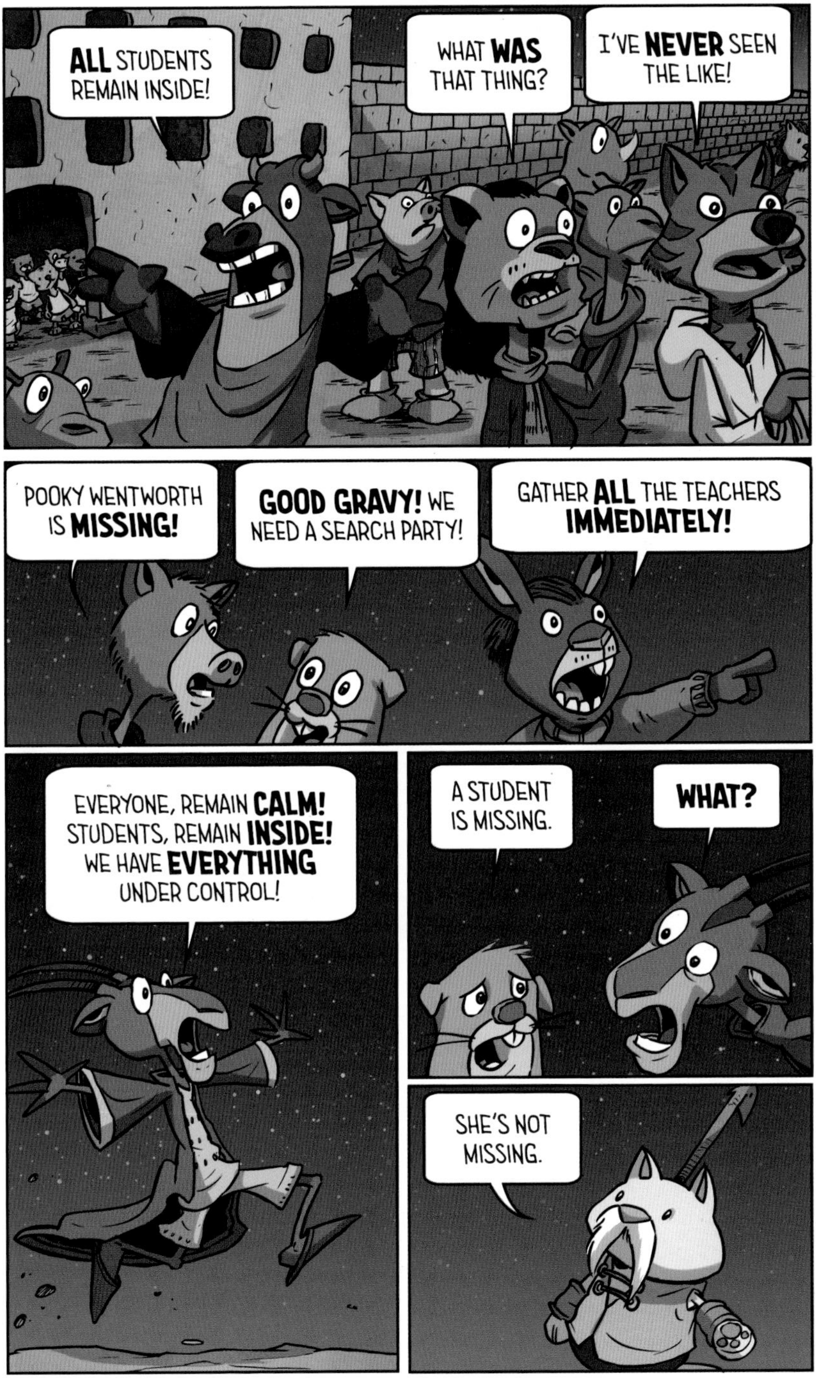

ALL STUDENTS REMAIN INSIDE!
WHAT WAS THAT THING?
I'VE NEVER SEEN THE LIKE!
POOKY WENTWORTH IS MISSING!
GOOD GRAVY! WE NEED A SEARCH PARTY!
GATHER ALL THE TEACHERS IMMEDIATELY!
EVERYONE, REMAIN CALM! STUDENTS, REMAIN INSIDE! WE HAVE EVERYTHING UNDER CONTROL!
A STUDENT IS MISSING.
WHAT?
SHE'S NOT MISSING.

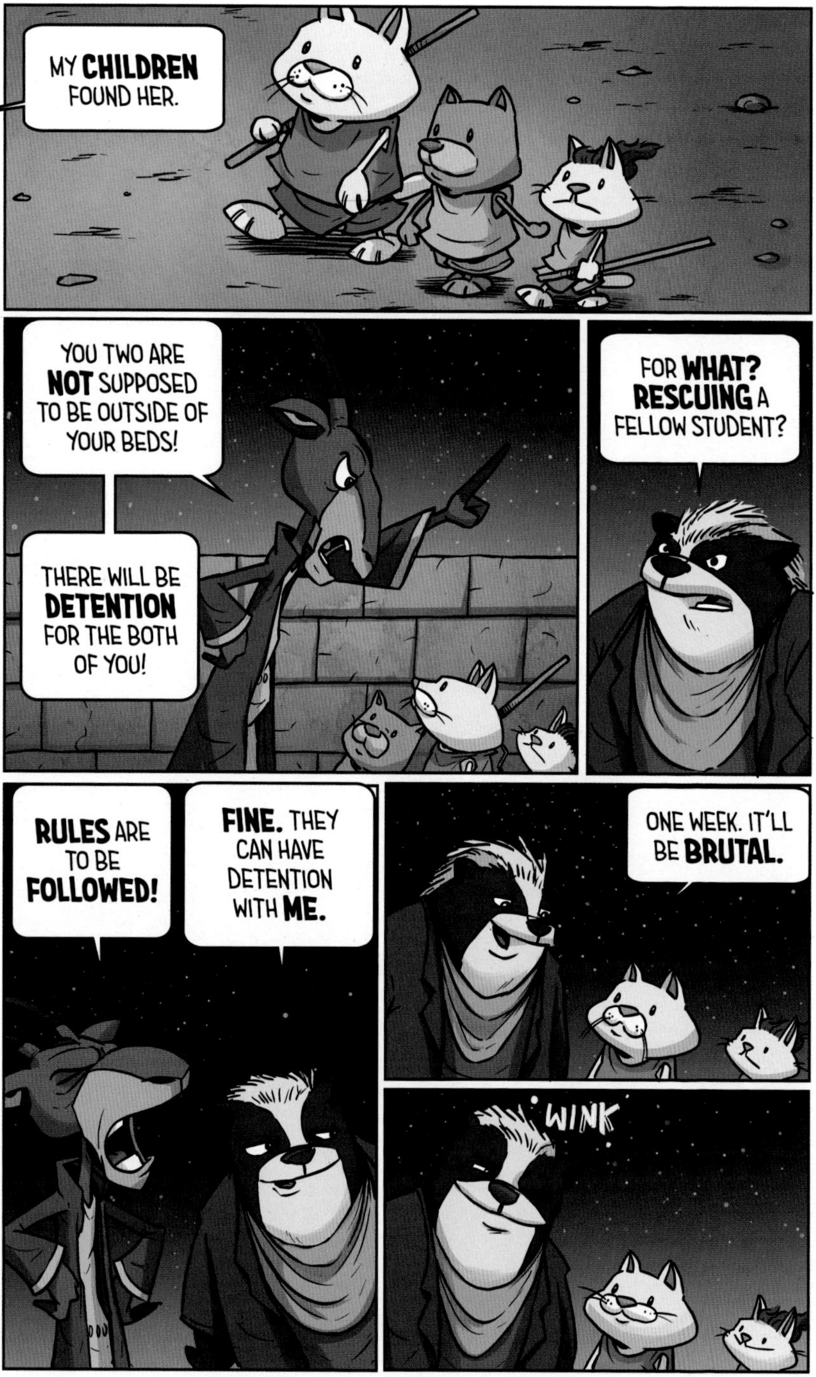
MY CHILDREN FOUND HER.
YOU TWO ARE NOT SUPPOSED TO BE OUTSIDE OF YOUR BEDS!
THERE WILL BE DETENTION FOR THE BOTH OF YOU!
FOR WHAT? RESCUING A FELLOW STUDENT?
RULES ARE TO BE FOLLOWED!
FINE. THEY CAN HAVE DETENTION WITH ME.
ONE WEEK. IT'LL BE BRUTAL.
WINK

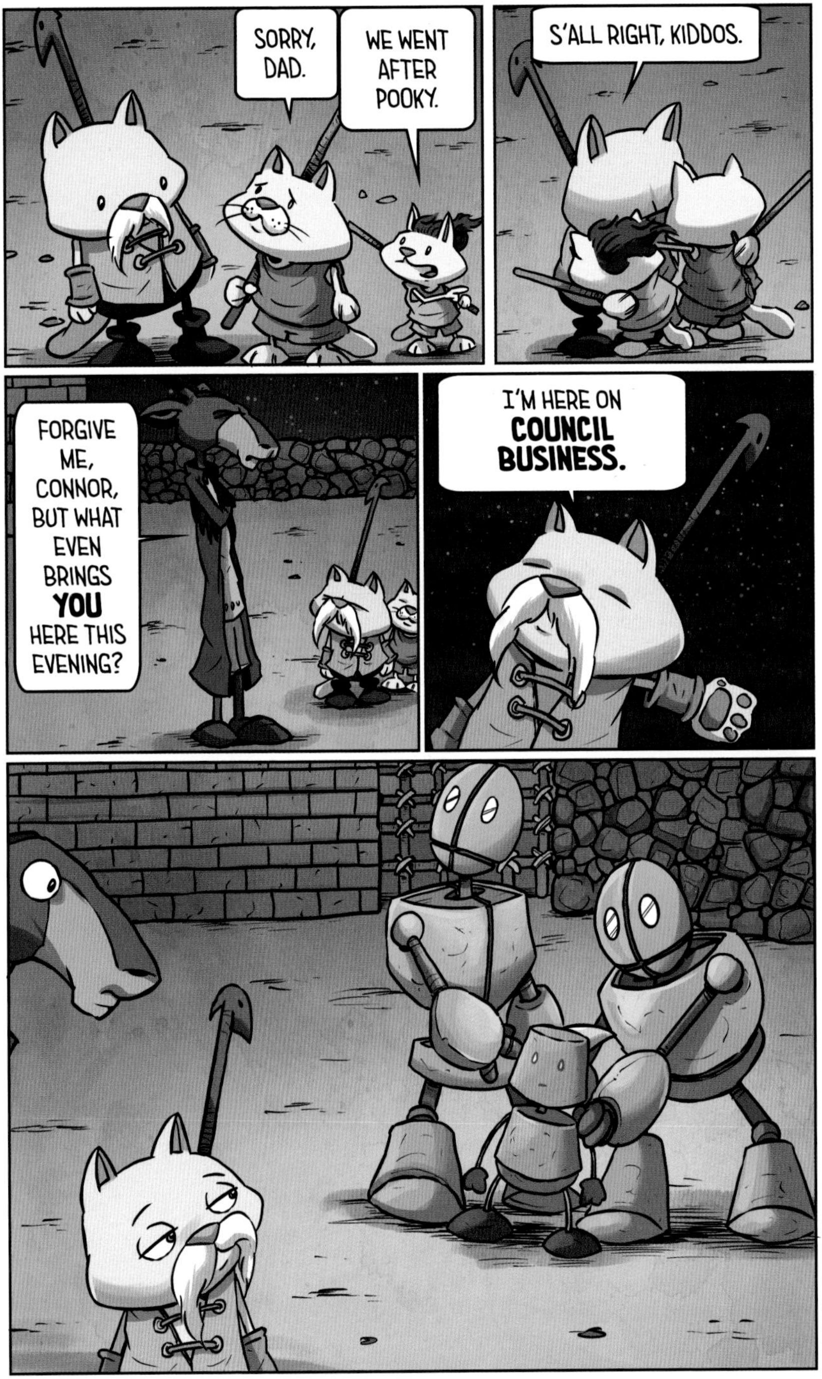
SORRY, DAD.
WE WENT AFTER POOKY.
S'ALL RIGHT, KIDDOS.
FORGIVE ME, CONNOR, BUT WHAT EVEN BRINGS **YOU** HERE THIS EVENING?
I'M HERE ON **COUNCIL BUSINESS.**

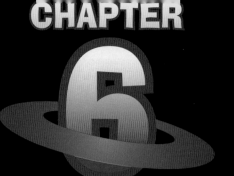

CHAPTER 6

BUNKMATES

COME ON.

AREN'T WE SUPPOSED TO BE IN **BED**?

I WANT TO HEAR THE GOINGS-ON.

OH, I **LIKE** IT WHEN YOU'RE **BAD.**

HUSH.

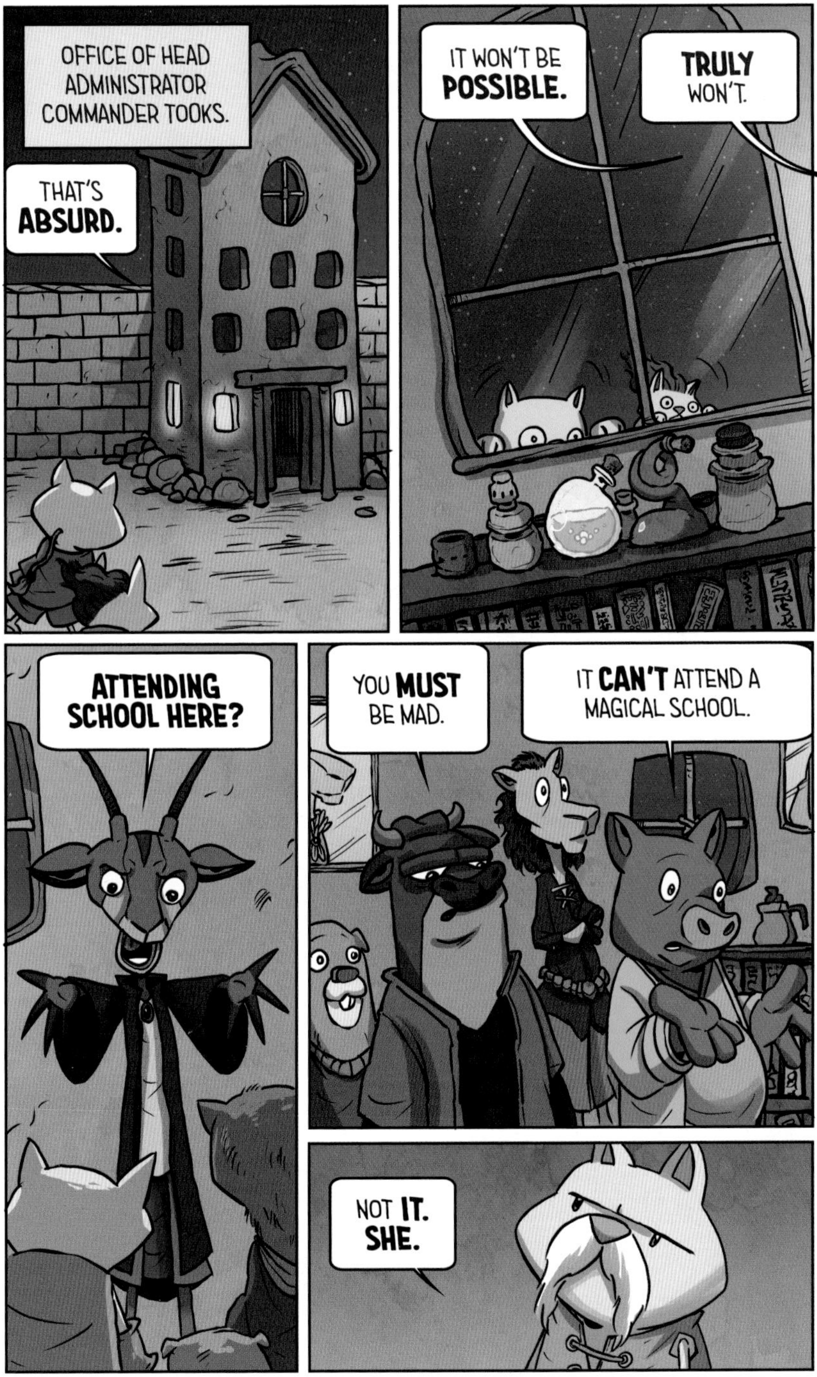
OFFICE OF HEAD ADMINISTRATOR COMMANDER TOOKS.
THAT'S **ABSURD.**
IT WON'T BE **POSSIBLE.**
TRULY WON'T.
ATTENDING SCHOOL HERE?
YOU **MUST** BE MAD.
IT **CAN'T** ATTEND A MAGICAL SCHOOL.
NOT **IT. SHE.**

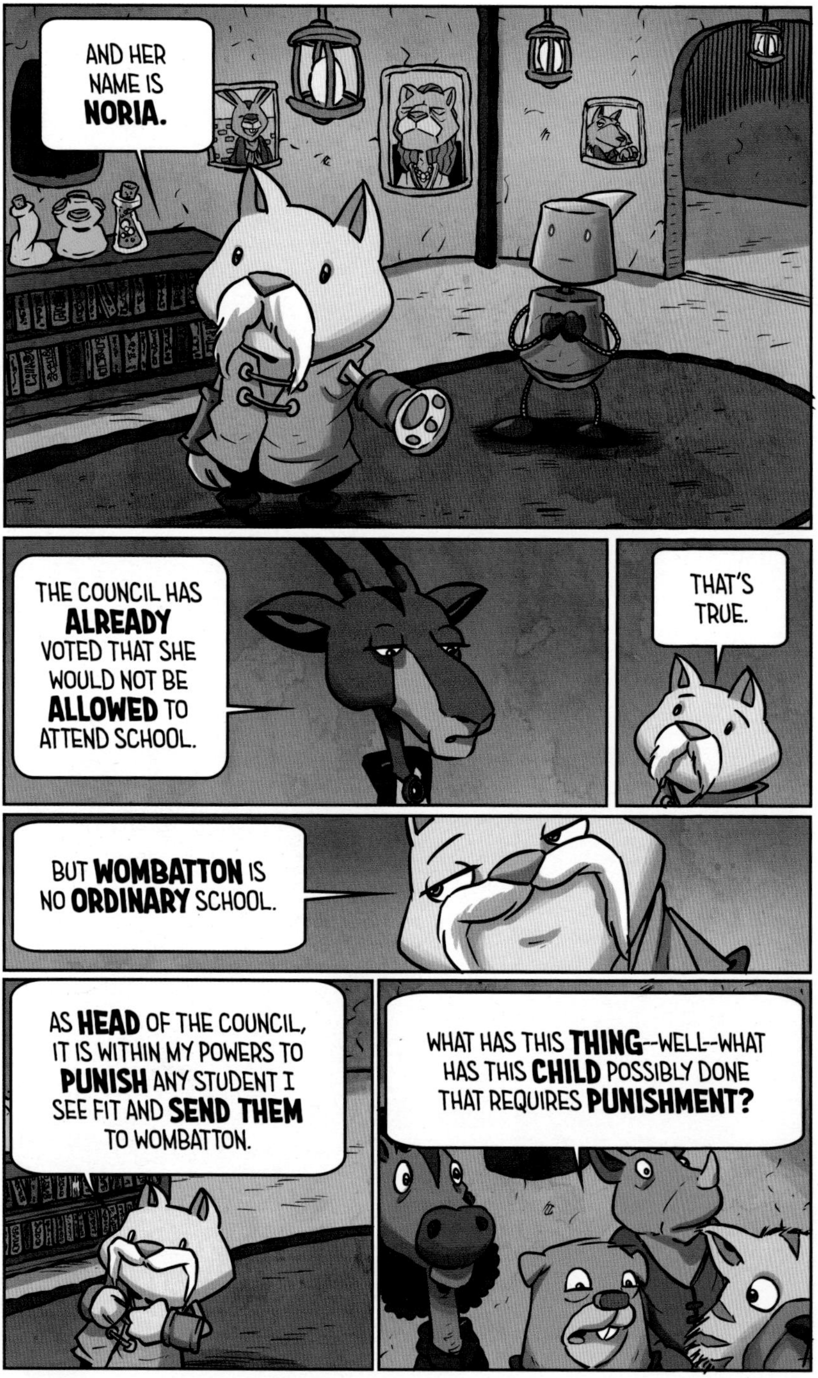
AND HER NAME IS **NORIA.**
THE COUNCIL HAS **ALREADY** VOTED THAT SHE WOULD NOT BE **ALLOWED** TO ATTEND SCHOOL.
THAT'S TRUE.
BUT **WOMBATTON** IS NO **ORDINARY** SCHOOL.
AS **HEAD** OF THE COUNCIL, IT IS WITHIN MY POWERS TO **PUNISH** ANY STUDENT I SEE FIT AND **SEND THEM** TO WOMBATTON.
WHAT HAS THIS **THING**--WELL--WHAT HAS THIS **CHILD** POSSIBLY DONE THAT REQUIRES **PUNISHMENT?**

SHE'S RUDE. **VERY** RUDE. AREN'T YOU, NORIA?

YOU'RE QUITE A POOP HEAD, SIR.

SEE? AWFUL.

YOU ARE TO BE SENT TO WOMBATTON.

YES, SIR.

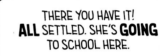

THERE YOU HAVE IT! **ALL** SETTLED. SHE'S **GOING** TO SCHOOL HERE.

AW, DAD'S A RASCAL.

I **LOVE** IT WHEN HE'S BAD.

THIS IS **HARDLY** THE TIME FOR SUCH, WELL, **DISTRACTIONS!** WE JUST HAD AN UNKNOWN **CREATURE** ATTACK THE **SCHOOL!**

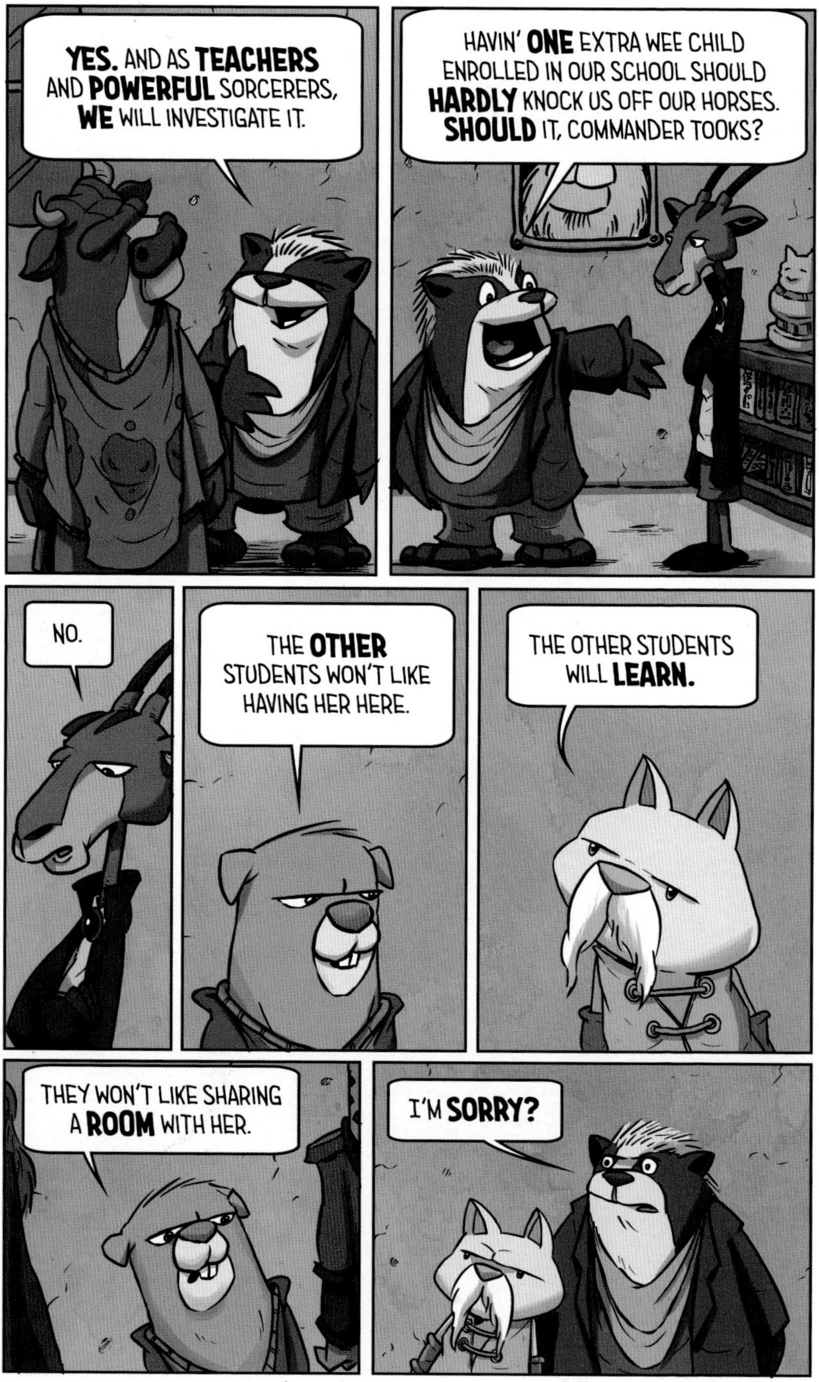
YES. AND AS TEACHERS AND POWERFUL SORCERERS, WE WILL INVESTIGATE IT.
HAVIN' ONE EXTRA WEE CHILD ENROLLED IN OUR SCHOOL SHOULD HARDLY KNOCK US OFF OUR HORSES. SHOULD IT, COMMANDER TOOKS?
NO.
THE OTHER STUDENTS WON'T LIKE HAVING HER HERE.
THE OTHER STUDENTS WILL LEARN.
THEY WON'T LIKE SHARING A ROOM WITH HER.
I'M SORRY?

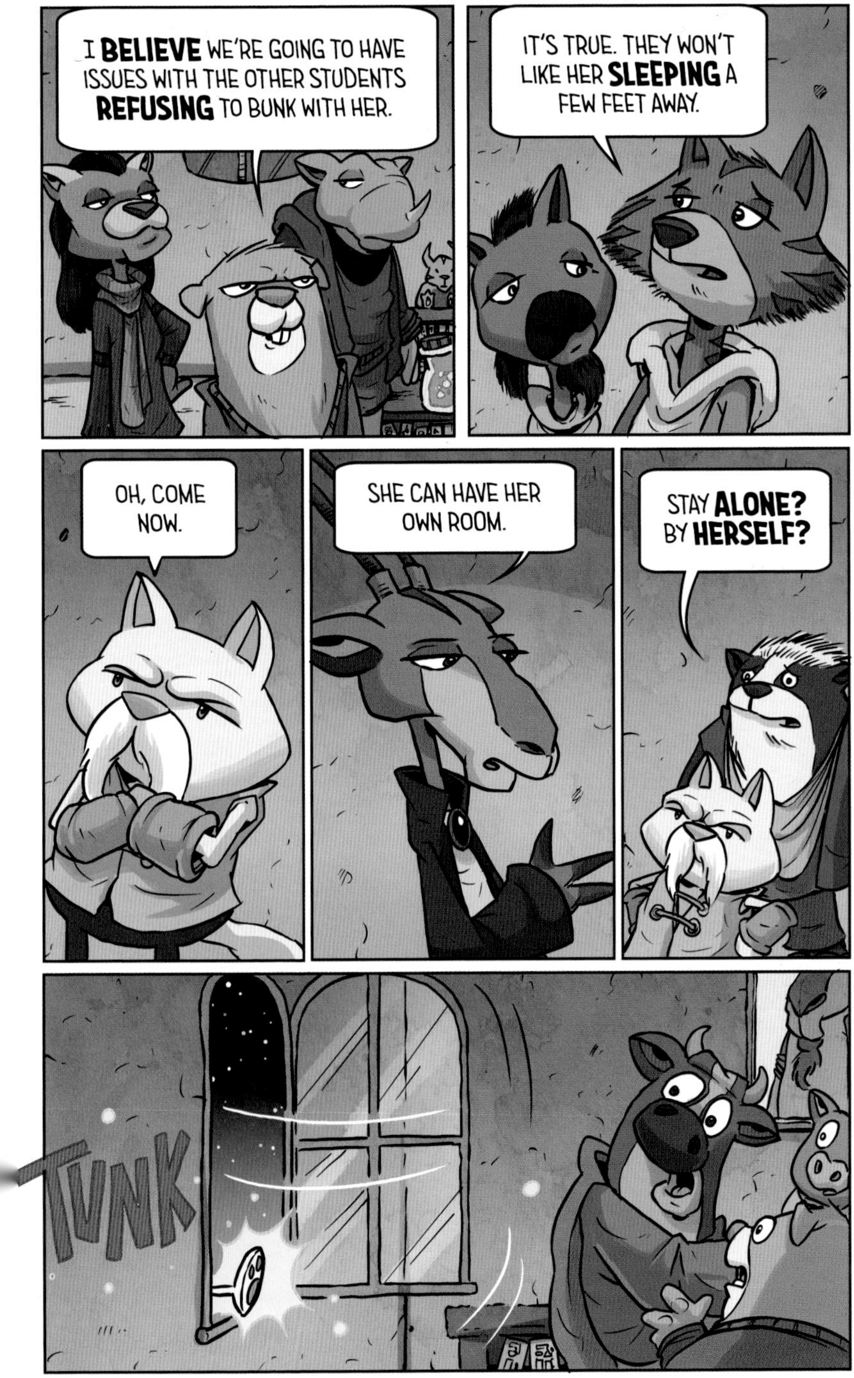
I BELIEVE WE'RE GOING TO HAVE ISSUES WITH THE OTHER STUDENTS REFUSING TO BUNK WITH HER.
IT'S TRUE. THEY WON'T LIKE HER SLEEPING A FEW FEET AWAY.
OH, COME NOW.
SHE CAN HAVE HER OWN ROOM.
STAY ALONE? BY HERSELF?
TUNK

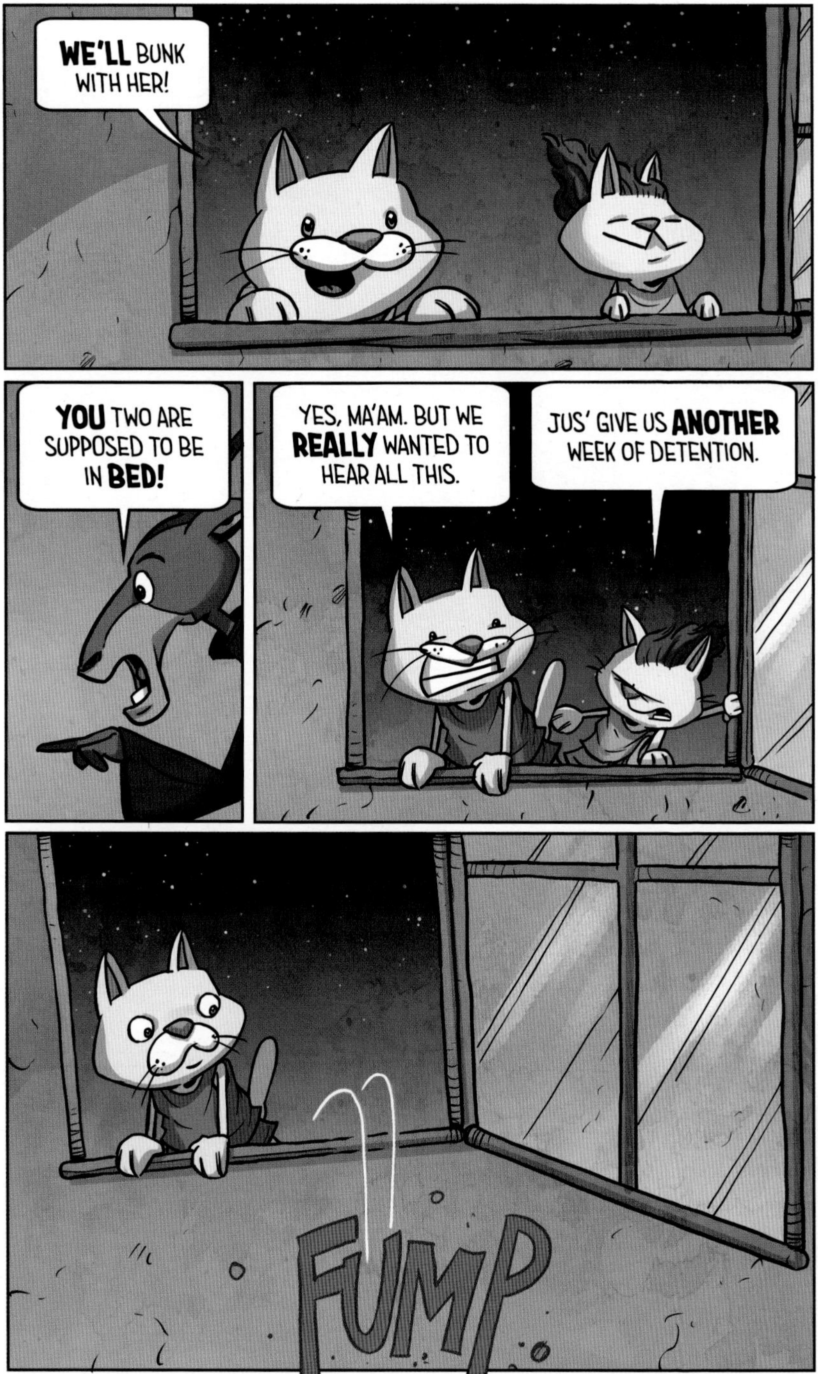
WE'LL BUNK WITH HER!
YOU TWO ARE SUPPOSED TO BE IN BED!
YES, MA'AM. BUT WE REALLY WANTED TO HEAR ALL THIS.
JUS' GIVE US ANOTHER WEEK OF DETENTION.
FUMP

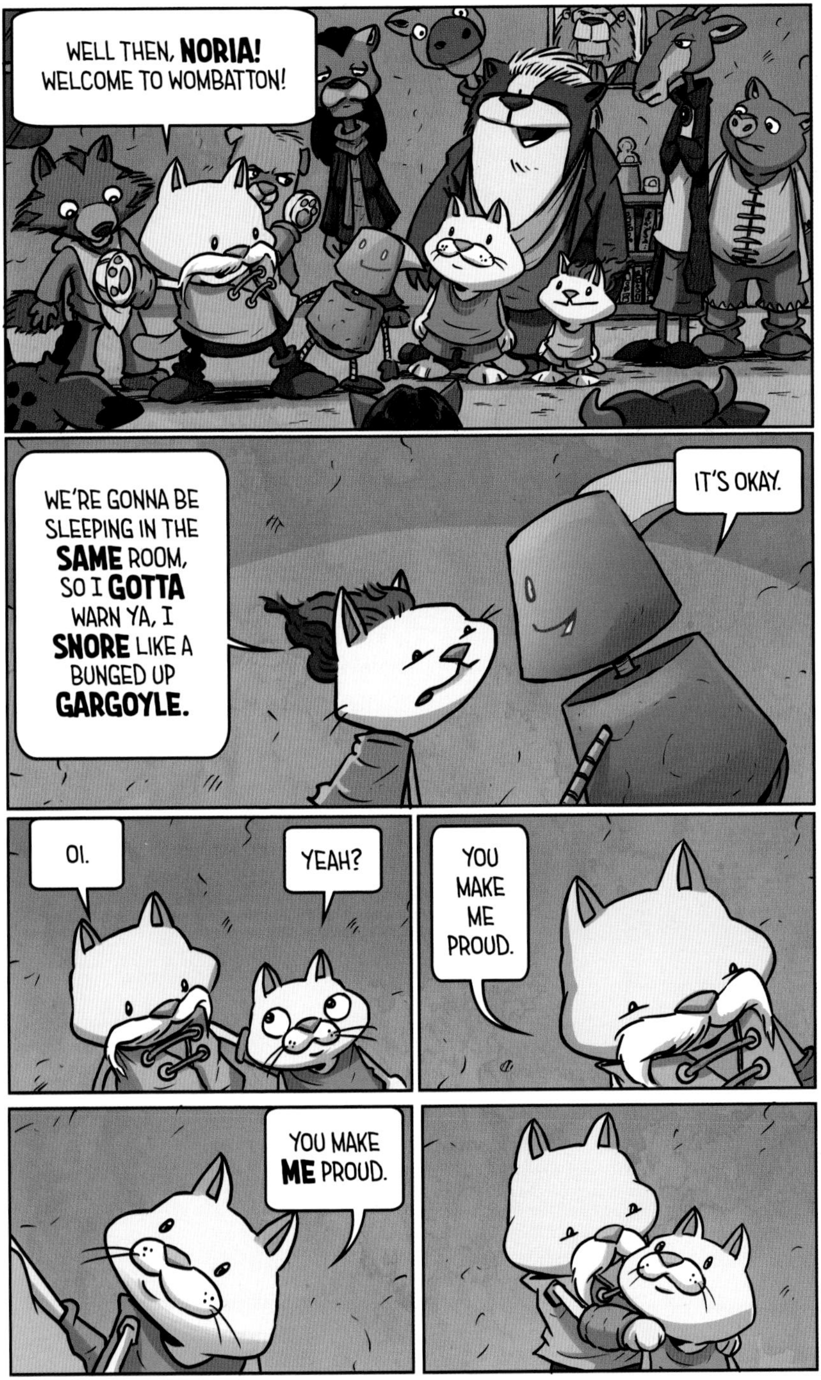

WELL THEN, **NORIA!** WELCOME TO WOMBATTON!
WE'RE GONNA BE SLEEPING IN THE **SAME** ROOM, SO I **GOTTA** WARN YA, I **SNORE** LIKE A BUNGED UP **GARGOYLE.**
IT'S OKAY.
OI.
YEAH?
YOU MAKE ME PROUD.
YOU MAKE **ME** PROUD.

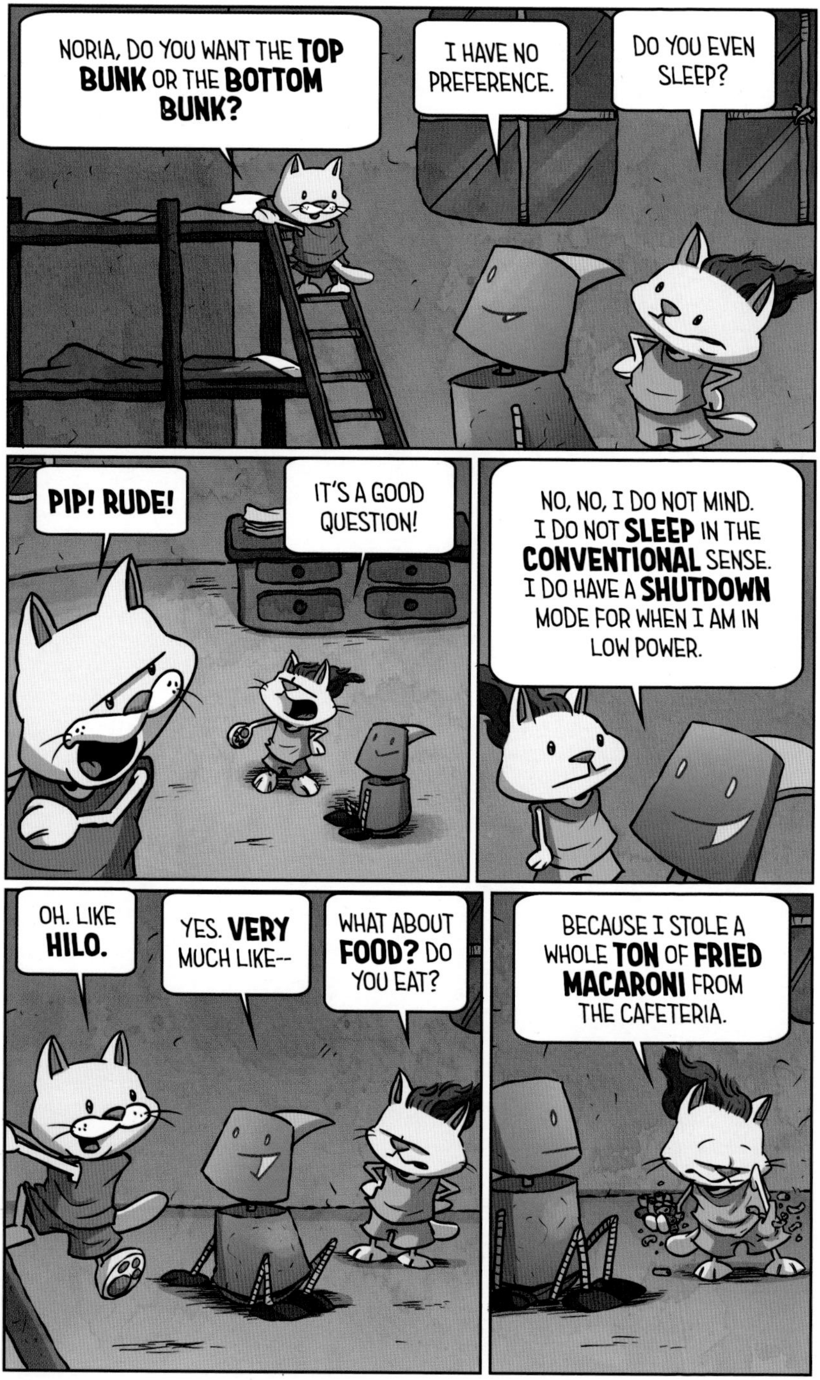
NORIA, DO YOU WANT THE **TOP BUNK** OR THE **BOTTOM BUNK?**
I HAVE NO PREFERENCE.
DO YOU EVEN SLEEP?
PIP! RUDE!
IT'S A GOOD QUESTION!
NO, NO, I DO NOT MIND. I DO NOT **SLEEP** IN THE **CONVENTIONAL** SENSE. I DO HAVE A **SHUTDOWN** MODE FOR WHEN I AM IN LOW POWER.
OH. LIKE **HILO.**
YES. **VERY** MUCH LIKE--
WHAT ABOUT **FOOD?** DO YOU EAT?
BECAUSE I STOLE A WHOLE **TON** OF **FRIED MACARONI** FROM THE CAFETERIA.

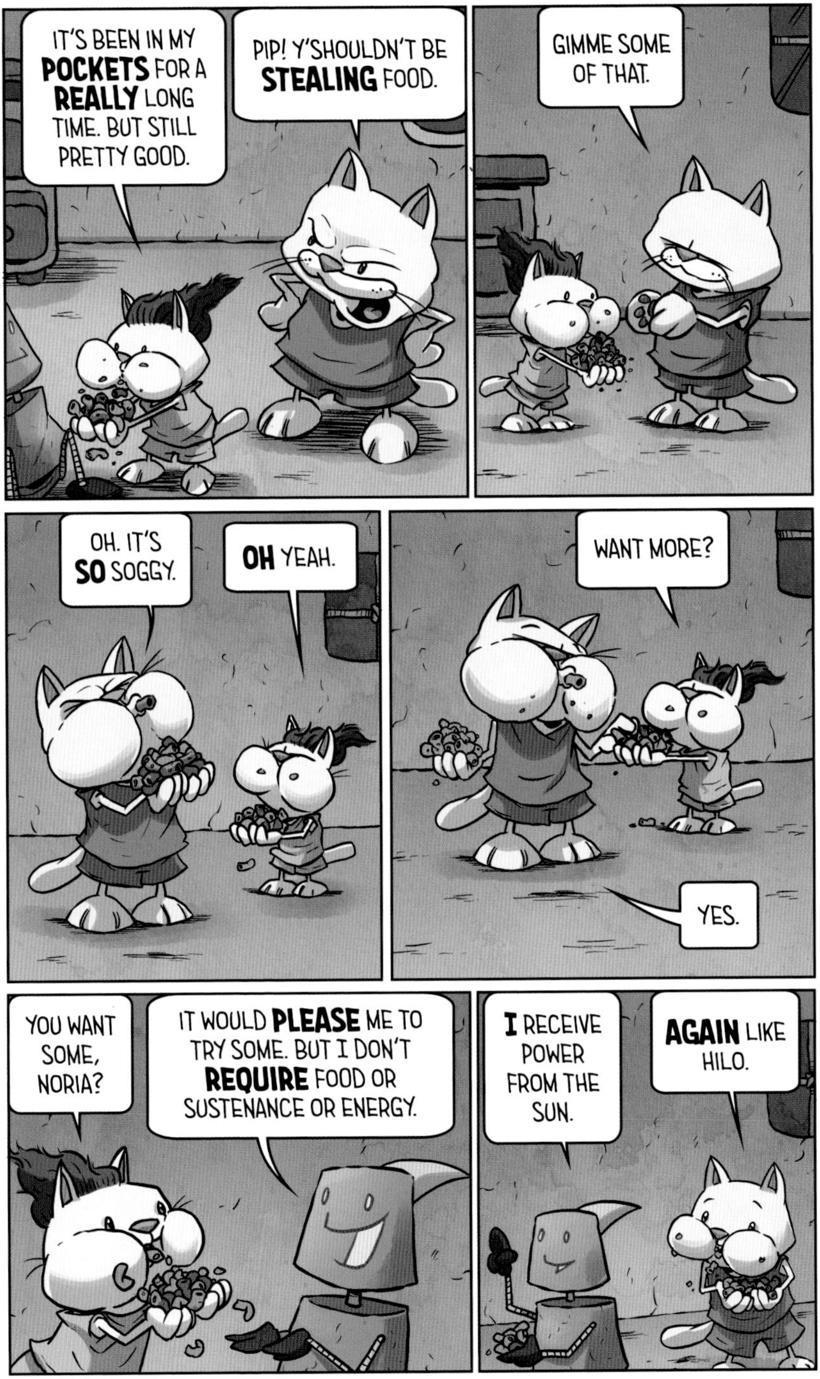
IT'S BEEN IN MY **POCKETS** FOR A **REALLY** LONG TIME. BUT STILL PRETTY GOOD.
PIP! Y'SHOULDN'T BE **STEALING** FOOD.
GIMME SOME OF THAT.
OH. IT'S **SO** SOGGY.
OH YEAH.
WANT MORE?
YES.
YOU WANT SOME, NORIA?
IT WOULD **PLEASE** ME TO TRY SOME. BUT I DON'T **REQUIRE** FOOD OR SUSTENANCE OR ENERGY.
I RECEIVE POWER FROM THE SUN.
AGAIN LIKE HILO.

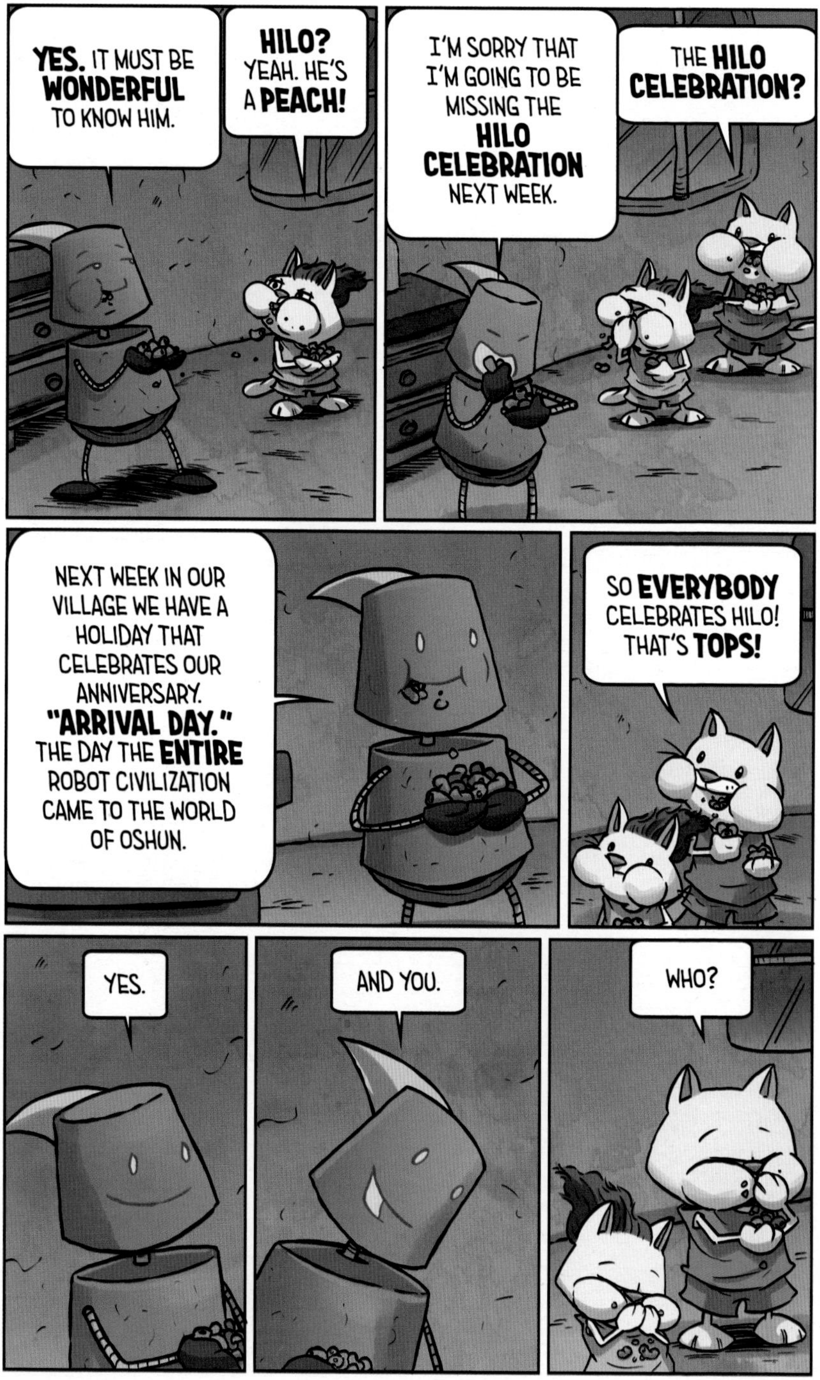
YES. IT MUST BE WONDERFUL TO KNOW HIM.
HILO? YEAH. HE'S A PEACH!
I'M SORRY THAT I'M GOING TO BE MISSING THE HILO CELEBRATION NEXT WEEK.
THE HILO CELEBRATION?
NEXT WEEK IN OUR VILLAGE WE HAVE A HOLIDAY THAT CELEBRATES OUR ANNIVERSARY. "ARRIVAL DAY." THE DAY THE ENTIRE ROBOT CIVILIZATION CAME TO THE WORLD OF OSHUN.
SO EVERYBODY CELEBRATES HILO! THAT'S TOPS!
YES.
AND YOU.
WHO?

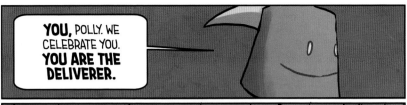

YOU, POLLY. WE CELEBRATE YOU. **YOU ARE THE DELIVERER.**

SPOORCH

WHAT NOW?

YOU ARE THE ONE WHO **BROUGHT** US TO OSHUN. WE OWE YOU AND HILO **EVERYTHING.**

SO YOU CELEBRATE **HER?** OH, CRIMITY. I'M NEVER GONNA HEAR THE END OF **THIS.**

A **HOLIDAY** FOR **ME!**

AND HILO.

YES.

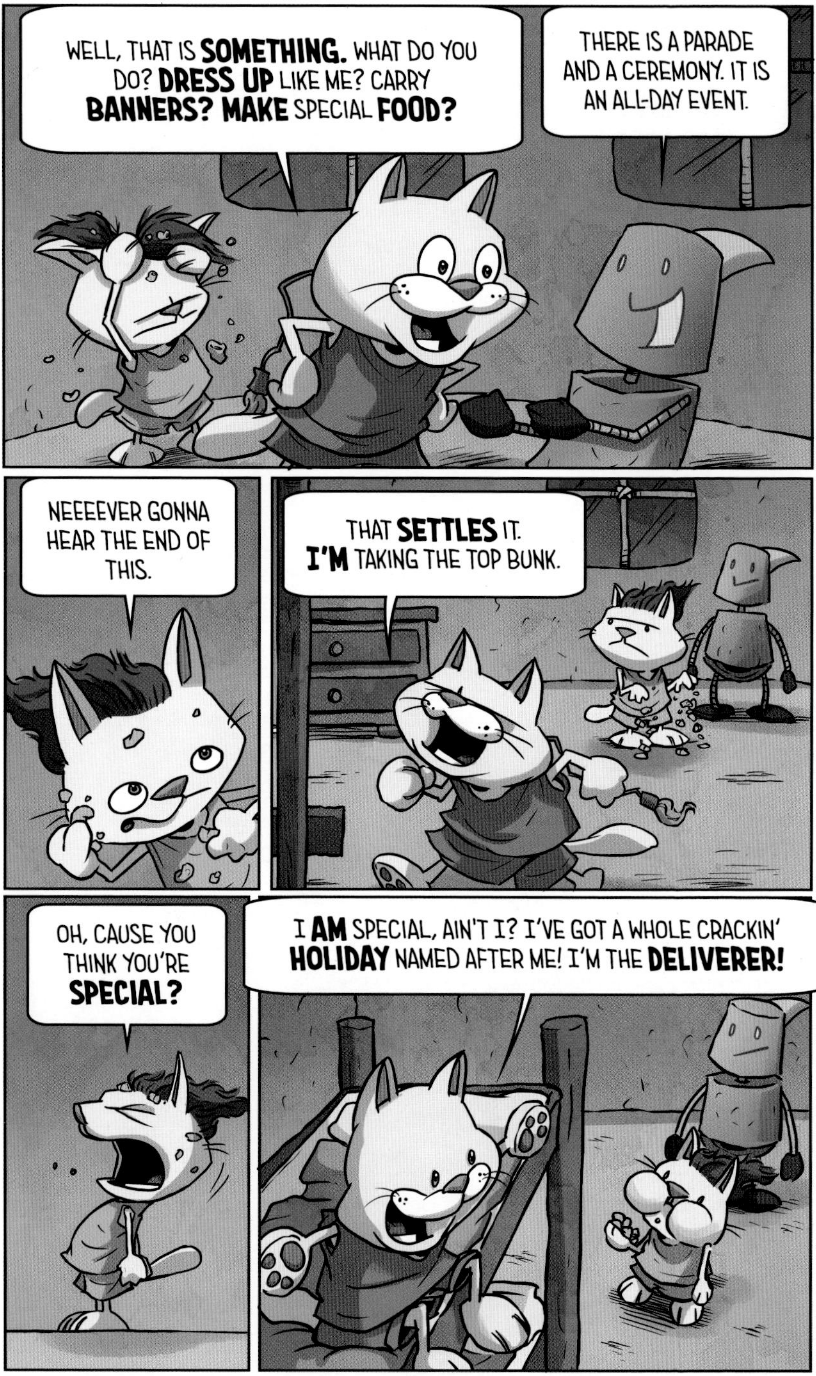

WELL, THAT IS SOMETHING. WHAT DO YOU DO? DRESS UP LIKE ME? CARRY BANNERS? MAKE SPECIAL FOOD?
THERE IS A PARADE AND A CEREMONY. IT IS AN ALL-DAY EVENT.
NEEEEVER GONNA HEAR THE END OF THIS.
THAT SETTLES IT. I'M TAKING THE TOP BUNK.
OH, CAUSE YOU THINK YOU'RE SPECIAL?
I AM SPECIAL, AIN'T I? I'VE GOT A WHOLE CRACKIN' HOLIDAY NAMED AFTER ME! I'M THE DELIVERER!

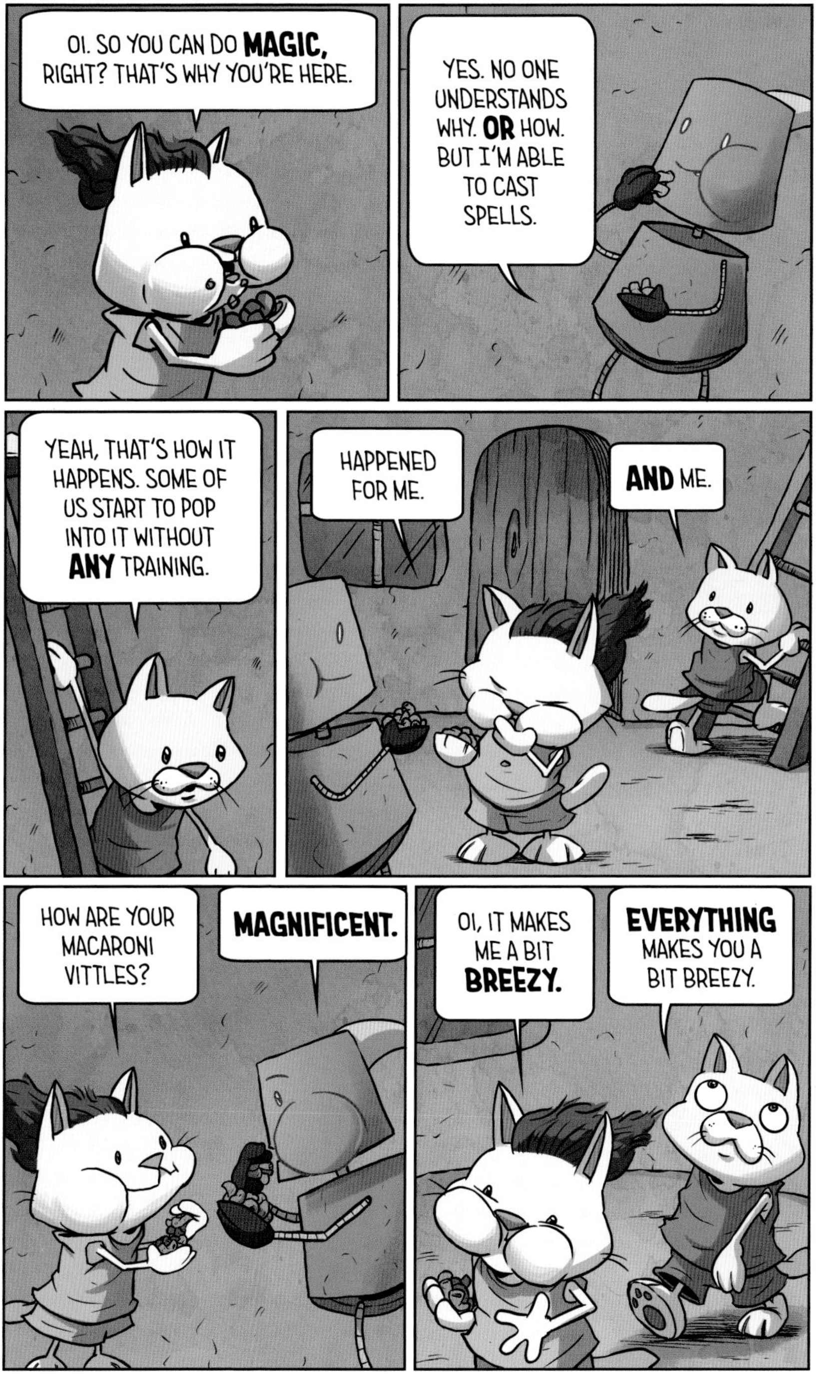

OI. SO YOU CAN DO **MAGIC,** RIGHT? THAT'S WHY YOU'RE HERE.
YES. NO ONE UNDERSTANDS WHY. **OR** HOW. BUT I'M ABLE TO CAST SPELLS.
YEAH, THAT'S HOW IT HAPPENS. SOME OF US START TO POP INTO IT WITHOUT **ANY** TRAINING.
HAPPENED FOR ME.
AND ME.
HOW ARE YOUR MACARONI VITTLES?
MAGNIFICENT.
OI, IT MAKES ME A BIT **BREEZY.**
EVERYTHING MAKES YOU A BIT BREEZY.

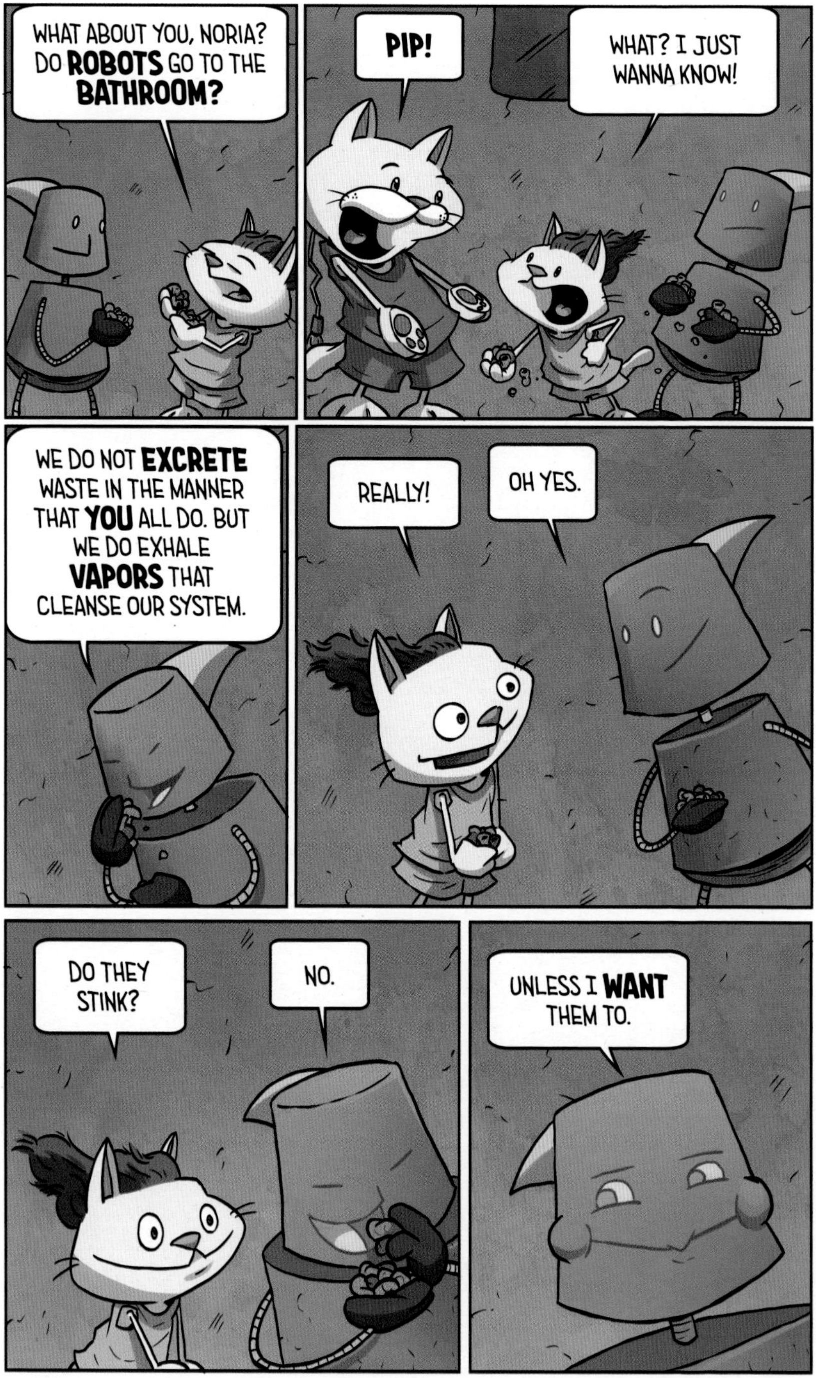
WHAT ABOUT YOU, NORIA? DO **ROBOTS** GO TO THE **BATHROOM?**
PIP!
WHAT? I JUST WANNA KNOW!
WE DO NOT **EXCRETE** WASTE IN THE MANNER THAT **YOU** ALL DO. BUT WE DO EXHALE **VAPORS** THAT CLEANSE OUR SYSTEM.
REALLY!
OH YES.
DO THEY STINK?
NO.
UNLESS I **WANT** THEM TO.

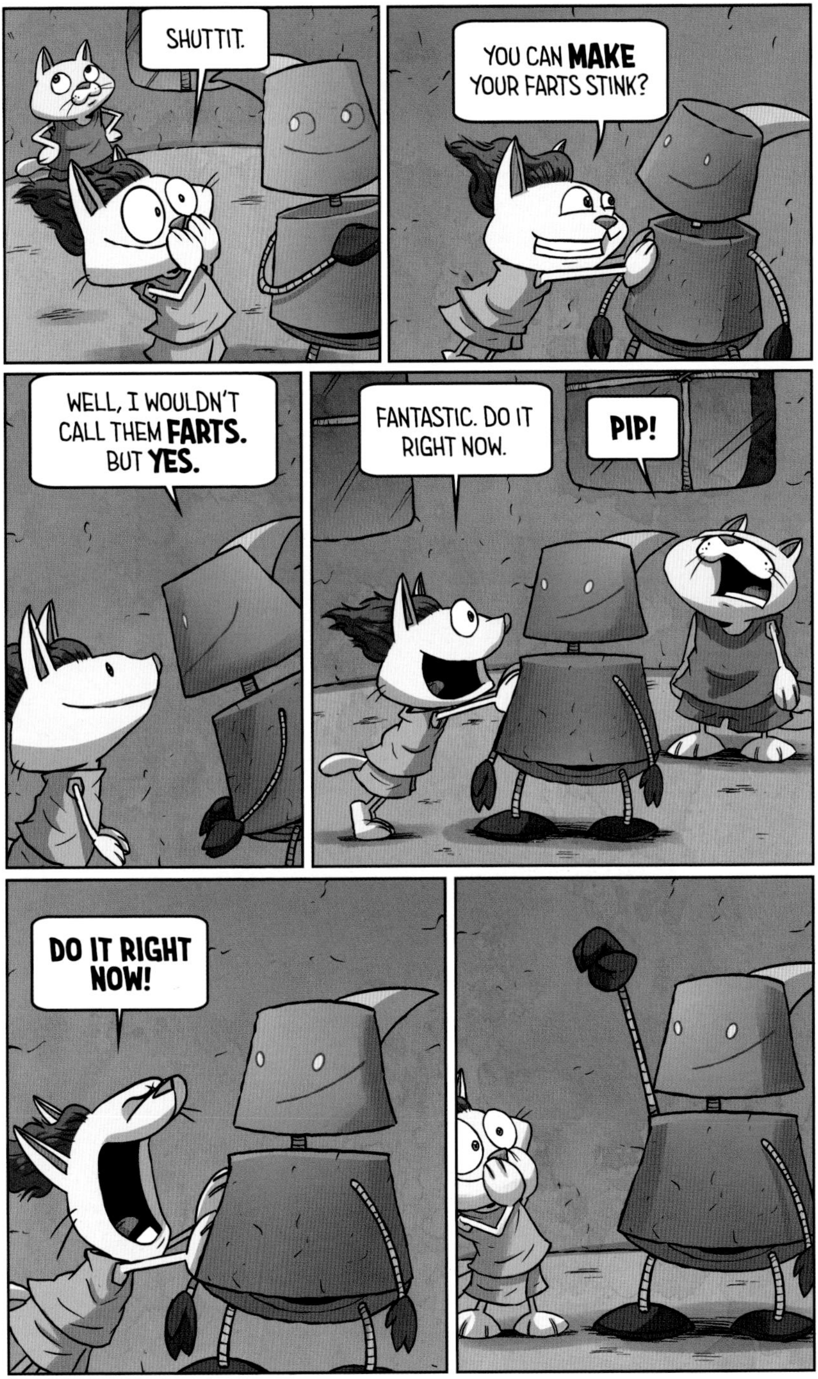
SHUTTIT.
YOU CAN **MAKE** YOUR FARTS STINK?
WELL, I WOULDN'T CALL THEM **FARTS.** BUT **YES.**
FANTASTIC. DO IT RIGHT NOW.
PIP!
DO IT RIGHT NOW!

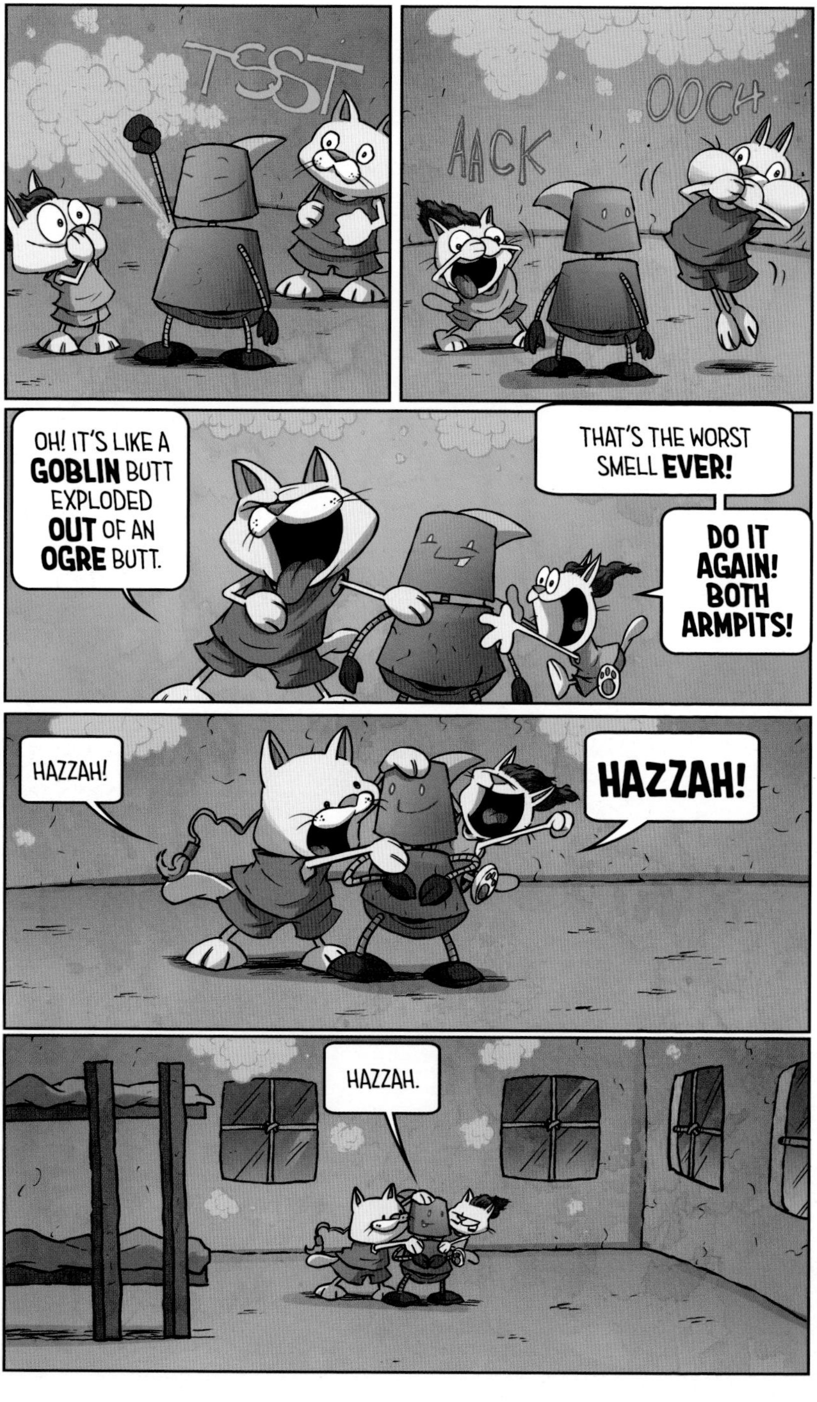
TSST
AACK
OOCH
OH! IT'S LIKE A **GOBLIN** BUTT EXPLODED **OUT** OF AN **OGRE** BUTT.
THAT'S THE WORST SMELL **EVER!**
DO IT AGAIN! BOTH ARMPITS!
HAZZAH!
HAZZAH!
HAZZAH.

CHAPTER 7

BOGWOGGLES

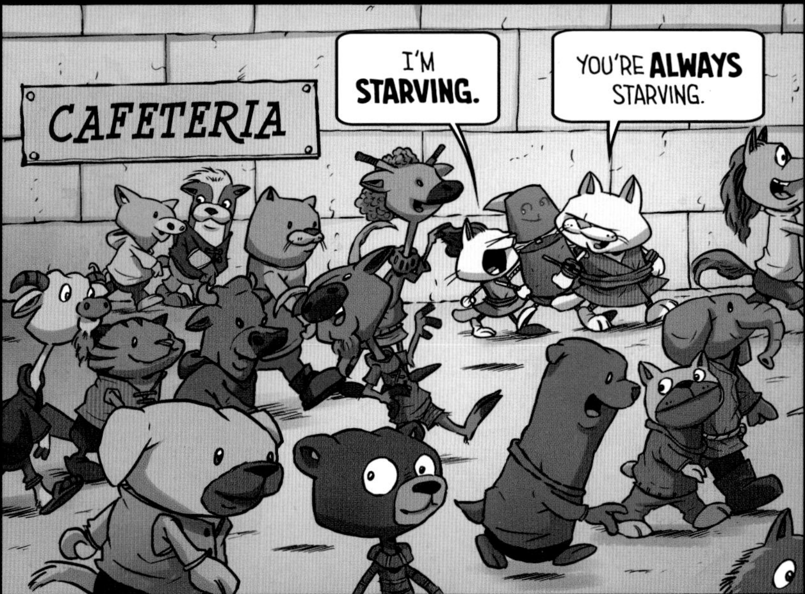
CAFETERIA
I'M STARVING.
YOU'RE ALWAYS STARVING.

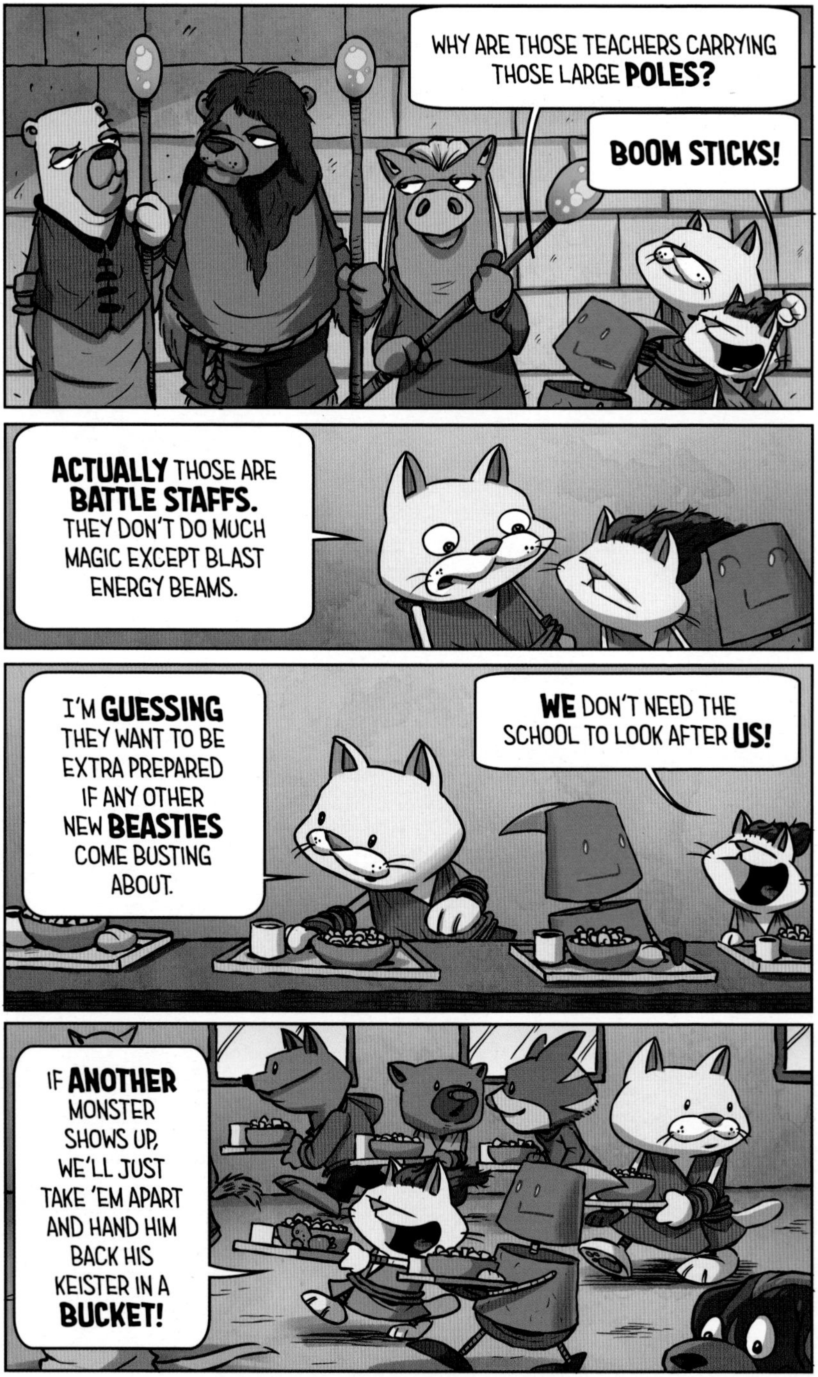
WHY ARE THOSE TEACHERS CARRYING THOSE LARGE **POLES?**
BOOM STICKS!
ACTUALLY THOSE ARE **BATTLE STAFFS.** THEY DON'T DO MUCH MAGIC EXCEPT BLAST ENERGY BEAMS.
I'M **GUESSING** THEY WANT TO BE EXTRA PREPARED IF ANY OTHER NEW **BEASTIES** COME BUSTING ABOUT.
WE DON'T NEED THE SCHOOL TO LOOK AFTER **US!**
IF **ANOTHER** MONSTER SHOWS UP, WE'LL JUST TAKE 'EM APART AND HAND HIM BACK HIS KEISTER IN A **BUCKET!**

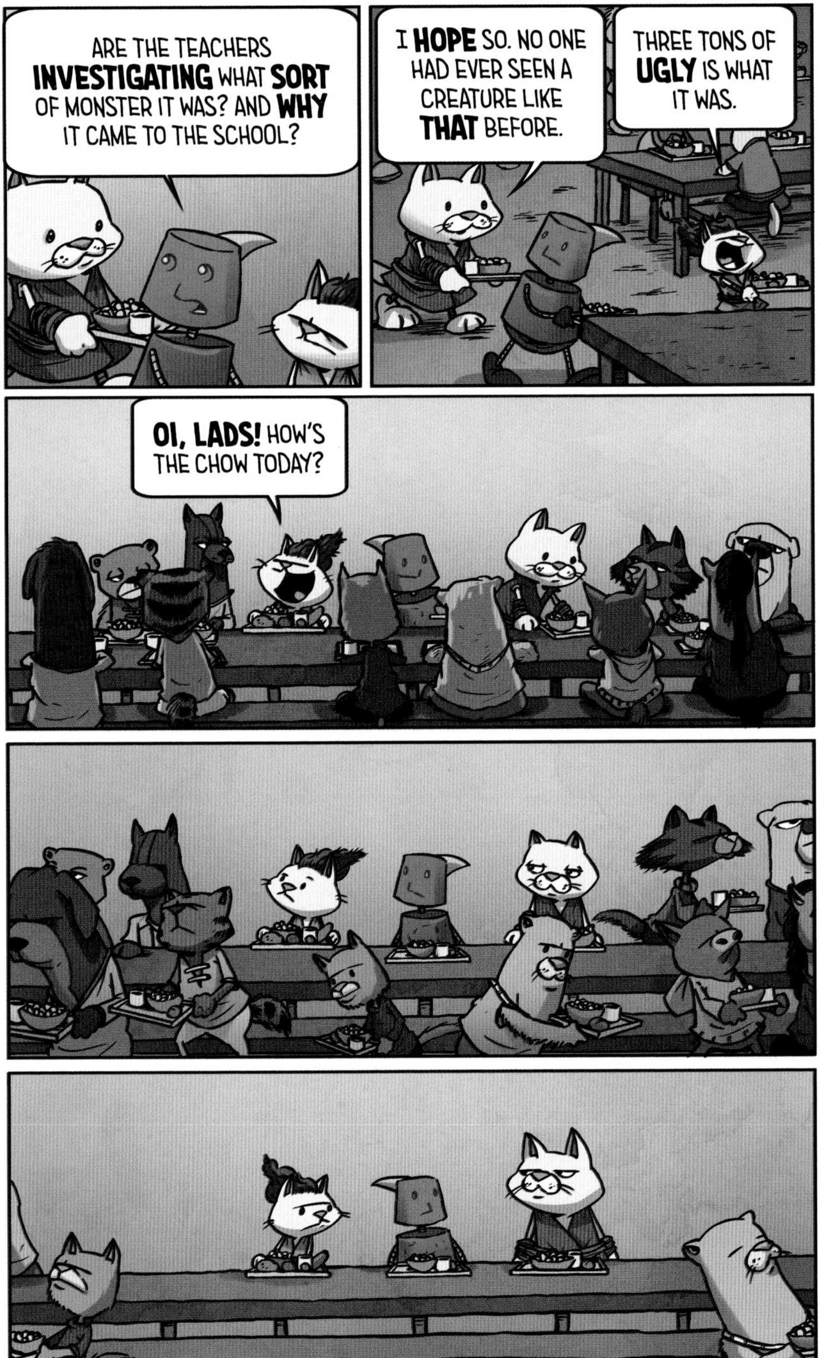
ARE THE TEACHERS INVESTIGATING WHAT SORT OF MONSTER IT WAS? AND WHY IT CAME TO THE SCHOOL?
I HOPE SO. NO ONE HAD EVER SEEN A CREATURE LIKE THAT BEFORE.
THREE TONS OF UGLY IS WHAT IT WAS.
OI, LADS! HOW'S THE CHOW TODAY?

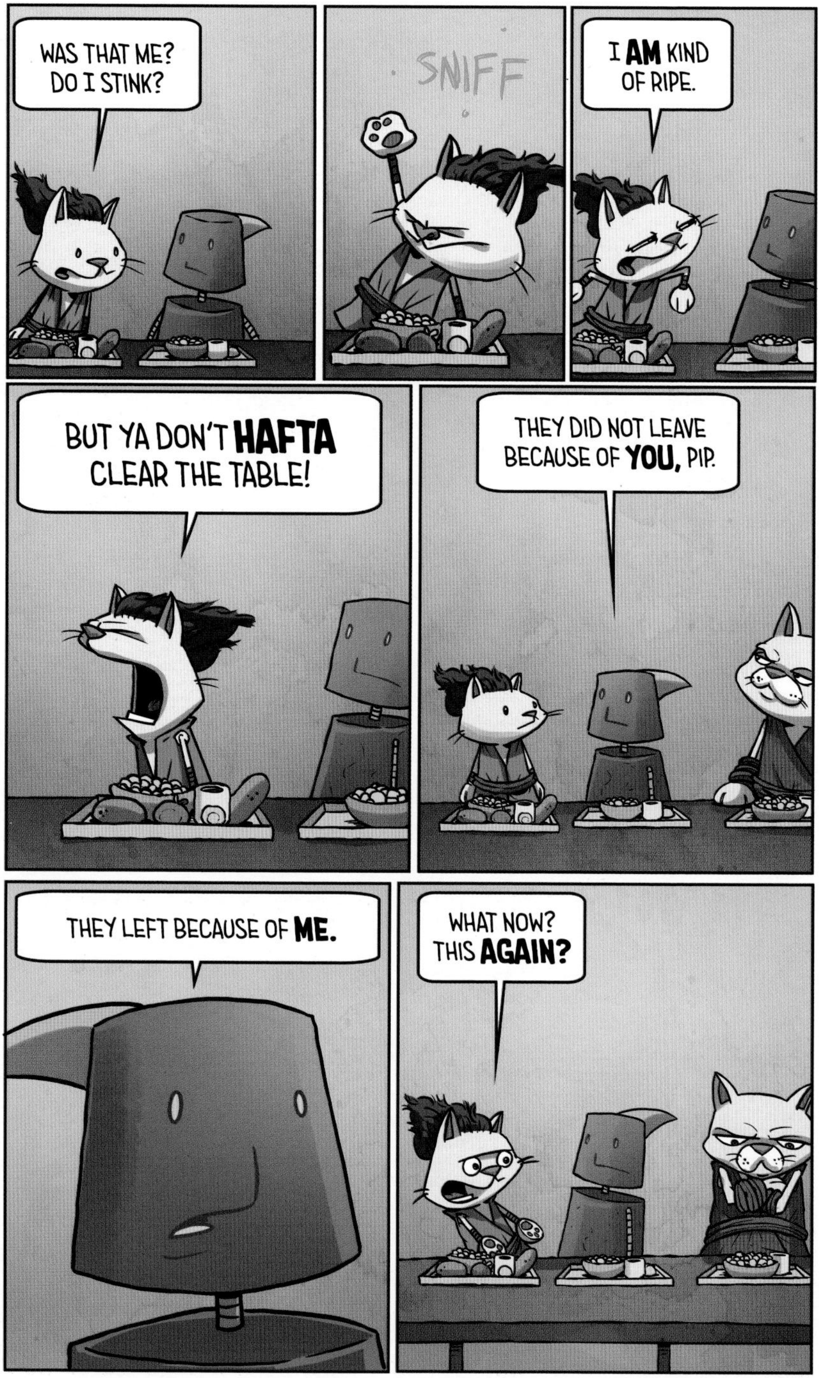
WAS THAT ME? DO I STINK?
SNIFF
I AM KIND OF RIPE.
BUT YA DON'T HAFTA CLEAR THE TABLE!
THEY DID NOT LEAVE BECAUSE OF YOU, PIP.
THEY LEFT BECAUSE OF ME.
WHAT NOW? THIS AGAIN?

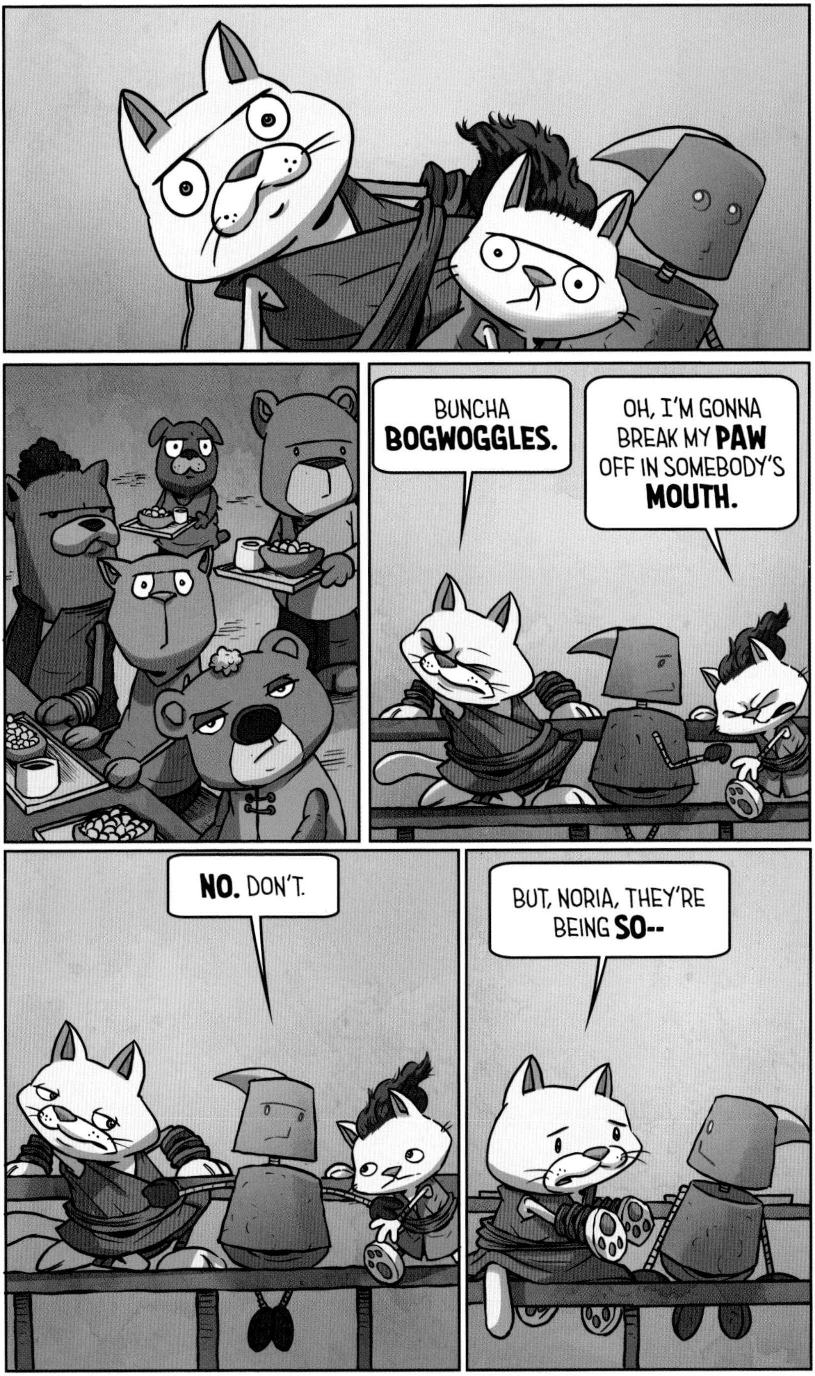
BUNCHA **BOGWOGGLES.**
OH, I'M GONNA BREAK MY **PAW** OFF IN SOMEBODY'S **MOUTH.**
NO. DON'T.
BUT, NORIA, THEY'RE BEING **SO--**

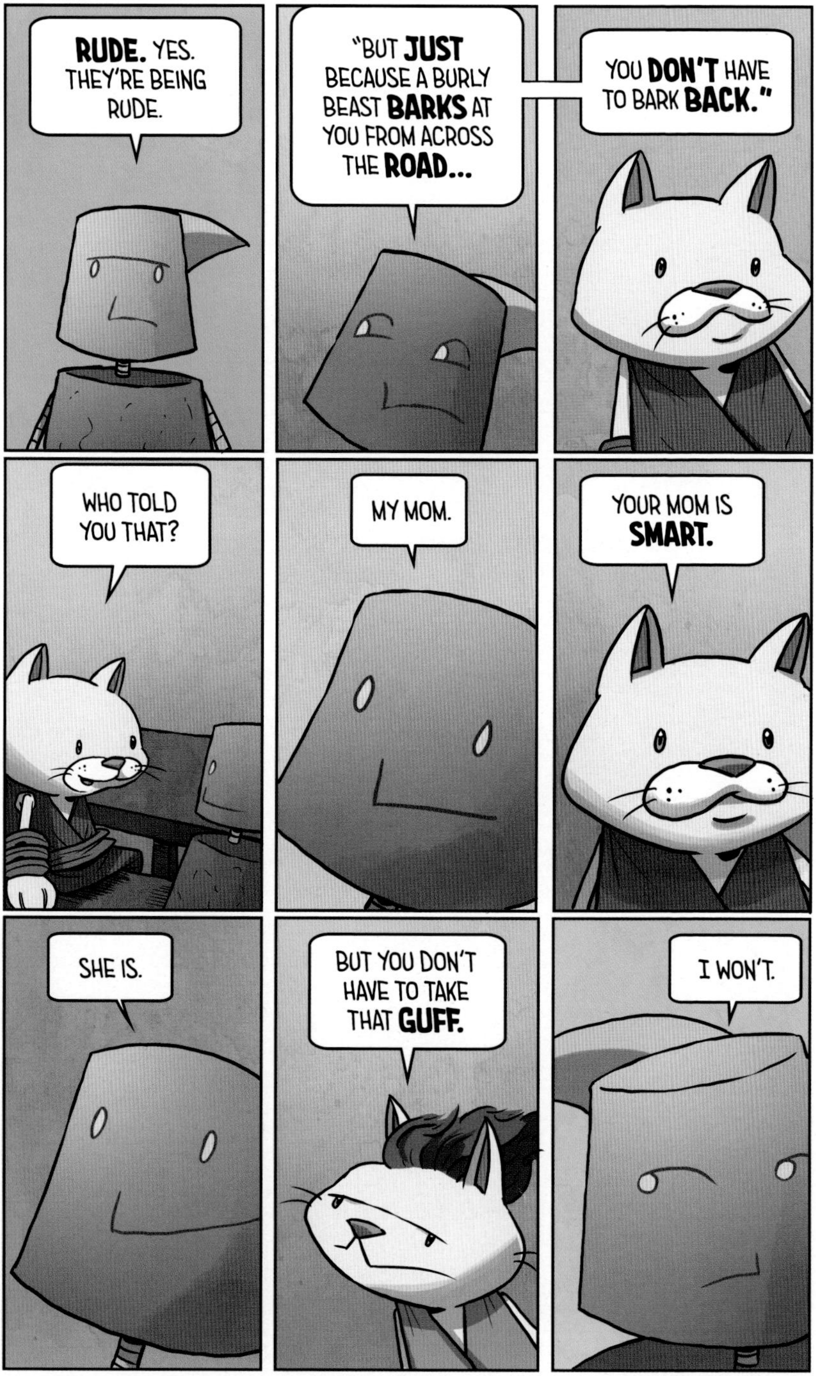
RUDE. YES. THEY'RE BEING RUDE.
"BUT JUST BECAUSE A BURLY BEAST BARKS AT YOU FROM ACROSS THE ROAD...
YOU DON'T HAVE TO BARK BACK."
WHO TOLD YOU THAT?
MY MOM.
YOUR MOM IS SMART.
SHE IS.
BUT YOU DON'T HAVE TO TAKE THAT GUFF.
I WON'T.

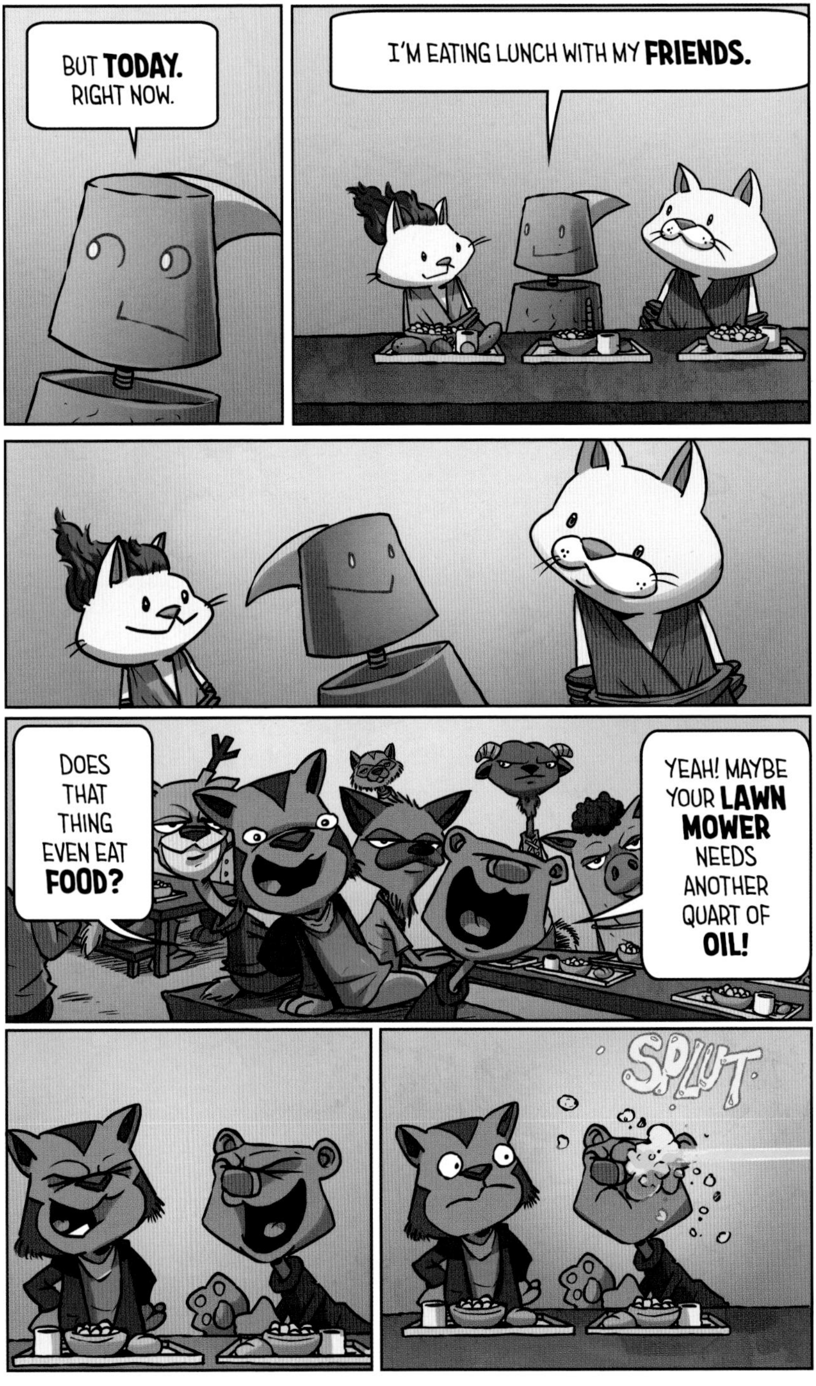
BUT **TODAY.** RIGHT NOW.
I'M EATING LUNCH WITH MY **FRIENDS.**
DOES THAT THING EVEN EAT **FOOD?**
YEAH! MAYBE YOUR **LAWN MOWER** NEEDS ANOTHER QUART OF **OIL!**
SPLUT

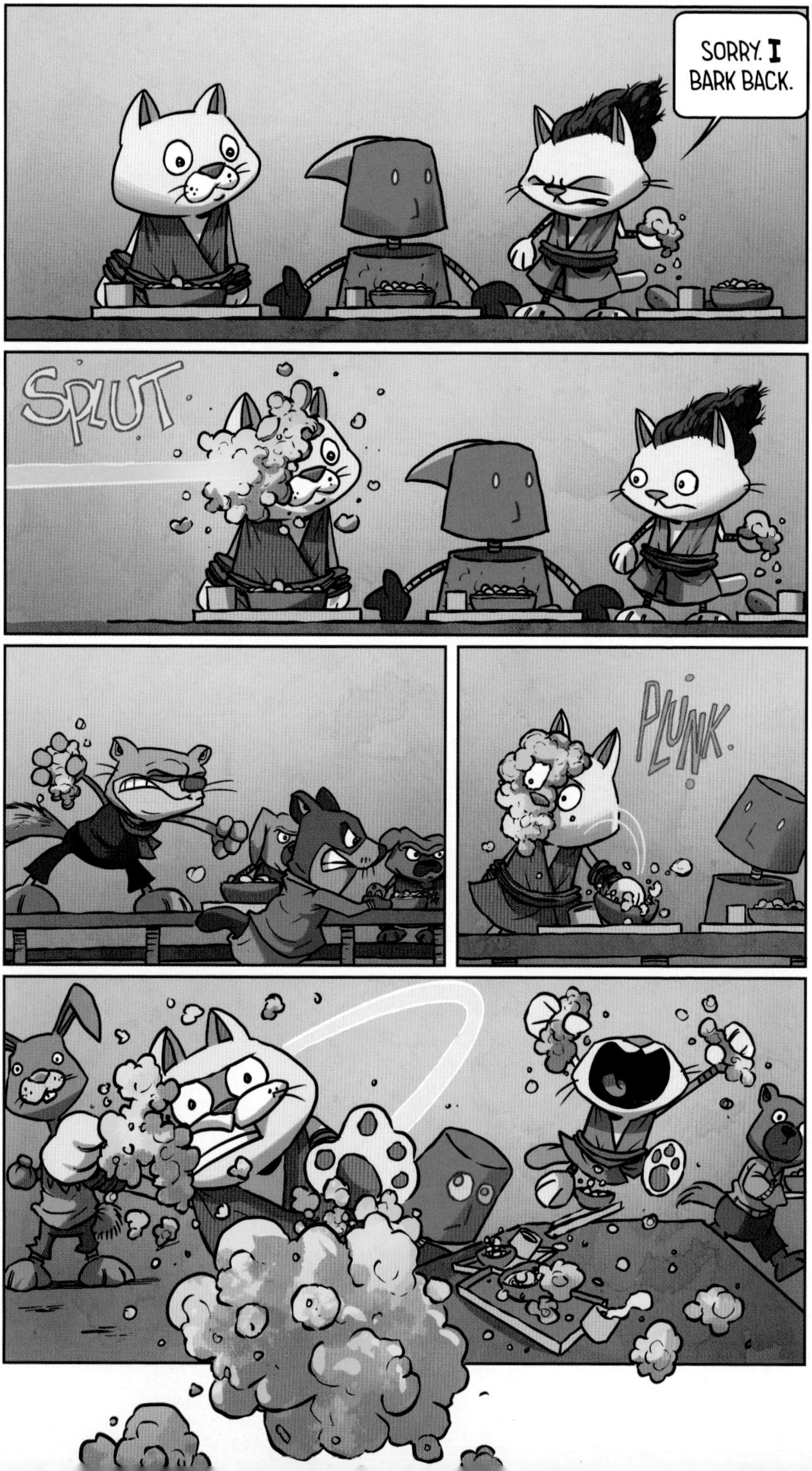
SORRY. I BARK BACK.
SPLUT
PLUNK.

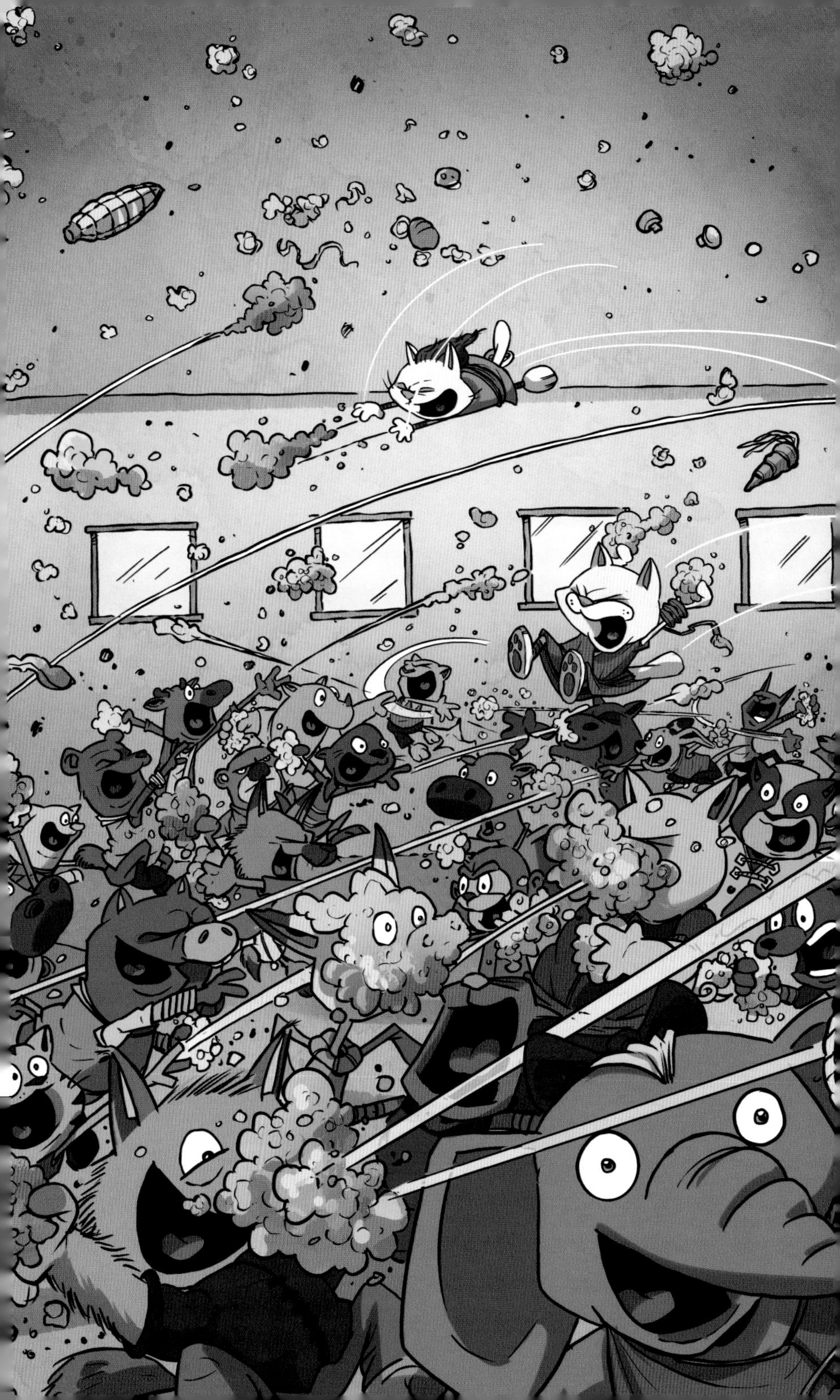

I DIDN'T **REALLY** HAVE TIME TO SIT WITH YOU TWO FOR **ANOTHER** DETENTION TODAY.

LIBRARY

I HAVE A BIT OF BUSINESS TO TAKE CARE OF MYSELF.

WE'RE SORRY.

IT WASN'T OUR FAULT.

YOU SAY THAT **A LOT.** "IT WASN'T **OUR** FAULT."

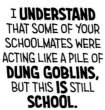

I **UNDERSTAND** THAT SOME OF YOUR SCHOOLMATES WERE ACTING LIKE A PILE OF **DUNG GOBLINS,** BUT THIS **IS** STILL **SCHOOL.**

AND THERE'S A TIME **AND** A PLACE TO HANDLE BULLIES.

IT'S KIND OF LIKE WHAT **NORIA** SAID.

YEAH.

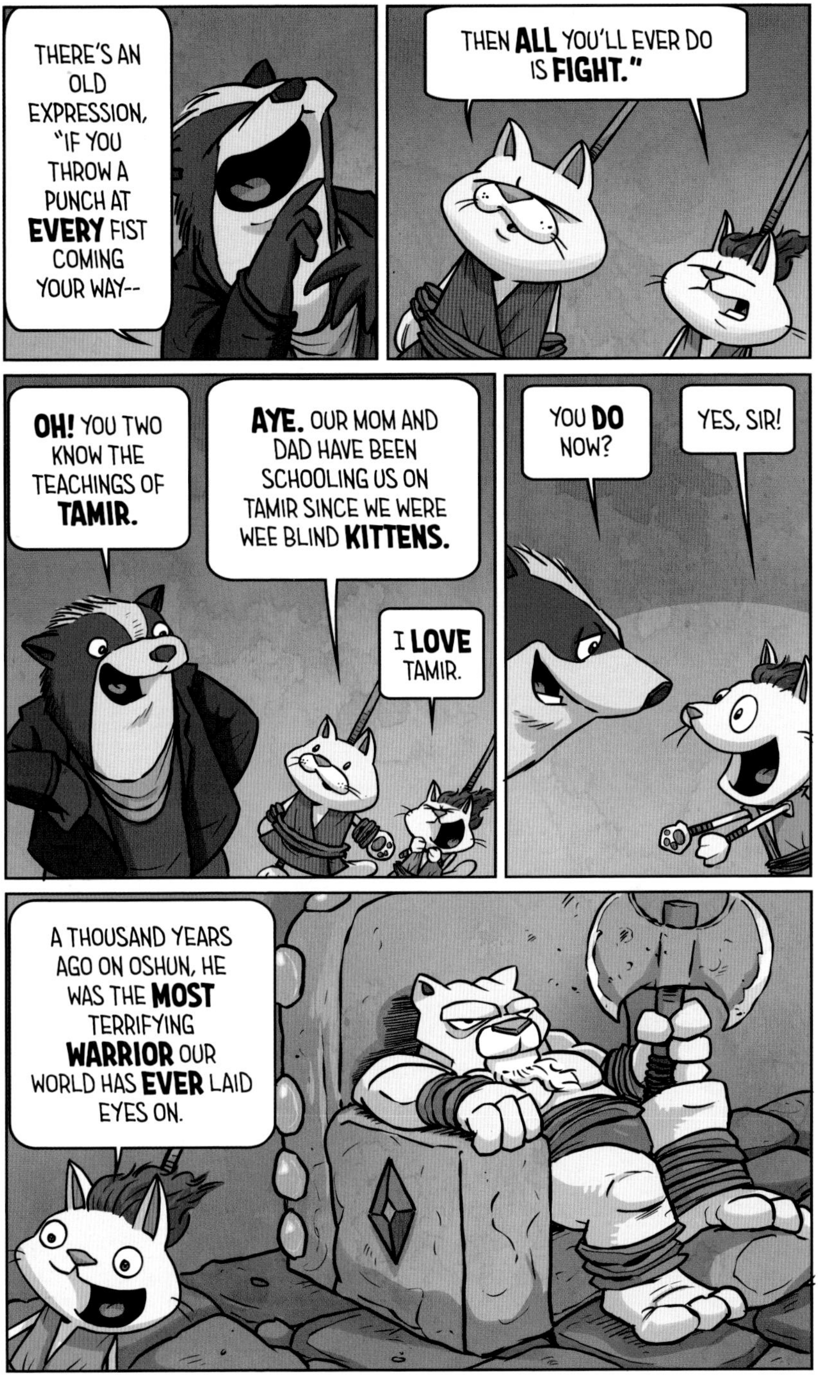

THERE'S AN OLD EXPRESSION, "IF YOU THROW A PUNCH AT **EVERY** FIST COMING YOUR WAY--
THEN **ALL** YOU'LL EVER DO IS **FIGHT.**"
OH! YOU TWO KNOW THE TEACHINGS OF **TAMIR.**
AYE. OUR MOM AND DAD HAVE BEEN SCHOOLING US ON TAMIR SINCE WE WERE WEE BLIND **KITTENS.**
I **LOVE** TAMIR.
YOU **DO** NOW?
YES, SIR!
A THOUSAND YEARS AGO ON OSHUN, HE WAS THE **MOST** TERRIFYING **WARRIOR** OUR WORLD HAS **EVER** LAID EYES ON.

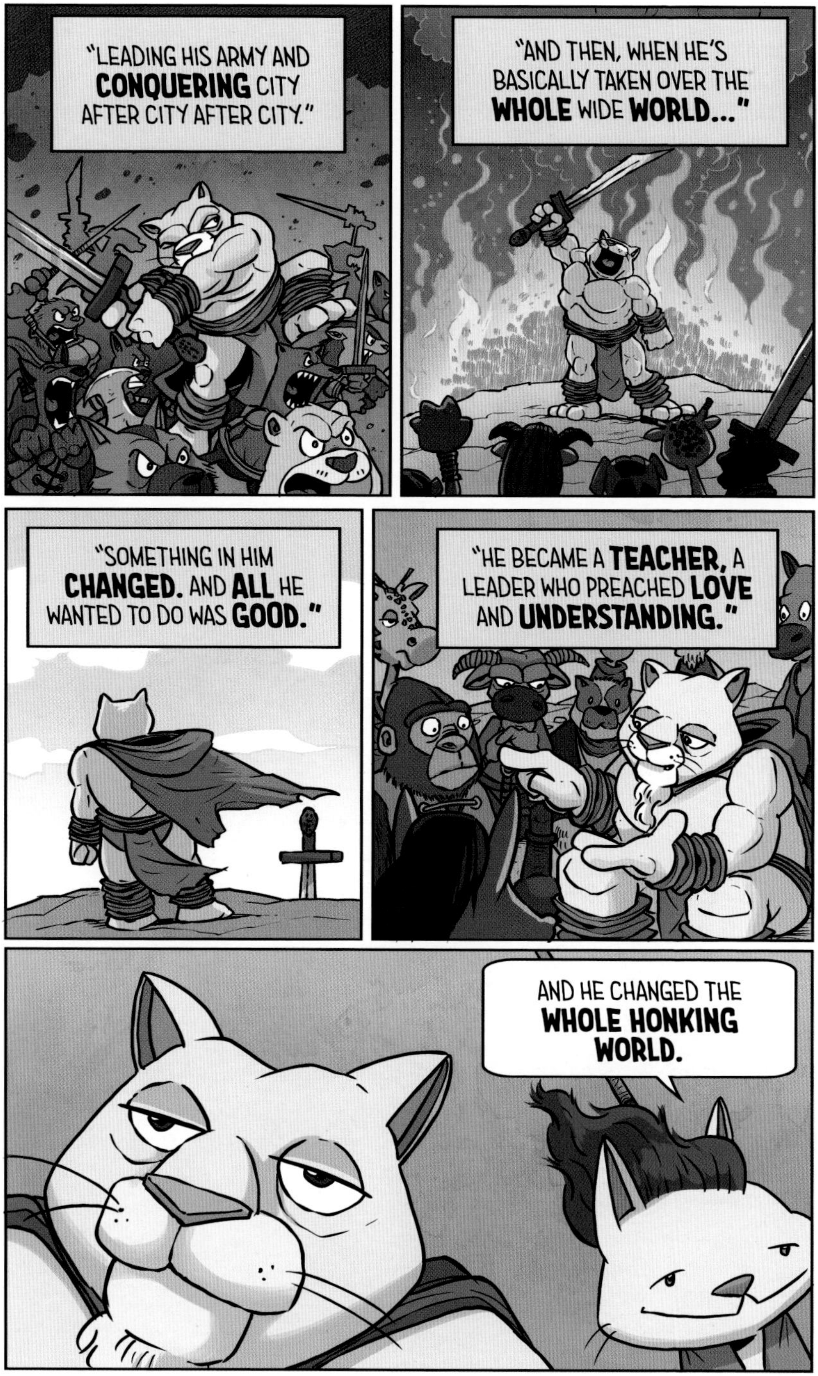
"LEADING HIS ARMY AND **CONQUERING** CITY AFTER CITY AFTER CITY."
"AND THEN, WHEN HE'S BASICALLY TAKEN OVER THE **WHOLE** WIDE **WORLD...**"
"SOMETHING IN HIM **CHANGED.** AND **ALL** HE WANTED TO DO WAS **GOOD.**"
"HE BECAME A **TEACHER,** A LEADER WHO PREACHED **LOVE** AND **UNDERSTANDING.**"
AND HE CHANGED THE **WHOLE HONKING WORLD.**

YOU **DO** KNOW YOUR TAMIR.

YOU CAN BET YOUR **WHISKERS** ON THAT! BUT **WE PLANET HOPPERS** LEARNED EVEN **MORE.**

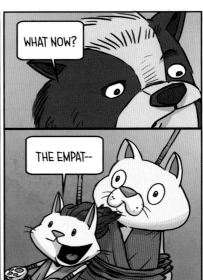

WHAT NOW?

THE EMPAT--

--UUMPH!

UH-WE-**YEAH!** WE **TOOK** THE LESSONS OF TAMIR ON OUR-- **Y'KNOW**--ADVENTURES TO **EARTH!**

YEP! **ALWAYS** REMEMBERING THE OPENNESS AND THE TRUTHINESS AND THE **CARING** AND THE **GOODNESS!**

NUDGE.

ALL THAT STUFF!

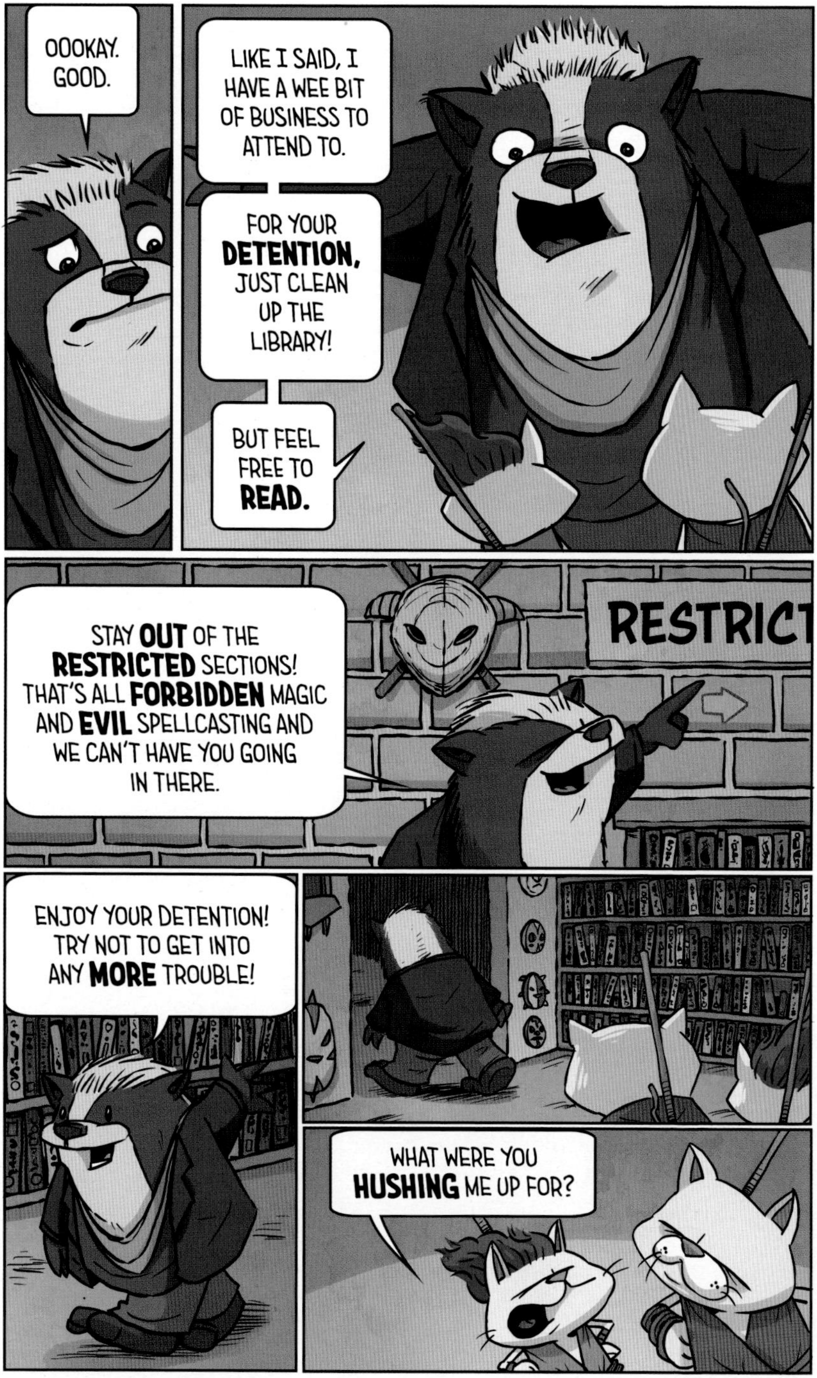
OOOKAY. GOOD.
LIKE I SAID, I HAVE A WEE BIT OF BUSINESS TO ATTEND TO.
FOR YOUR DETENTION, JUST CLEAN UP THE LIBRARY!
BUT FEEL FREE TO READ.
RESTRICT
STAY OUT OF THE RESTRICTED SECTIONS! THAT'S ALL FORBIDDEN MAGIC AND EVIL SPELLCASTING AND WE CAN'T HAVE YOU GOING IN THERE.
ENJOY YOUR DETENTION! TRY NOT TO GET INTO ANY MORE TROUBLE!
WHAT WERE YOU HUSHING ME UP FOR?

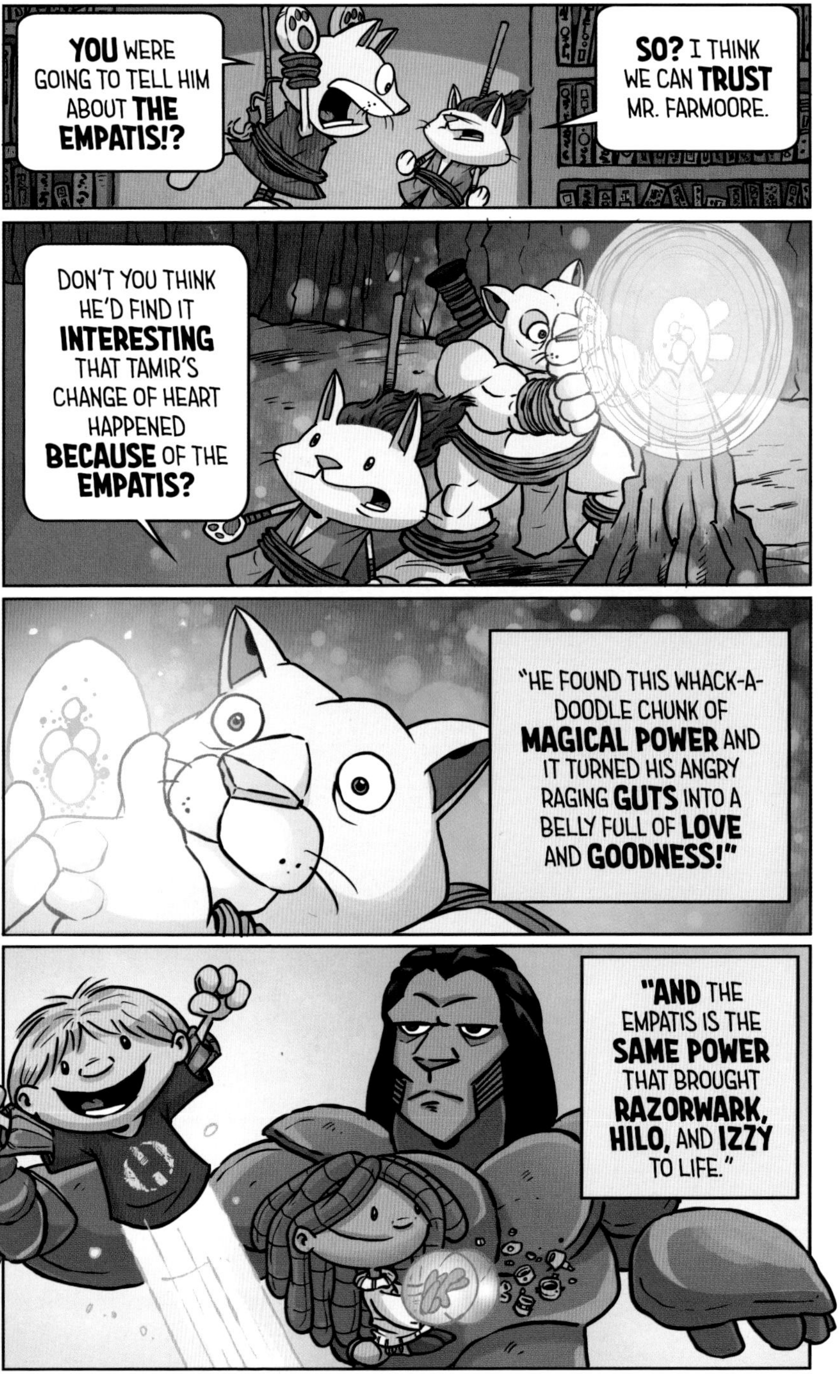
YOU WERE GOING TO TELL HIM ABOUT THE EMPATIS!?
SO? I THINK WE CAN TRUST MR. FARMOORE.
DON'T YOU THINK HE'D FIND IT INTERESTING THAT TAMIR'S CHANGE OF HEART HAPPENED BECAUSE OF THE EMPATIS?
"HE FOUND THIS WHACK-A-DOODLE CHUNK OF MAGICAL POWER AND IT TURNED HIS ANGRY RAGING GUTS INTO A BELLY FULL OF LOVE AND GOODNESS!"
"AND THE EMPATIS IS THE SAME POWER THAT BROUGHT RAZORWARK, HILO, AND IZZY TO LIFE."

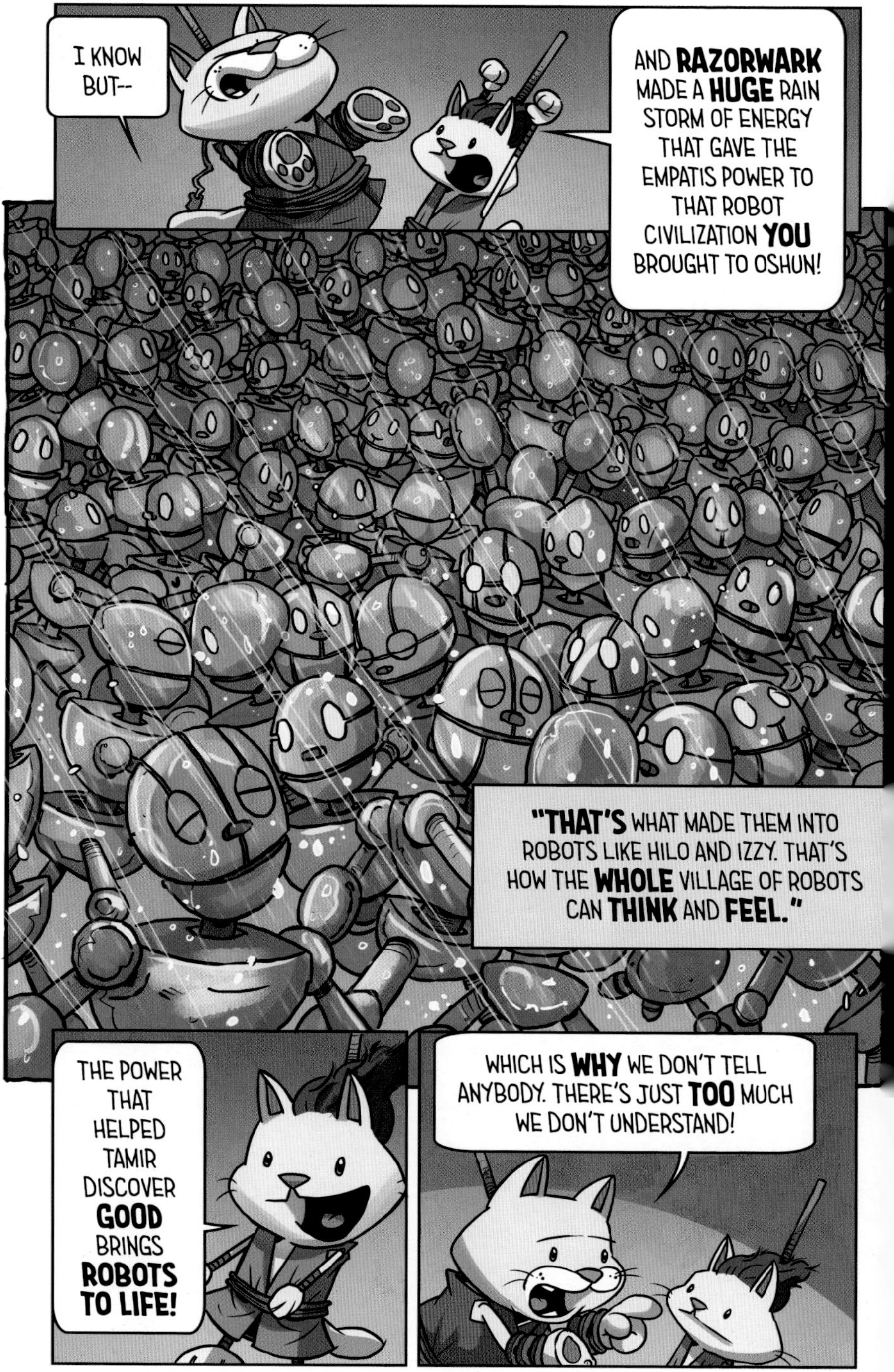

I KNOW BUT--
AND **RAZORWARK** MADE A **HUGE** RAIN STORM OF ENERGY THAT GAVE THE EMPATIS POWER TO THAT ROBOT CIVILIZATION **YOU** BROUGHT TO OSHUN!
"**THAT'S** WHAT MADE THEM INTO ROBOTS LIKE HILO AND IZZY. THAT'S HOW THE **WHOLE** VILLAGE OF ROBOTS CAN **THINK** AND **FEEL.**"
THE POWER THAT HELPED TAMIR DISCOVER **GOOD** BRINGS **ROBOTS TO LIFE!**
WHICH IS **WHY** WE DON'T TELL ANYBODY. THERE'S JUST **TOO** MUCH WE DON'T UNDERSTAND!

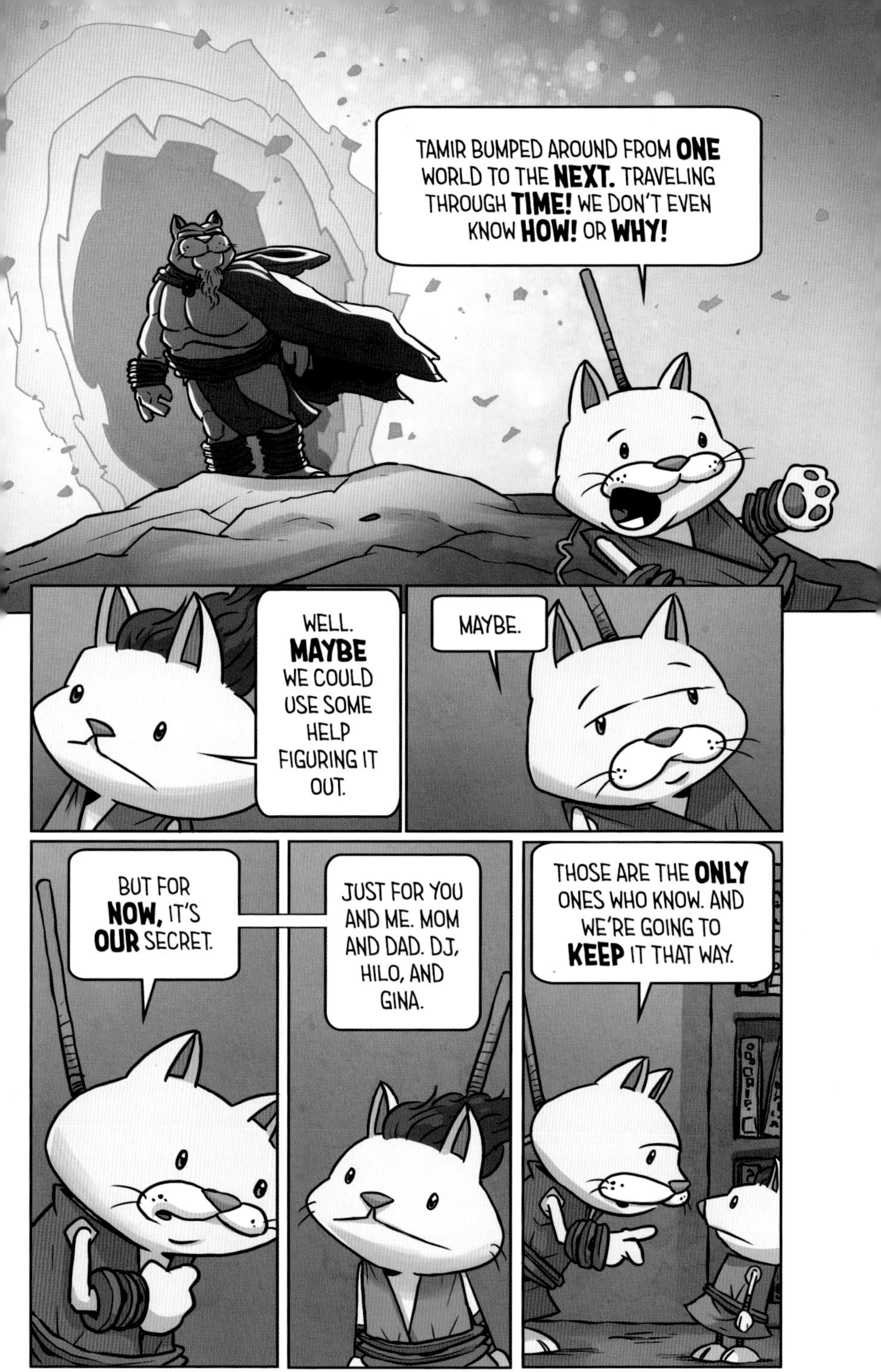
TAMIR BUMPED AROUND FROM **ONE** WORLD TO THE **NEXT.** TRAVELING THROUGH **TIME!** WE DON'T EVEN KNOW **HOW!** OR **WHY!**
WELL. **MAYBE** WE COULD USE SOME HELP FIGURING IT OUT.
MAYBE.
BUT FOR **NOW,** IT'S **OUR** SECRET.
JUST FOR YOU AND ME. MOM AND DAD. DJ, HILO, AND GINA.
THOSE ARE THE **ONLY** ONES WHO KNOW. AND WE'RE GOING TO **KEEP** IT THAT WAY.

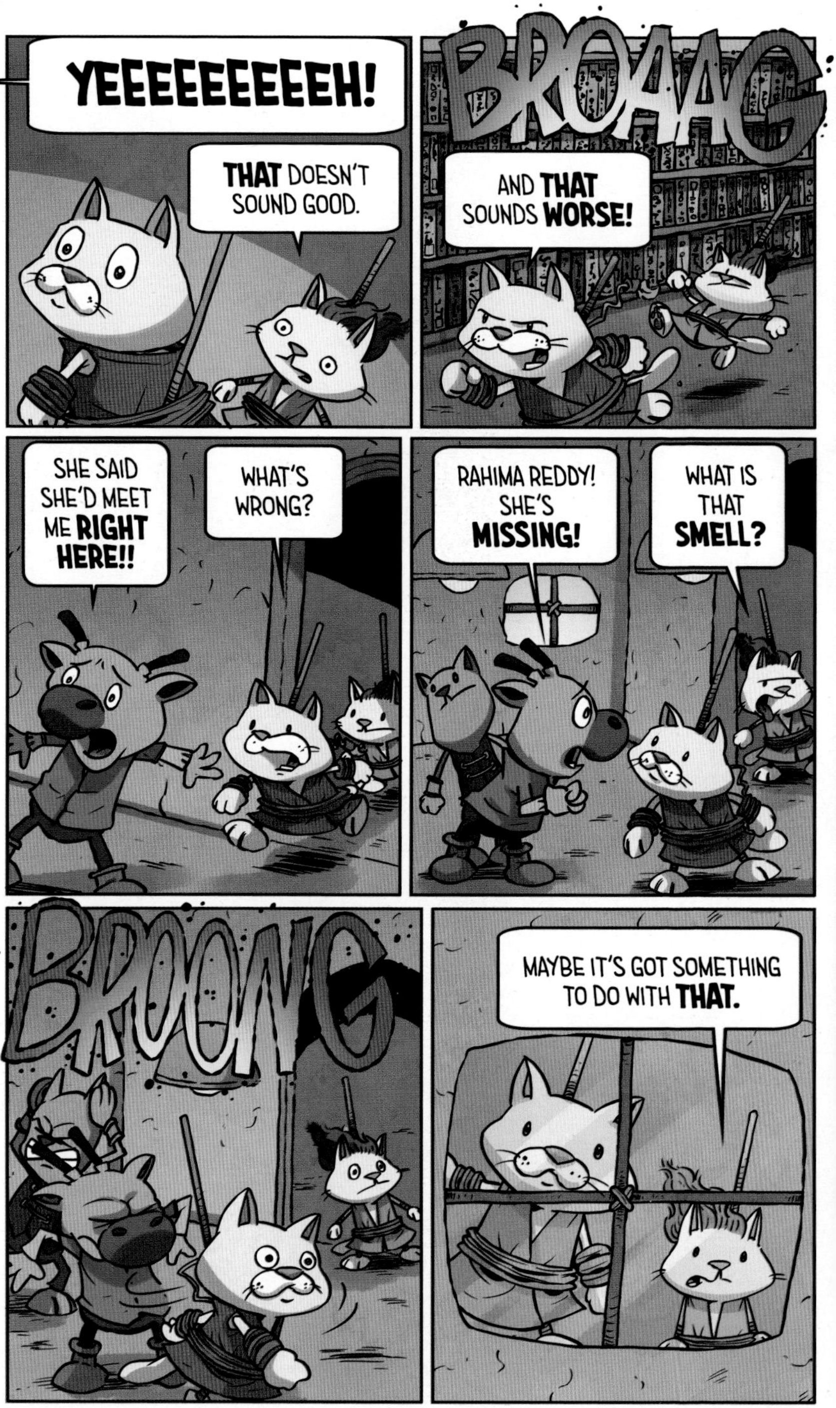
YEEEEEEEEEEH!
THAT DOESN'T SOUND GOOD.
BROAAG
AND THAT SOUNDS WORSE!
SHE SAID SHE'D MEET ME RIGHT HERE!!
WHAT'S WRONG?
RAHIMA REDDY! SHE'S MISSING!
WHAT IS THAT SMELL?
BROOONG
MAYBE IT'S GOT SOMETHING TO DO WITH THAT.

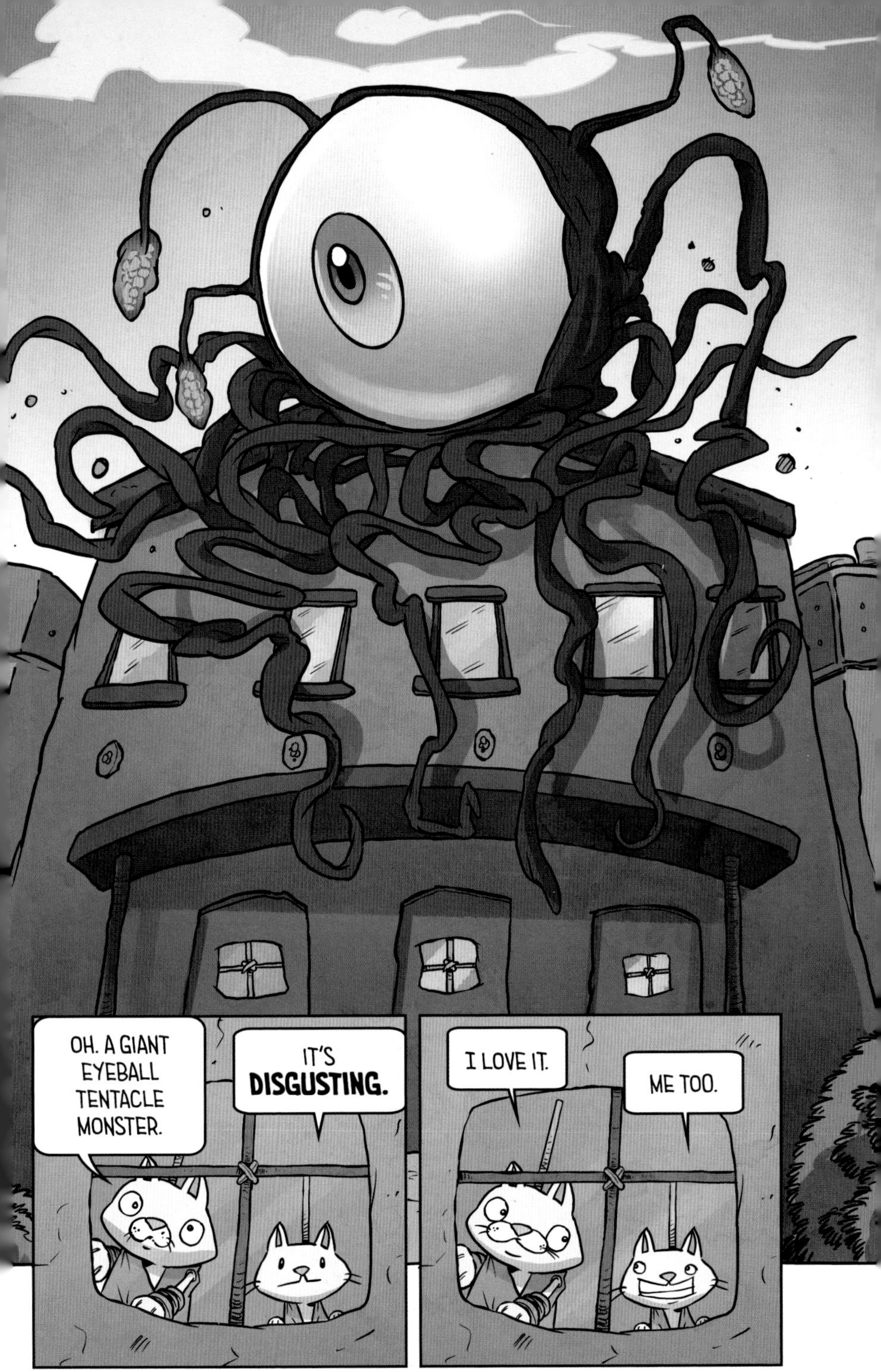

OH. A GIANT EYEBALL TENTACLE MONSTER.
IT'S DISGUSTING.
I LOVE IT.
ME TOO.

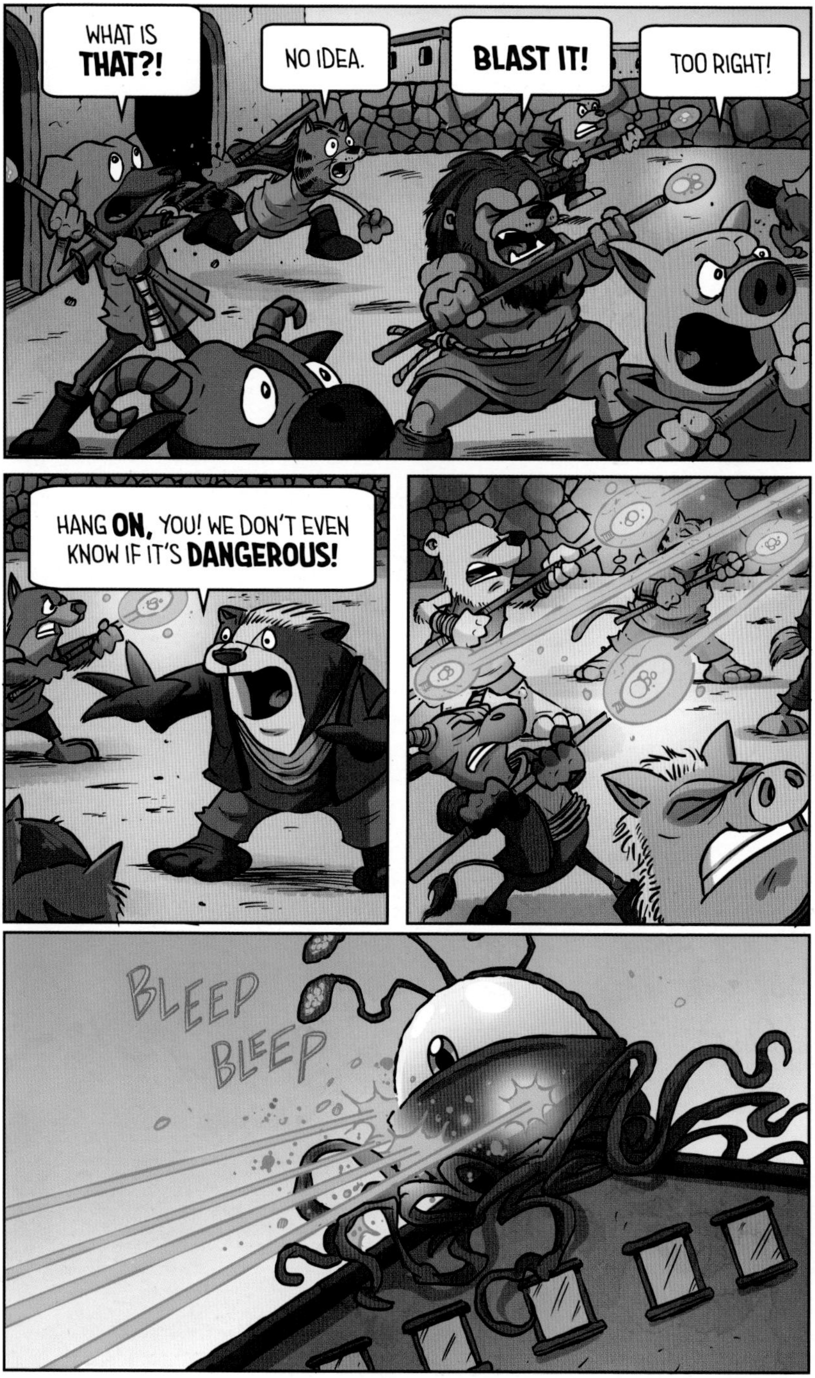
WHAT IS **THAT?!**
NO IDEA.
BLAST IT!
TOO RIGHT!
HANG **ON,** YOU! WE DON'T EVEN KNOW IF IT'S **DANGEROUS!**
BLEEP
BLEEP

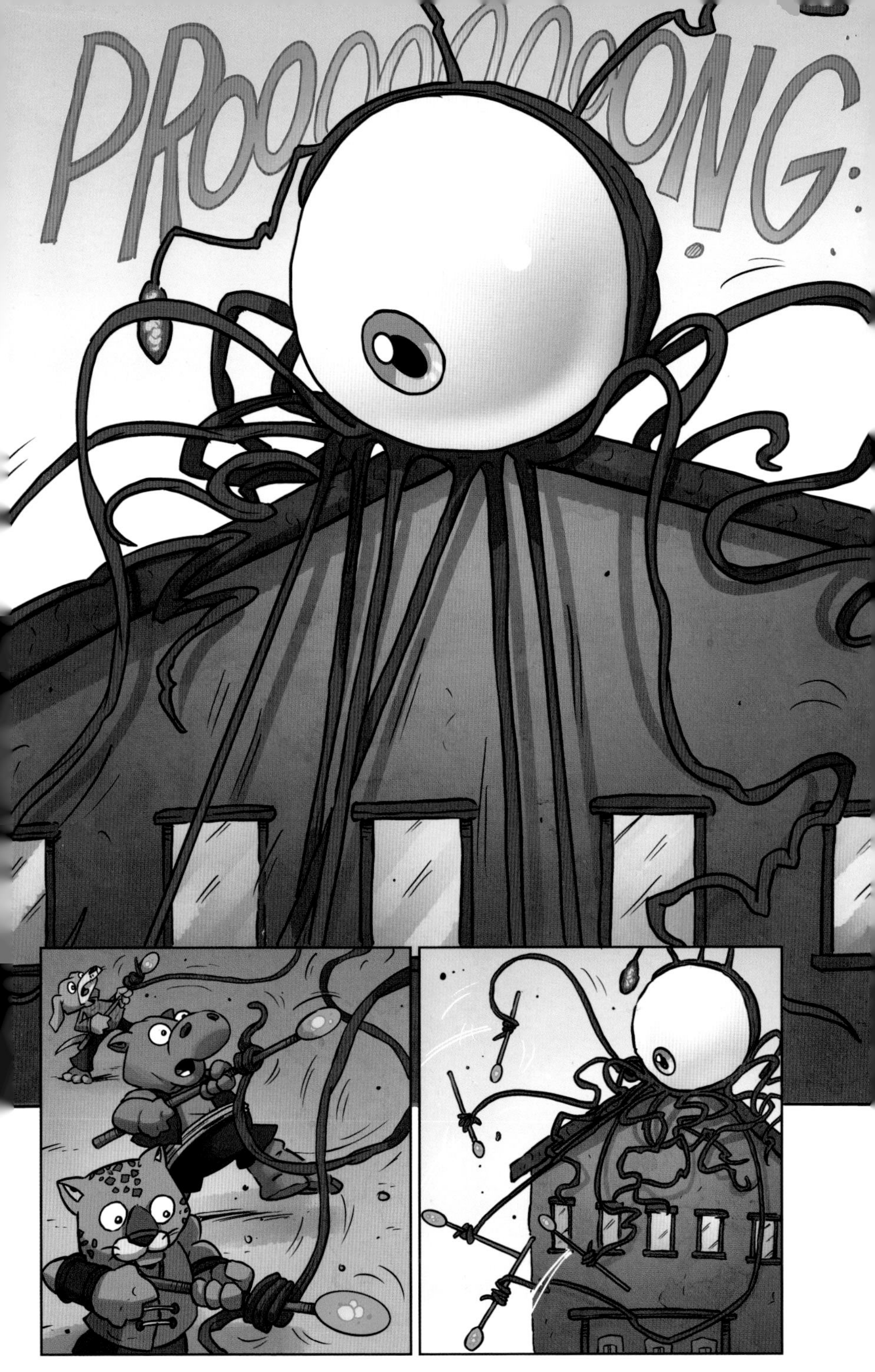
PROOOOOOOONG

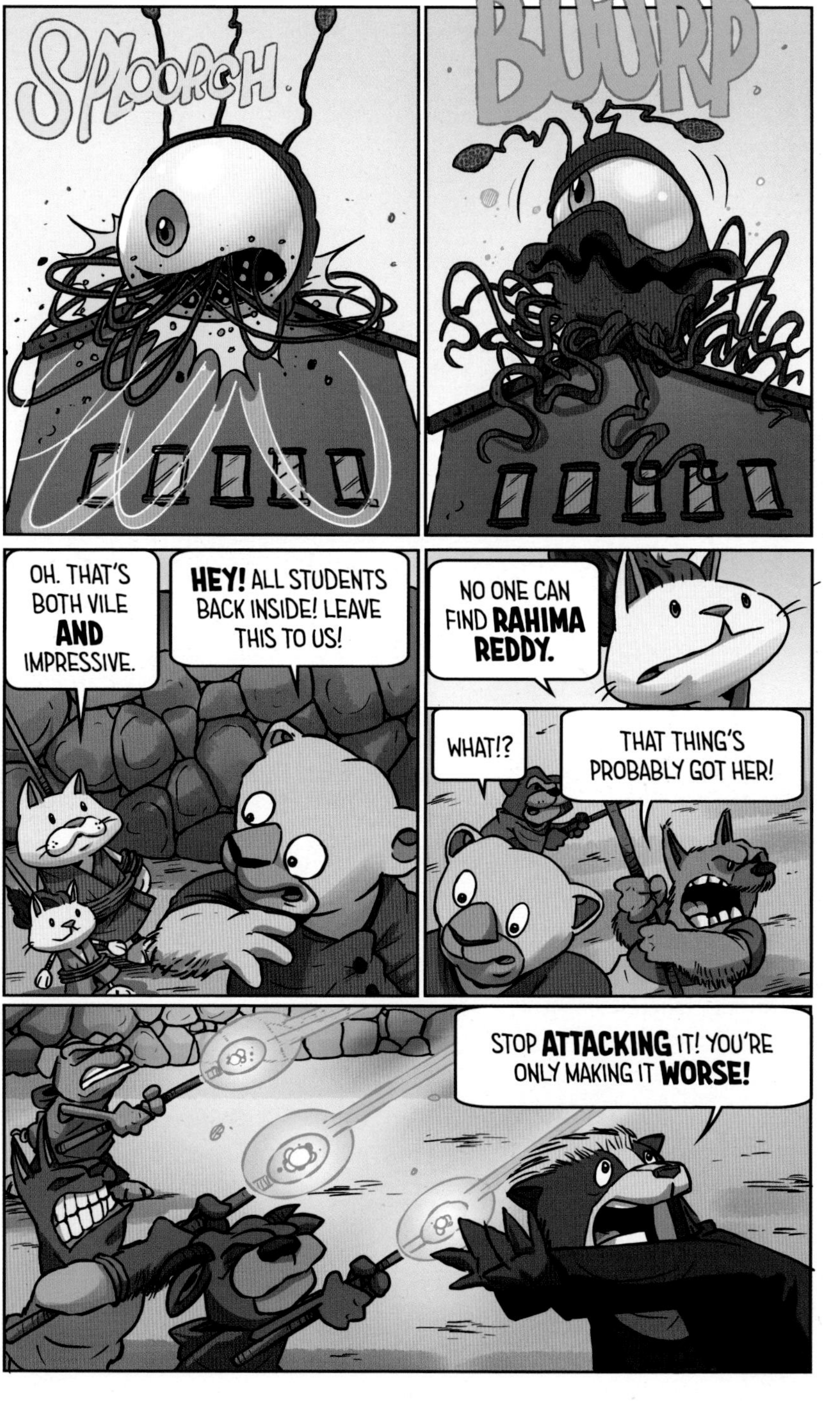
SPLOORCH
BUURP
OH. THAT'S BOTH VILE AND IMPRESSIVE.
HEY! ALL STUDENTS BACK INSIDE! LEAVE THIS TO US!
NO ONE CAN FIND RAHIMA REDDY.
WHAT!?
THAT THING'S PROBABLY GOT HER!
STOP ATTACKING IT! YOU'RE ONLY MAKING IT WORSE!

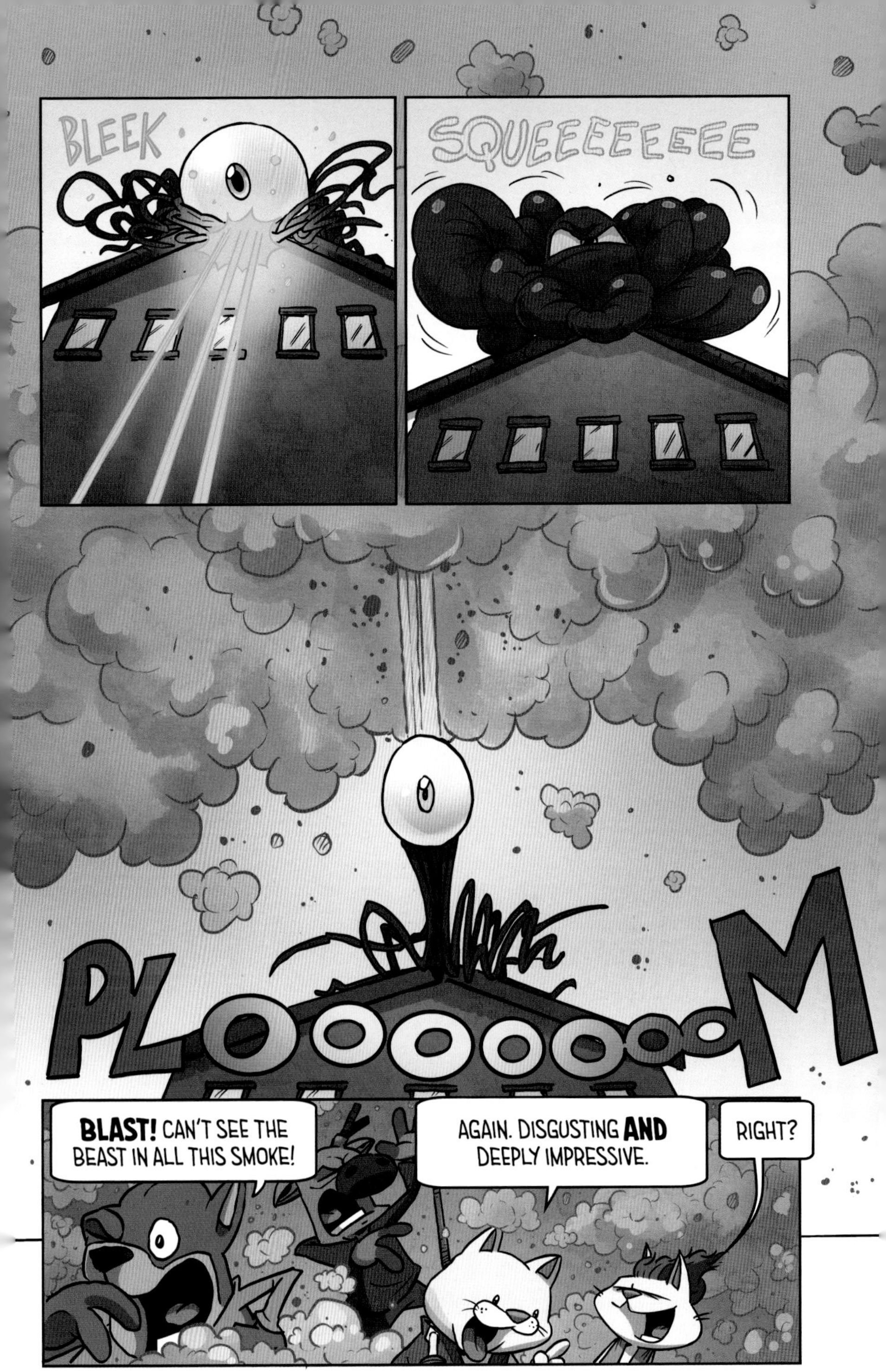
BLEEK
SQUEEEEEEEEE
PLOOOOOOOM
BLAST! CAN'T SEE THE BEAST IN ALL THIS SMOKE!
AGAIN. DISGUSTING AND DEEPLY IMPRESSIVE.
RIGHT?

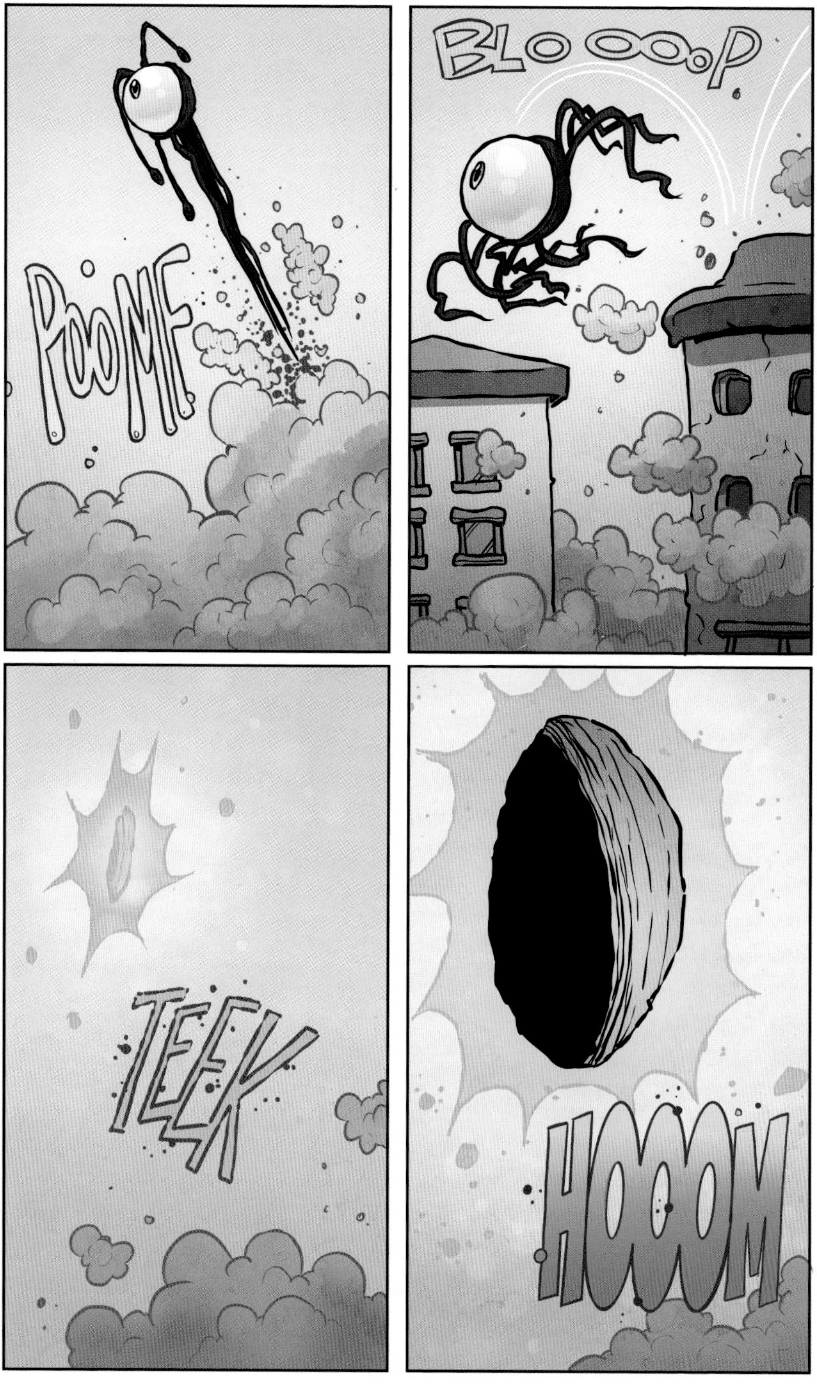
POOMF
BLOOOOP
TEEK
HOOOM

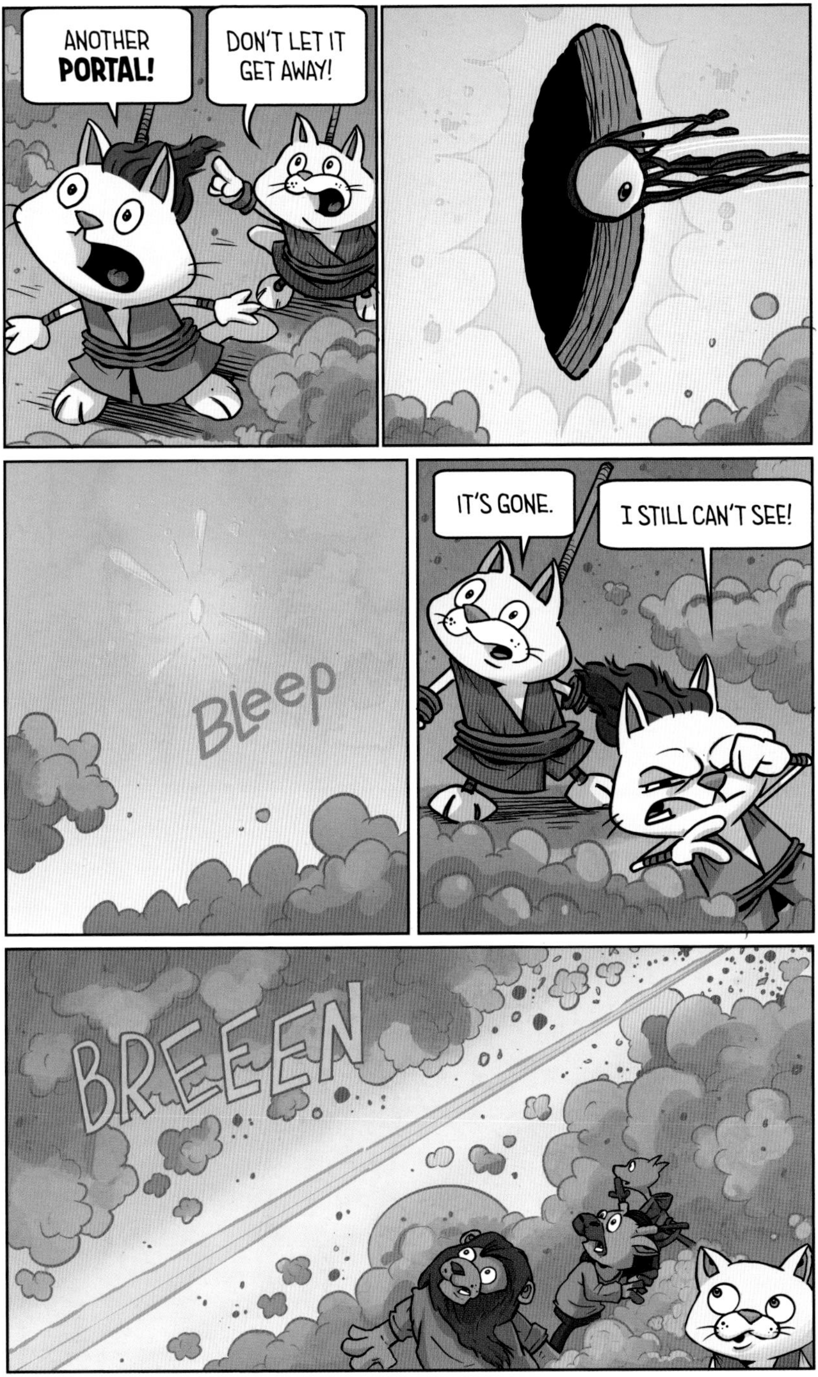
ANOTHER **PORTAL!**
DON'T LET IT GET AWAY!
BLEEP
IT'S GONE.
I STILL CAN'T SEE!
BREEEN

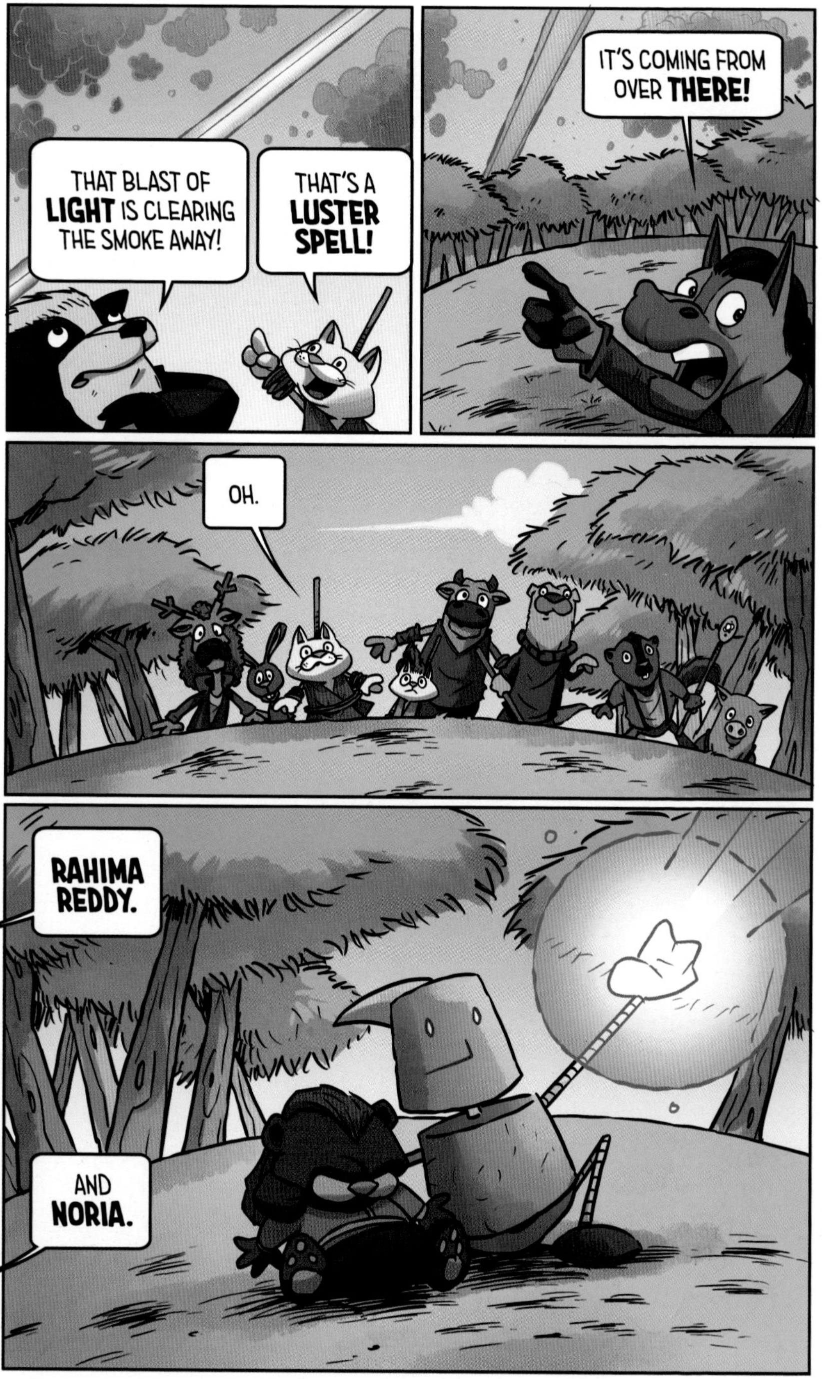
THAT BLAST OF **LIGHT** IS CLEARING THE SMOKE AWAY!
THAT'S A **LUSTER SPELL!**
IT'S COMING FROM OVER **THERE!**
OH.
RAHIMA REDDY.
AND **NORIA.**

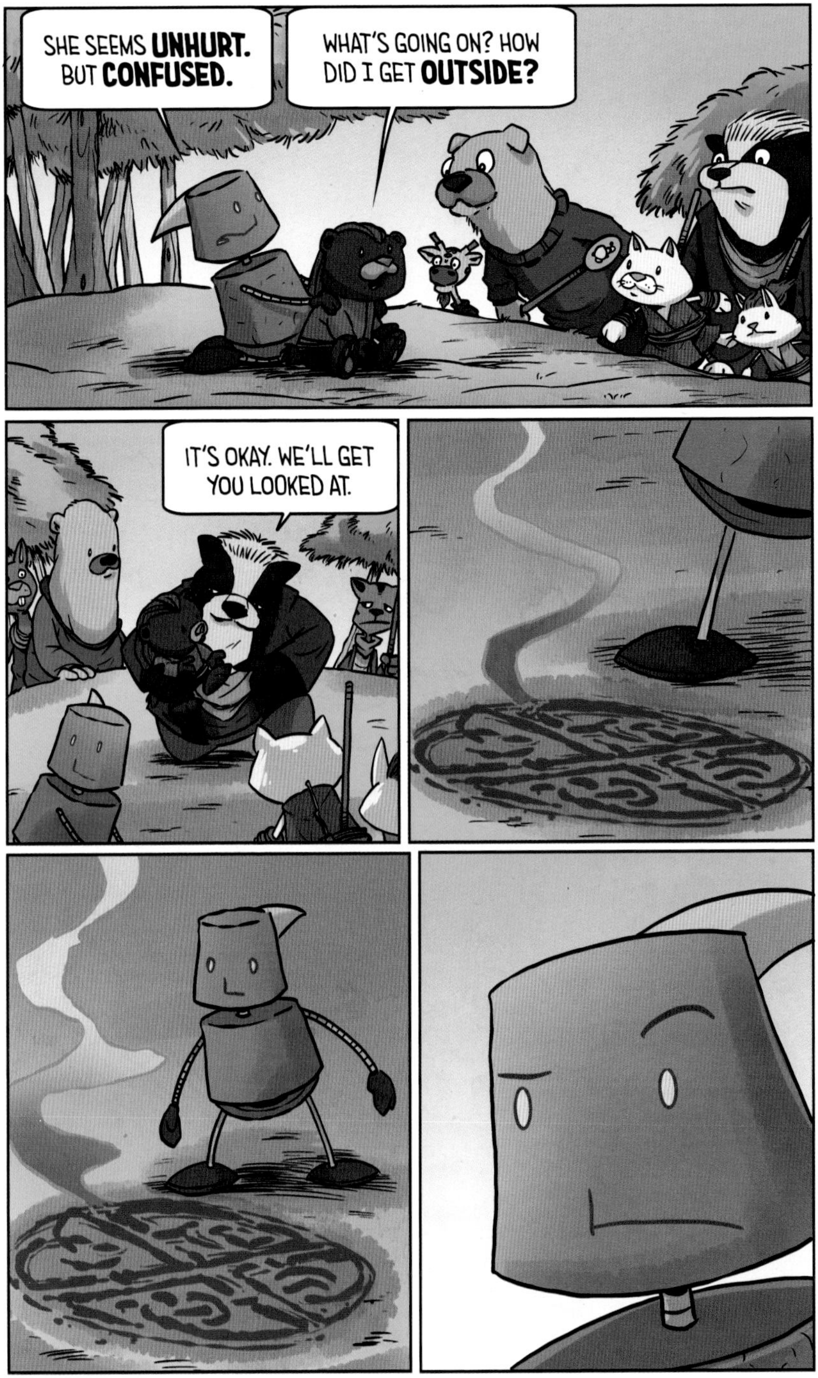
SHE SEEMS **UNHURT.** BUT **CONFUSED.**
WHAT'S GOING ON? HOW DID I GET **OUTSIDE?**
IT'S OKAY. WE'LL GET YOU LOOKED AT.

DEGRADING

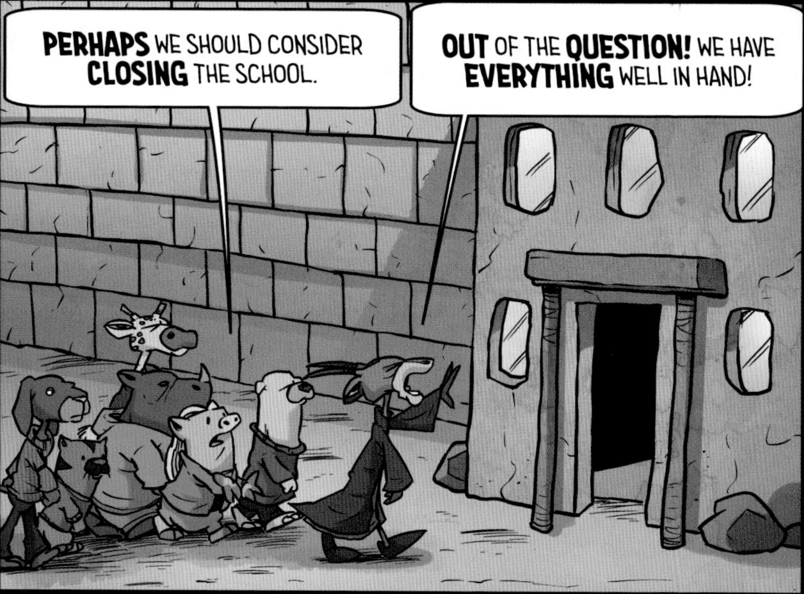
PERHAPS WE SHOULD CONSIDER CLOSING THE SCHOOL.
OUT OF THE QUESTION! WE HAVE EVERYTHING WELL IN HAND!

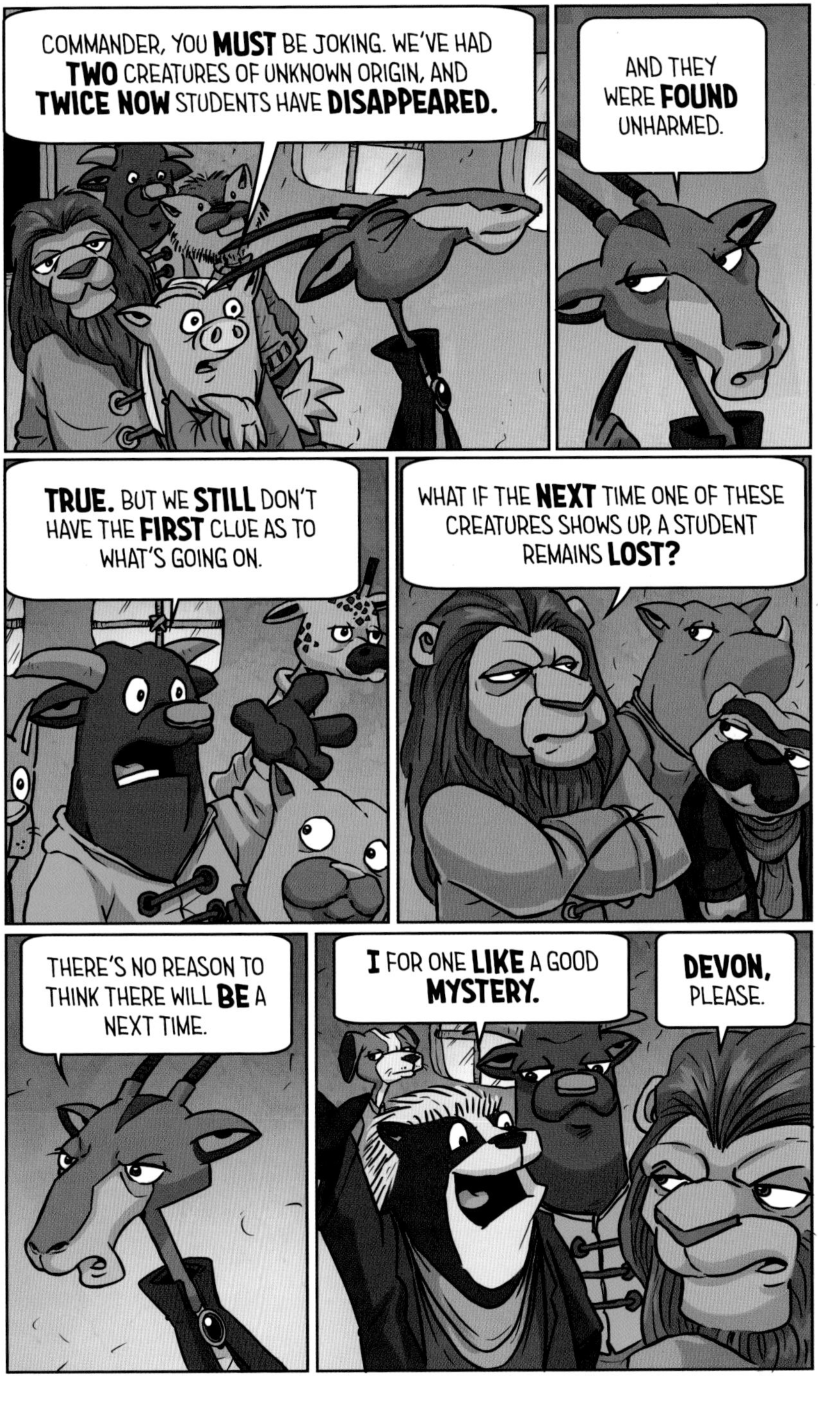

COMMANDER, YOU MUST BE JOKING. WE'VE HAD TWO CREATURES OF UNKNOWN ORIGIN, AND TWICE NOW STUDENTS HAVE DISAPPEARED.
AND THEY WERE FOUND UNHARMED.
TRUE. BUT WE STILL DON'T HAVE THE FIRST CLUE AS TO WHAT'S GOING ON.
WHAT IF THE NEXT TIME ONE OF THESE CREATURES SHOWS UP, A STUDENT REMAINS LOST?
THERE'S NO REASON TO THINK THERE WILL BE A NEXT TIME.
I FOR ONE LIKE A GOOD MYSTERY.
DEVON, PLEASE.

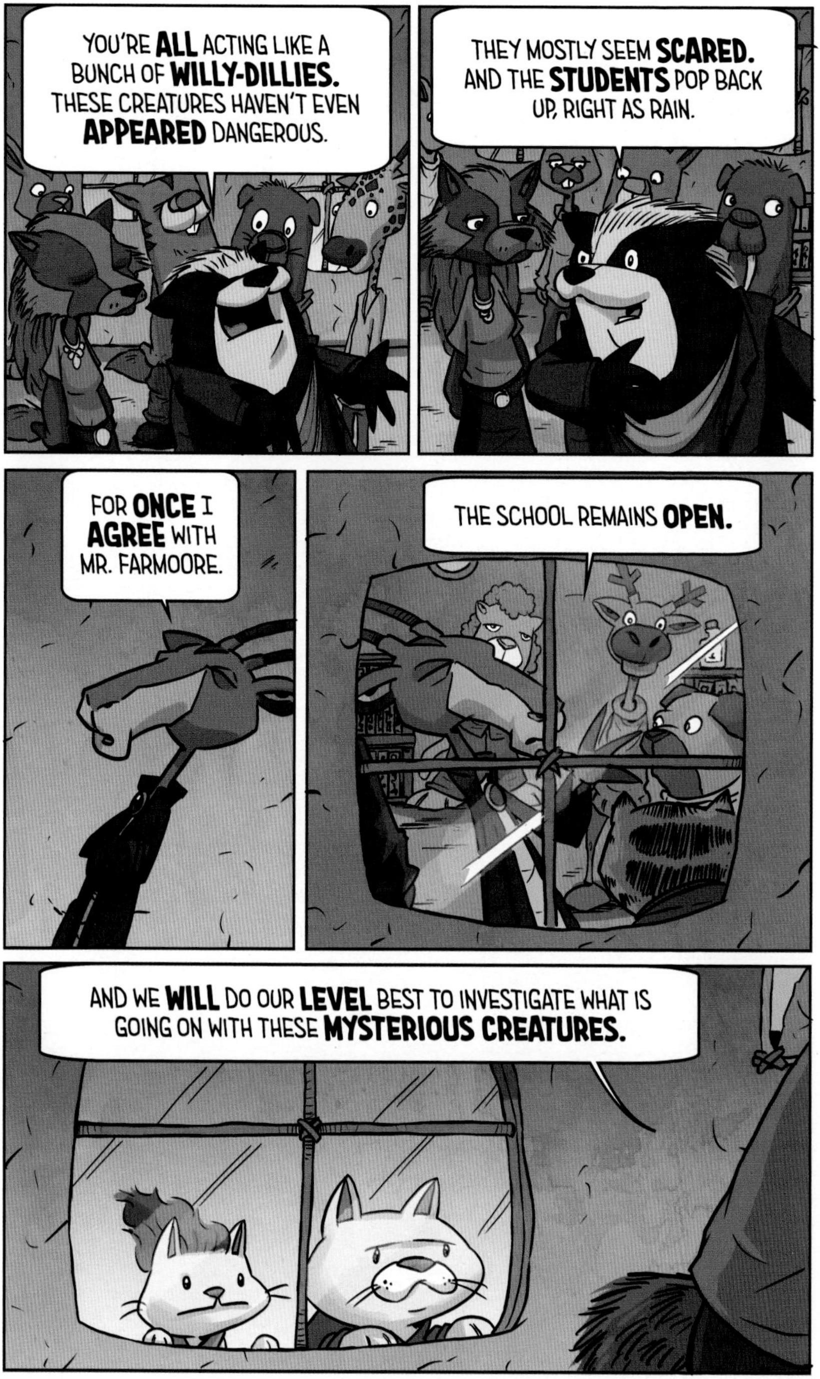

YOU'RE ALL ACTING LIKE A BUNCH OF WILLY-DILLIES. THESE CREATURES HAVEN'T EVEN APPEARED DANGEROUS.
THEY MOSTLY SEEM SCARED. AND THE STUDENTS POP BACK UP, RIGHT AS RAIN.
FOR ONCE I AGREE WITH MR. FARMOORE.
THE SCHOOL REMAINS OPEN.
AND WE WILL DO OUR LEVEL BEST TO INVESTIGATE WHAT IS GOING ON WITH THESE MYSTERIOUS CREATURES.

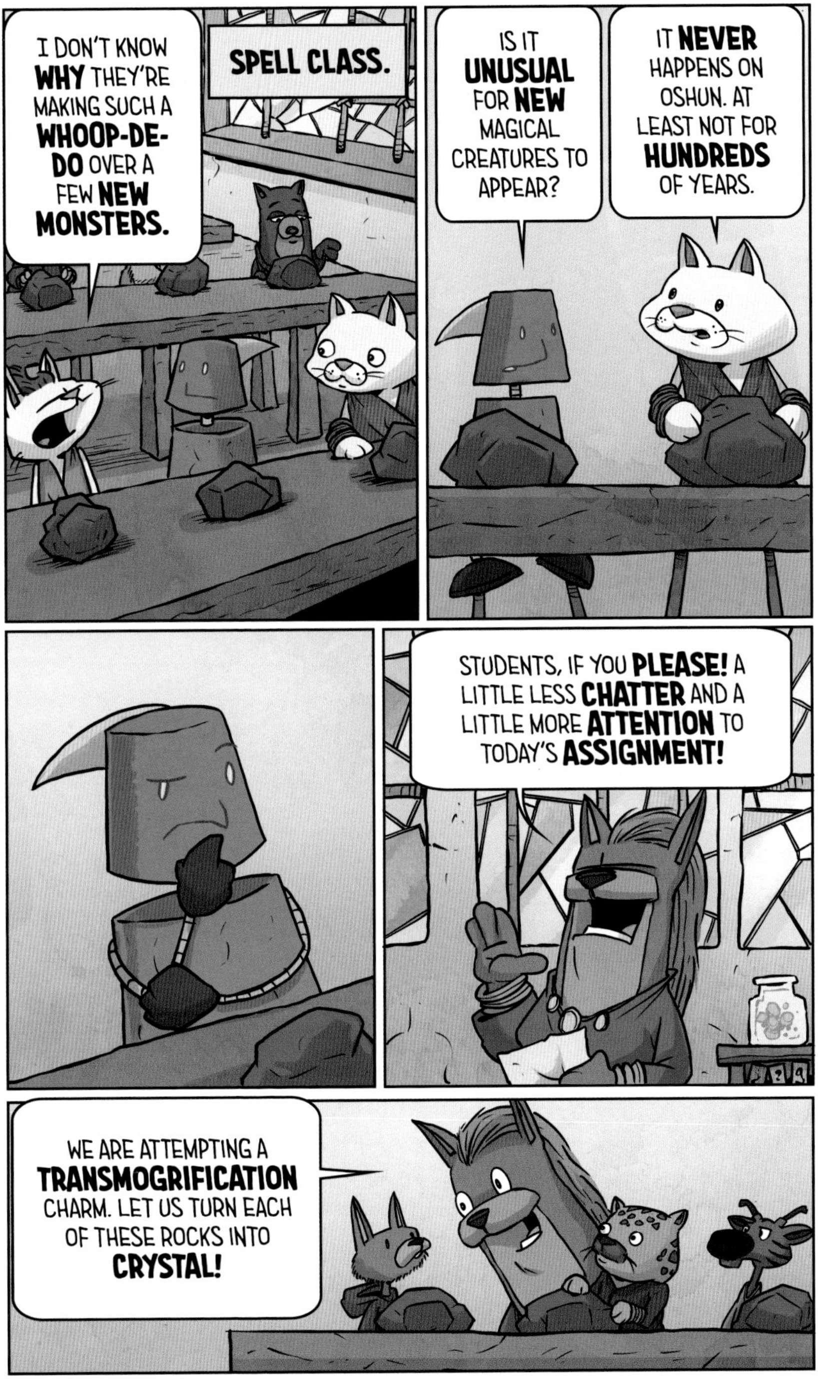

I DON'T KNOW WHY THEY'RE MAKING SUCH A WHOOP-DE-DO OVER A FEW NEW MONSTERS.
SPELL CLASS.
IS IT UNUSUAL FOR NEW MAGICAL CREATURES TO APPEAR?
IT NEVER HAPPENS ON OSHUN. AT LEAST NOT FOR HUNDREDS OF YEARS.
STUDENTS, IF YOU PLEASE! A LITTLE LESS CHATTER AND A LITTLE MORE ATTENTION TO TODAY'S ASSIGNMENT!
WE ARE ATTEMPTING A TRANSMOGRIFICATION CHARM. LET US TURN EACH OF THESE ROCKS INTO CRYSTAL!

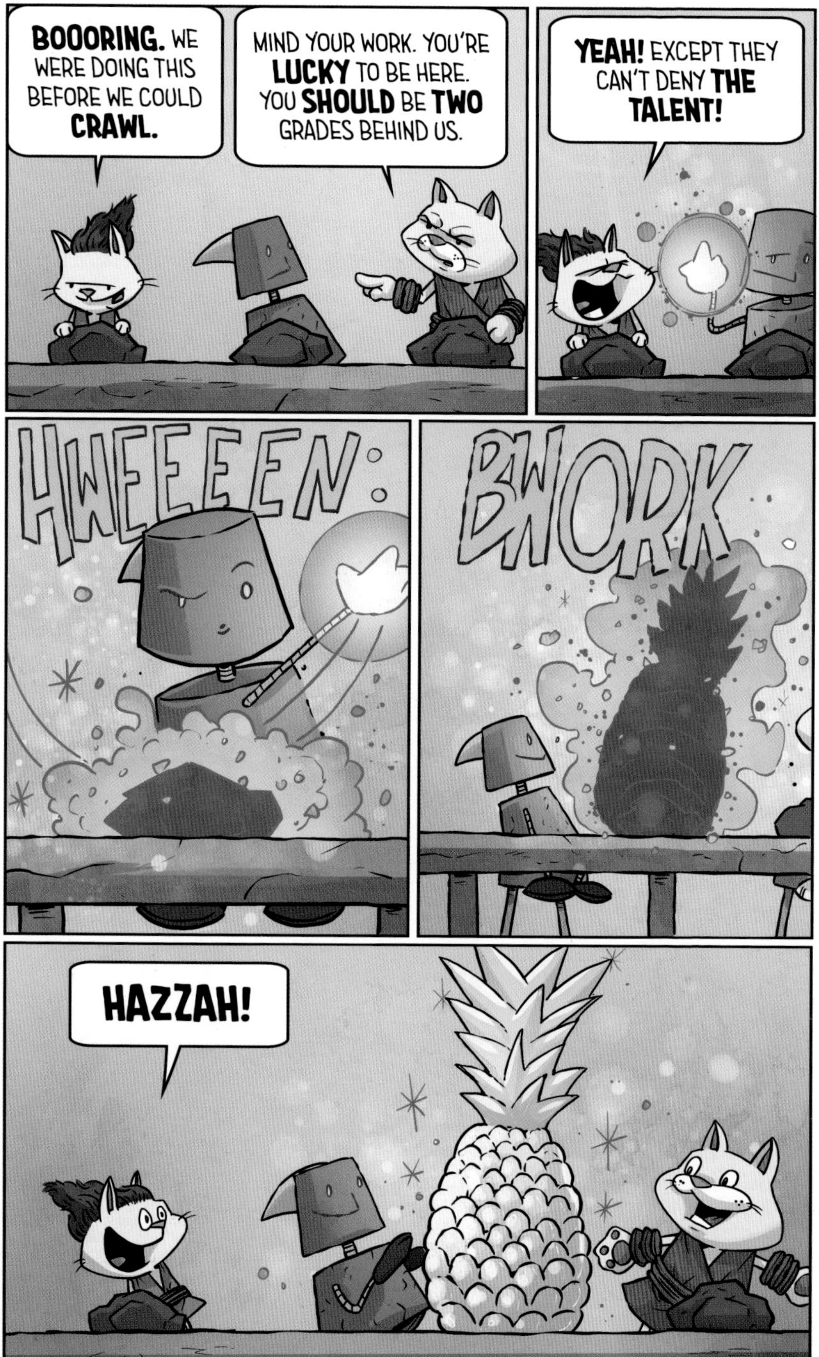
BOOORING. WE WERE DOING THIS BEFORE WE COULD CRAWL.
MIND YOUR WORK. YOU'RE LUCKY TO BE HERE. YOU SHOULD BE TWO GRADES BEHIND US.
YEAH! EXCEPT THEY CAN'T DENY THE TALENT!
HWEEEEN
BWORK
HAZZAH!

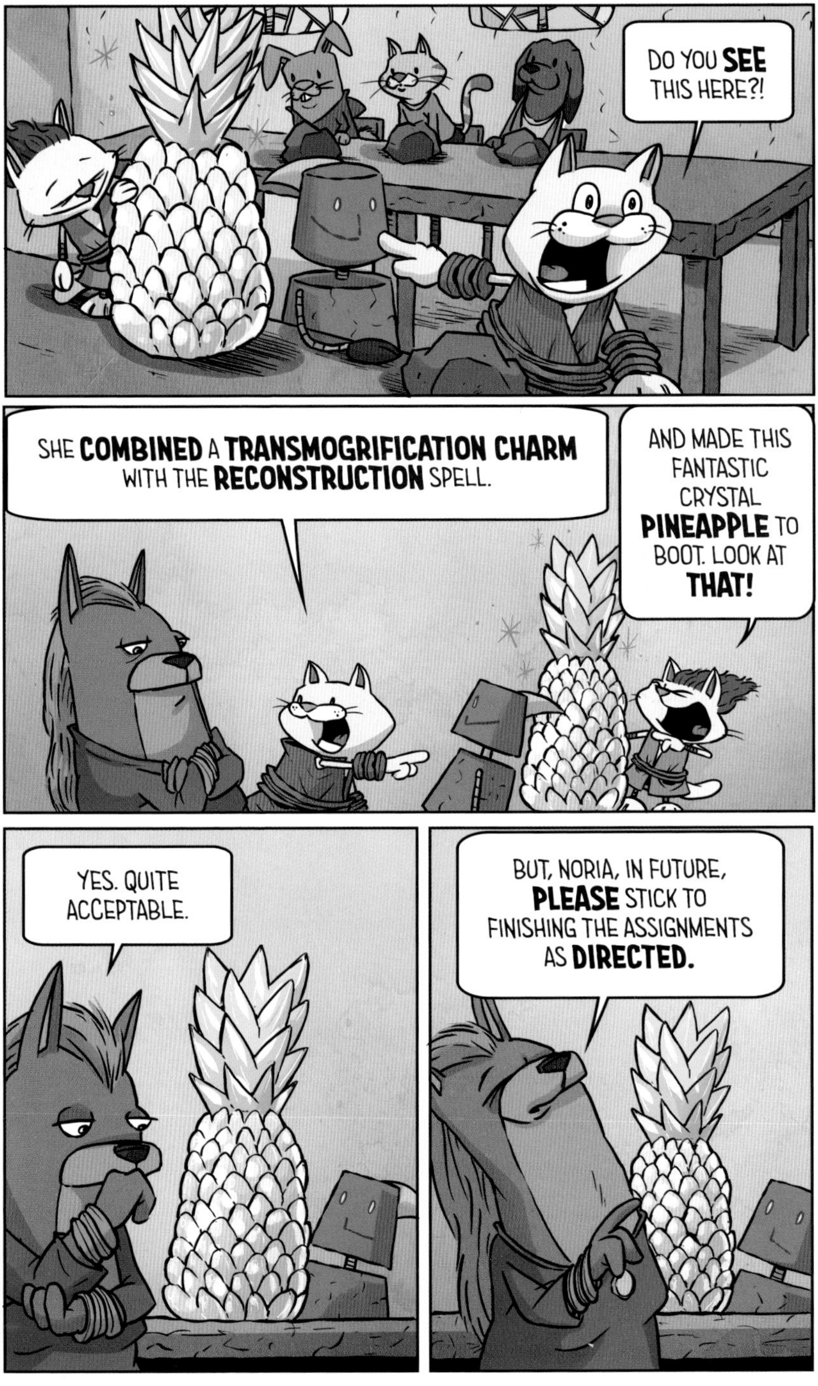
DO YOU **SEE** THIS HERE?!
SHE **COMBINED** A **TRANSMOGRIFICATION CHARM** WITH THE **RECONSTRUCTION** SPELL.
AND MADE THIS FANTASTIC CRYSTAL **PINEAPPLE** TO BOOT. LOOK AT **THAT!**
YES. QUITE ACCEPTABLE.
BUT, NORIA, IN FUTURE, **PLEASE** STICK TO FINISHING THE ASSIGNMENTS AS **DIRECTED.**

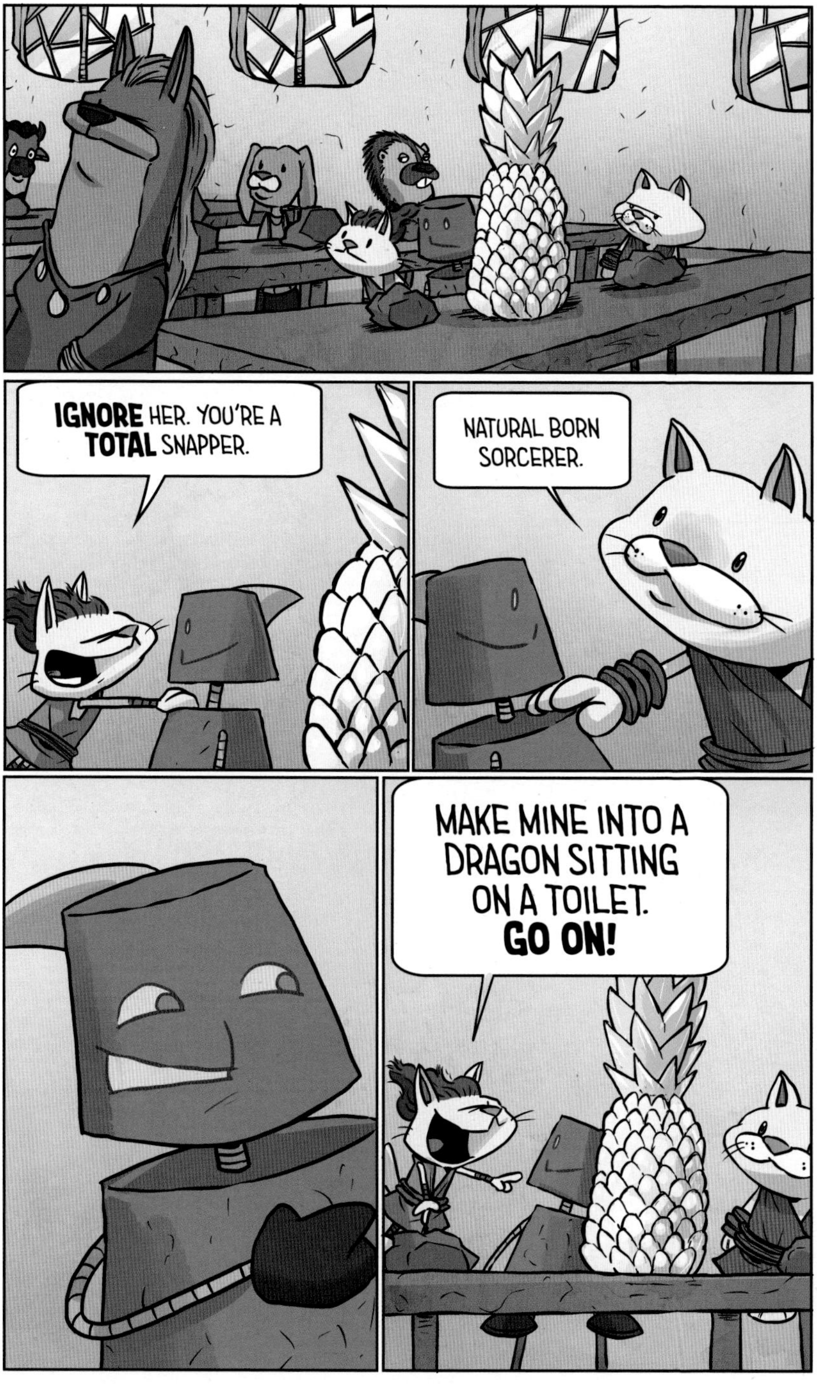
IGNORE HER. YOU'RE A TOTAL SNAPPER.
NATURAL BORN SORCERER.
MAKE MINE INTO A DRAGON SITTING ON A TOILET. GO ON!

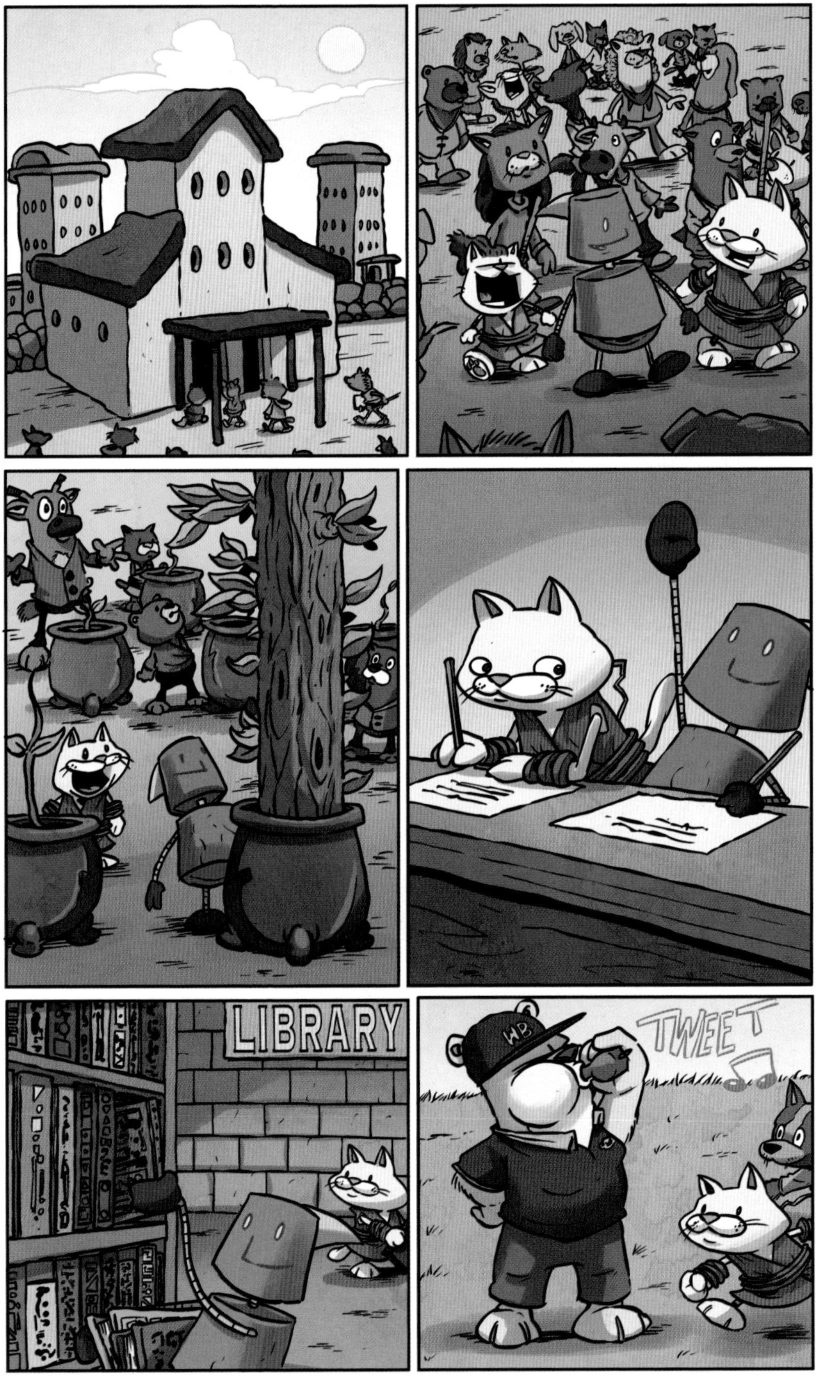
LIBRARY
TWEET

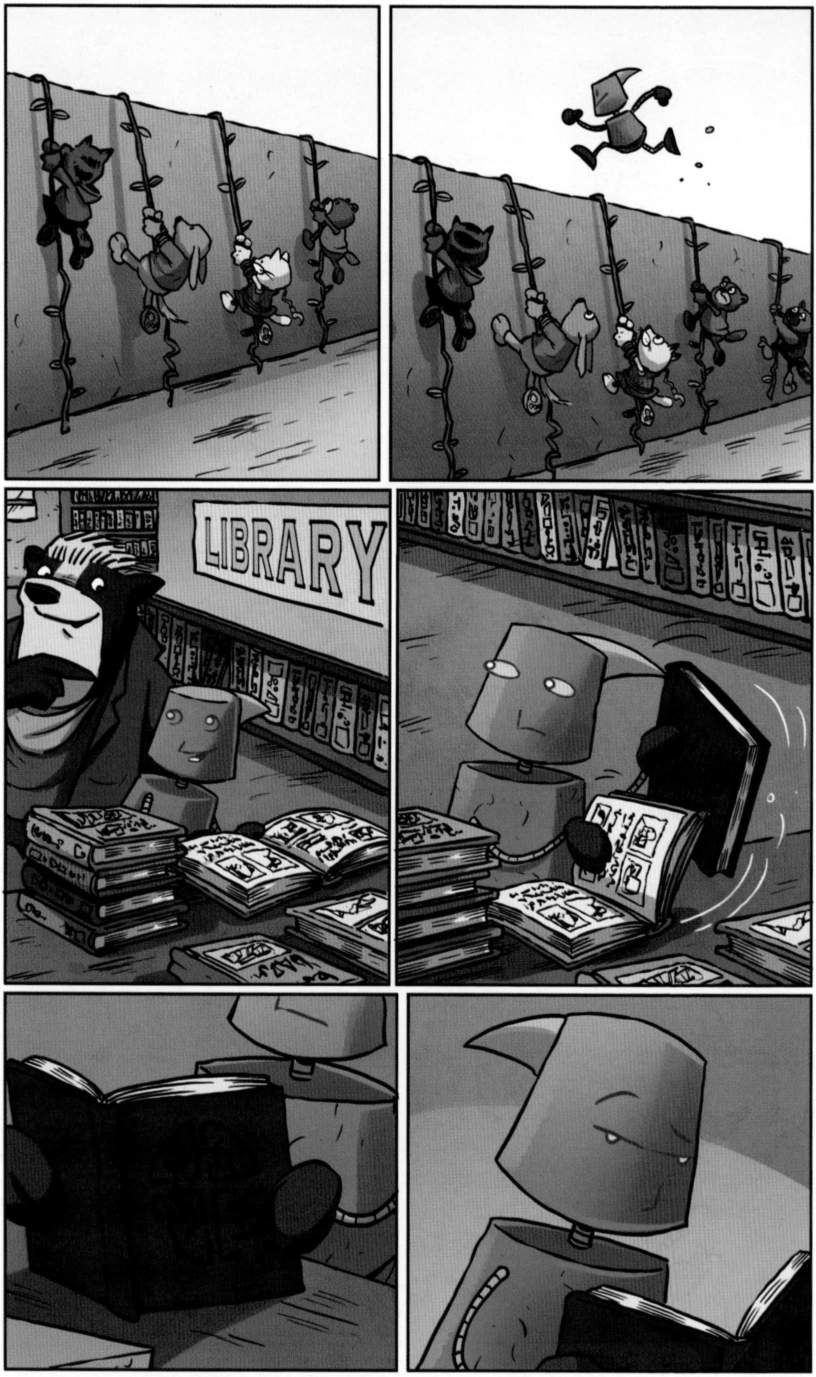
LIBRARY

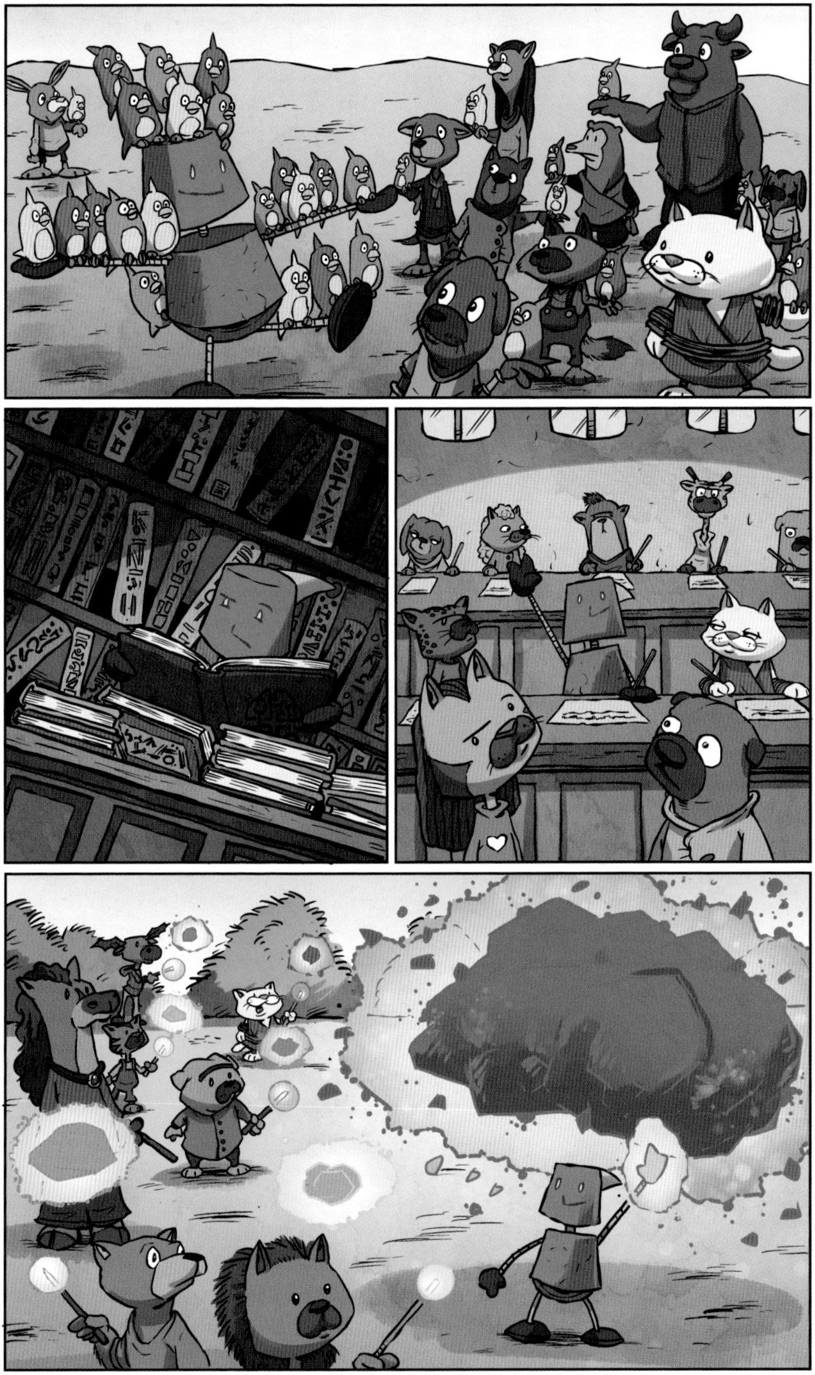

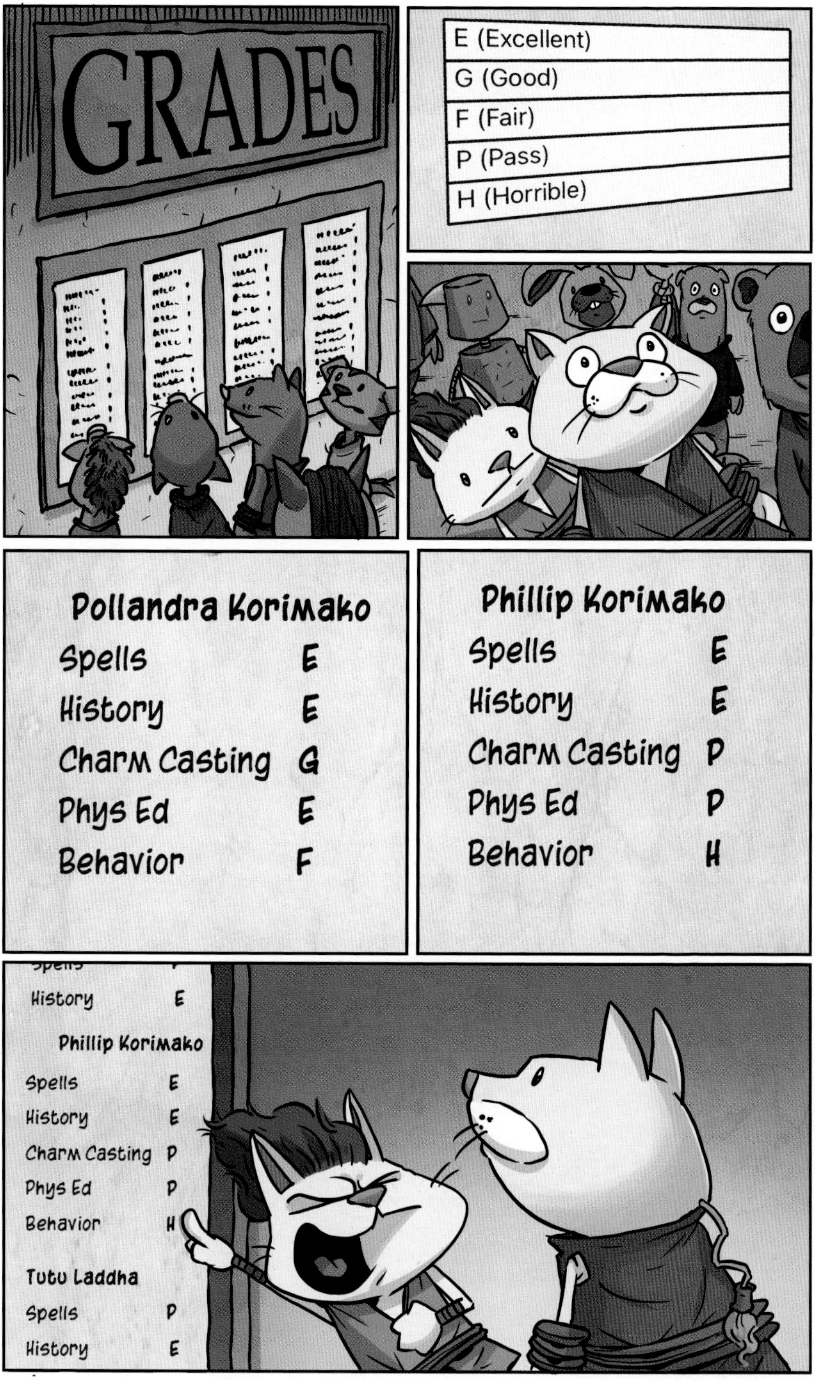
GRADES
E (Excellent)
G (Good)
F (Fair)
P (Pass)
H (Horrible)
Pollandra Korimako
Spells E
History E
Charm Casting G
Phys Ed E
Behavior F
Phillip Korimako
Spells E
History E
Charm Casting P
Phys Ed P
Behavior H
History E
Phillip Korimako
Spells E
History E
Charm Casting P
Phys Ed P
Behavior H
Tutu Laddha
Spells P
History E

Noria

Spells	P
History	E
Charm Casting	P
Phys Ed	P
Behavior	P

Felipe Noriega

Spells	P

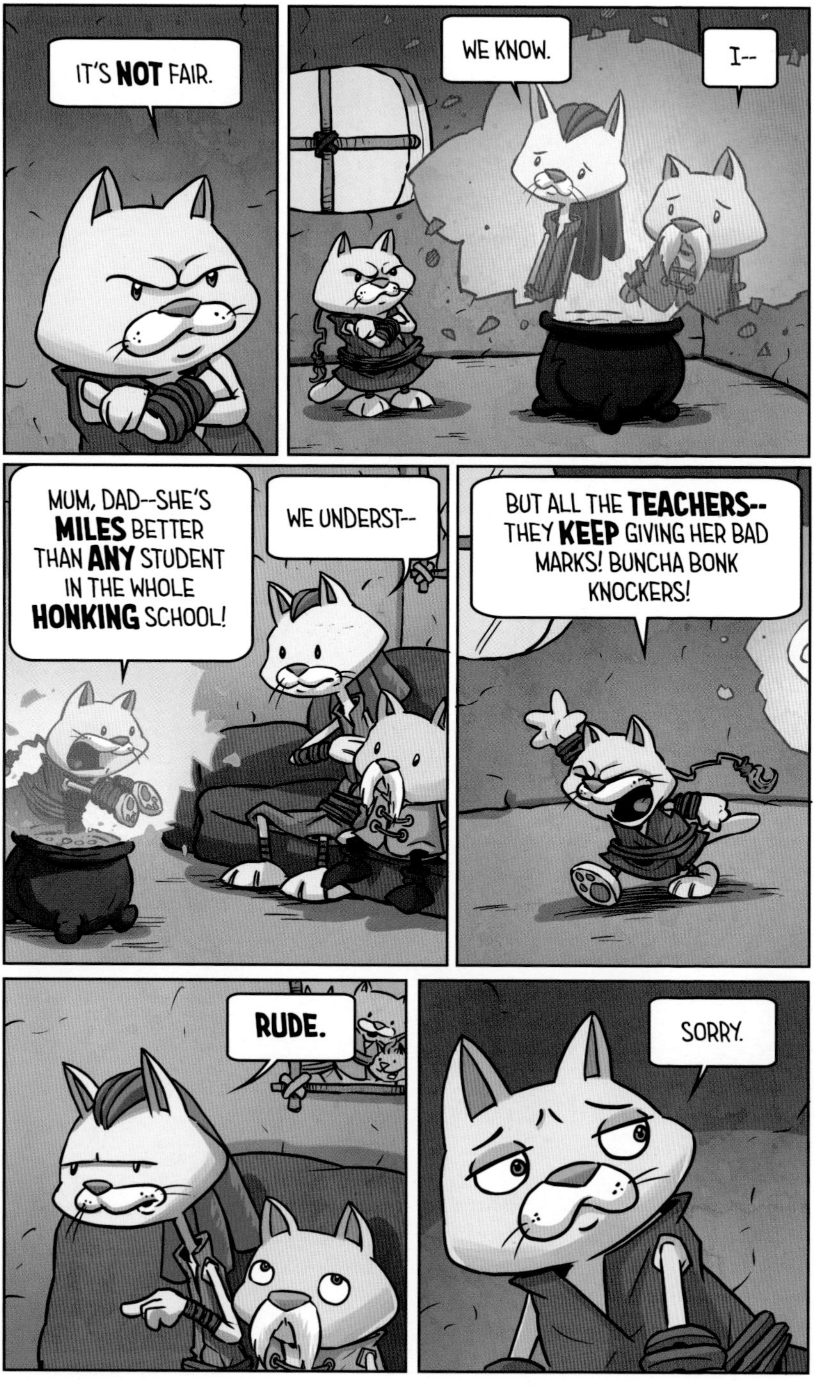
IT'S **NOT** FAIR.
WE KNOW.
I--
MUM, DAD--SHE'S **MILES** BETTER THAN **ANY** STUDENT IN THE WHOLE **HONKING** SCHOOL!
WE UNDERST--
BUT ALL THE **TEACHERS**-- THEY **KEEP** GIVING HER BAD MARKS! BUNCHA BONK KNOCKERS!
RUDE.
SORRY.

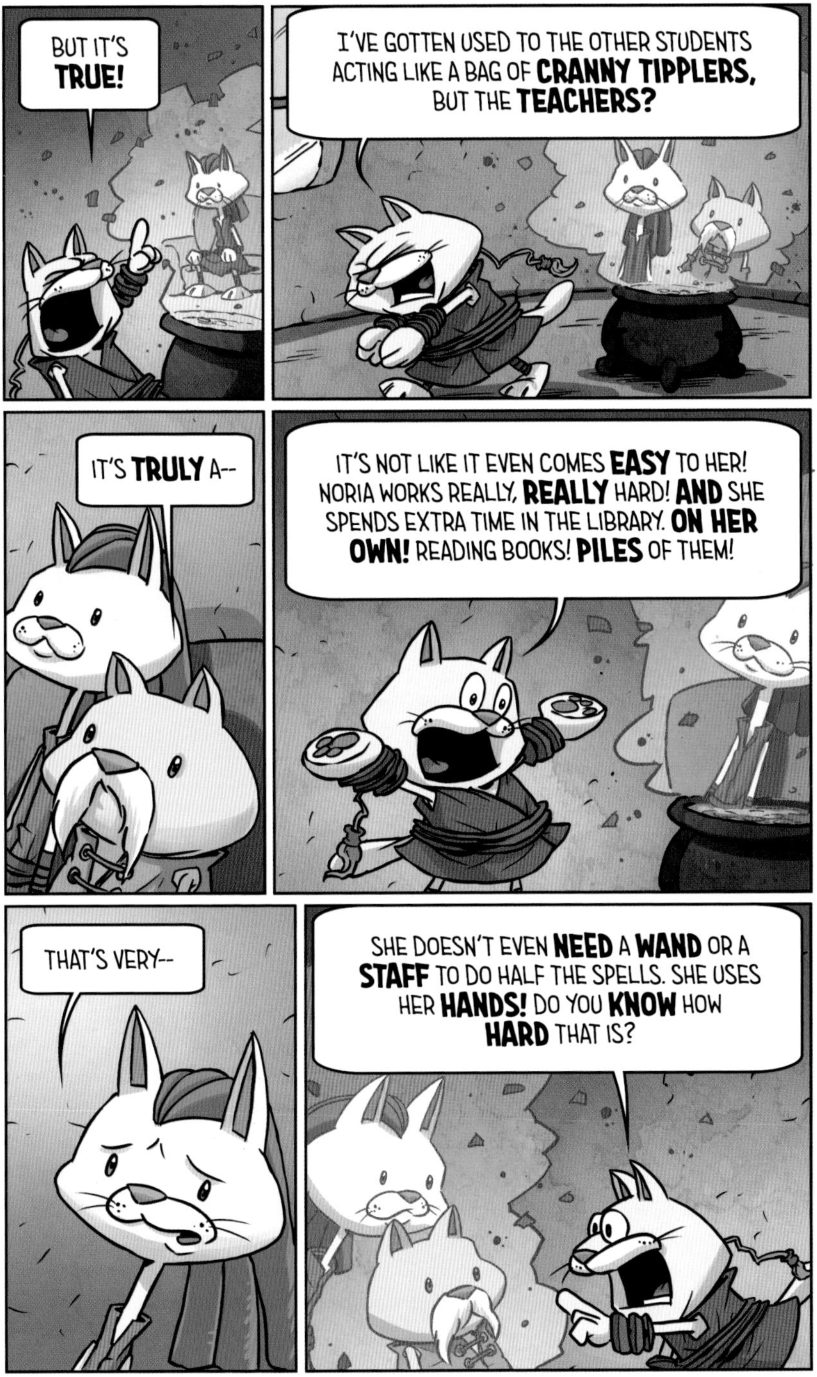
BUT IT'S **TRUE!**
I'VE GOTTEN USED TO THE OTHER STUDENTS ACTING LIKE A BAG OF **CRANNY TIPPLERS,** BUT THE **TEACHERS?**
IT'S **TRULY** A--
IT'S NOT LIKE IT EVEN COMES **EASY** TO HER! NORIA WORKS REALLY, **REALLY** HARD! **AND** SHE SPENDS EXTRA TIME IN THE LIBRARY. **ON HER OWN!** READING BOOKS! **PILES** OF THEM!
THAT'S VERY--
SHE DOESN'T EVEN **NEED** A **WAND** OR A **STAFF** TO DO HALF THE SPELLS. SHE USES HER **HANDS!** DO YOU **KNOW** HOW **HARD** THAT IS?

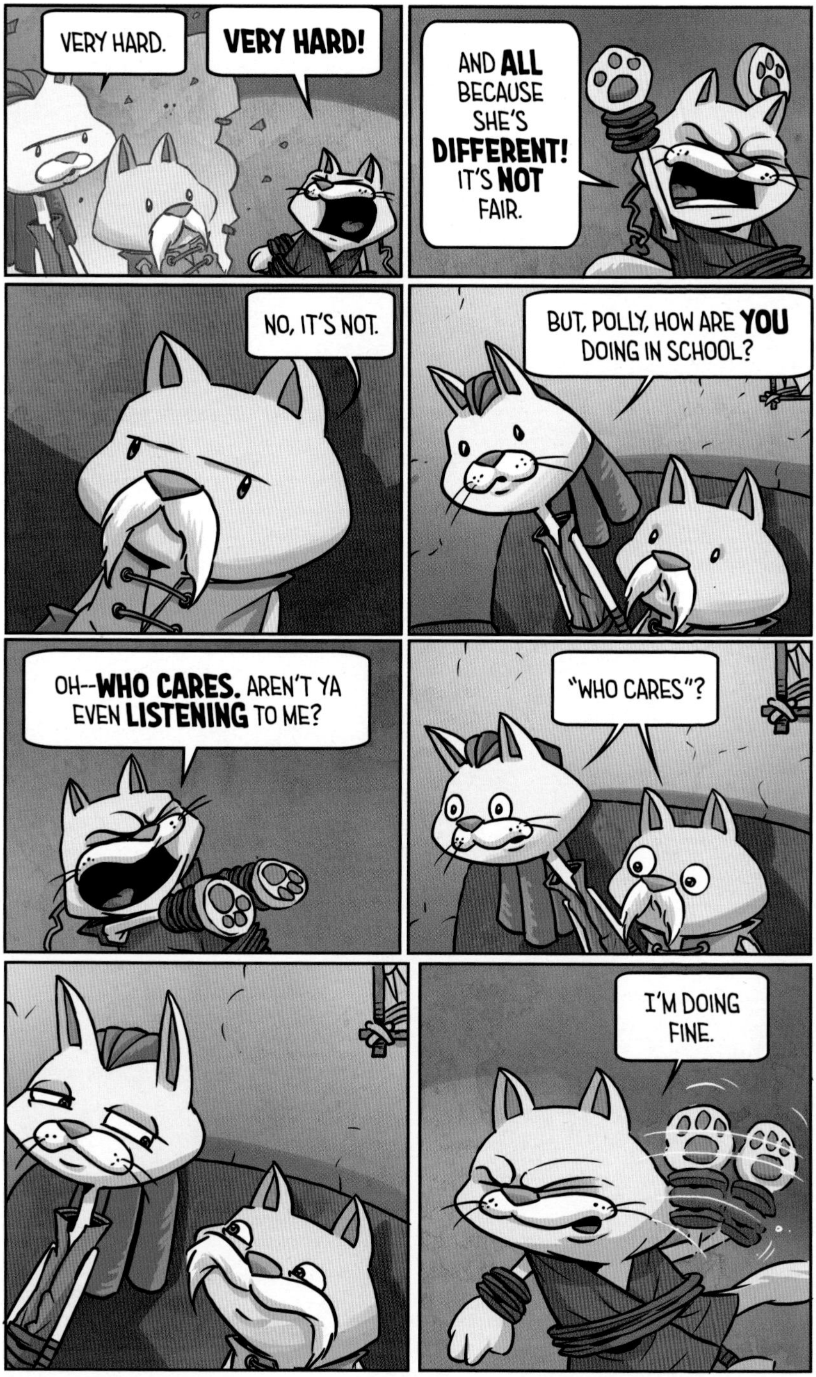
VERY HARD.
VERY HARD!
AND ALL BECAUSE SHE'S DIFFERENT! IT'S NOT FAIR.
NO, IT'S NOT.
BUT, POLLY, HOW ARE YOU DOING IN SCHOOL?
OH--WHO CARES. AREN'T YA EVEN LISTENING TO ME?
"WHO CARES"?
I'M DOING FINE.

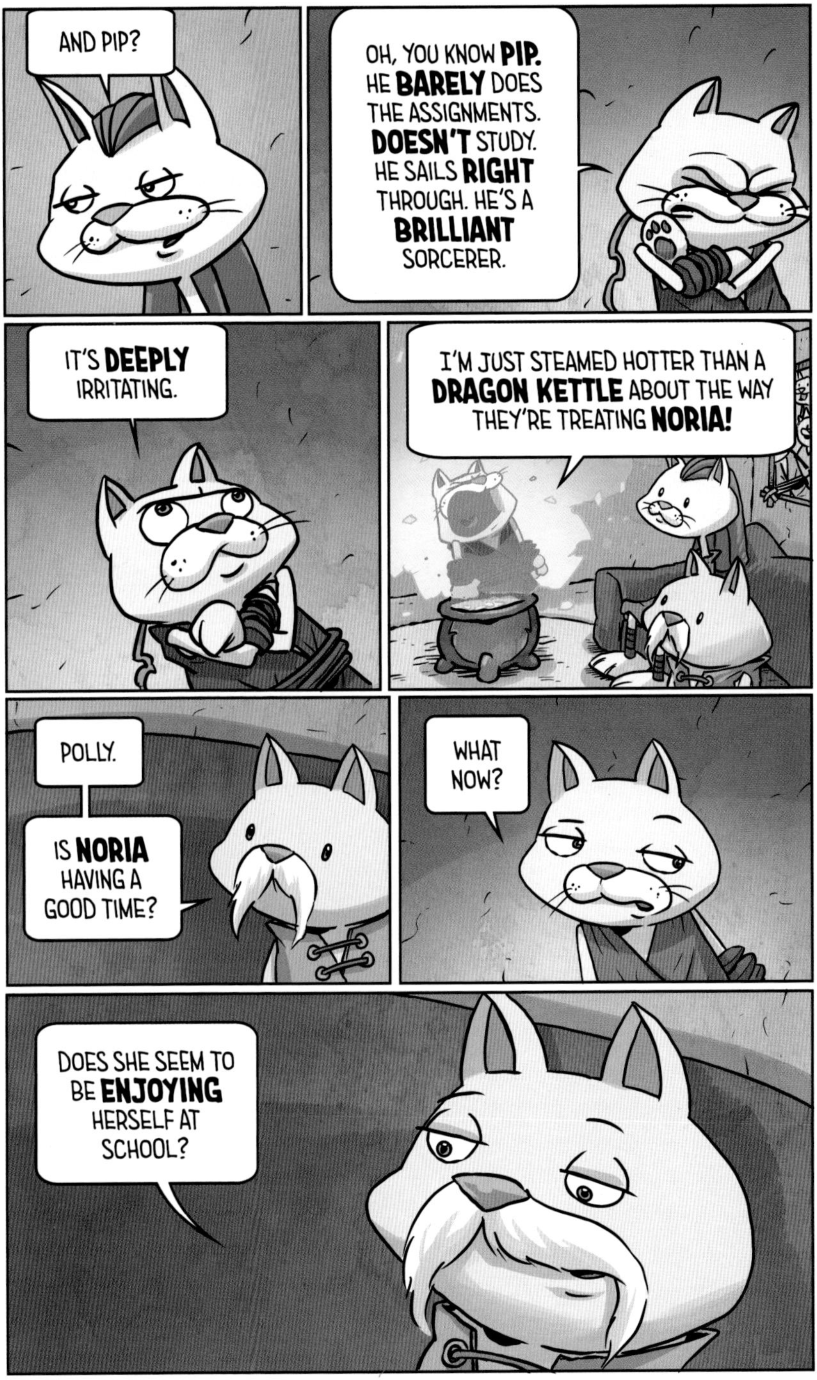
AND PIP?
OH, YOU KNOW **PIP.** HE **BARELY** DOES THE ASSIGNMENTS. **DOESN'T** STUDY. HE SAILS **RIGHT** THROUGH. HE'S A **BRILLIANT** SORCERER.
IT'S **DEEPLY** IRRITATING.
I'M JUST STEAMED HOTTER THAN A **DRAGON KETTLE** ABOUT THE WAY THEY'RE TREATING **NORIA!**
POLLY.
IS **NORIA** HAVING A GOOD TIME?
WHAT NOW?
DOES SHE SEEM TO BE **ENJOYING** HERSELF AT SCHOOL?

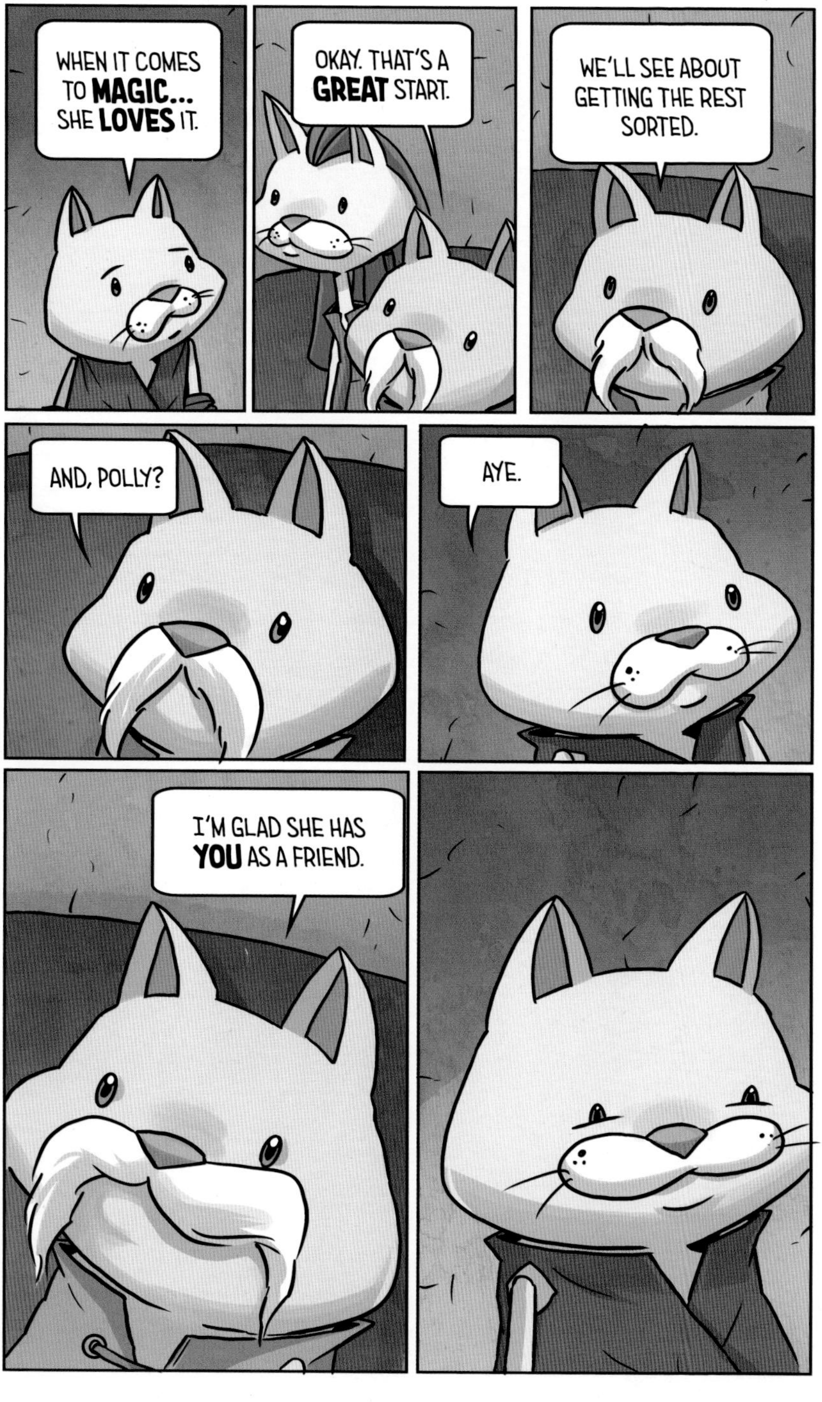
WHEN IT COMES TO **MAGIC...** SHE **LOVES** IT.
OKAY. THAT'S A **GREAT** START.
WE'LL SEE ABOUT GETTING THE REST SORTED.
AND, POLLY?
AYE.
I'M GLAD SHE HAS **YOU** AS A FRIEND.

CHAPTER 9

OUTDOOR ED

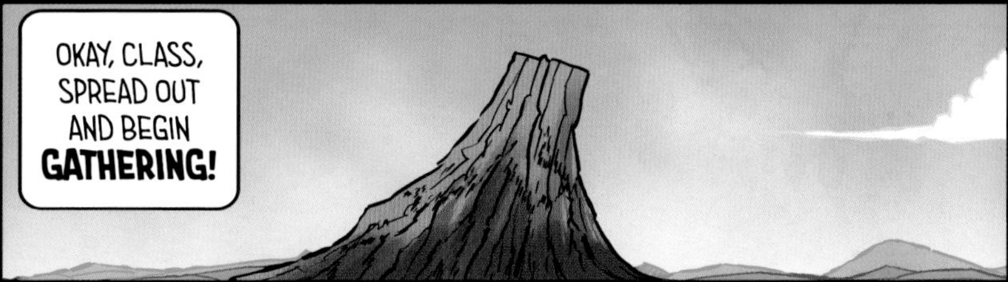
OKAY, CLASS, SPREAD OUT AND BEGIN **GATHERING!**

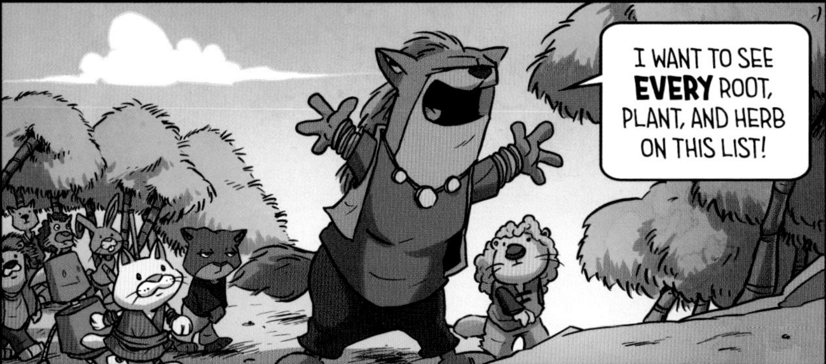
I WANT TO SEE **EVERY** ROOT, PLANT, AND HERB ON THIS LIST!

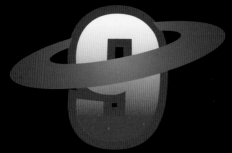

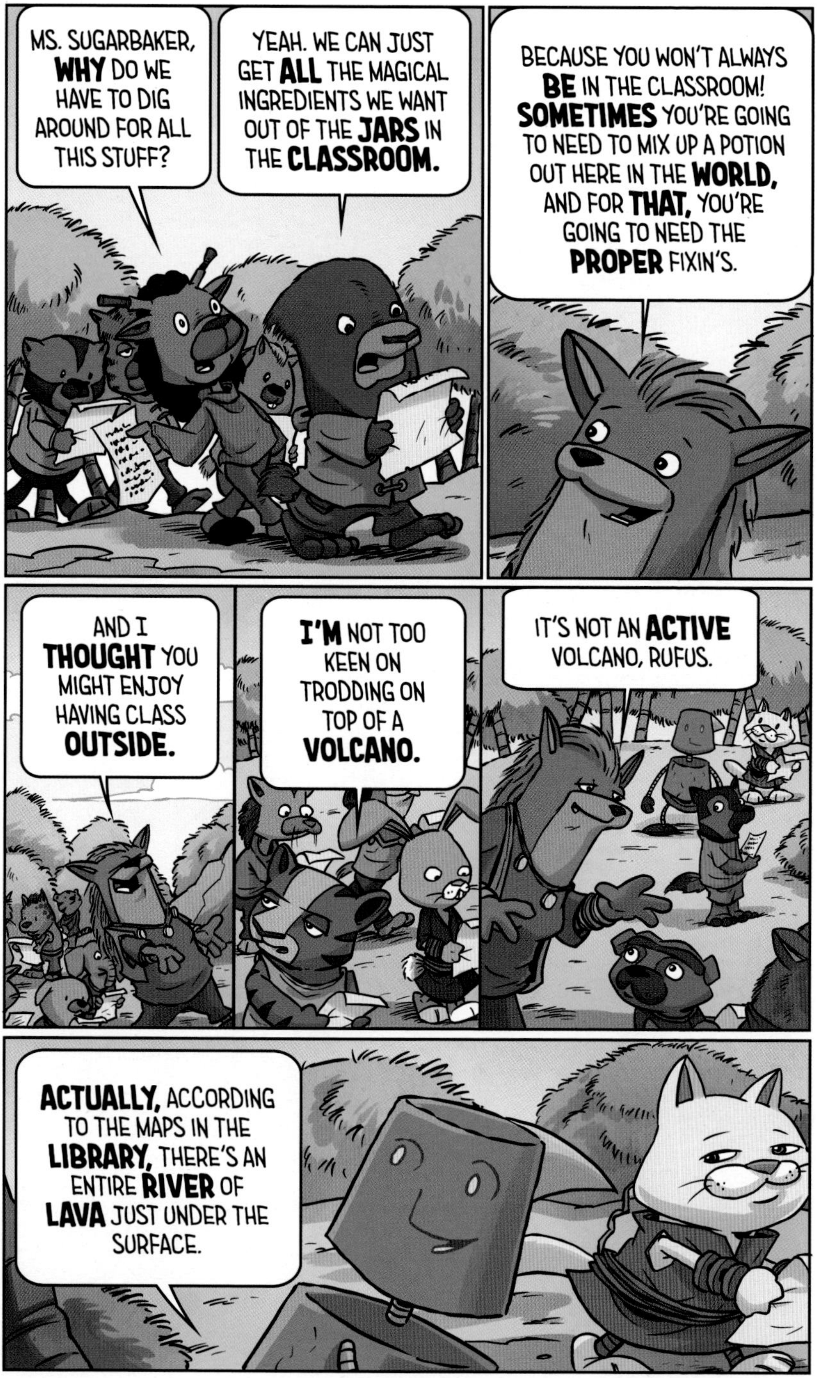

MS. SUGARBAKER, **WHY** DO WE HAVE TO DIG AROUND FOR ALL THIS STUFF?
YEAH. WE CAN JUST GET **ALL** THE MAGICAL INGREDIENTS WE WANT OUT OF THE **JARS** IN THE **CLASSROOM.**
BECAUSE YOU WON'T ALWAYS **BE** IN THE CLASSROOM! **SOMETIMES** YOU'RE GOING TO NEED TO MIX UP A POTION OUT HERE IN THE **WORLD,** AND FOR **THAT,** YOU'RE GOING TO NEED THE **PROPER** FIXIN'S.
AND I **THOUGHT** YOU MIGHT ENJOY HAVING CLASS **OUTSIDE.**
I'M NOT TOO KEEN ON TRODDING ON TOP OF A **VOLCANO.**
IT'S NOT AN **ACTIVE** VOLCANO, RUFUS.
ACTUALLY, ACCORDING TO THE MAPS IN THE **LIBRARY,** THERE'S AN ENTIRE **RIVER** OF **LAVA** JUST UNDER THE SURFACE.

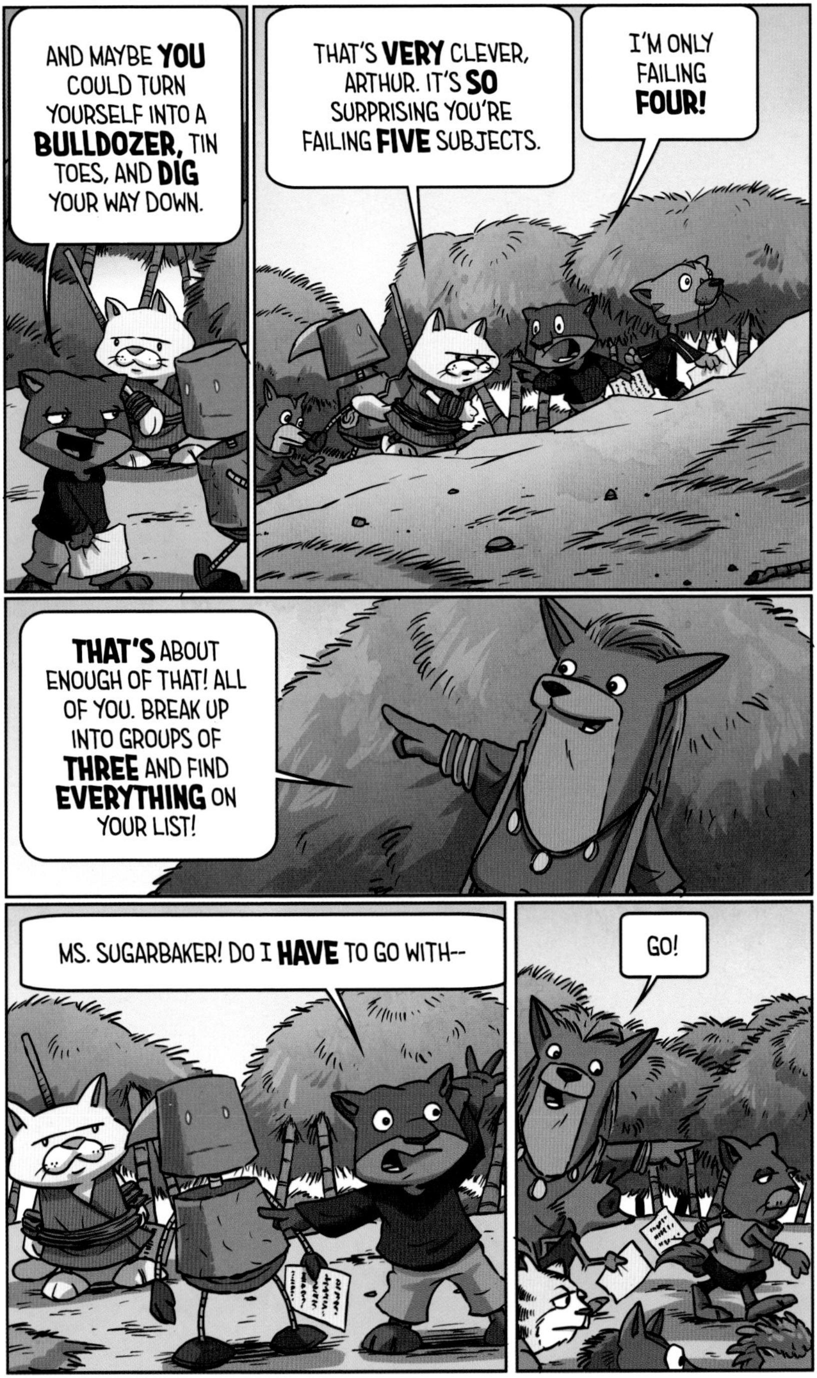
AND MAYBE **YOU** COULD TURN YOURSELF INTO A **BULLDOZER,** TIN TOES, AND **DIG** YOUR WAY DOWN.
THAT'S **VERY** CLEVER, ARTHUR. IT'S **SO** SURPRISING YOU'RE FAILING **FIVE** SUBJECTS.
I'M ONLY FAILING **FOUR!**
THAT'S ABOUT ENOUGH OF THAT! ALL OF YOU. BREAK UP INTO GROUPS OF **THREE** AND FIND **EVERYTHING** ON YOUR LIST!
MS. SUGARBAKER! DO I **HAVE** TO GO WITH--
GO!

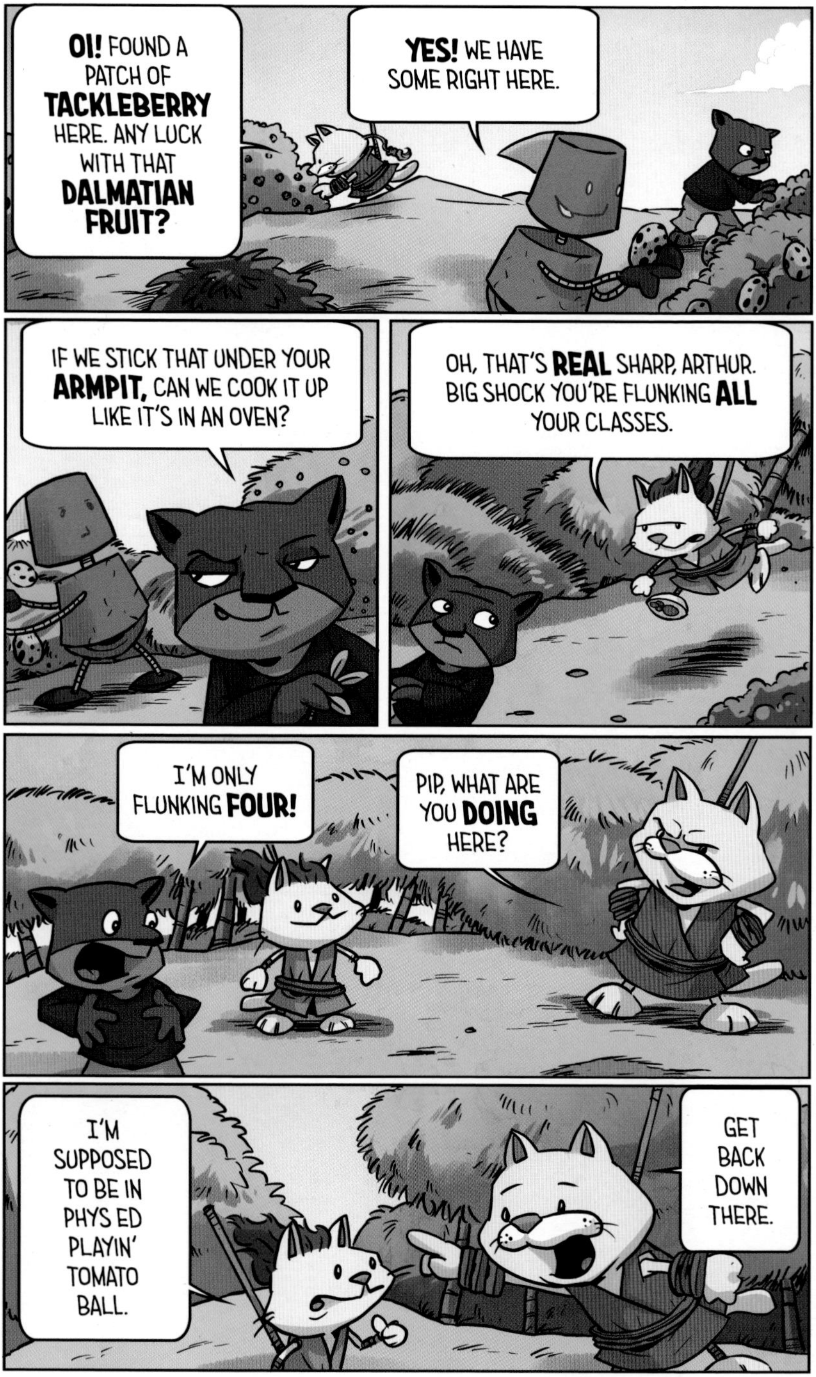
OI! FOUND A PATCH OF TACKLEBERRY HERE. ANY LUCK WITH THAT DALMATIAN FRUIT?
YES! WE HAVE SOME RIGHT HERE.
IF WE STICK THAT UNDER YOUR ARMPIT, CAN WE COOK IT UP LIKE IT'S IN AN OVEN?
OH, THAT'S REAL SHARP, ARTHUR. BIG SHOCK YOU'RE FLUNKING ALL YOUR CLASSES.
I'M ONLY FLUNKING FOUR!
PIP, WHAT ARE YOU DOING HERE?
I'M SUPPOSED TO BE IN PHYS ED PLAYIN' TOMATO BALL.
GET BACK DOWN THERE.

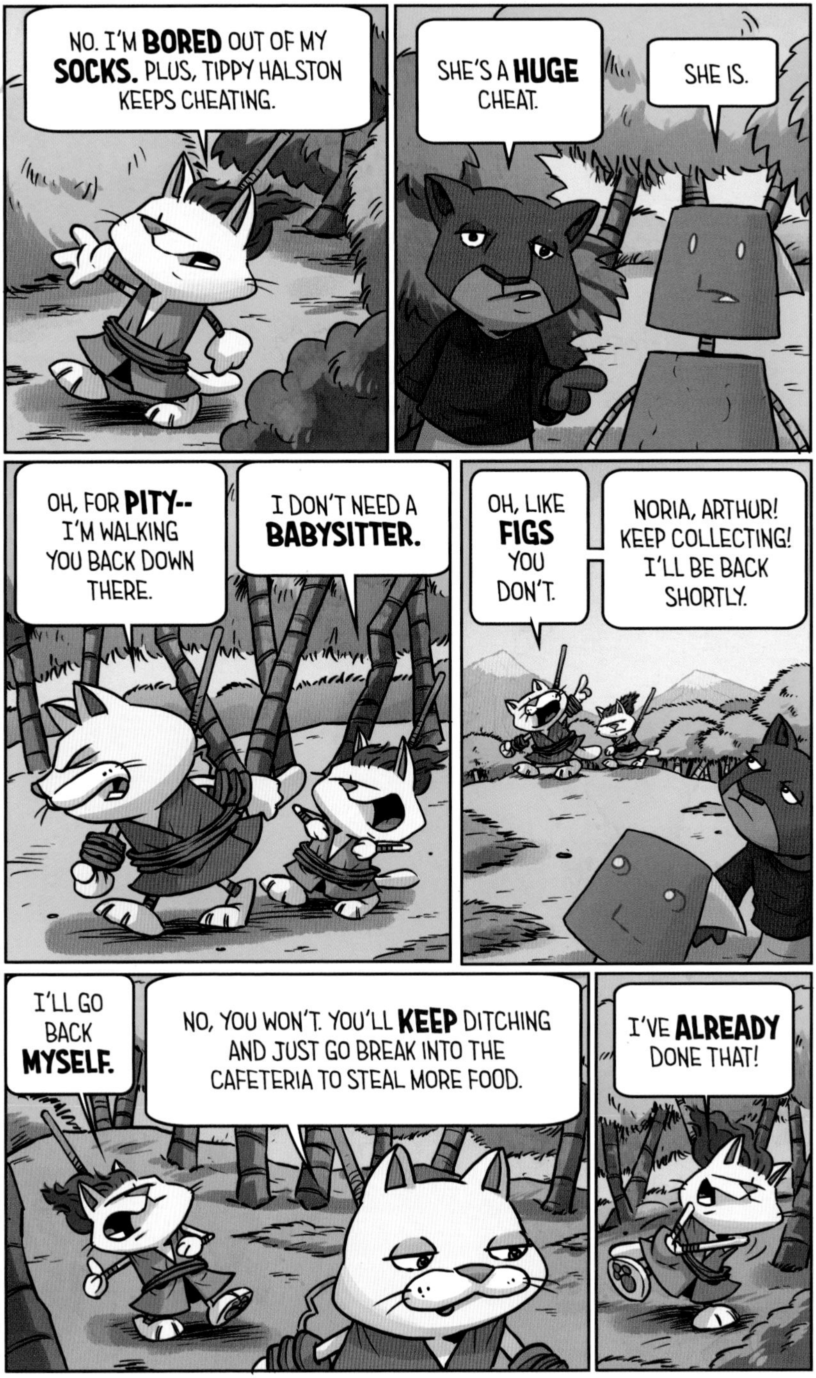
NO. I'M **BORED** OUT OF MY **SOCKS.** PLUS, TIPPY HALSTON KEEPS CHEATING.
SHE'S A **HUGE** CHEAT.
SHE IS.
OH, FOR **PITY--** I'M WALKING YOU BACK DOWN THERE.
I DON'T NEED A **BABYSITTER.**
OH, LIKE **FIGS** YOU DON'T.
NORIA, ARTHUR! KEEP COLLECTING! I'LL BE BACK SHORTLY.
I'LL GO BACK **MYSELF.**
NO, YOU WON'T. YOU'LL **KEEP** DITCHING AND JUST GO BREAK INTO THE CAFETERIA TO STEAL MORE FOOD.
I'VE **ALREADY** DONE THAT!

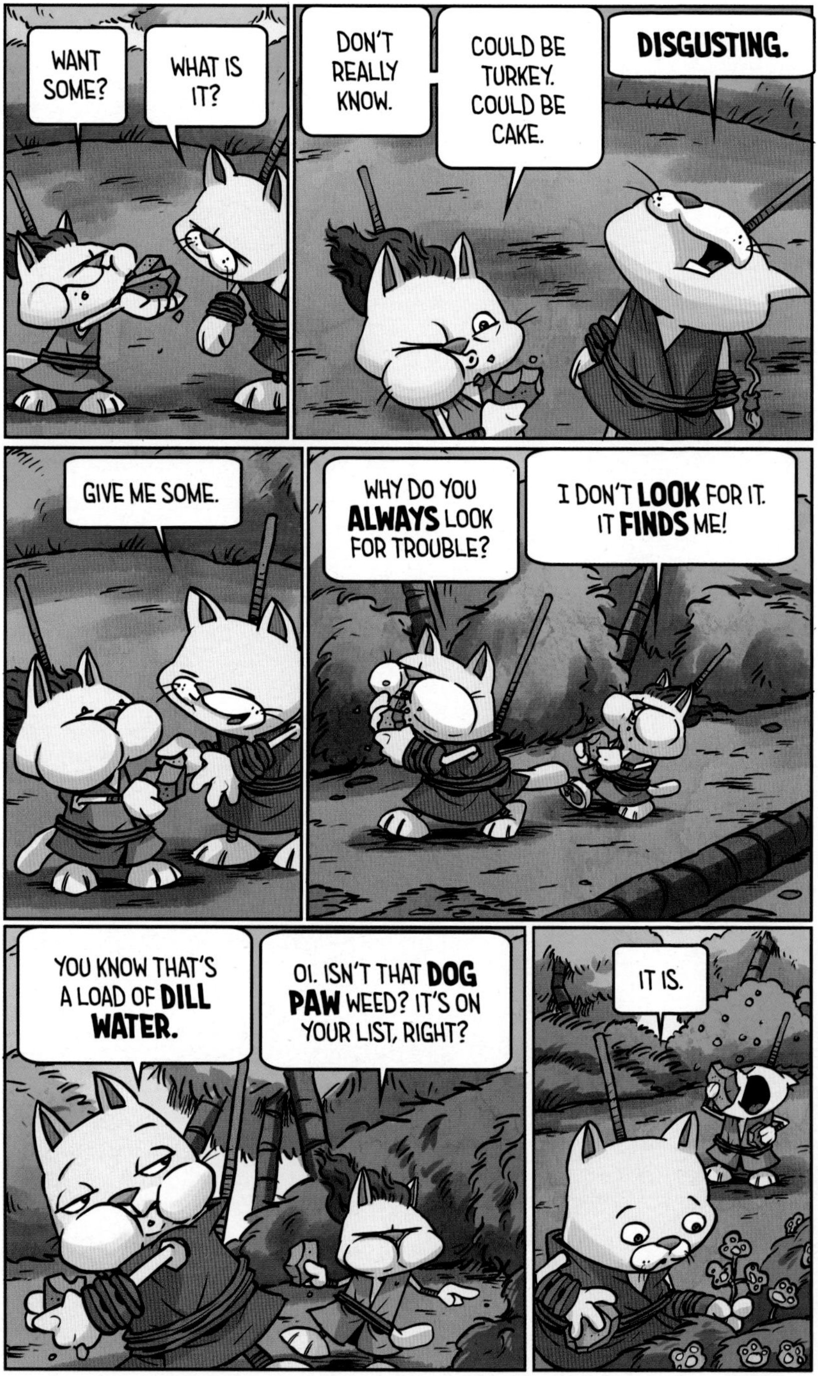
WANT SOME?
WHAT IS IT?
DON'T REALLY KNOW.
COULD BE TURKEY. COULD BE CAKE.
DISGUSTING.
GIVE ME SOME.
WHY DO YOU ALWAYS LOOK FOR TROUBLE?
I DON'T LOOK FOR IT. IT FINDS ME!
YOU KNOW THAT'S A LOAD OF DILL WATER.
OI. ISN'T THAT DOG PAW WEED? IT'S ON YOUR LIST, RIGHT?
IT IS.

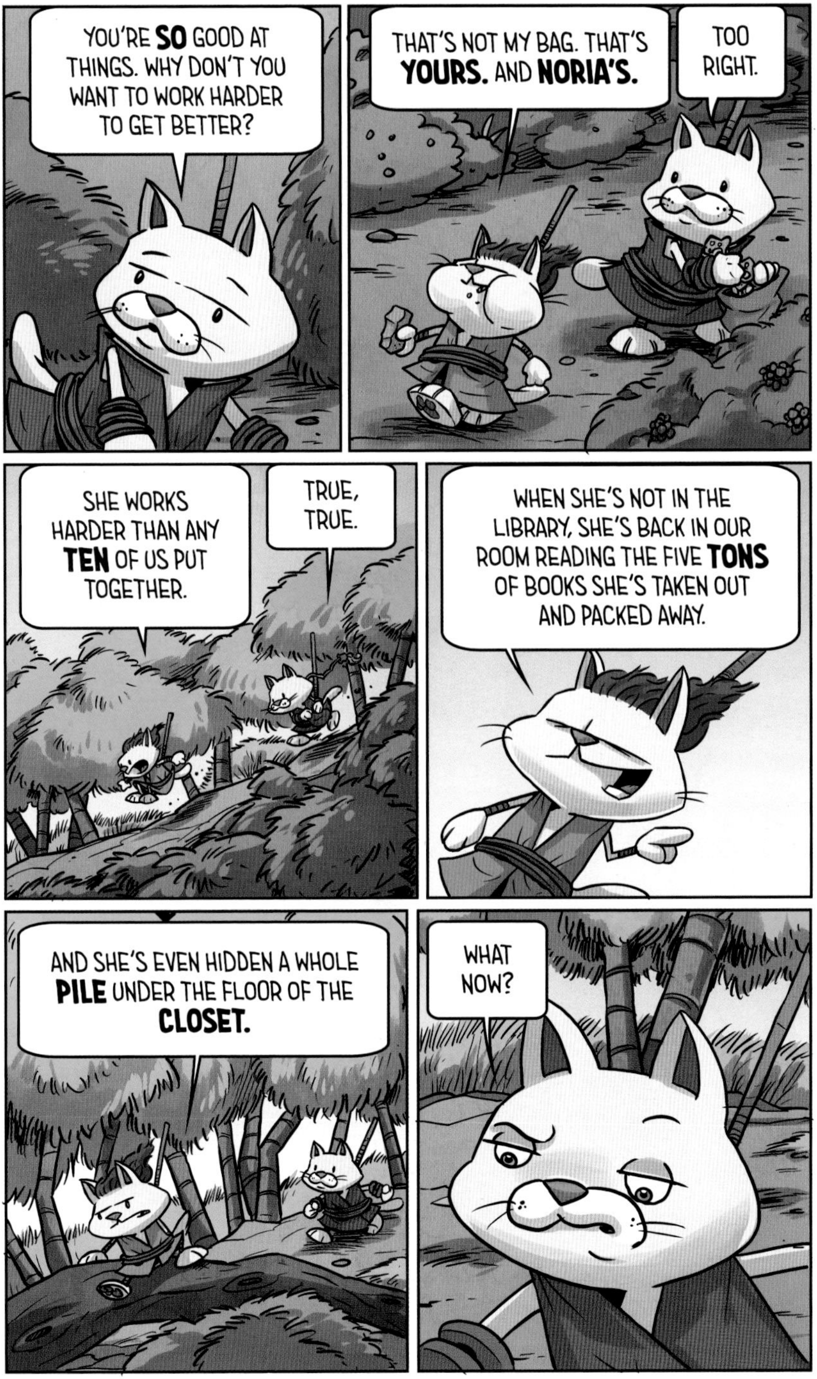
YOU'RE **SO** GOOD AT THINGS. WHY DON'T YOU WANT TO WORK HARDER TO GET BETTER?
THAT'S NOT MY BAG. THAT'S **YOURS.** AND **NORIA'S.**
TOO RIGHT.
SHE WORKS HARDER THAN ANY **TEN** OF US PUT TOGETHER.
TRUE, TRUE.
WHEN SHE'S NOT IN THE LIBRARY, SHE'S BACK IN OUR ROOM READING THE FIVE **TONS** OF BOOKS SHE'S TAKEN OUT AND PACKED AWAY.
AND SHE'S EVEN HIDDEN A WHOLE **PILE** UNDER THE FLOOR OF THE **CLOSET.**
WHAT NOW?

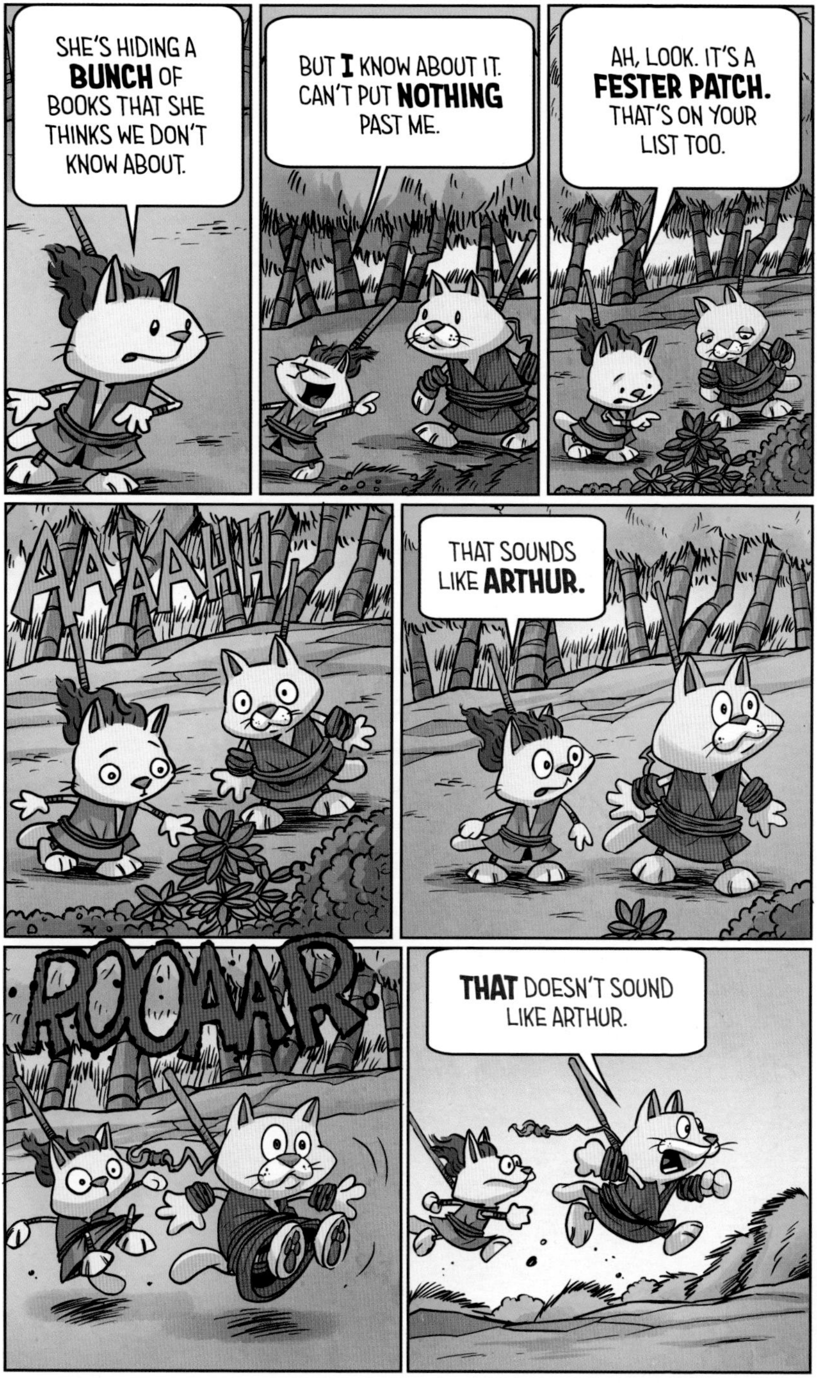

SHE'S HIDING A **BUNCH** OF BOOKS THAT SHE THINKS WE DON'T KNOW ABOUT.
BUT **I** KNOW ABOUT IT. CAN'T PUT **NOTHING** PAST ME.
AH, LOOK. IT'S A **FESTER PATCH.** THAT'S ON YOUR LIST TOO.
AAAAHH!
THAT SOUNDS LIKE **ARTHUR.**
ROOAAR!
THAT DOESN'T SOUND LIKE ARTHUR.

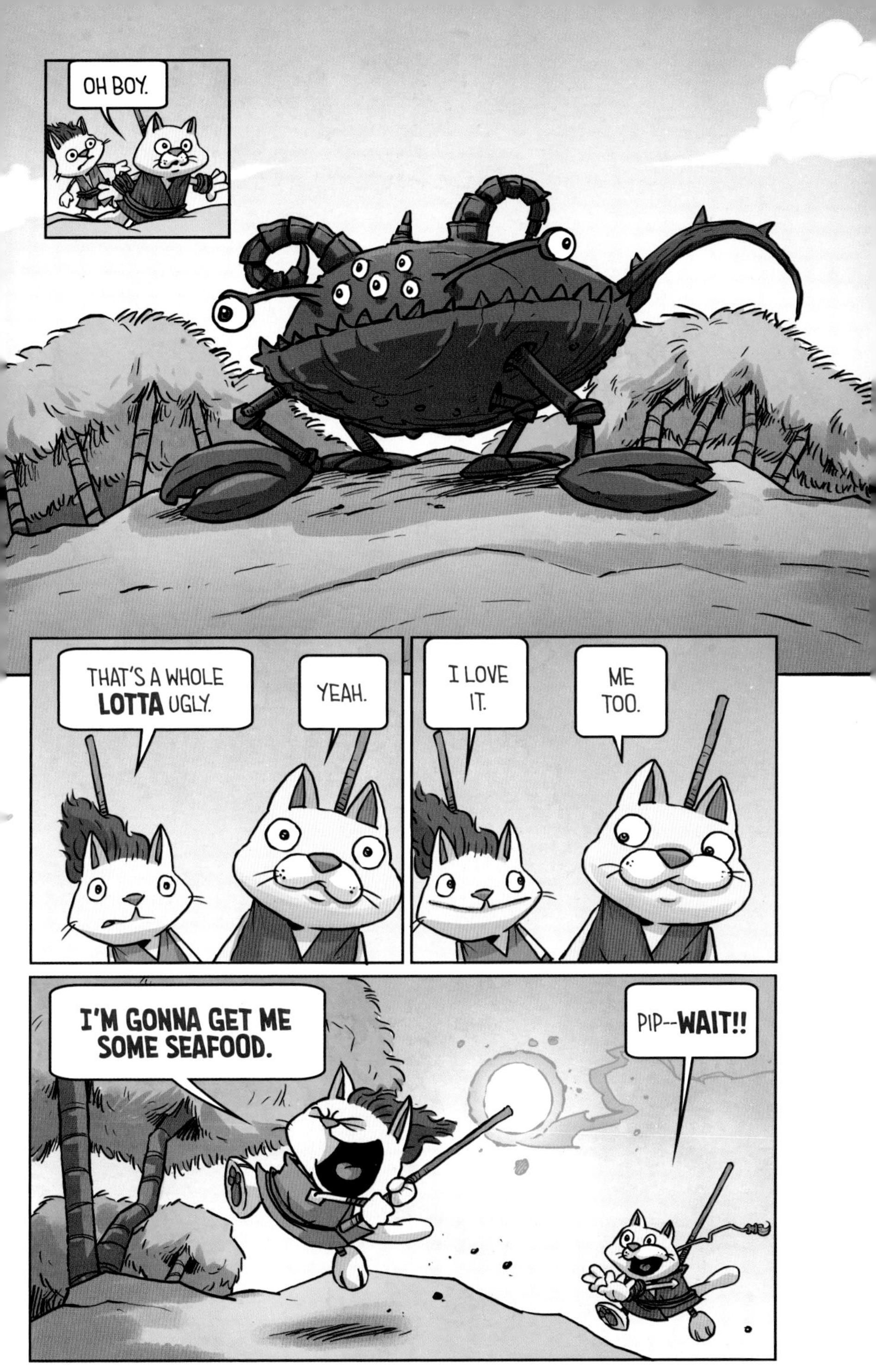
OH BOY.
THAT'S A WHOLE **LOTTA** UGLY.
YEAH.
I LOVE IT.
ME TOO.
I'M GONNA GET ME SOME SEAFOOD.
PIP--**WAIT!!**

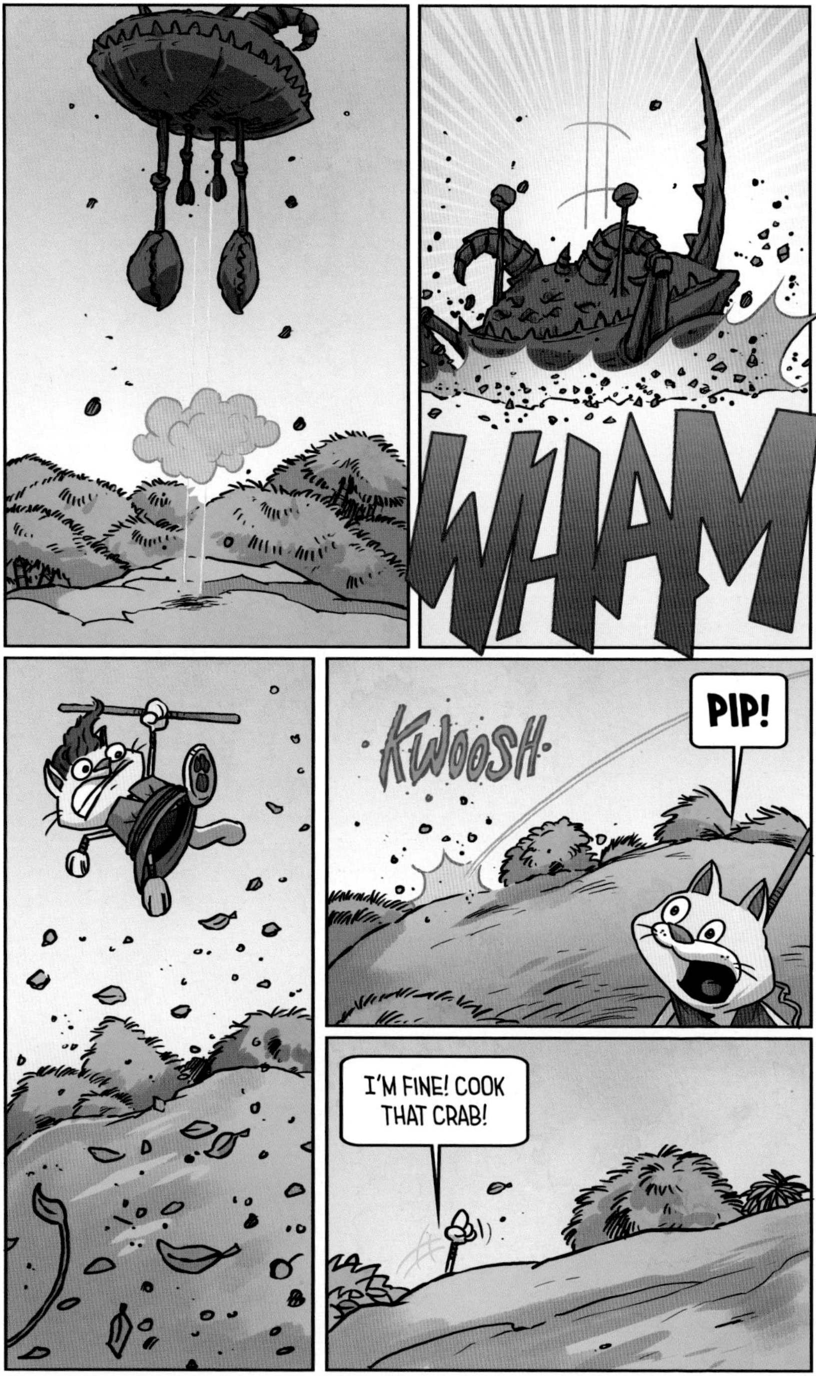
WHAM
KWOOSH
PIP!
I'M FINE! COOK THAT CRAB!

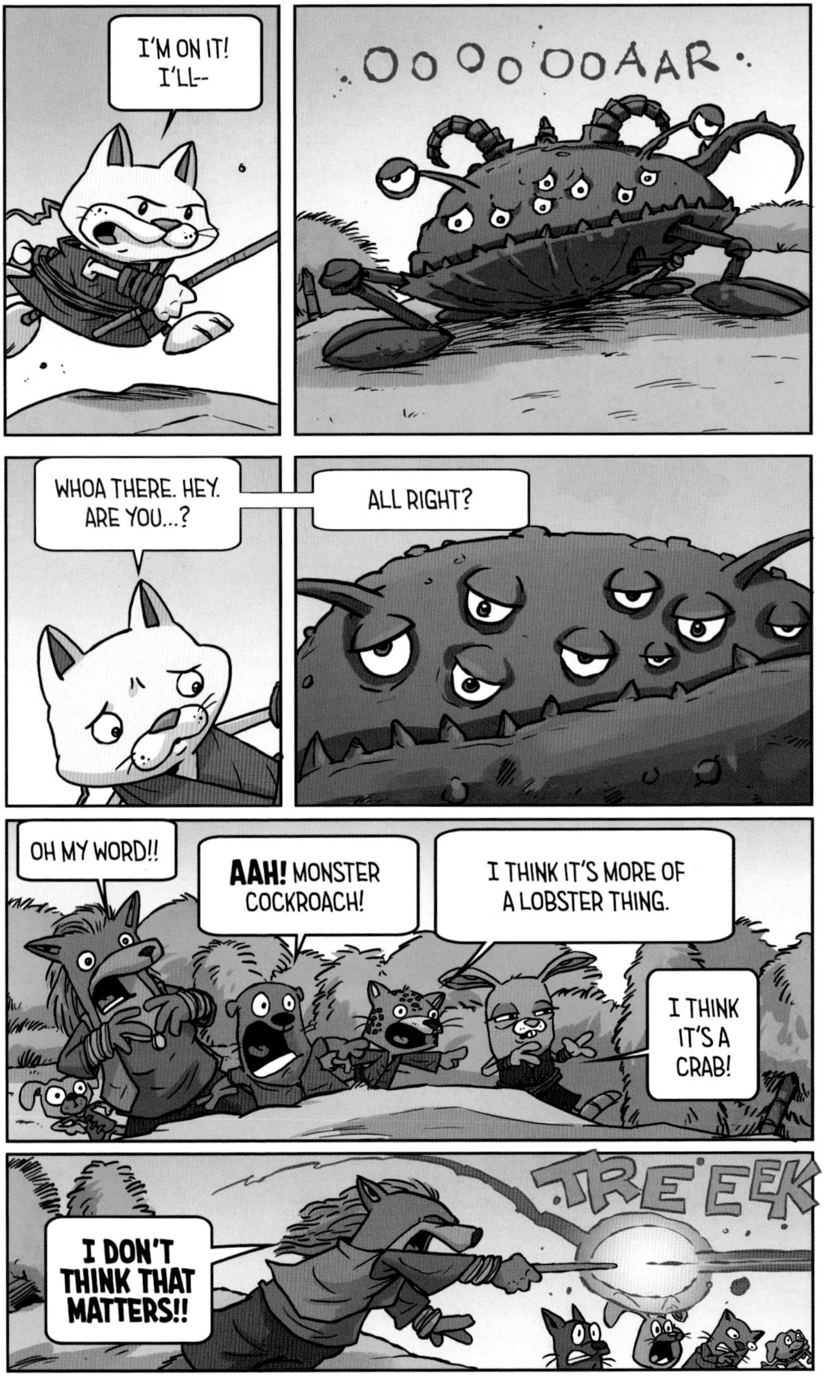

I'M ON IT! I'LL--
OOOOOOOAAR
WHOA THERE. HEY. ARE YOU...?
ALL RIGHT?
OH MY WORD!!
AAH! MONSTER COCKROACH!
I THINK IT'S MORE OF A LOBSTER THING.
I THINK IT'S A CRAB!
TREEEK
I DON'T THINK THAT MATTERS!!

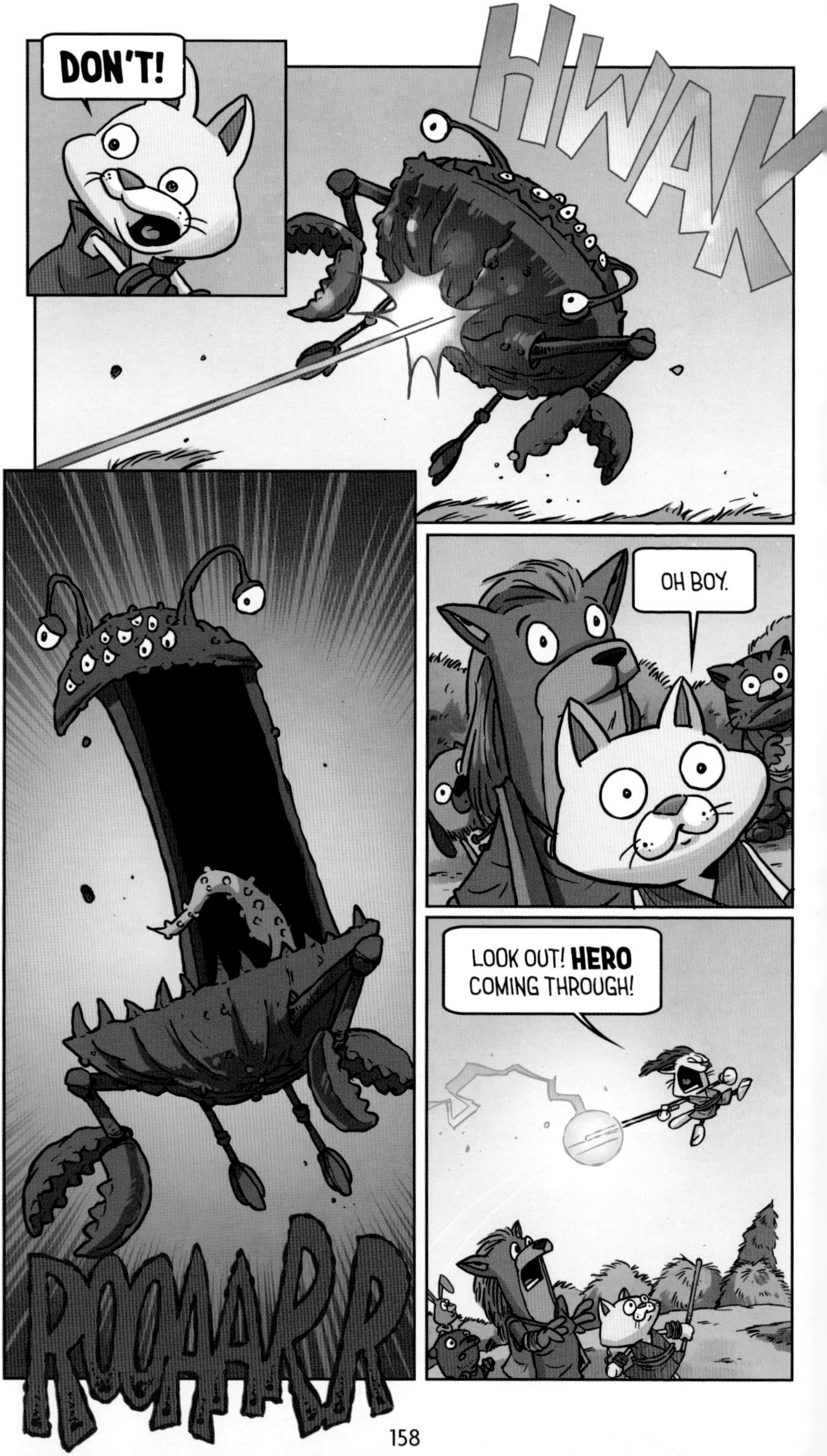
DON'T!
HWAK
ROOAARR
OH BOY.
LOOK OUT! **HERO** COMING THROUGH!

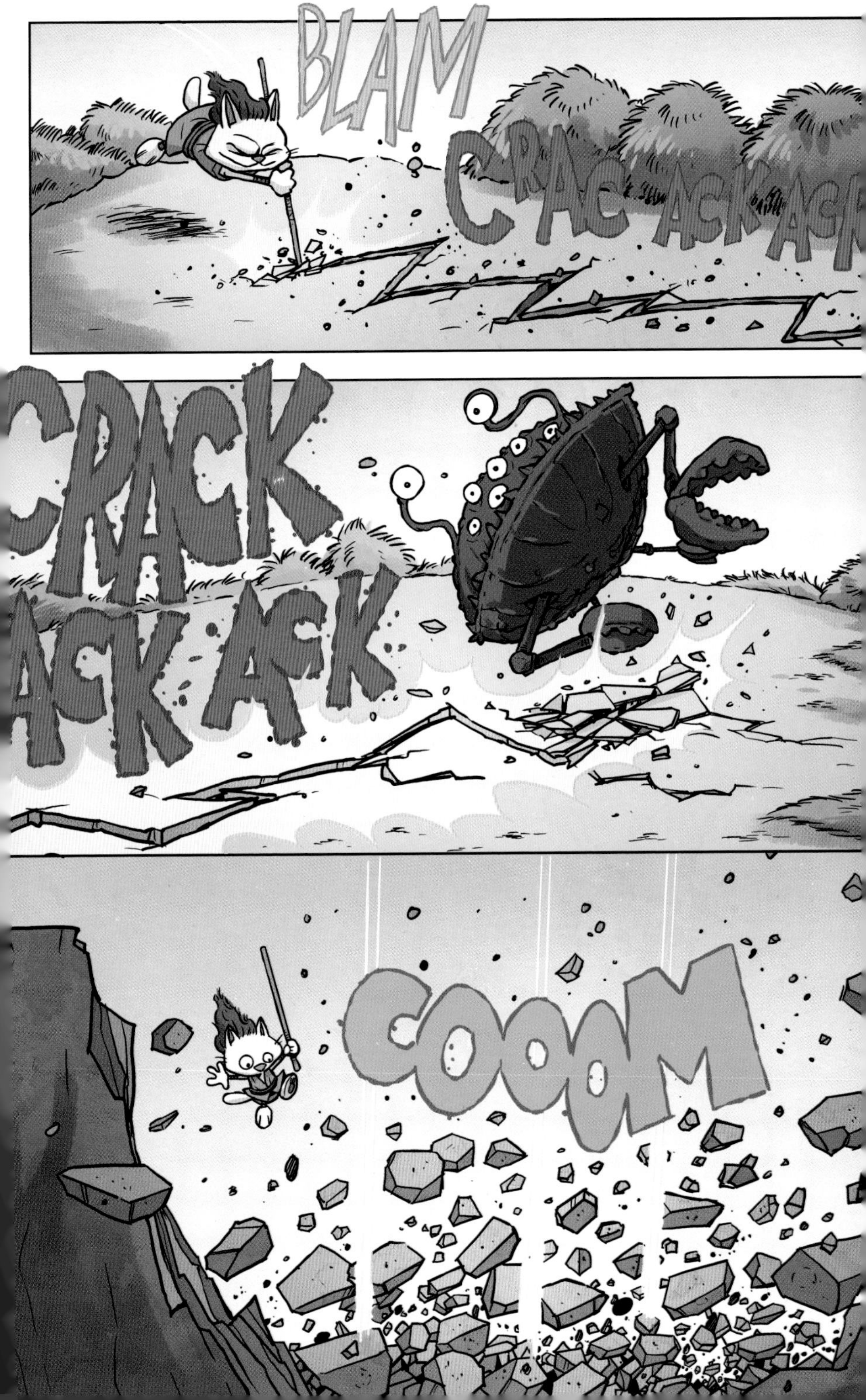

BLAM
CRACK
COOOM

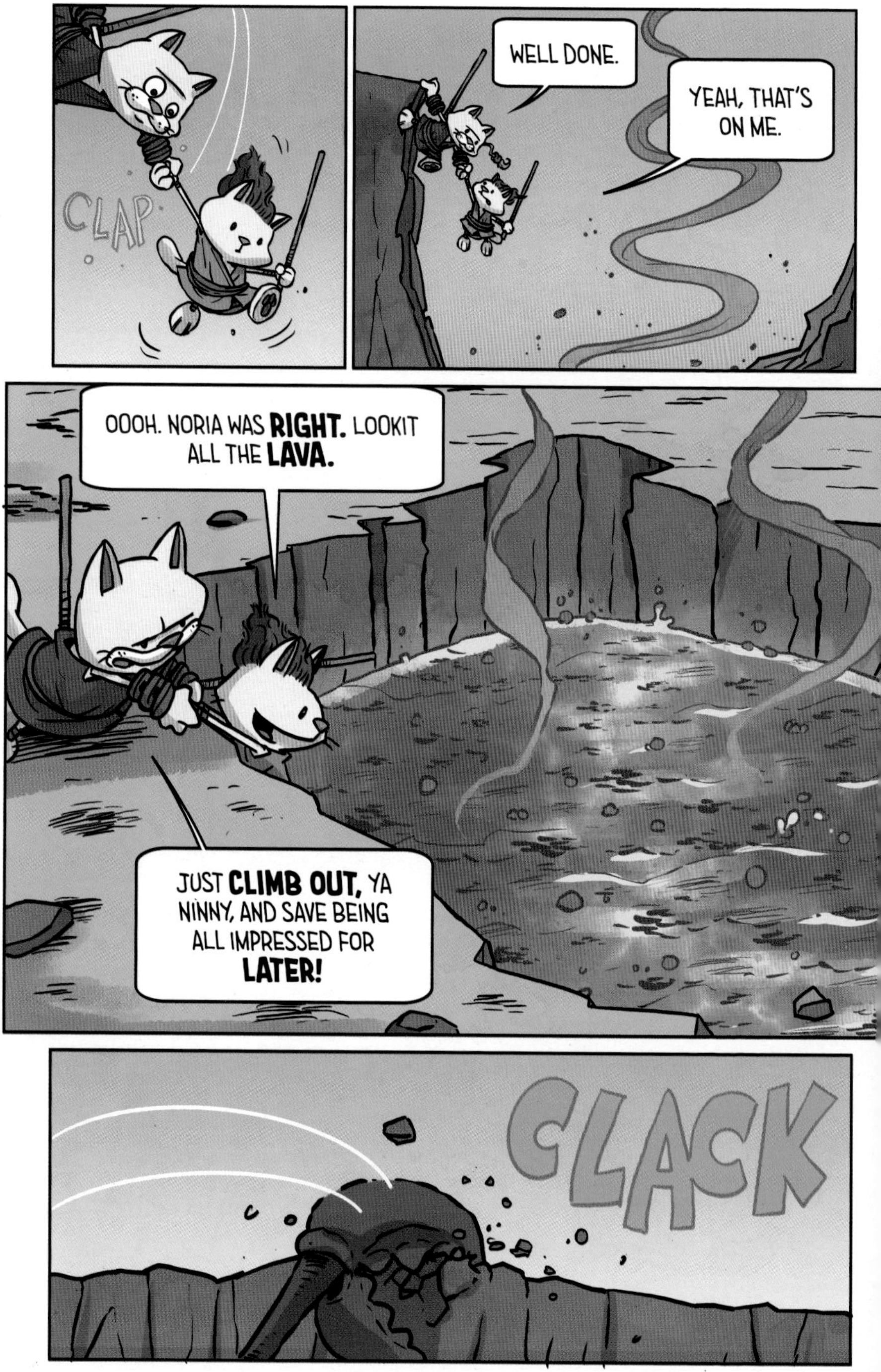
CLAP
WELL DONE.
YEAH, THAT'S ON ME.
OOOH. NORIA WAS **RIGHT.** LOOKIT ALL THE **LAVA.**
JUST **CLIMB OUT,** YA NINNY, AND SAVE BEING ALL IMPRESSED FOR **LATER!**
CLACK

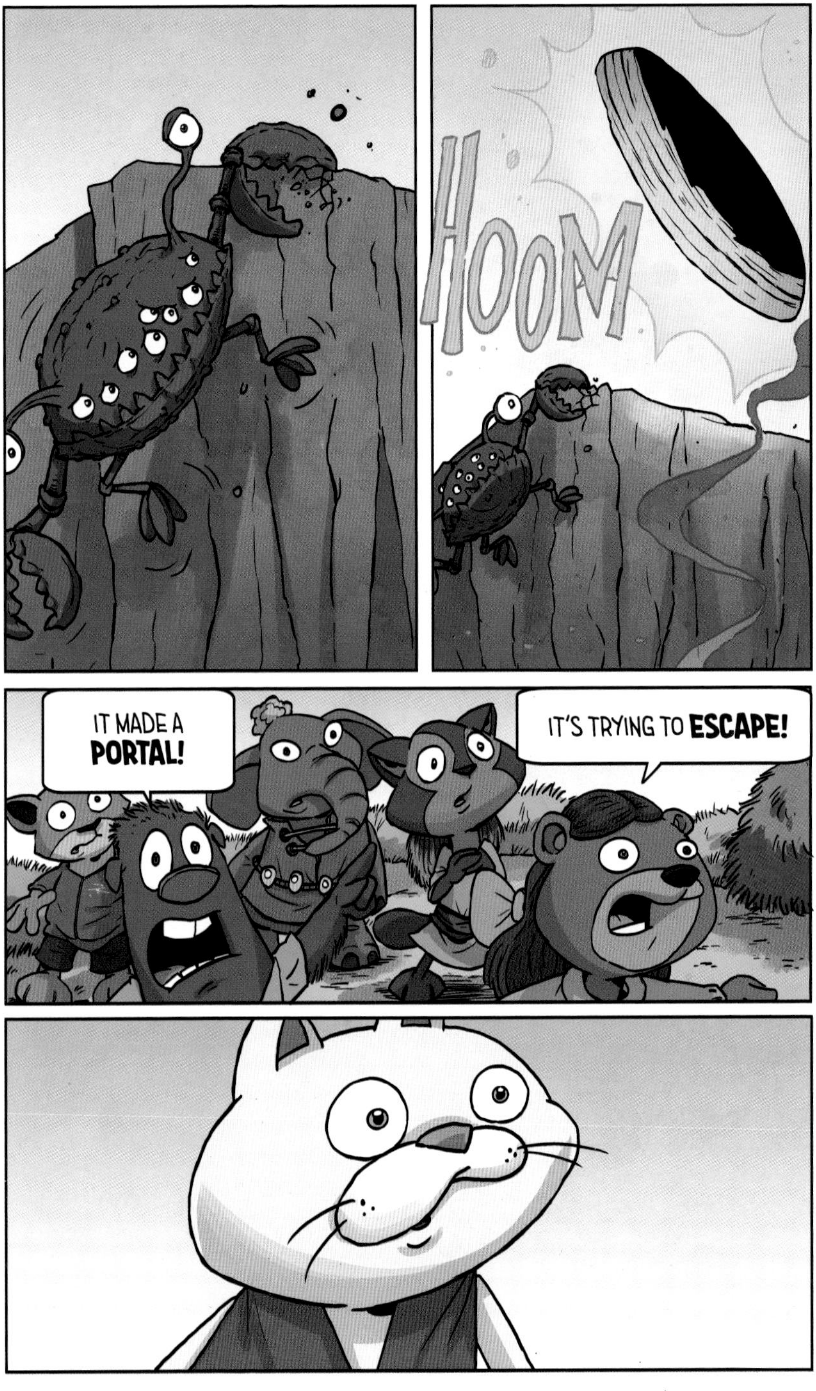
HOOM
IT MADE A PORTAL!
IT'S TRYING TO ESCAPE!

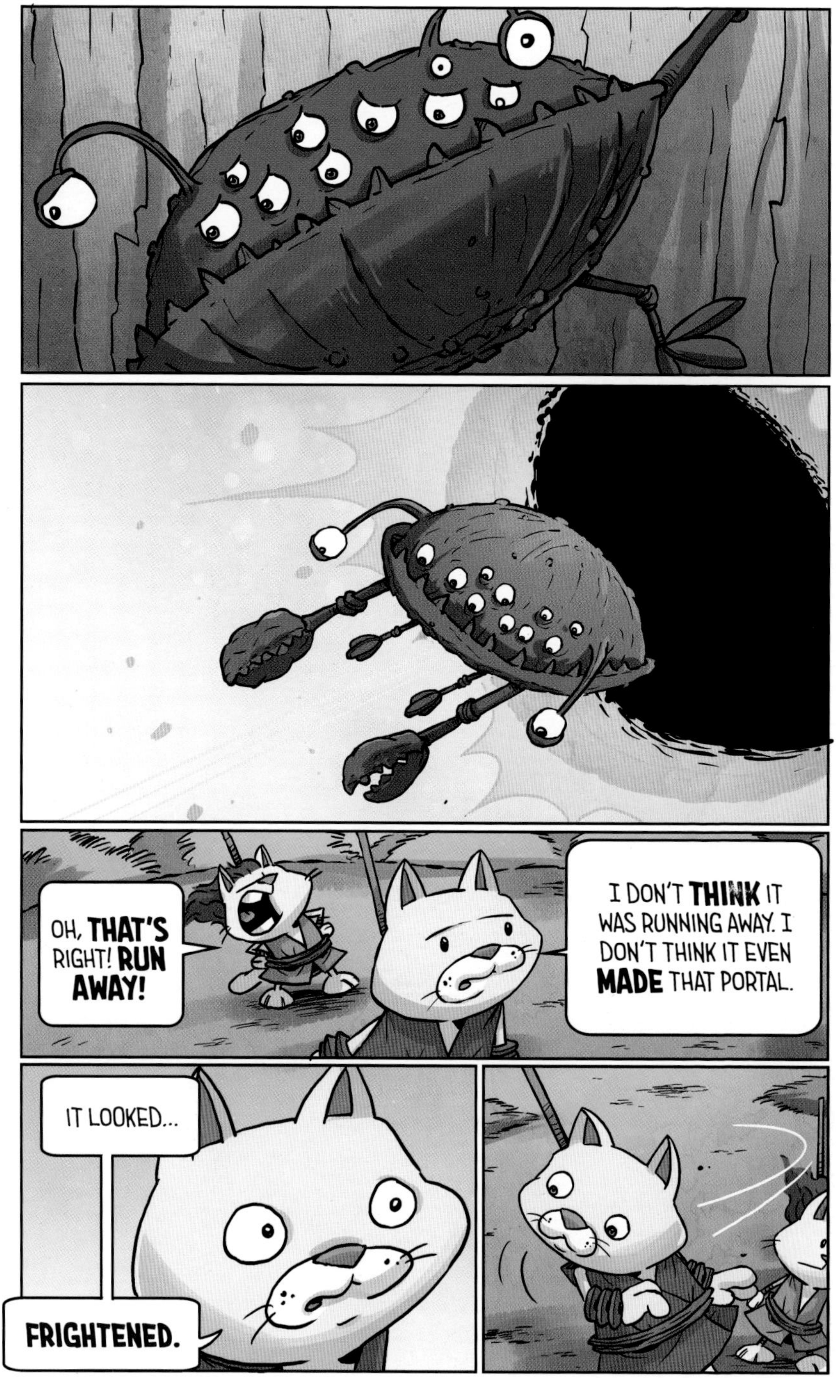
OH, THAT'S RIGHT! RUN AWAY!
I DON'T THINK IT WAS RUNNING AWAY. I DON'T THINK IT EVEN MADE THAT PORTAL.
IT LOOKED...
FRIGHTENED.

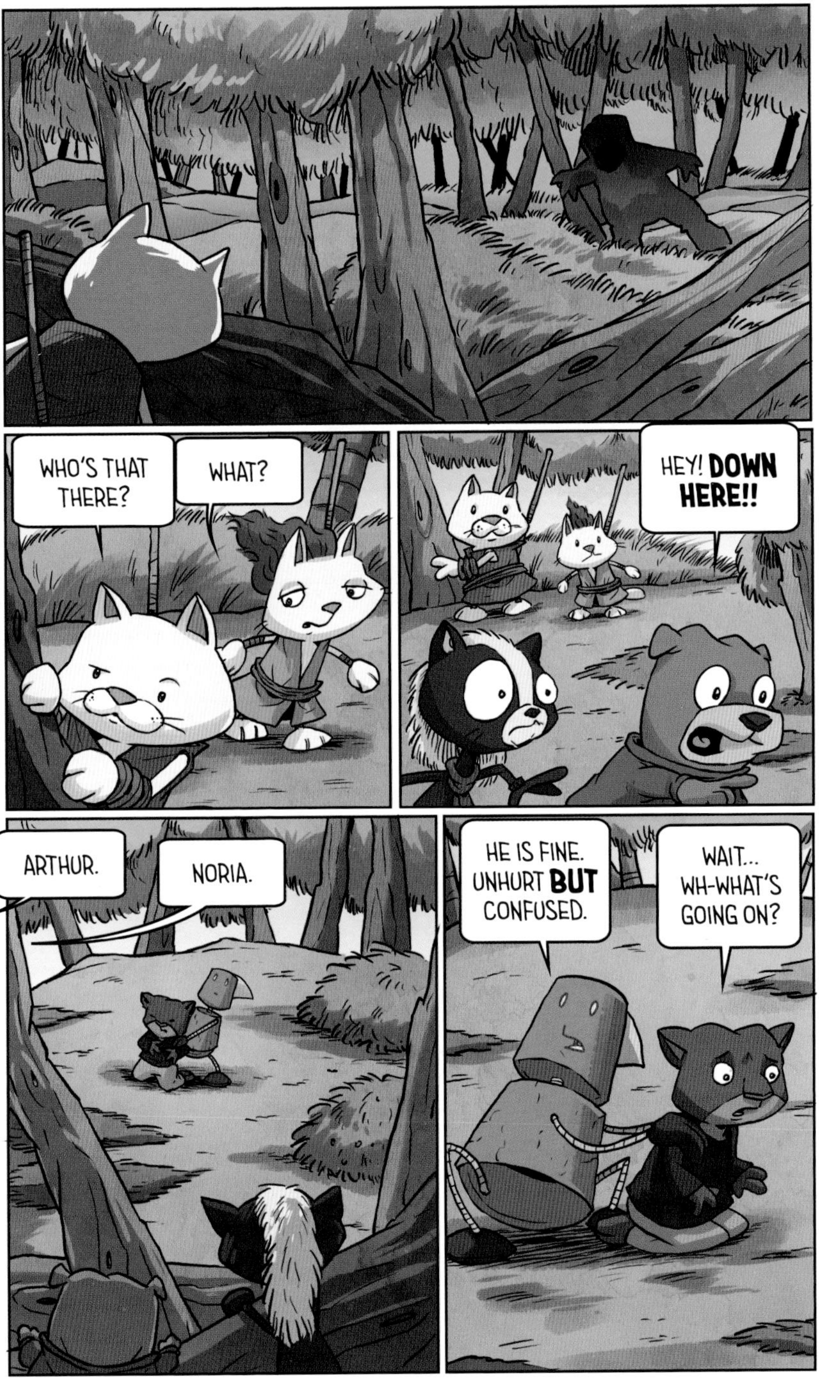

WHO'S THAT THERE?
WHAT?
HEY! **DOWN HERE!!**
ARTHUR.
NORIA.
HE IS FINE. UNHURT **BUT** CONFUSED.
WAIT... WH-WHAT'S GOING ON?

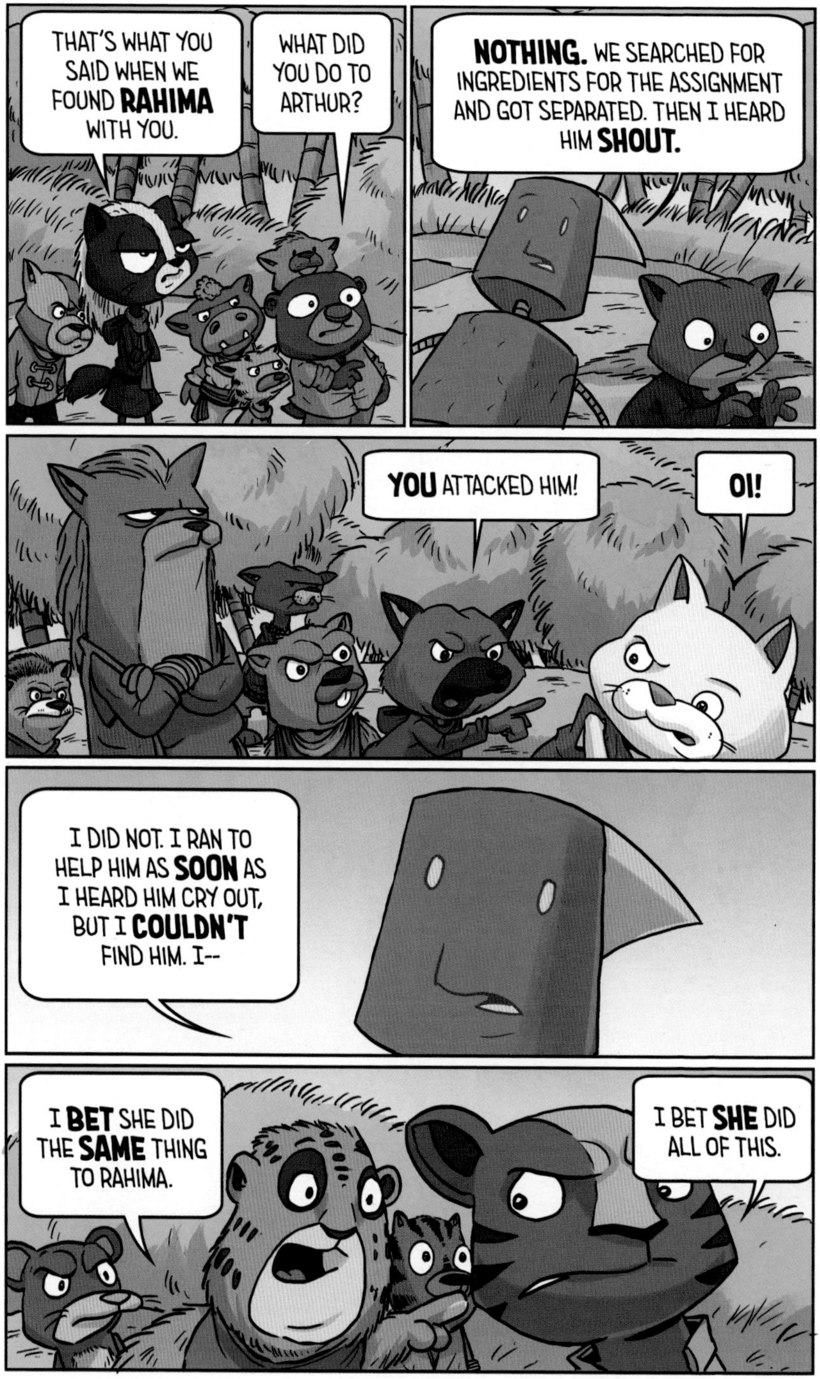
THAT'S WHAT YOU SAID WHEN WE FOUND **RAHIMA** WITH YOU.
WHAT DID YOU DO TO ARTHUR?
NOTHING. WE SEARCHED FOR INGREDIENTS FOR THE ASSIGNMENT AND GOT SEPARATED. THEN I HEARD HIM **SHOUT.**
YOU ATTACKED HIM!
OI!
I DID NOT. I RAN TO HELP HIM AS **SOON** AS I HEARD HIM CRY OUT, BUT I **COULDN'T** FIND HIM. I--
I **BET** SHE DID THE **SAME** THING TO RAHIMA.
I BET **SHE** DID ALL OF THIS.

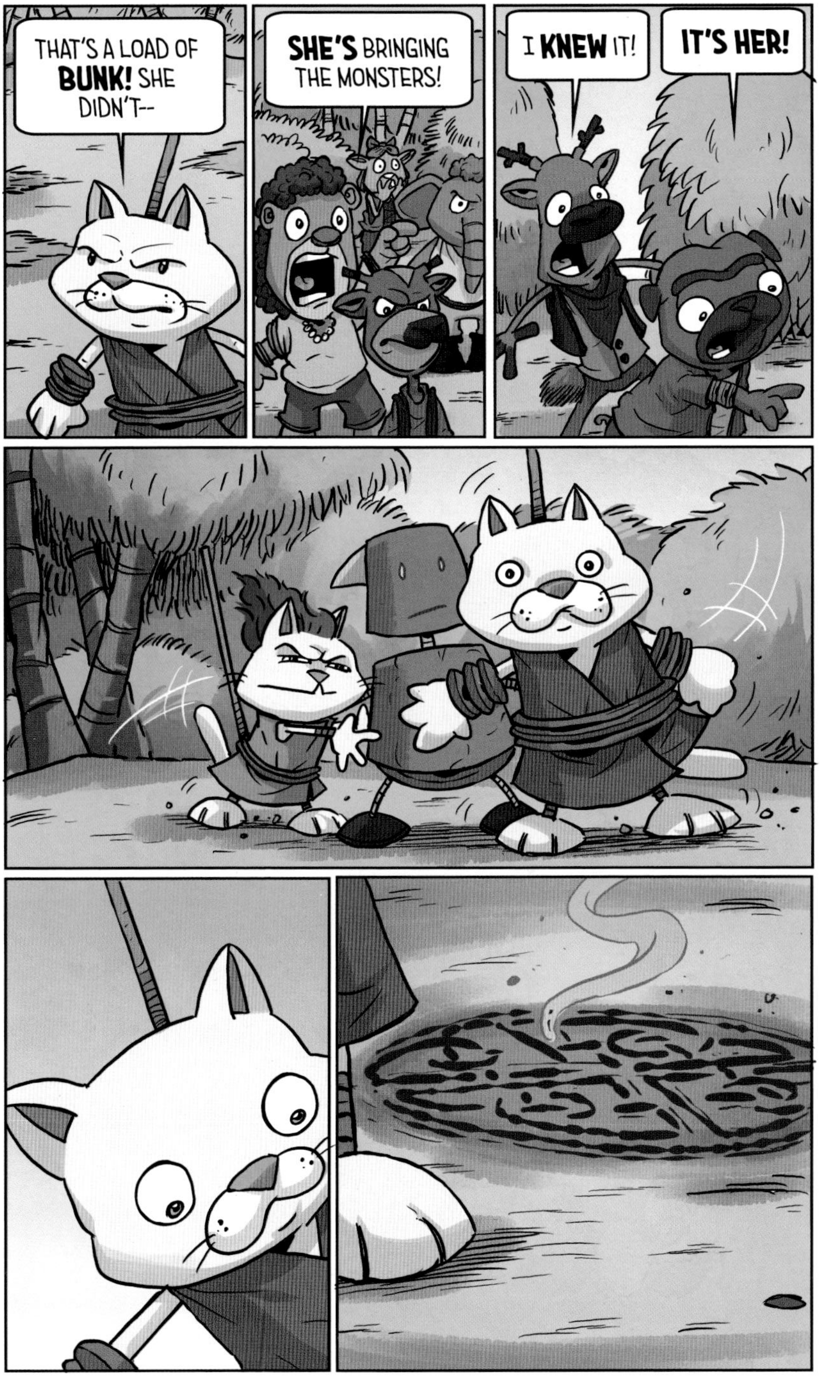

THAT'S A LOAD OF **BUNK!** SHE DIDN'T--
SHE'S BRINGING THE MONSTERS!
I **KNEW** IT!
IT'S HER!

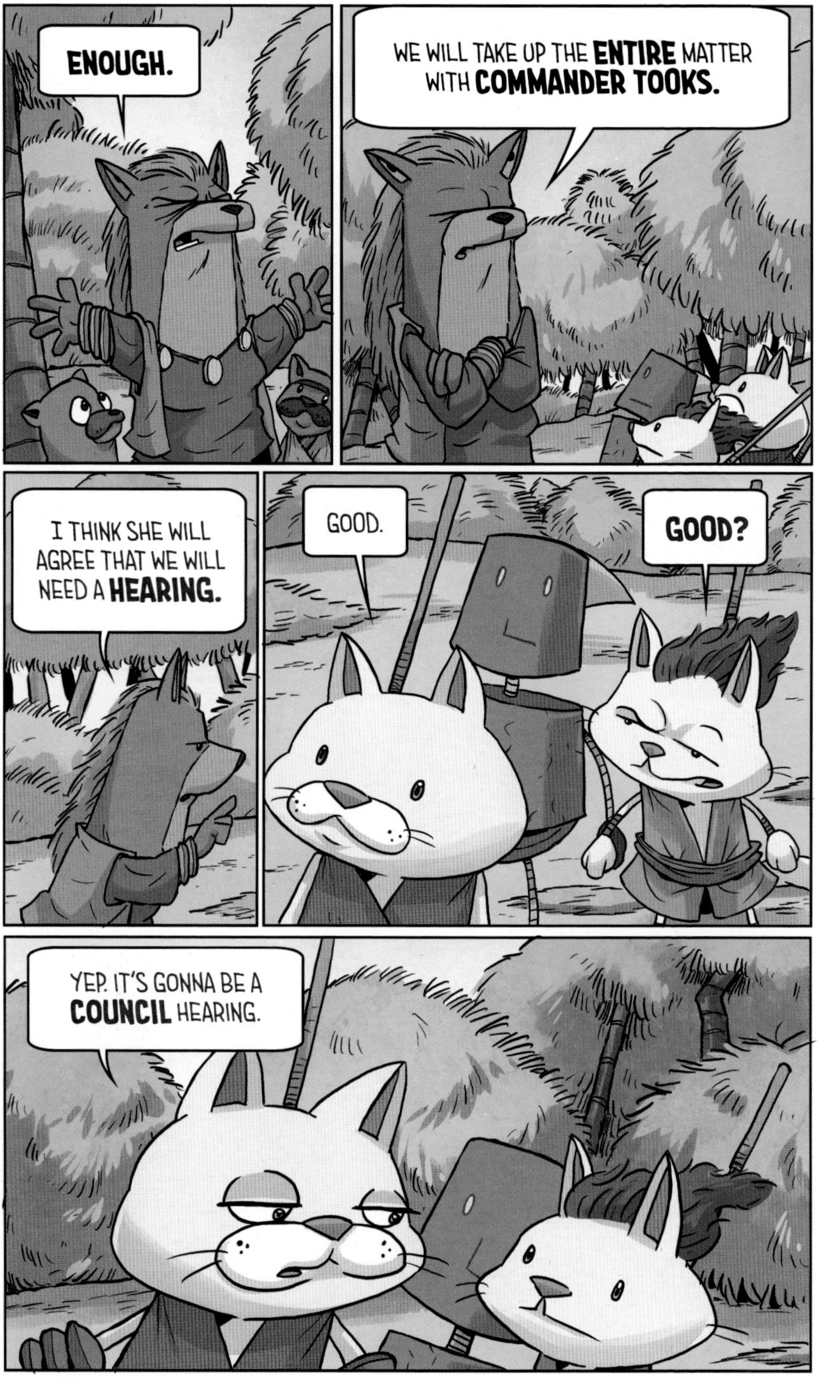
ENOUGH.
WE WILL TAKE UP THE ENTIRE MATTER WITH COMMANDER TOOKS.
I THINK SHE WILL AGREE THAT WE WILL NEED A HEARING.
GOOD.
GOOD?
YEP. IT'S GONNA BE A COUNCIL HEARING.

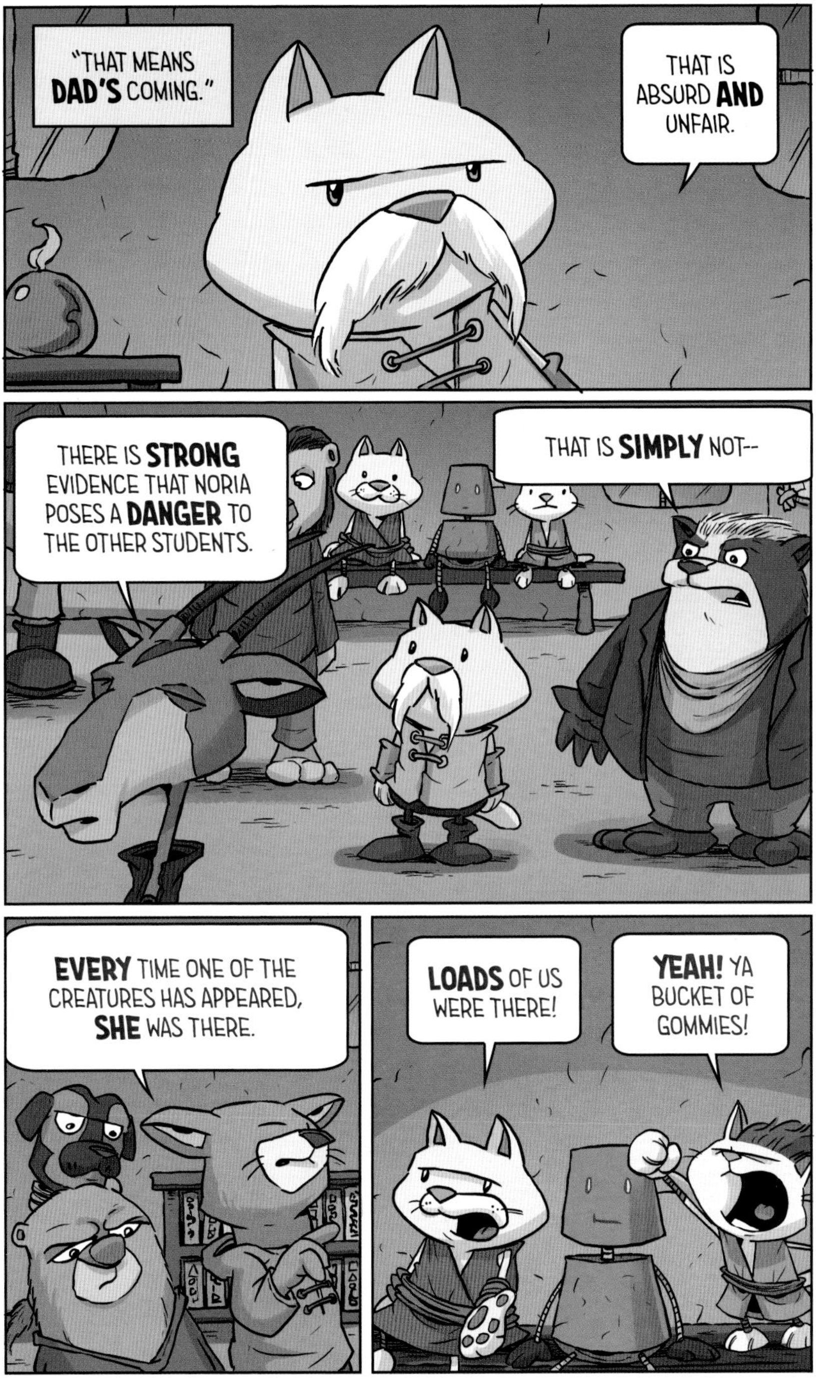
"THAT MEANS **DAD'S** COMING."
THAT IS ABSURD **AND** UNFAIR.
THERE IS **STRONG** EVIDENCE THAT NORIA POSES A **DANGER** TO THE OTHER STUDENTS.
THAT IS **SIMPLY** NOT--
EVERY TIME ONE OF THE CREATURES HAS APPEARED, **SHE** WAS THERE.
LOADS OF US WERE THERE!
YEAH! YA BUCKET OF GOMMIES!

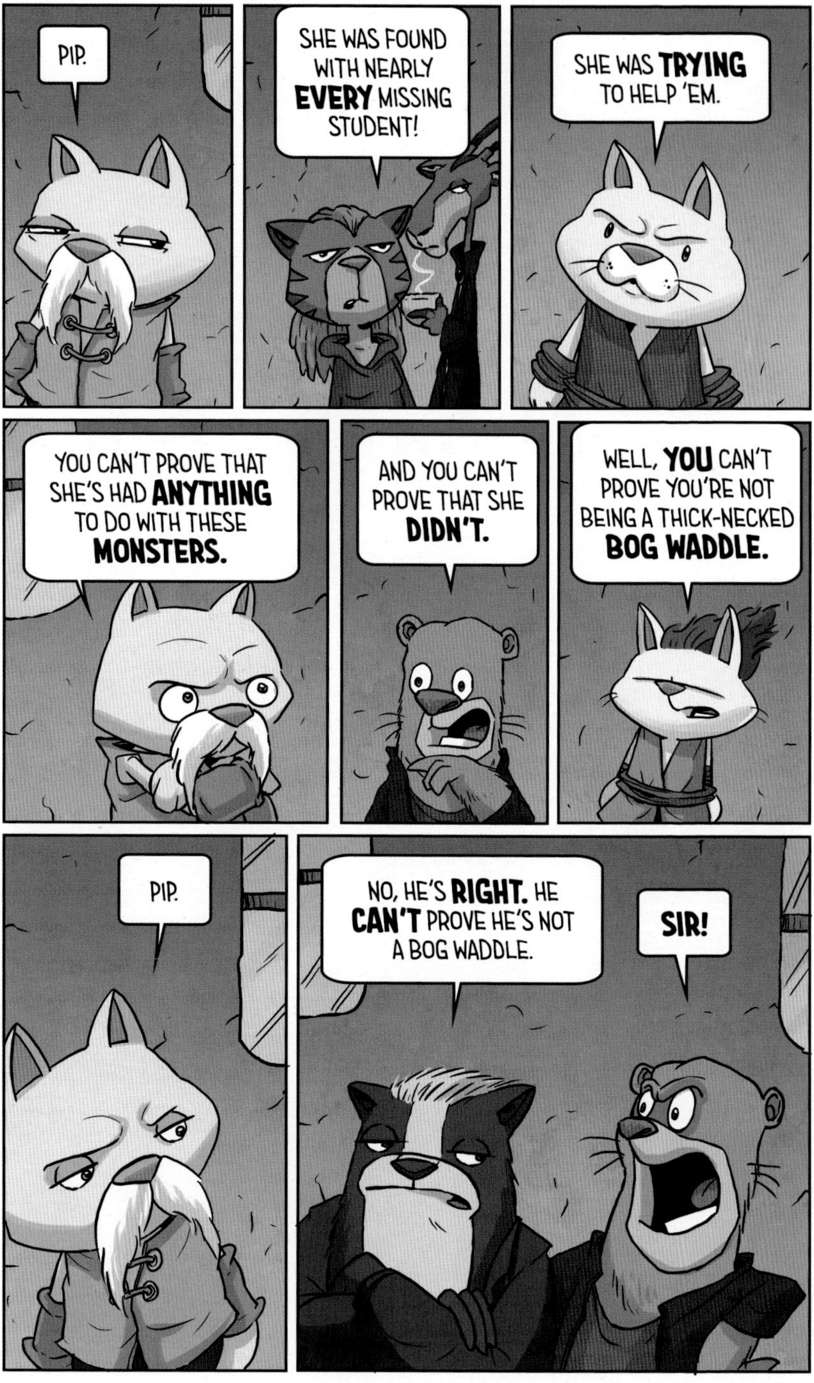
PIP.
SHE WAS FOUND WITH NEARLY **EVERY** MISSING STUDENT!
SHE WAS **TRYING** TO HELP 'EM.
YOU CAN'T PROVE THAT SHE'S HAD **ANYTHING** TO DO WITH THESE **MONSTERS.**
AND YOU CAN'T PROVE THAT SHE **DIDN'T.**
WELL, **YOU** CAN'T PROVE YOU'RE NOT BEING A THICK-NECKED **BOG WADDLE.**
PIP.
NO, HE'S **RIGHT.** HE **CAN'T** PROVE HE'S NOT A BOG WADDLE.
SIR!

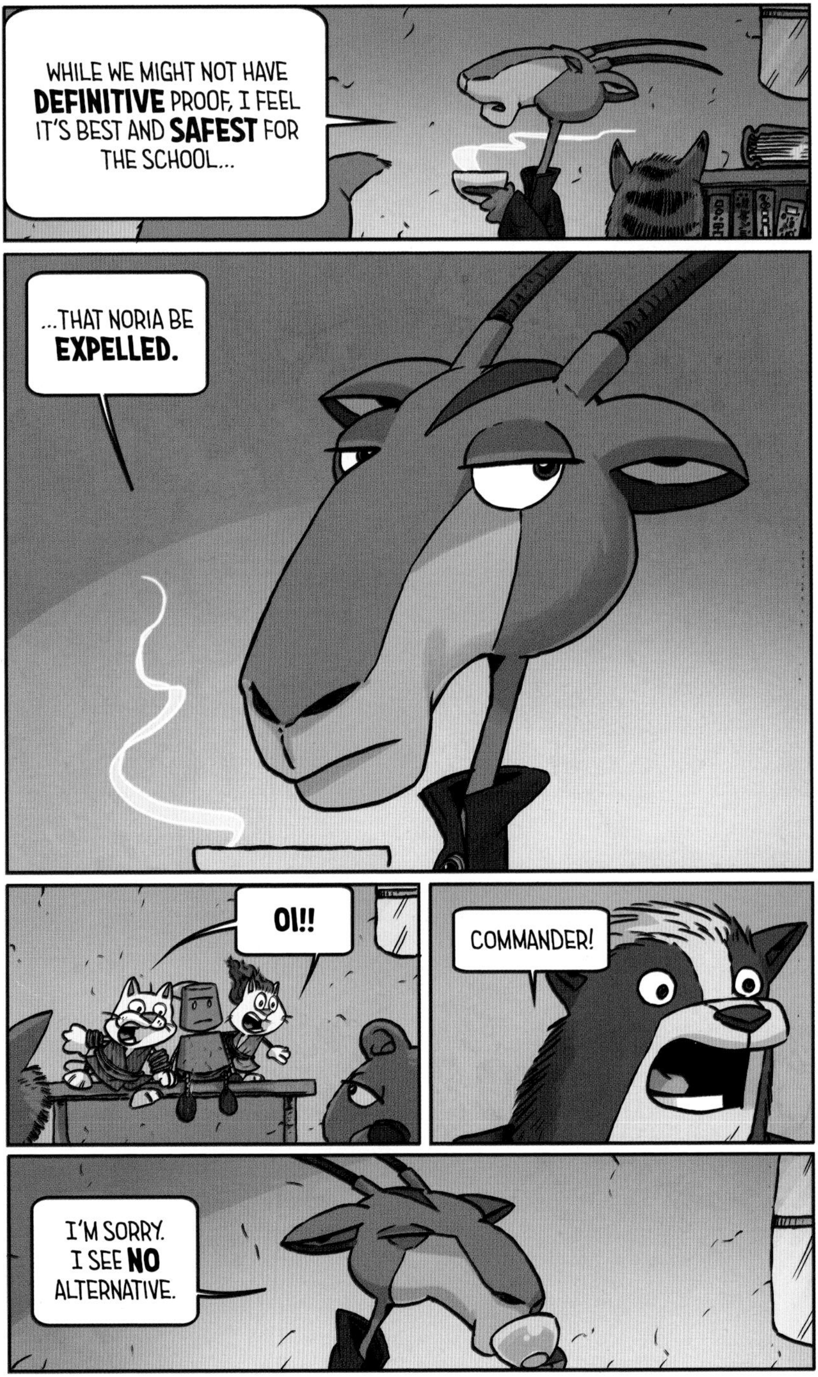
WHILE WE MIGHT NOT HAVE **DEFINITIVE** PROOF, I FEEL IT'S BEST AND **SAFEST** FOR THE SCHOOL...
...THAT NORIA BE **EXPELLED.**
OI!!
COMMANDER!
I'M SORRY. I SEE **NO** ALTERNATIVE.

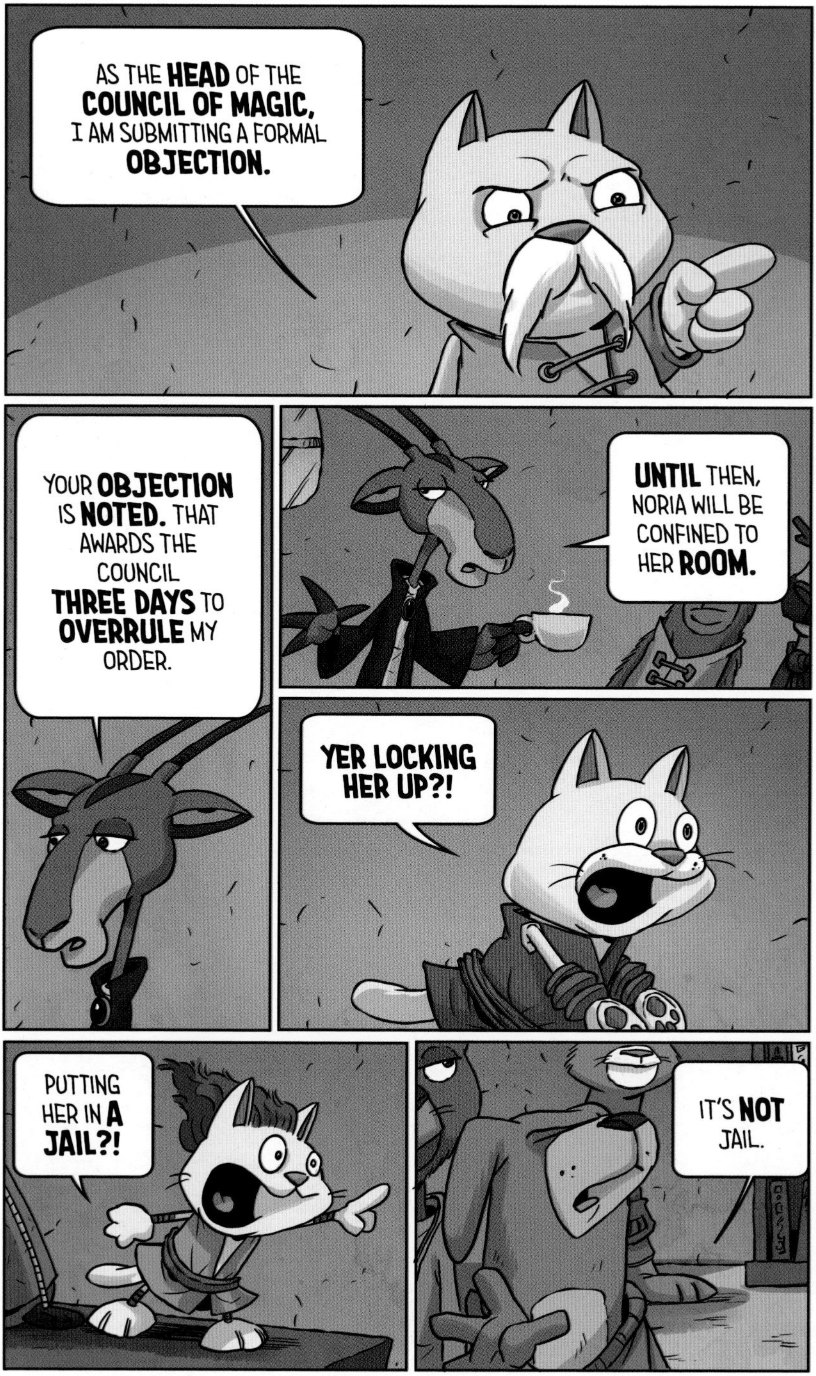

AS THE **HEAD** OF THE **COUNCIL OF MAGIC,** I AM SUBMITTING A FORMAL **OBJECTION.**
YOUR **OBJECTION** IS **NOTED.** THAT AWARDS THE COUNCIL **THREE DAYS** TO **OVERRULE** MY ORDER.
UNTIL THEN, NORIA WILL BE CONFINED TO HER **ROOM.**
YER LOCKING HER UP?!
PUTTING HER IN **A JAIL?!**
IT'S **NOT** JAIL.

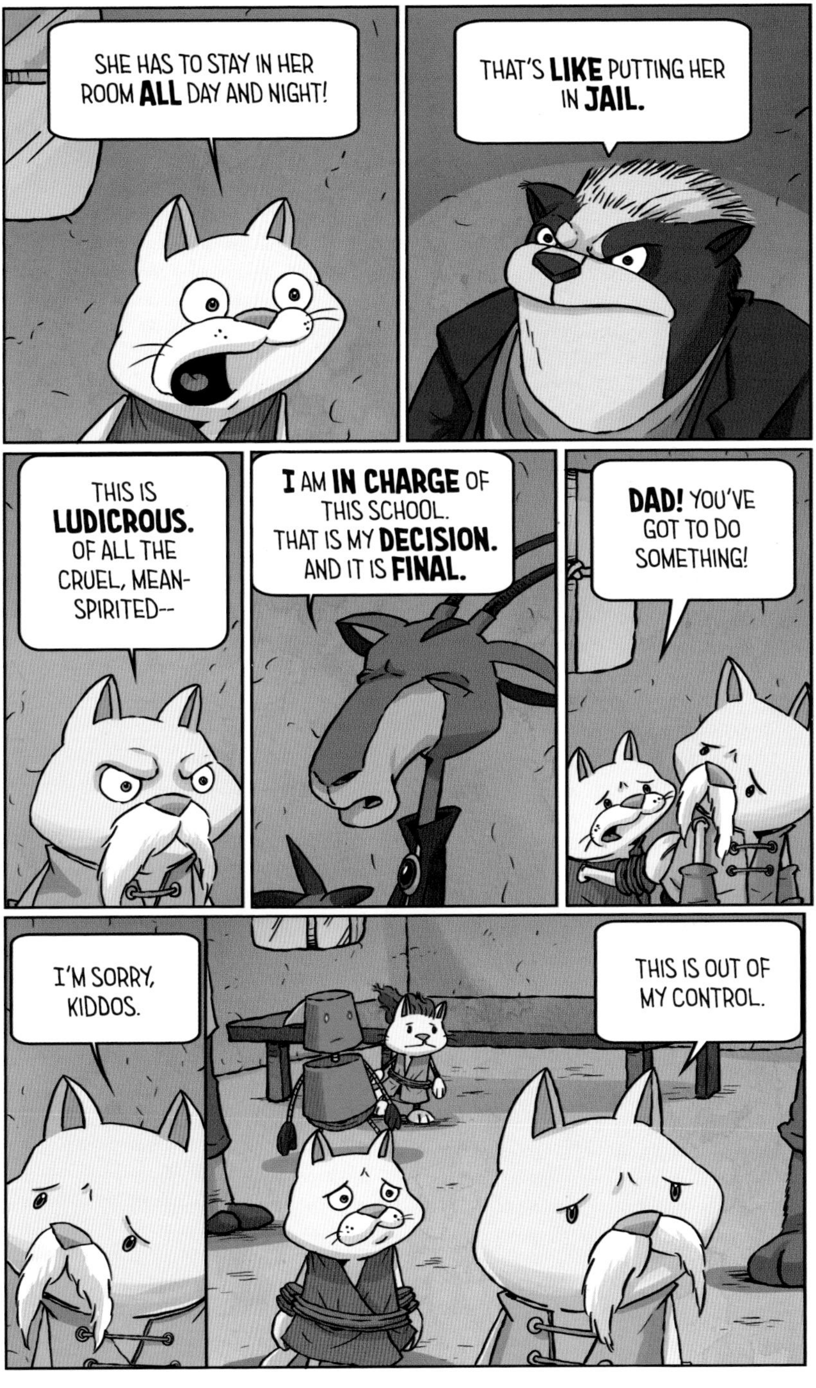

SHE HAS TO STAY IN HER ROOM **ALL** DAY AND NIGHT!
THAT'S **LIKE** PUTTING HER IN **JAIL.**
THIS IS **LUDICROUS.** OF ALL THE CRUEL, MEAN-SPIRITED--
I AM **IN CHARGE** OF THIS SCHOOL. THAT IS MY **DECISION.** AND IT IS **FINAL.**
DAD! YOU'VE GOT TO DO SOMETHING!
I'M SORRY, KIDDOS.
THIS IS OUT OF MY CONTROL.

CHAPTER 10

STAND WITH THE ONES WHO NEED US

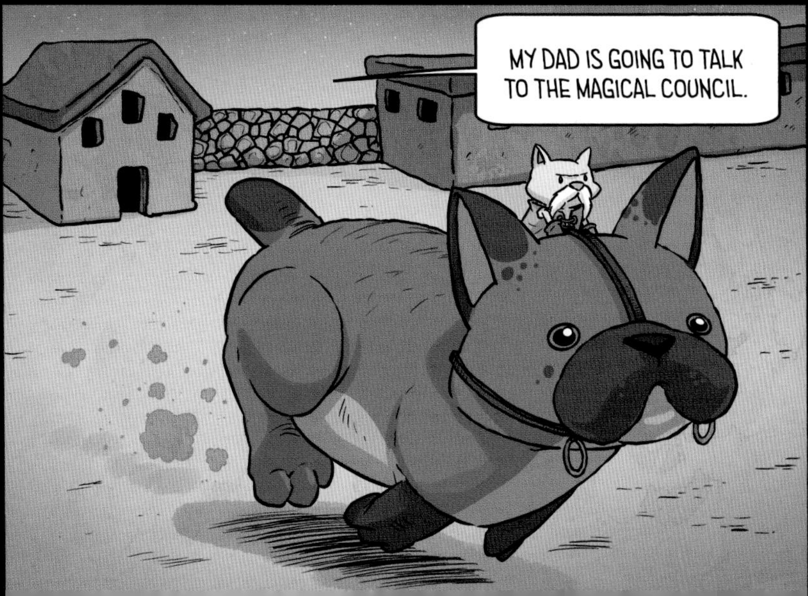
MY DAD IS GOING TO TALK TO THE MAGICAL COUNCIL.

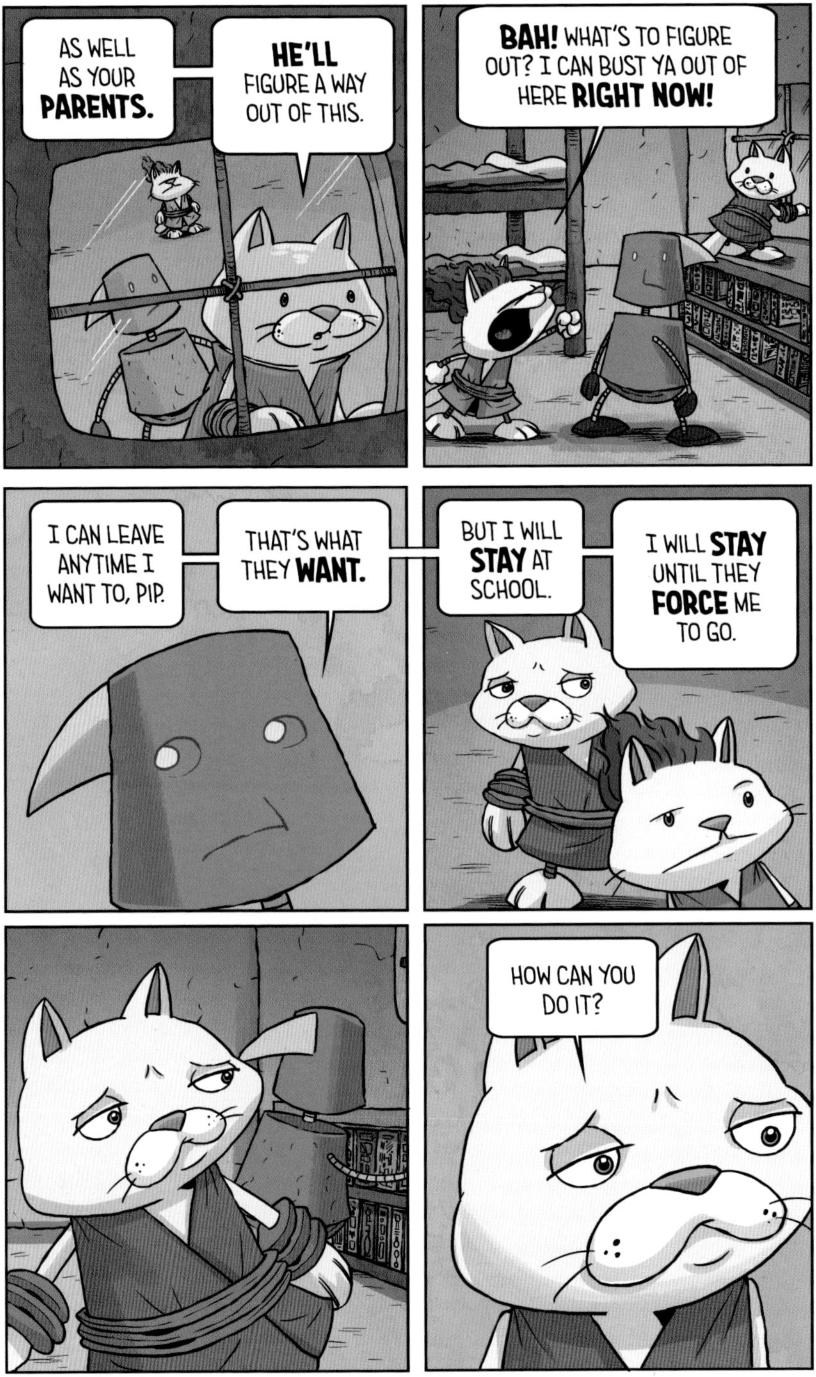
AS WELL AS YOUR **PARENTS.**
HE'LL FIGURE A WAY OUT OF THIS.
BAH! WHAT'S TO FIGURE OUT? I CAN BUST YA OUT OF HERE **RIGHT NOW!**
I CAN LEAVE ANYTIME I WANT TO, PIP.
THAT'S WHAT THEY **WANT.**
BUT I WILL **STAY** AT SCHOOL.
I WILL **STAY** UNTIL THEY **FORCE** ME TO GO.
HOW CAN YOU DO IT?

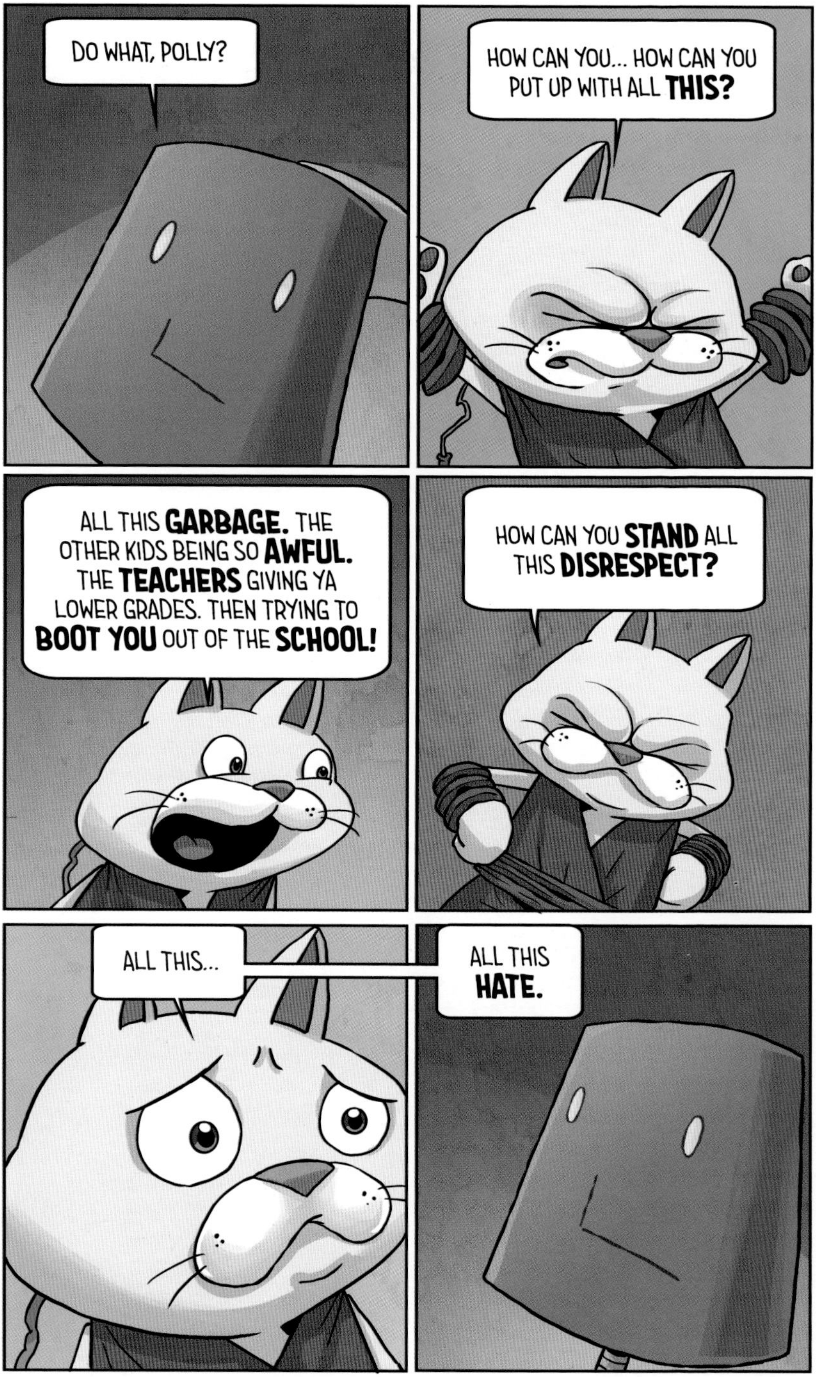
DO WHAT, POLLY?
HOW CAN YOU... HOW CAN YOU PUT UP WITH ALL **THIS?**
ALL THIS **GARBAGE.** THE OTHER KIDS BEING SO **AWFUL.** THE **TEACHERS** GIVING YA LOWER GRADES. THEN TRYING TO **BOOT YOU** OUT OF THE **SCHOOL!**
HOW CAN YOU **STAND** ALL THIS **DISRESPECT?**
ALL THIS...
ALL THIS **HATE.**

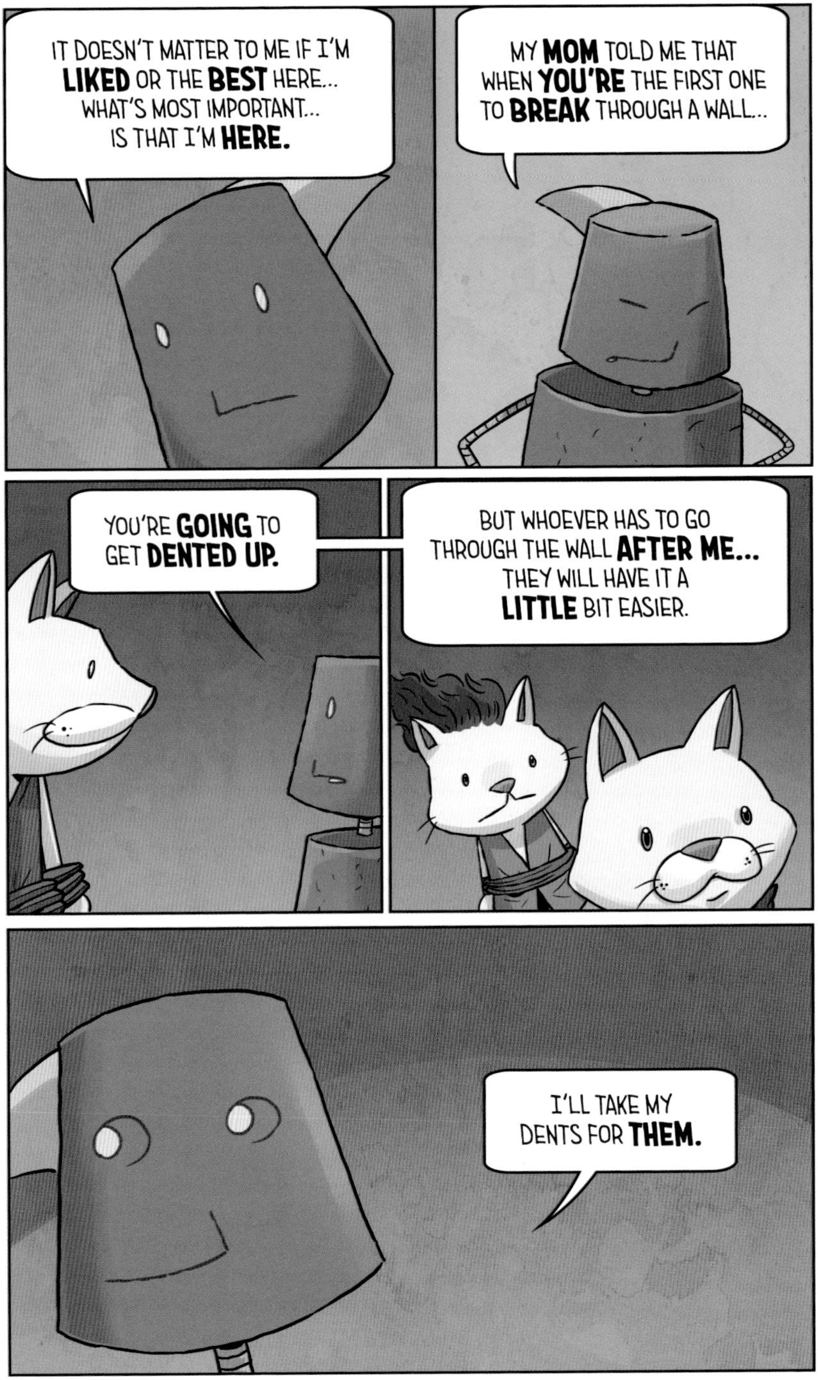
IT DOESN'T MATTER TO ME IF I'M LIKED OR THE BEST HERE... WHAT'S MOST IMPORTANT... IS THAT I'M HERE.
MY MOM TOLD ME THAT WHEN YOU'RE THE FIRST ONE TO BREAK THROUGH A WALL...
YOU'RE GOING TO GET DENTED UP.
BUT WHOEVER HAS TO GO THROUGH THE WALL AFTER ME... THEY WILL HAVE IT A LITTLE BIT EASIER.
I'LL TAKE MY DENTS FOR THEM.

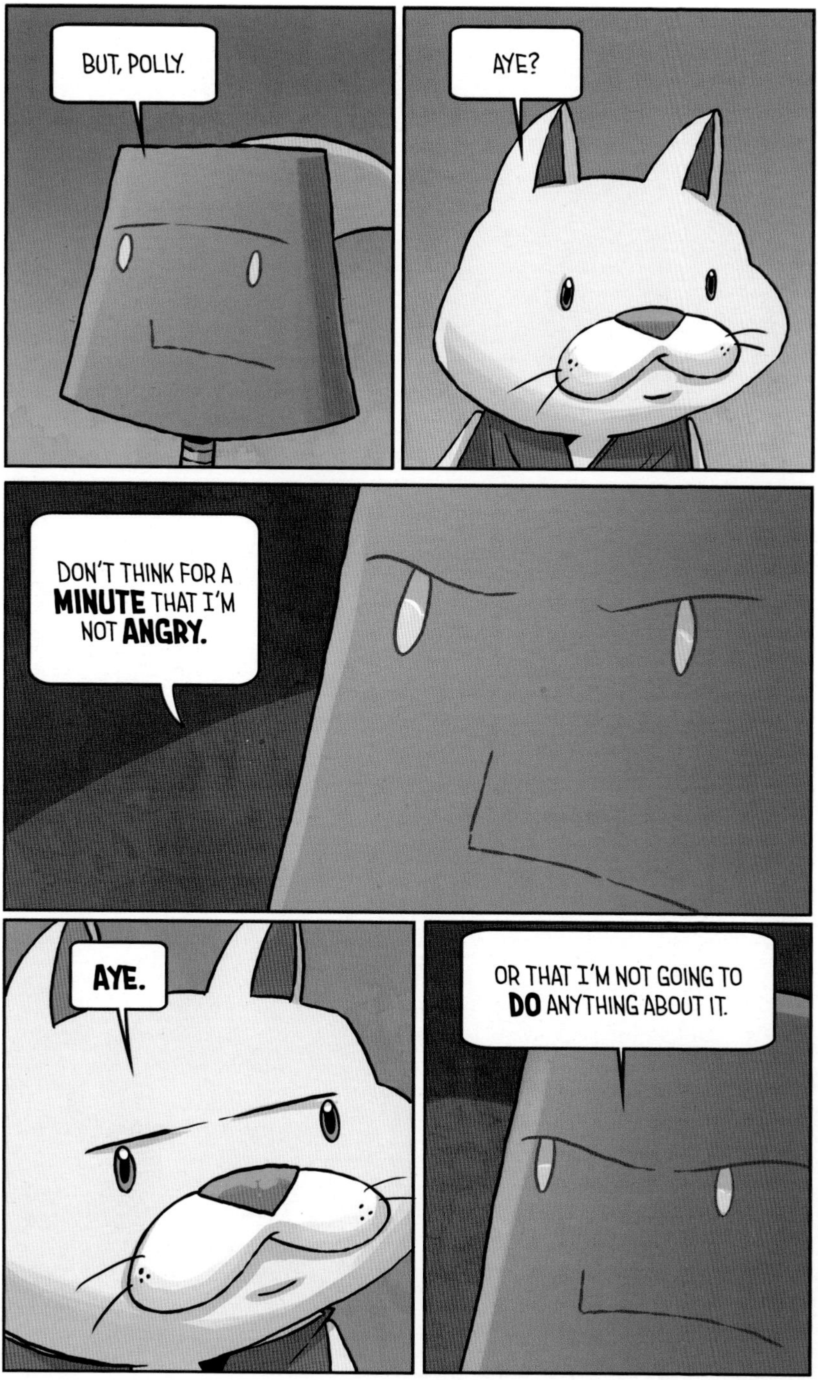

BUT, POLLY.
AYE?
DON'T THINK FOR A **MINUTE** THAT I'M NOT **ANGRY.**
AYE.
OR THAT I'M NOT GOING TO **DO** ANYTHING ABOUT IT.

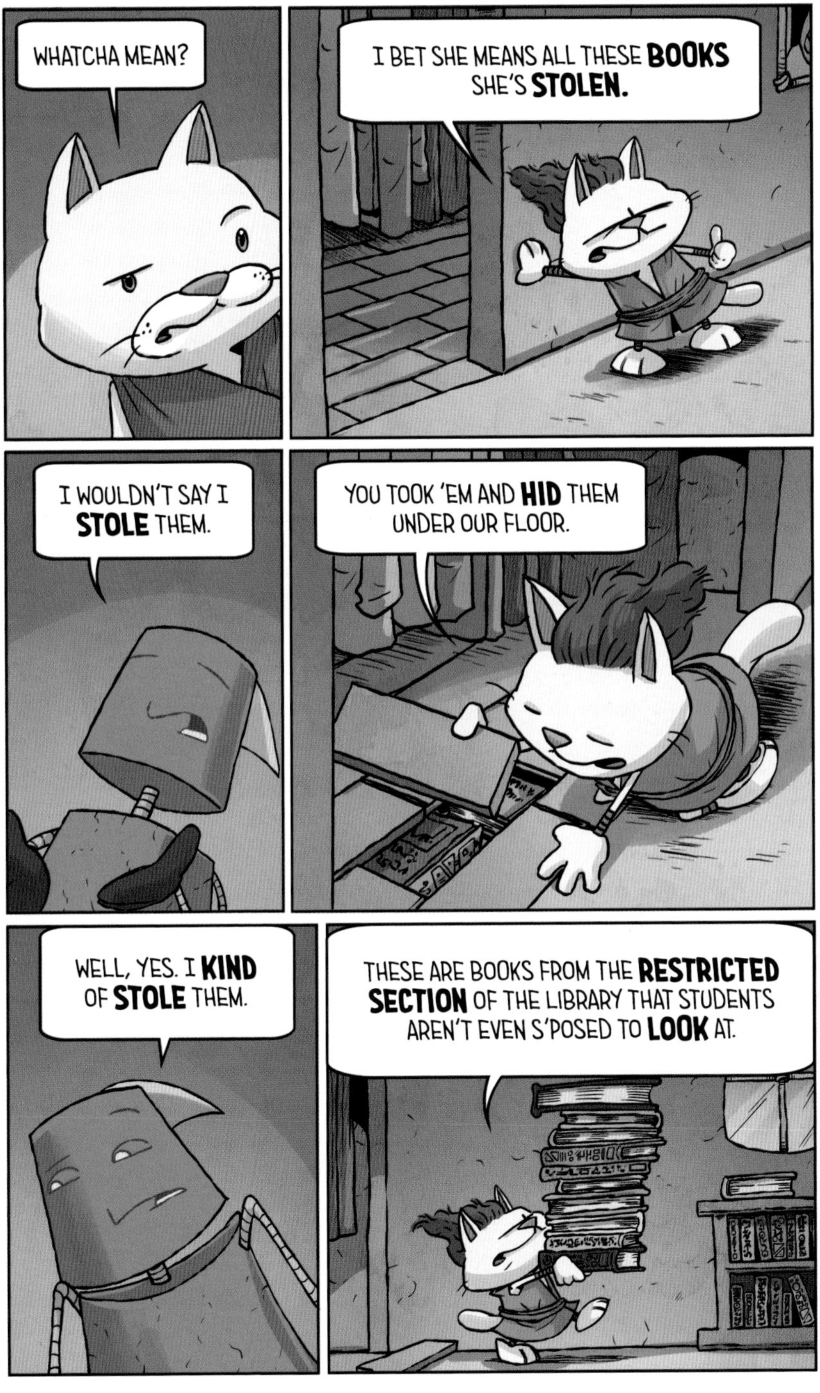
WHATCHA MEAN?
I BET SHE MEANS ALL THESE **BOOKS** SHE'S **STOLEN.**
I WOULDN'T SAY I **STOLE** THEM.
YOU TOOK 'EM AND **HID** THEM UNDER OUR FLOOR.
WELL, YES. I **KIND** OF **STOLE** THEM.
THESE ARE BOOKS FROM THE **RESTRICTED SECTION** OF THE LIBRARY THAT STUDENTS AREN'T EVEN S'POSED TO **LOOK** AT.

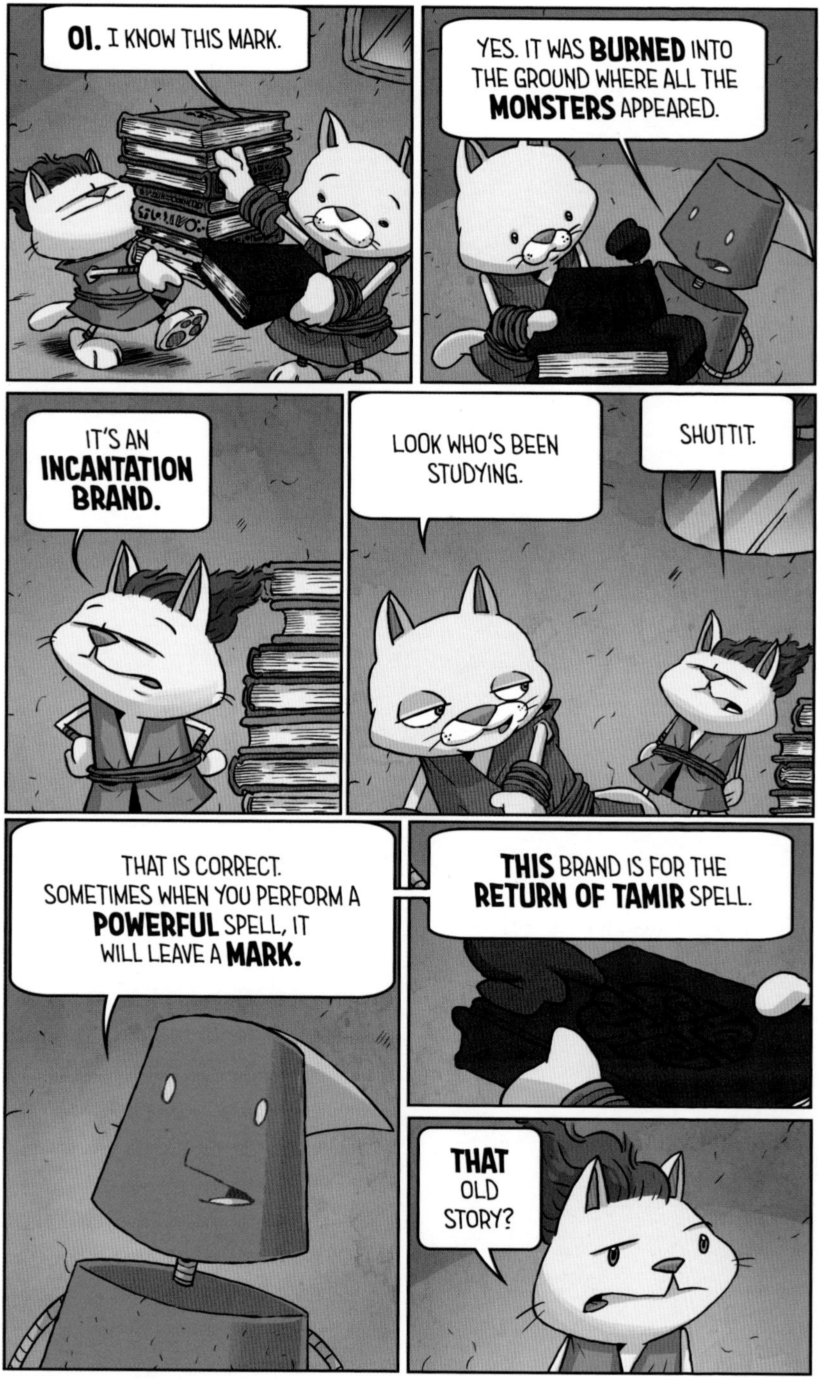
OI. I KNOW THIS MARK.
YES. IT WAS BURNED INTO THE GROUND WHERE ALL THE MONSTERS APPEARED.
IT'S AN INCANTATION BRAND.
LOOK WHO'S BEEN STUDYING.
SHUTTIT.
THAT IS CORRECT. SOMETIMES WHEN YOU PERFORM A POWERFUL SPELL, IT WILL LEAVE A MARK.
THIS BRAND IS FOR THE RETURN OF TAMIR SPELL.
THAT OLD STORY?

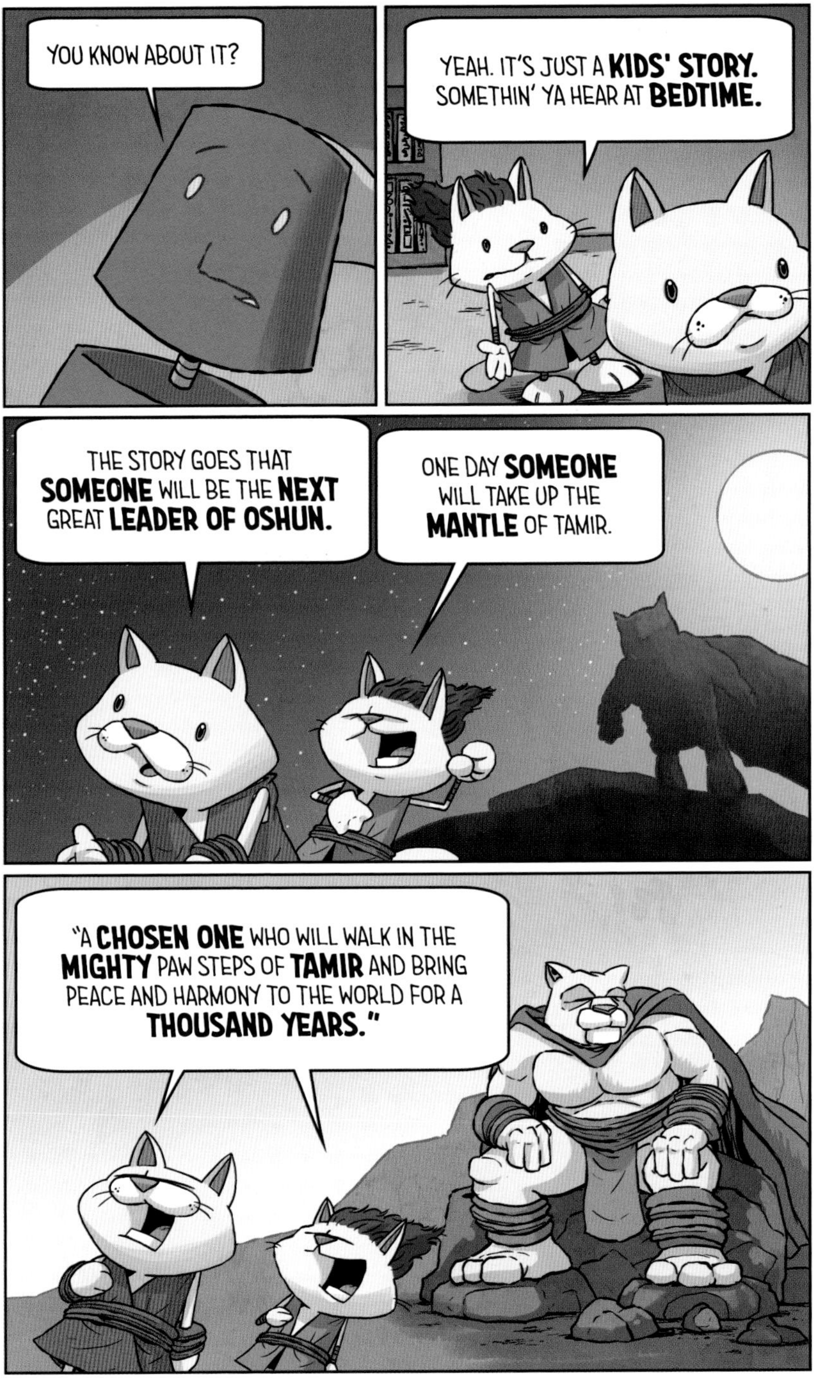
YOU KNOW ABOUT IT?
YEAH. IT'S JUST A **KIDS' STORY.** SOMETHIN' YA HEAR AT **BEDTIME.**
THE STORY GOES THAT **SOMEONE** WILL BE THE **NEXT** GREAT **LEADER OF OSHUN.**
ONE DAY **SOMEONE** WILL TAKE UP THE **MANTLE** OF TAMIR.
"A **CHOSEN ONE** WHO WILL WALK IN THE **MIGHTY** PAW STEPS OF **TAMIR** AND BRING PEACE AND HARMONY TO THE WORLD FOR A **THOUSAND YEARS.**"

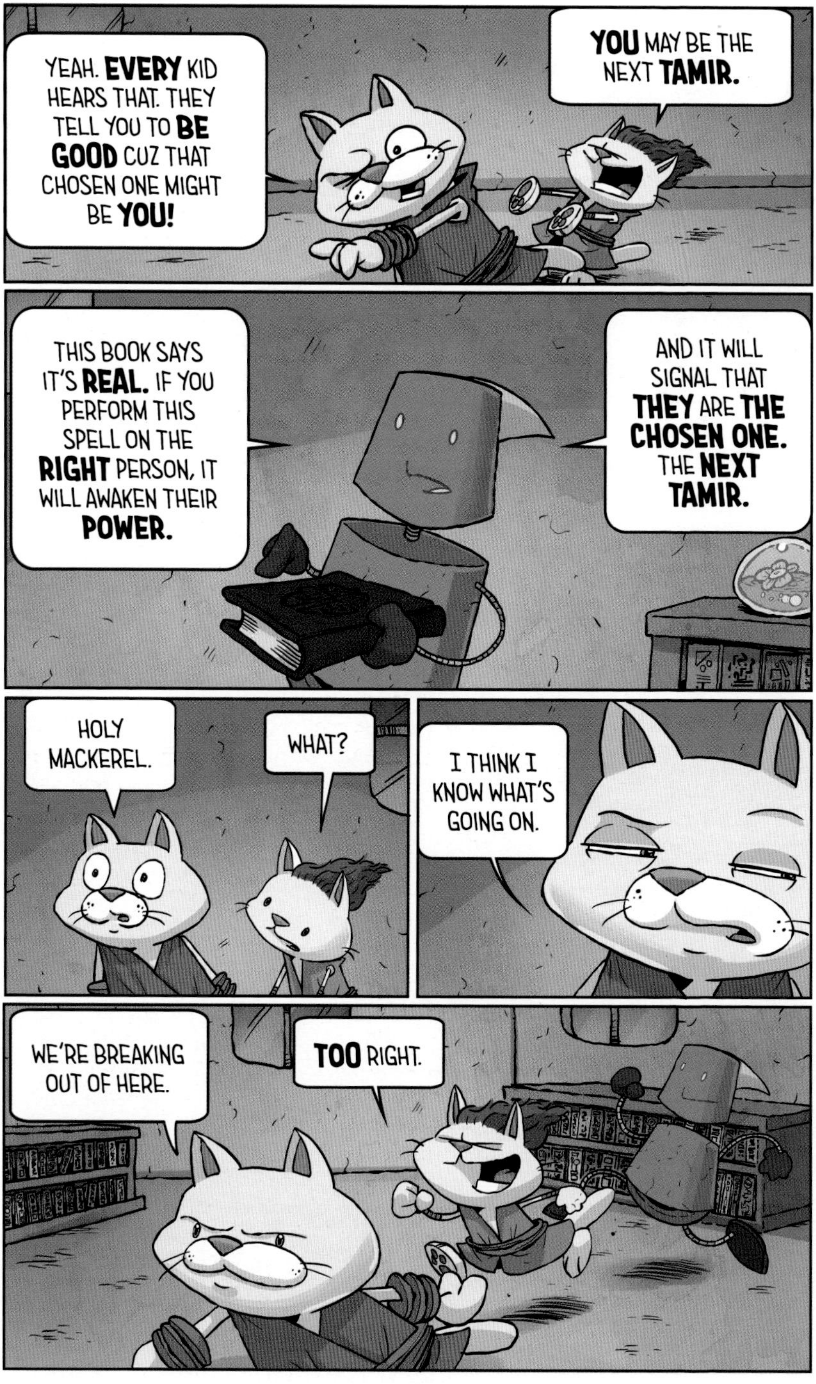
YEAH. **EVERY** KID HEARS THAT. THEY TELL YOU TO **BE GOOD** CUZ THAT CHOSEN ONE MIGHT BE **YOU!**
YOU MAY BE THE NEXT **TAMIR.**
THIS BOOK SAYS IT'S **REAL.** IF YOU PERFORM THIS SPELL ON THE **RIGHT** PERSON, IT WILL AWAKEN THEIR **POWER.**
AND IT WILL SIGNAL THAT **THEY** ARE **THE CHOSEN ONE.** THE **NEXT TAMIR.**
HOLY MACKEREL.
WHAT?
I THINK I KNOW WHAT'S GOING ON.
WE'RE BREAKING OUT OF HERE.
TOO RIGHT.

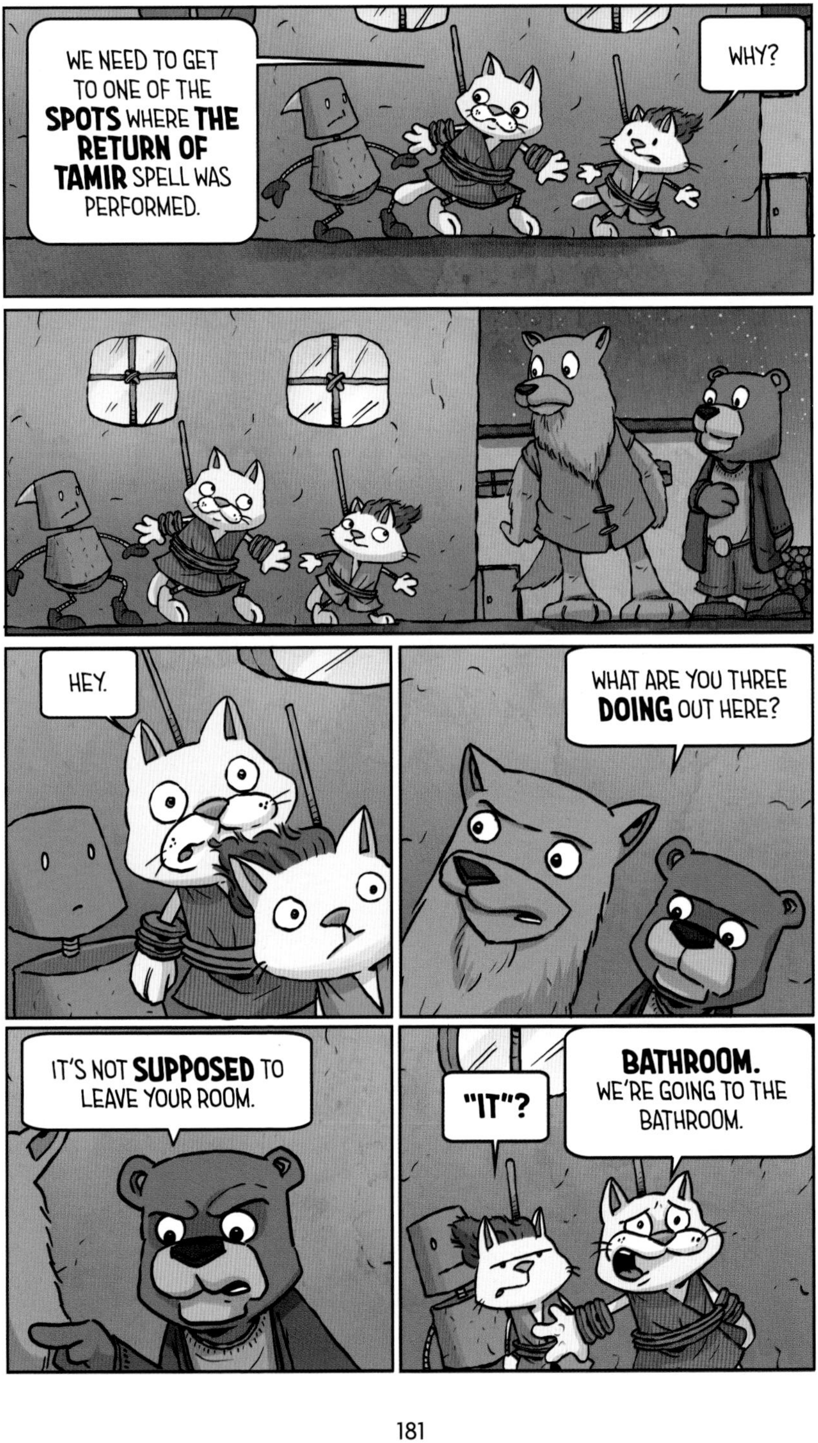
WE NEED TO GET TO ONE OF THE **SPOTS** WHERE **THE RETURN OF TAMIR** SPELL WAS PERFORMED.
WHY?
HEY.
WHAT ARE YOU THREE **DOING** OUT HERE?
IT'S NOT **SUPPOSED** TO LEAVE YOUR ROOM.
"IT"?
BATHROOM. WE'RE GOING TO THE BATHROOM.

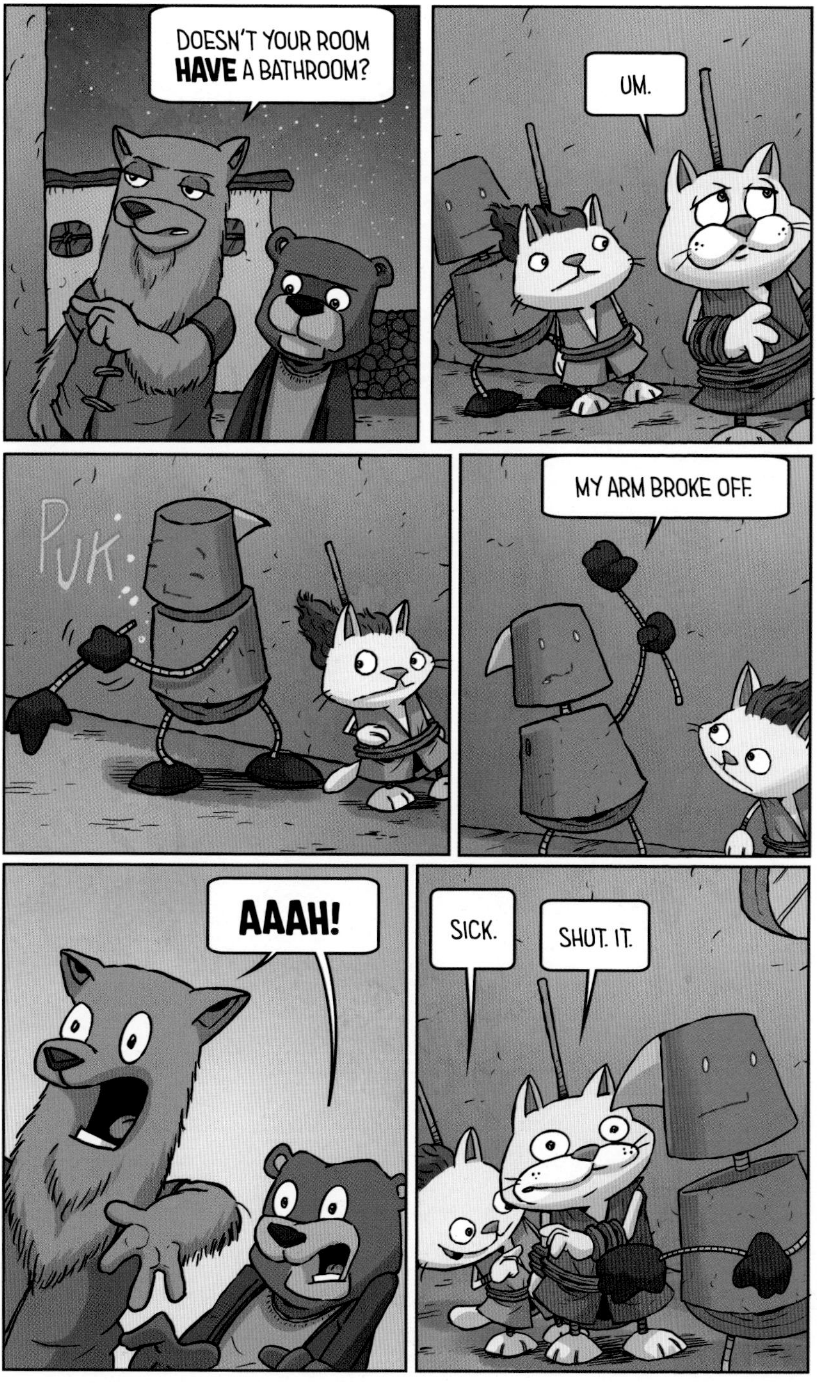
DOESN'T YOUR ROOM **HAVE** A BATHROOM?
UM.
PUK
MY ARM BROKE OFF.
AAAH!
SICK.
SHUT. IT.

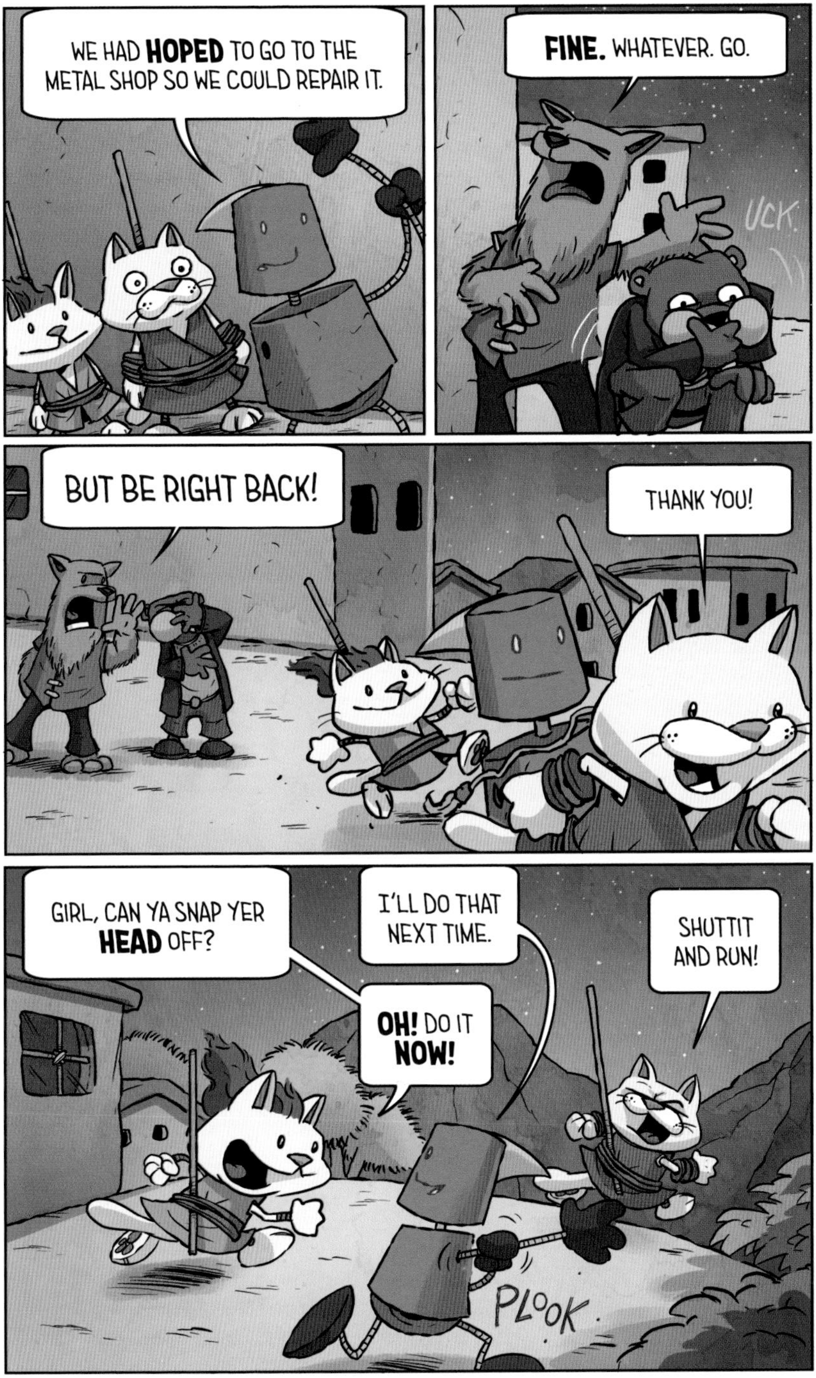

WE HAD HOPED TO GO TO THE METAL SHOP SO WE COULD REPAIR IT.
FINE. WHATEVER. GO.
UCK
BUT BE RIGHT BACK!
THANK YOU!
GIRL, CAN YA SNAP YER HEAD OFF?
I'LL DO THAT NEXT TIME.
OH! DO IT NOW!
SHUTTIT AND RUN!
PLOOK

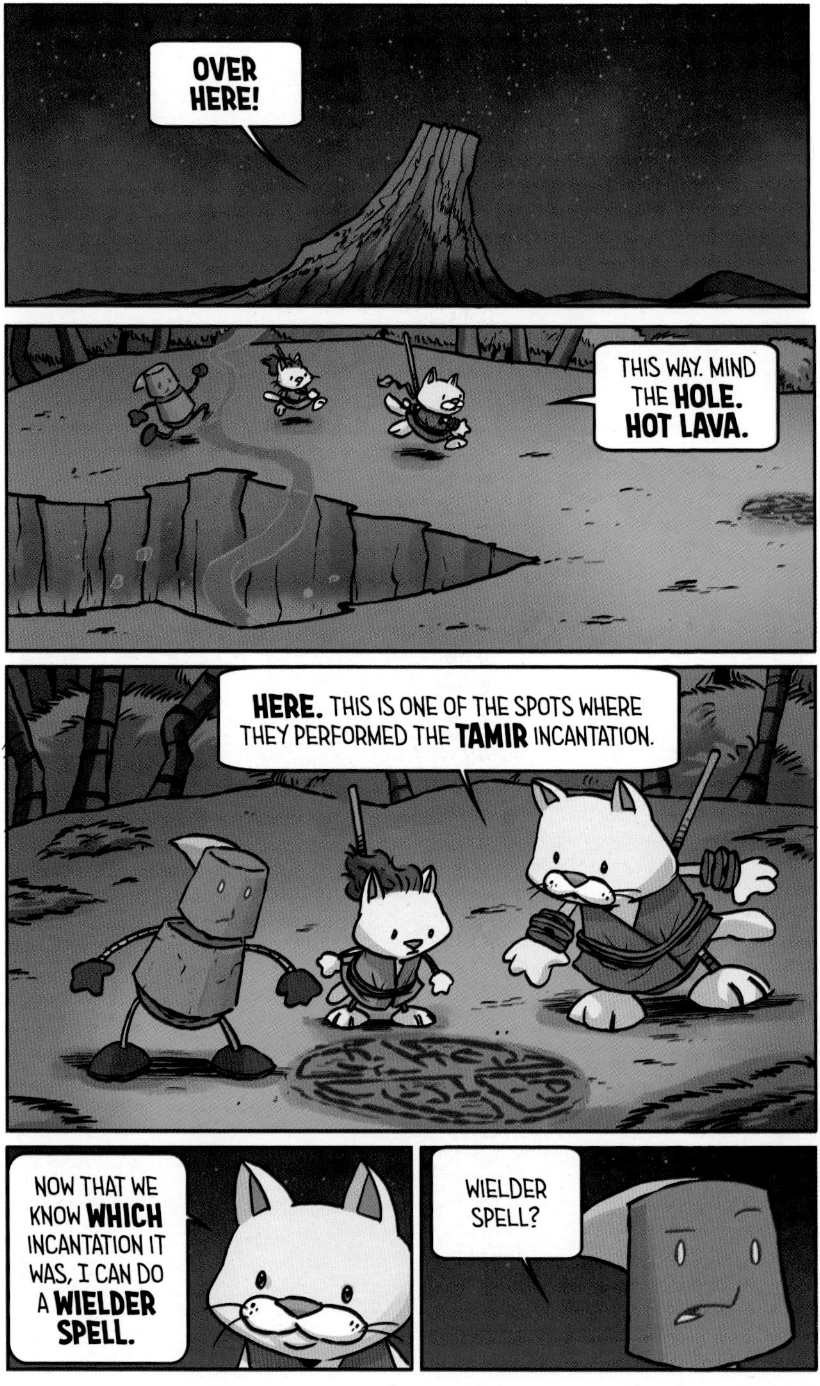

OVER HERE!
THIS WAY. MIND THE HOLE. HOT LAVA.
HERE. THIS IS ONE OF THE SPOTS WHERE THEY PERFORMED THE TAMIR INCANTATION.
NOW THAT WE KNOW WHICH INCANTATION IT WAS, I CAN DO A WIELDER SPELL.
WIELDER SPELL?

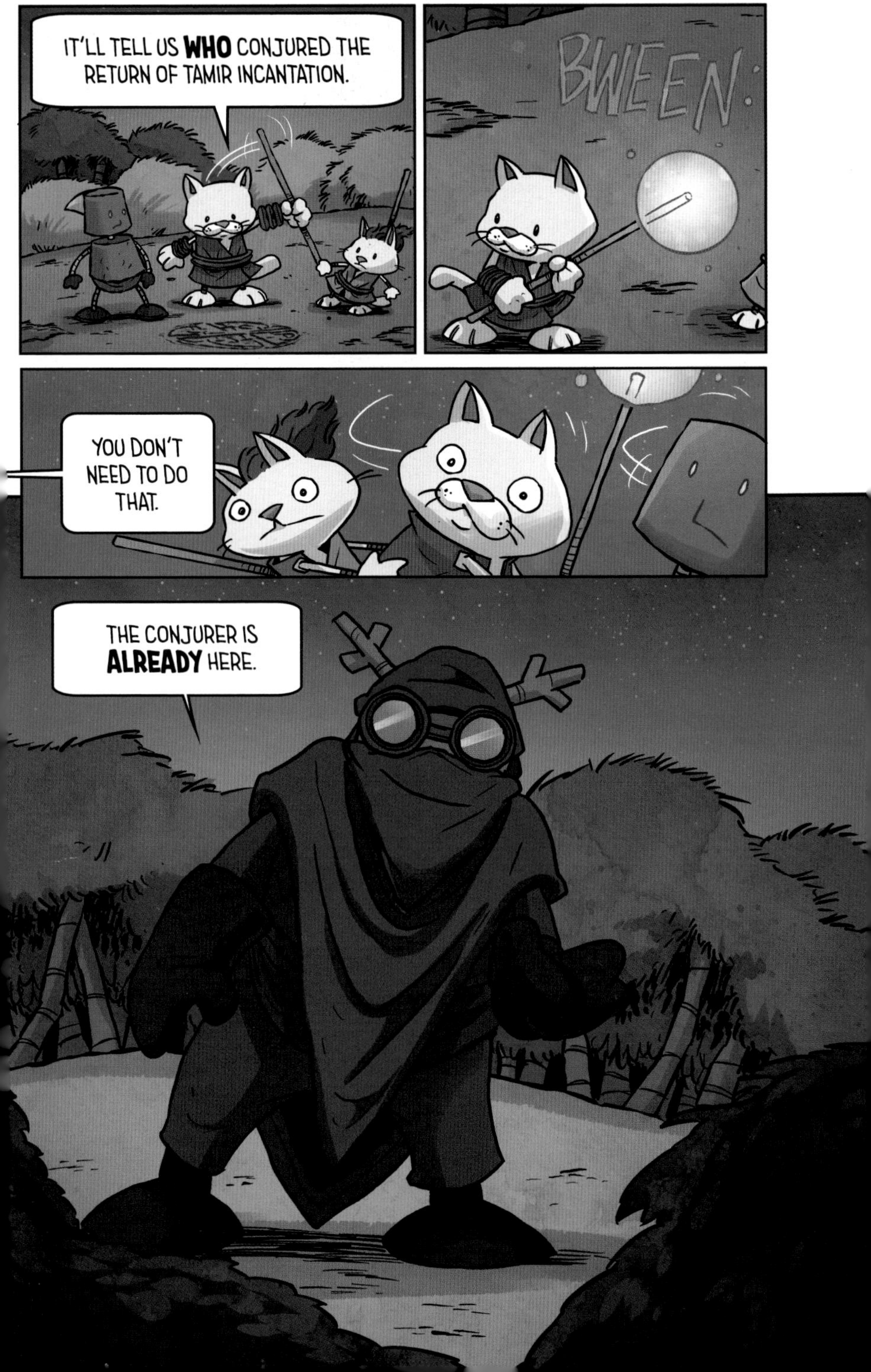
IT'LL TELL US **WHO** CONJURED THE RETURN OF TAMIR INCANTATION.
BWEEN
YOU DON'T NEED TO DO THAT.
THE CONJURER IS **ALREADY** HERE.

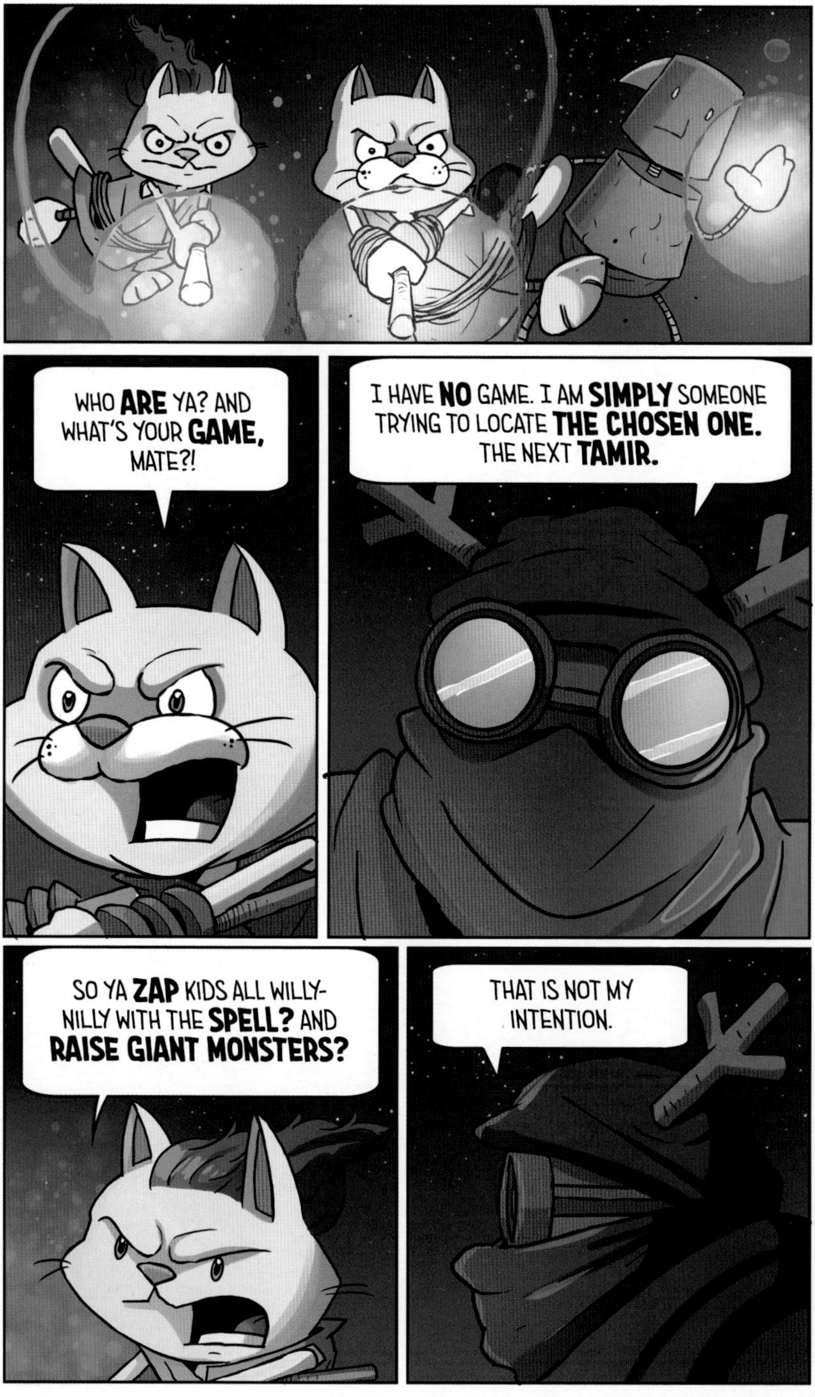
WHO ARE YA? AND WHAT'S YOUR GAME, MATE?!
I HAVE NO GAME. I AM SIMPLY SOMEONE TRYING TO LOCATE THE CHOSEN ONE. THE NEXT TAMIR.
SO YA ZAP KIDS ALL WILLY-NILLY WITH THE SPELL? AND RAISE GIANT MONSTERS?
THAT IS NOT MY INTENTION.

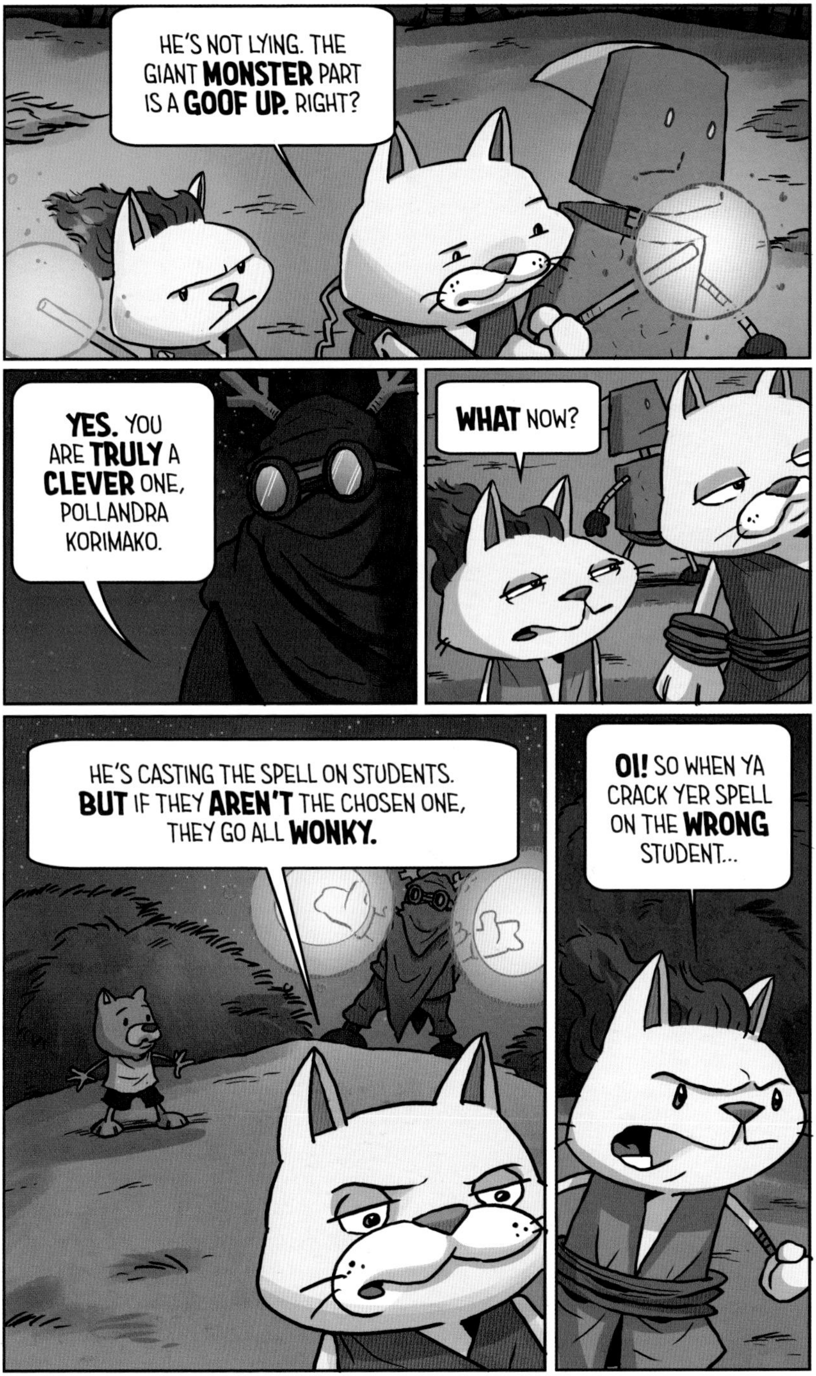
HE'S NOT LYING. THE GIANT MONSTER PART IS A GOOF UP. RIGHT?
YES. YOU ARE TRULY A CLEVER ONE, POLLANDRA KORIMAKO.
WHAT NOW?
HE'S CASTING THE SPELL ON STUDENTS. BUT IF THEY AREN'T THE CHOSEN ONE, THEY GO ALL WONKY.
OI! SO WHEN YA CRACK YER SPELL ON THE WRONG STUDENT...

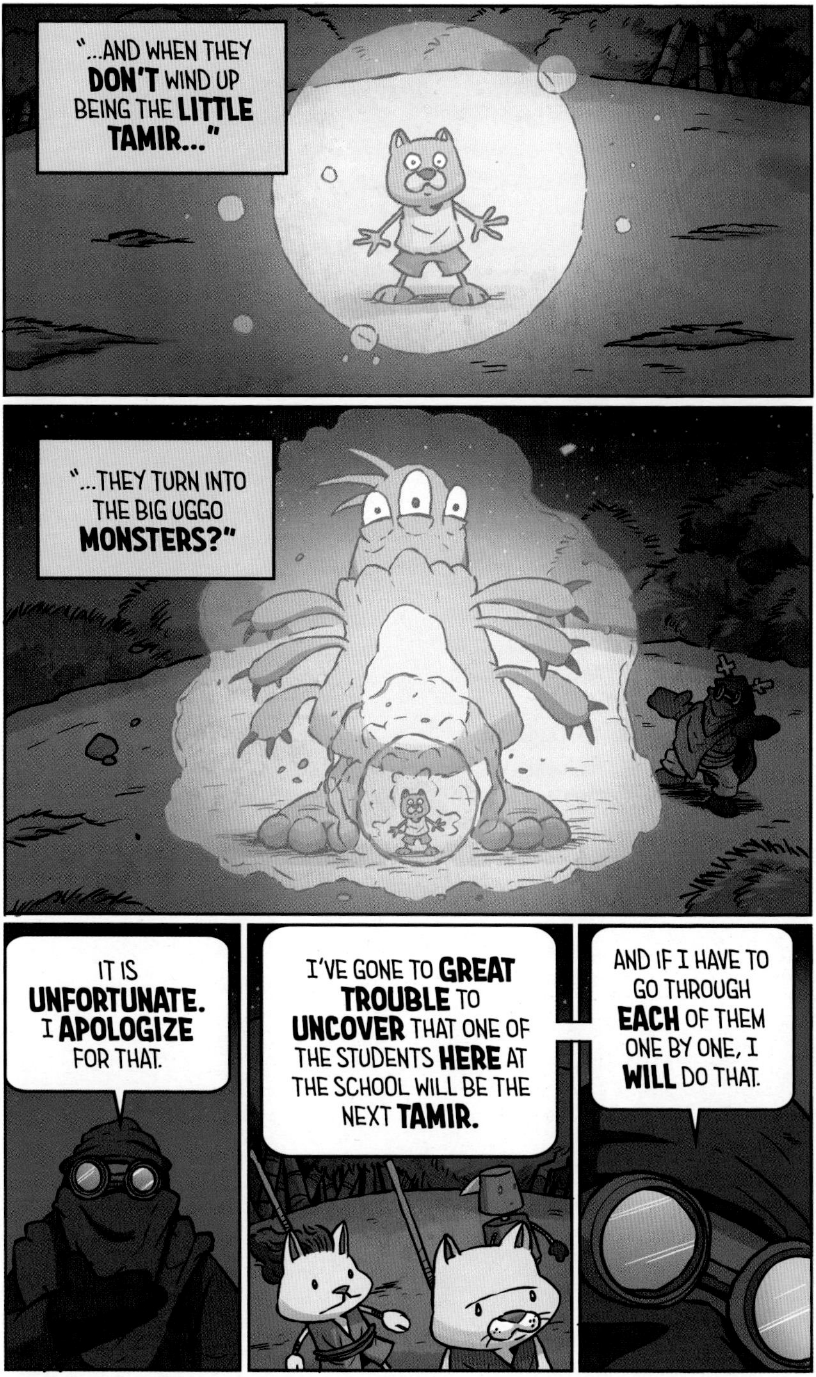
"...AND WHEN THEY DON'T WIND UP BEING THE LITTLE TAMIR..."
"...THEY TURN INTO THE BIG UGGO MONSTERS?"
IT IS UNFORTUNATE. I APOLOGIZE FOR THAT.
I'VE GONE TO GREAT TROUBLE TO UNCOVER THAT ONE OF THE STUDENTS HERE AT THE SCHOOL WILL BE THE NEXT TAMIR.
AND IF I HAVE TO GO THROUGH EACH OF THEM ONE BY ONE, I WILL DO THAT.

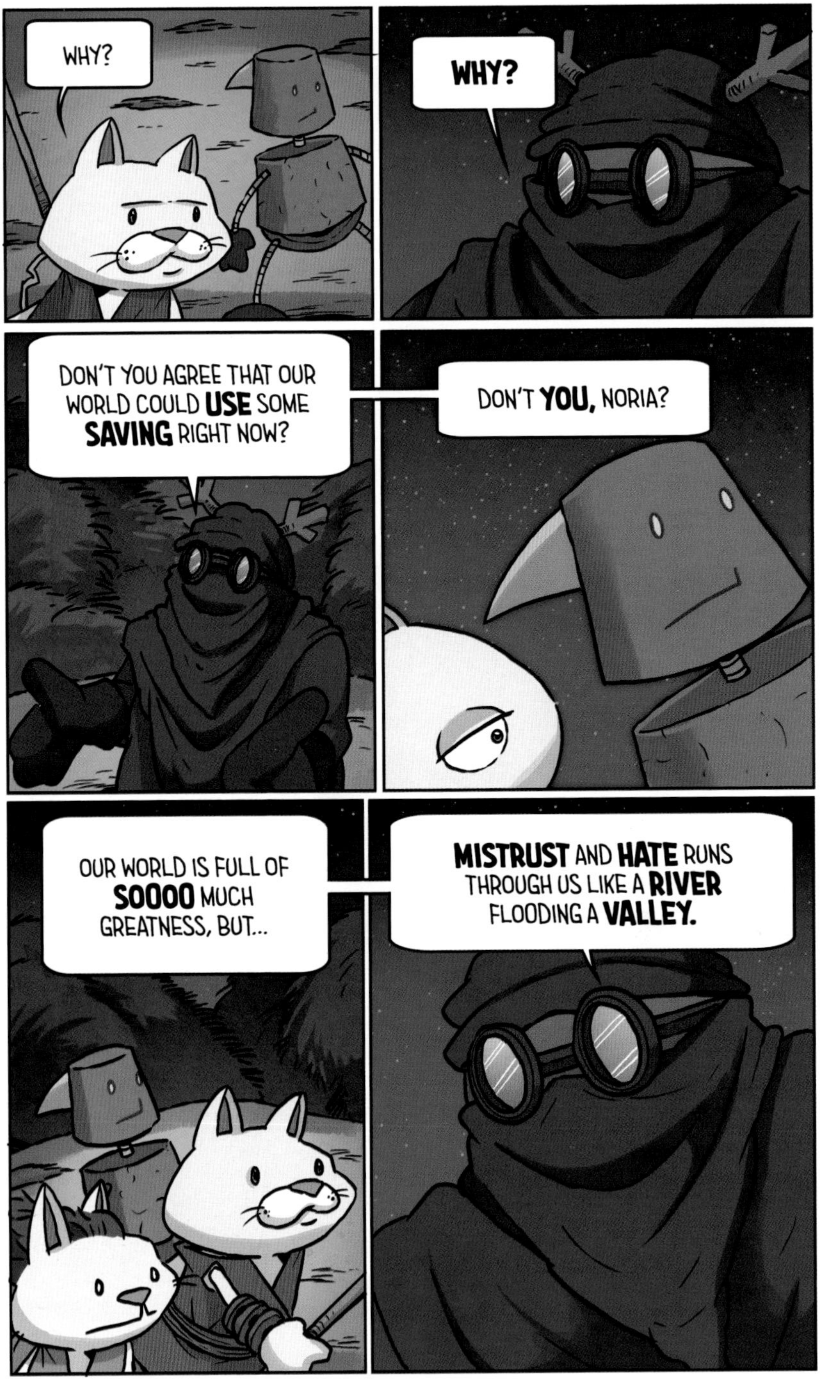

WHY?
WHY?
DON'T YOU AGREE THAT OUR WORLD COULD **USE** SOME **SAVING** RIGHT NOW?
DON'T **YOU,** NORIA?
OUR WORLD IS FULL OF **SOOOO** MUCH GREATNESS, BUT...
MISTRUST AND **HATE** RUNS THROUGH US LIKE A **RIVER** FLOODING A **VALLEY.**

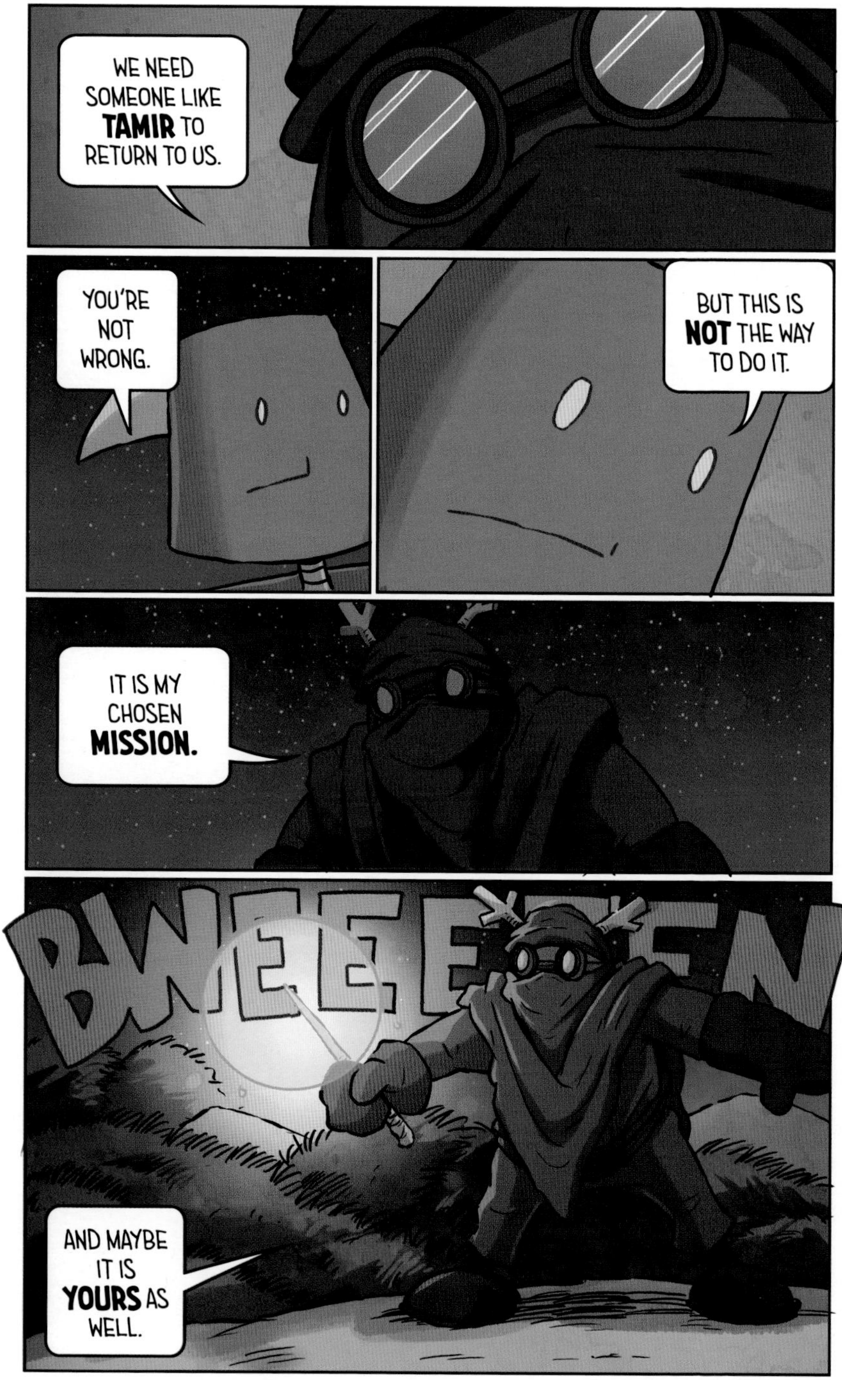
WE NEED SOMEONE LIKE **TAMIR** TO RETURN TO US.
YOU'RE NOT WRONG.
BUT THIS IS **NOT** THE WAY TO DO IT.
IT IS MY CHOSEN **MISSION.**
AND MAYBE IT IS **YOURS** AS WELL.

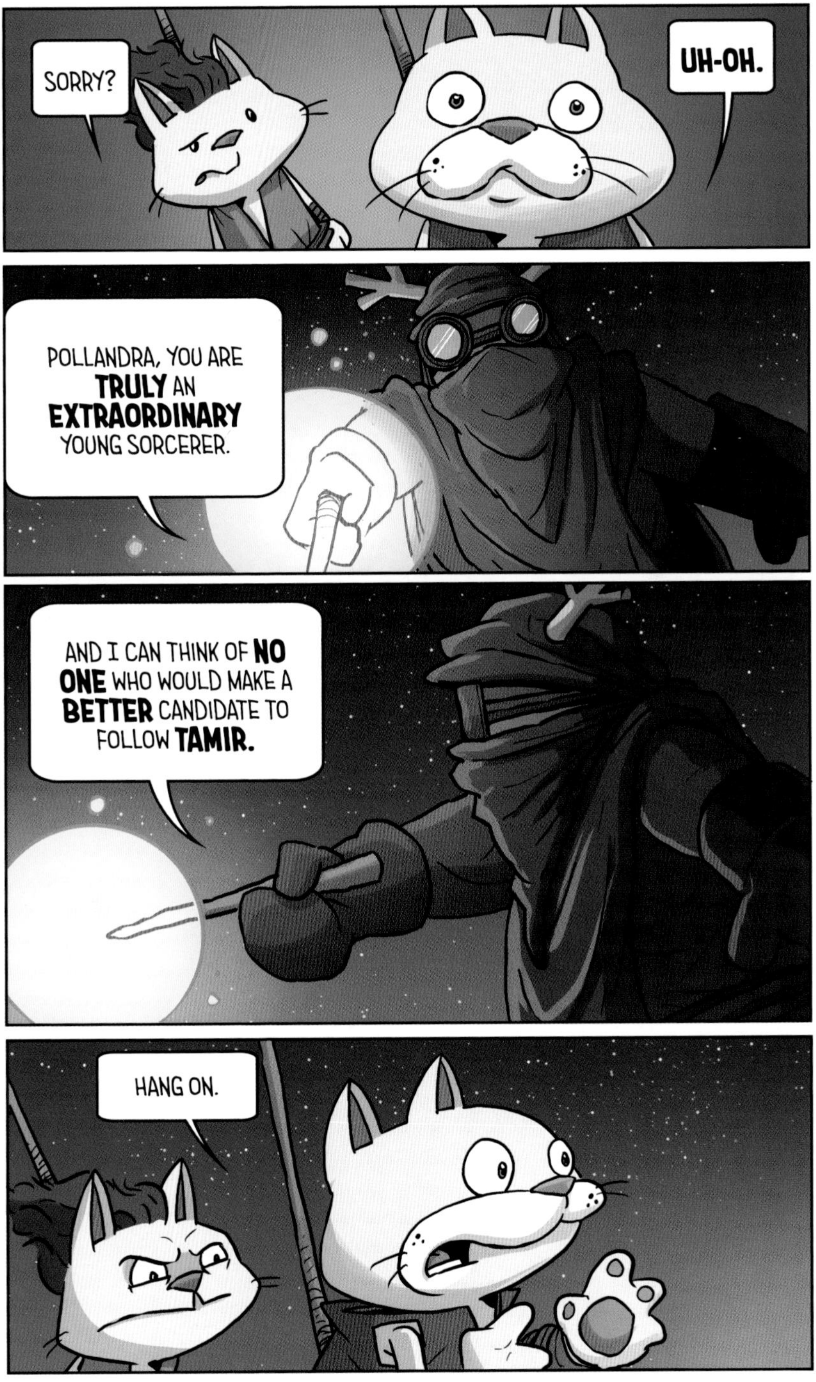
SORRY?
UH-OH.
POLLANDRA, YOU ARE **TRULY** AN **EXTRAORDINARY** YOUNG SORCERER.
AND I CAN THINK OF **NO ONE** WHO WOULD MAKE A **BETTER** CANDIDATE TO FOLLOW **TAMIR.**
HANG ON.

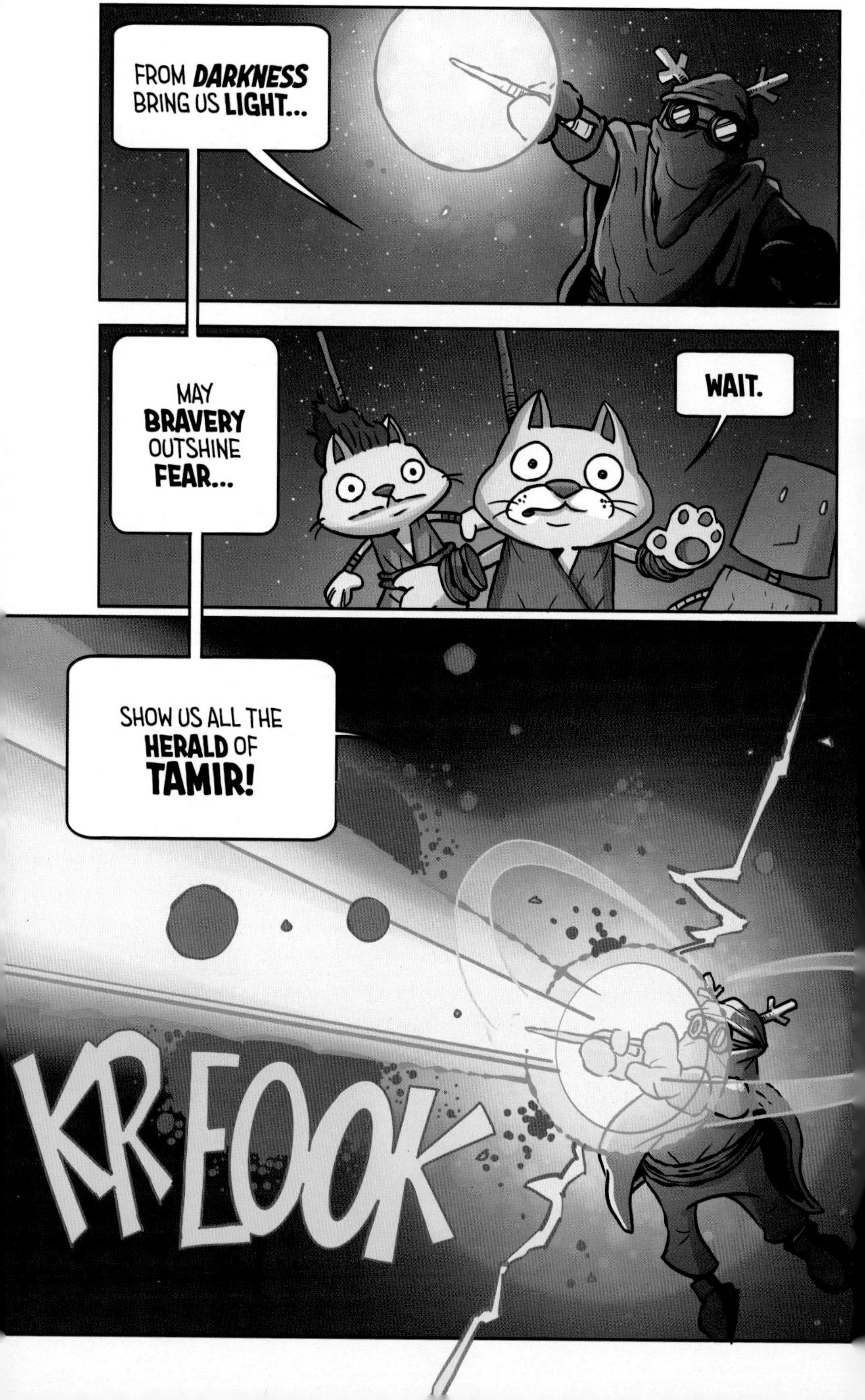
FROM DARKNESS BRING US LIGHT...
MAY BRAVERY OUTSHINE FEAR...
WAIT.
SHOW US ALL THE HERALD OF TAMIR!
KREOOK

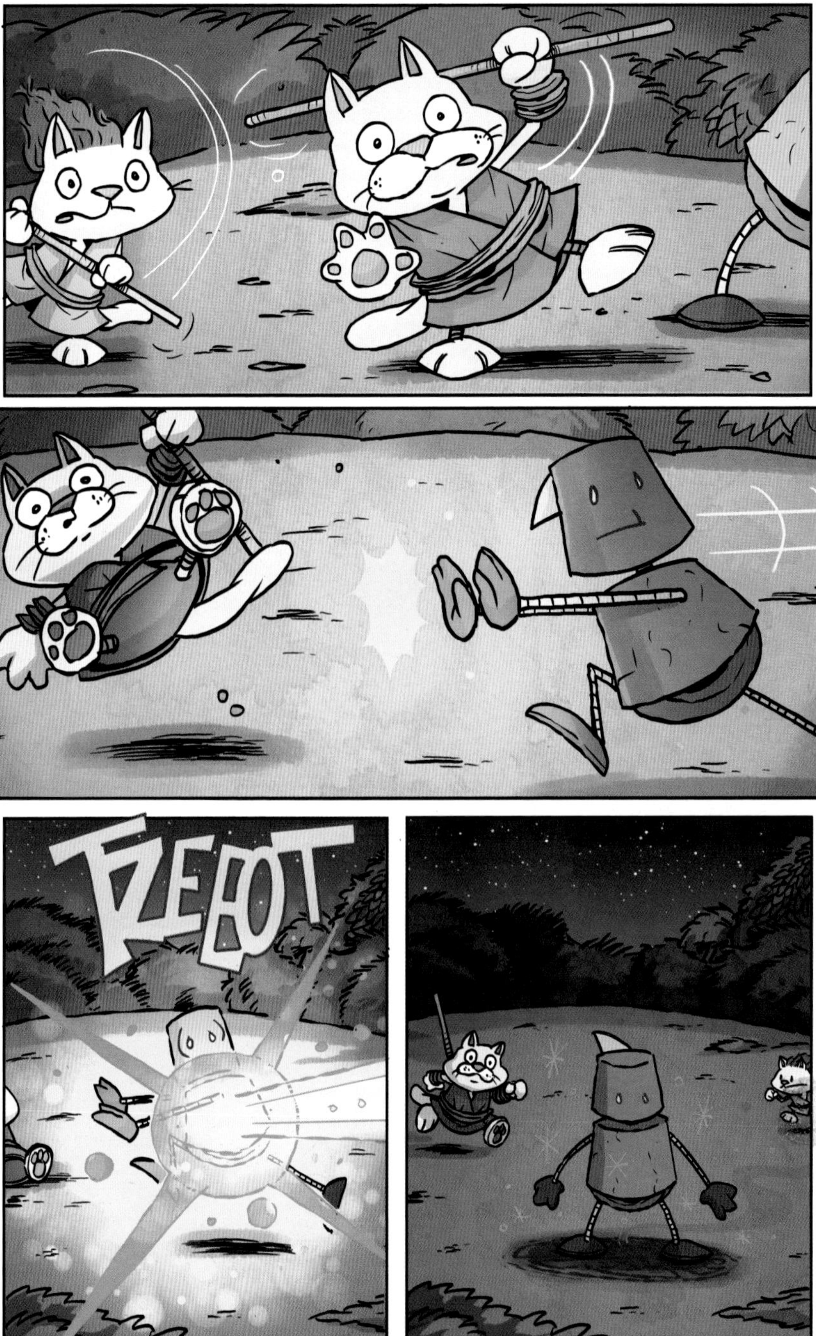
TZEEOT

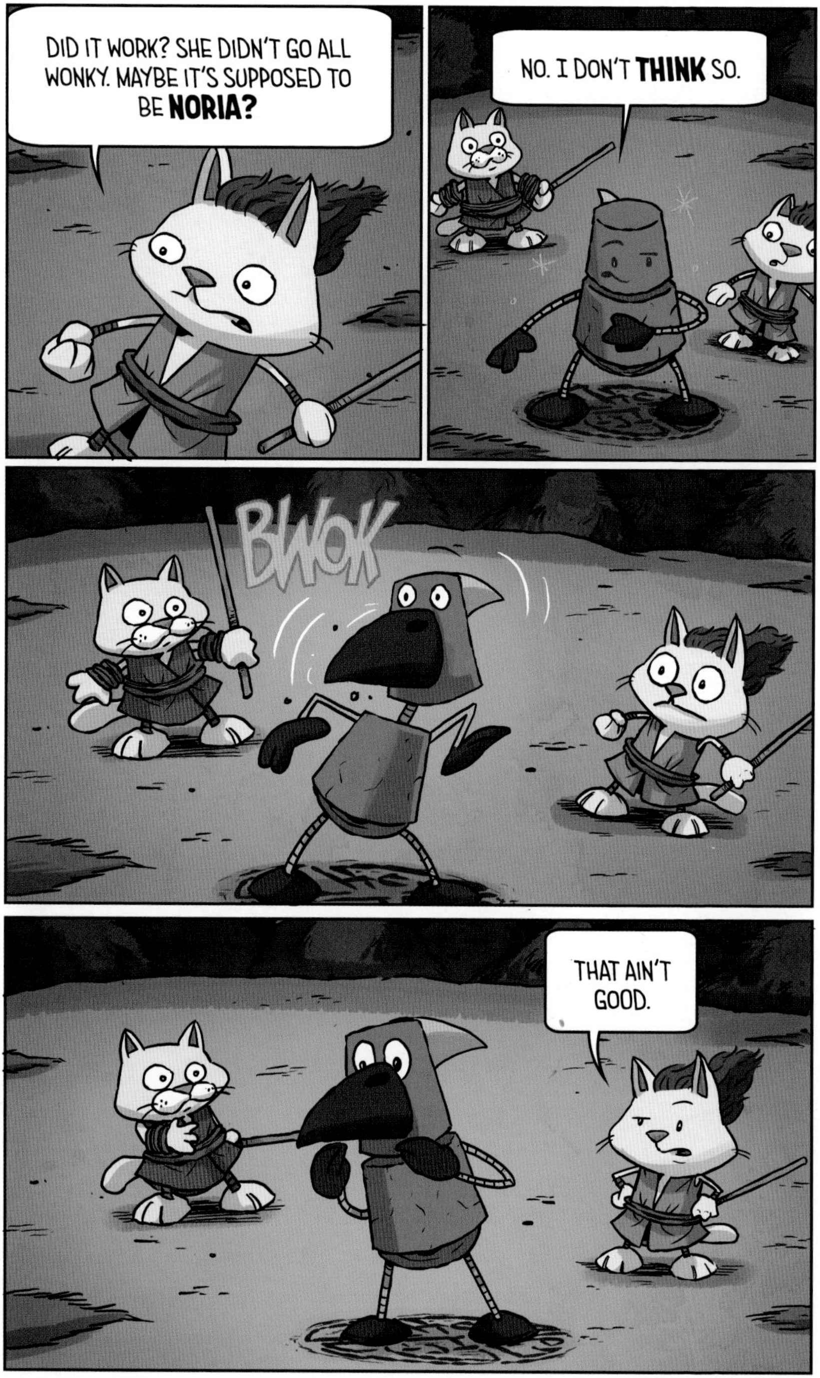
DID IT WORK? SHE DIDN'T GO ALL WONKY. MAYBE IT'S SUPPOSED TO BE **NORIA?**
NO. I DON'T **THINK** SO.
BWOK
THAT AIN'T GOOD.

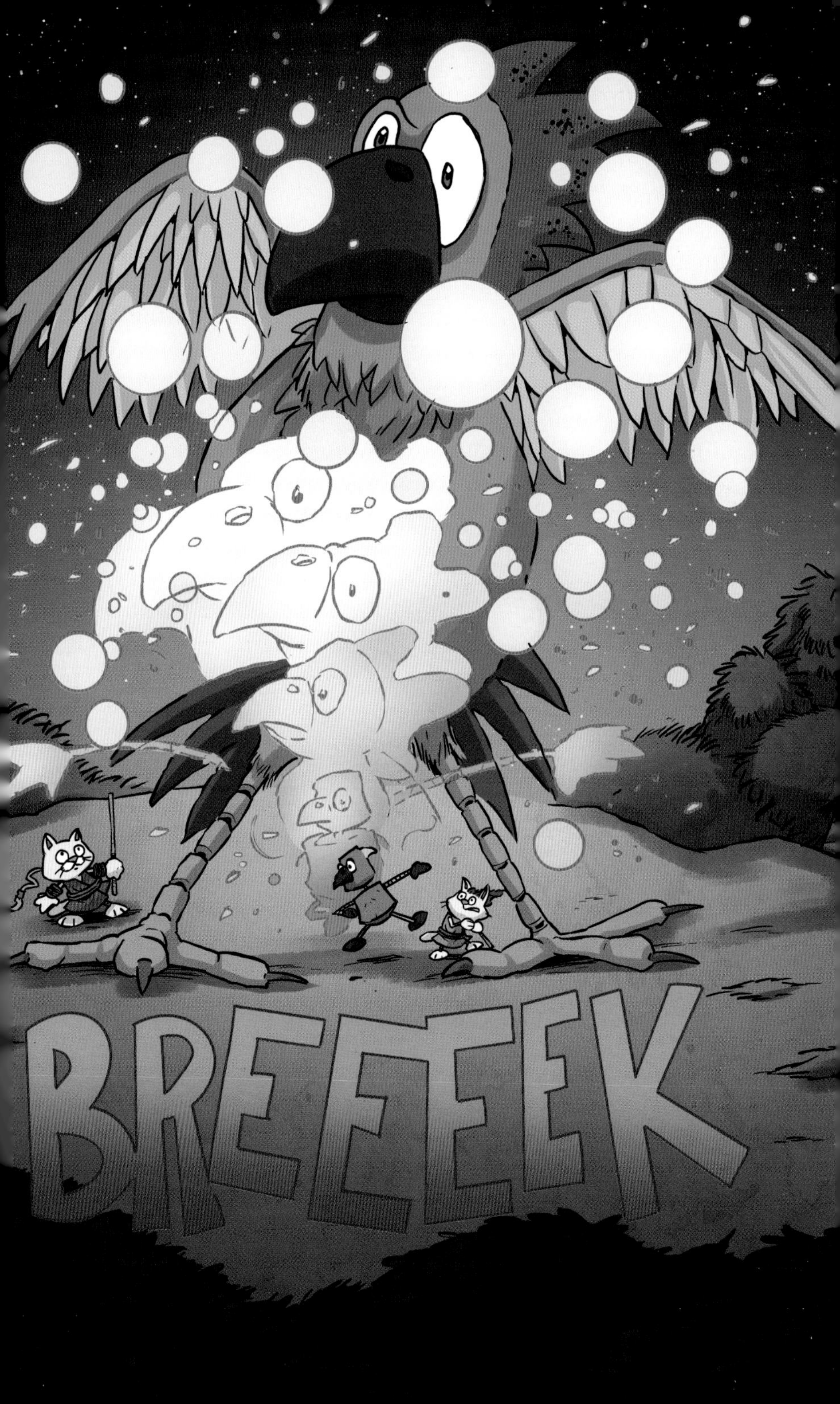
BREEEK

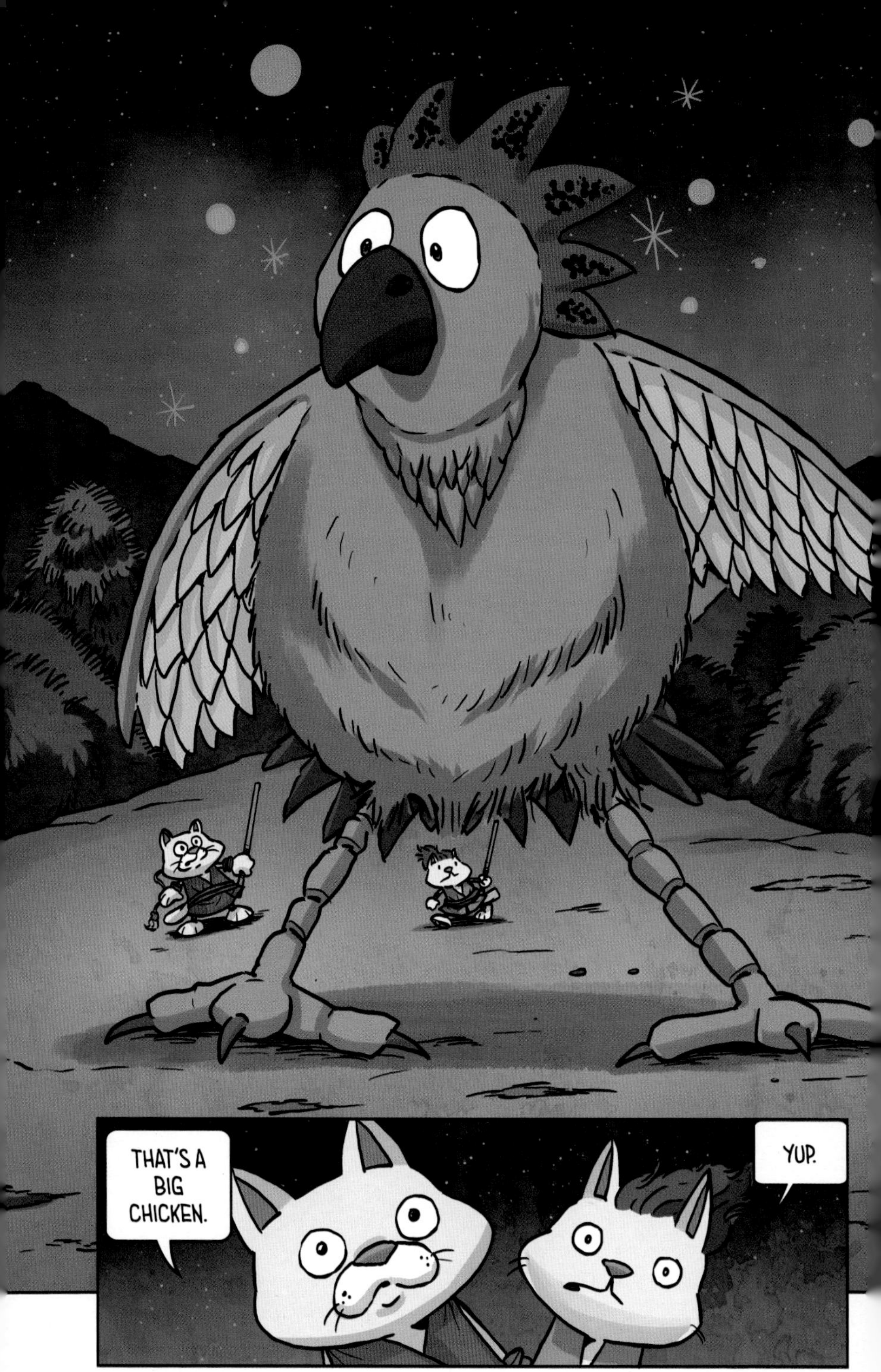
THAT'S A BIG CHICKEN.
YUP.

CHAPTER 11

BIG CHICKEN

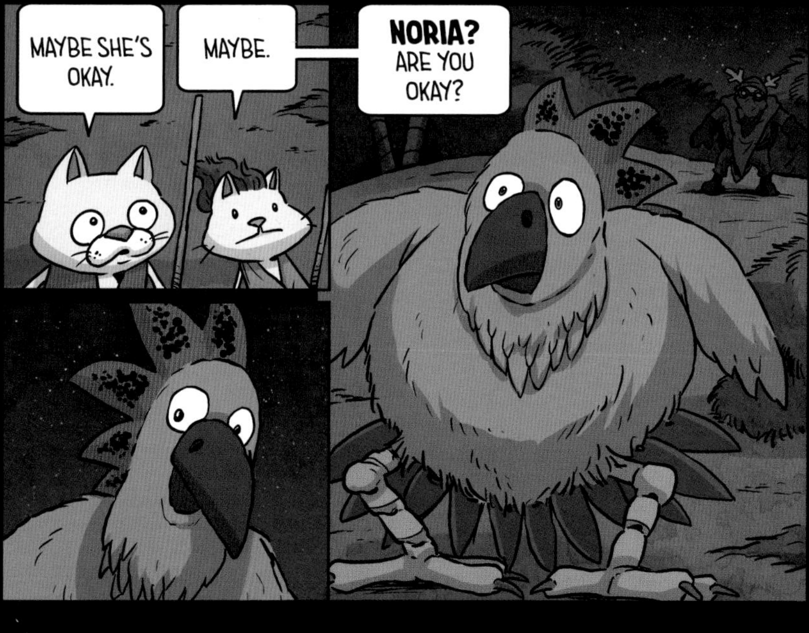
MAYBE SHE'S OKAY.
MAYBE.
NORIA? ARE YOU OKAY?

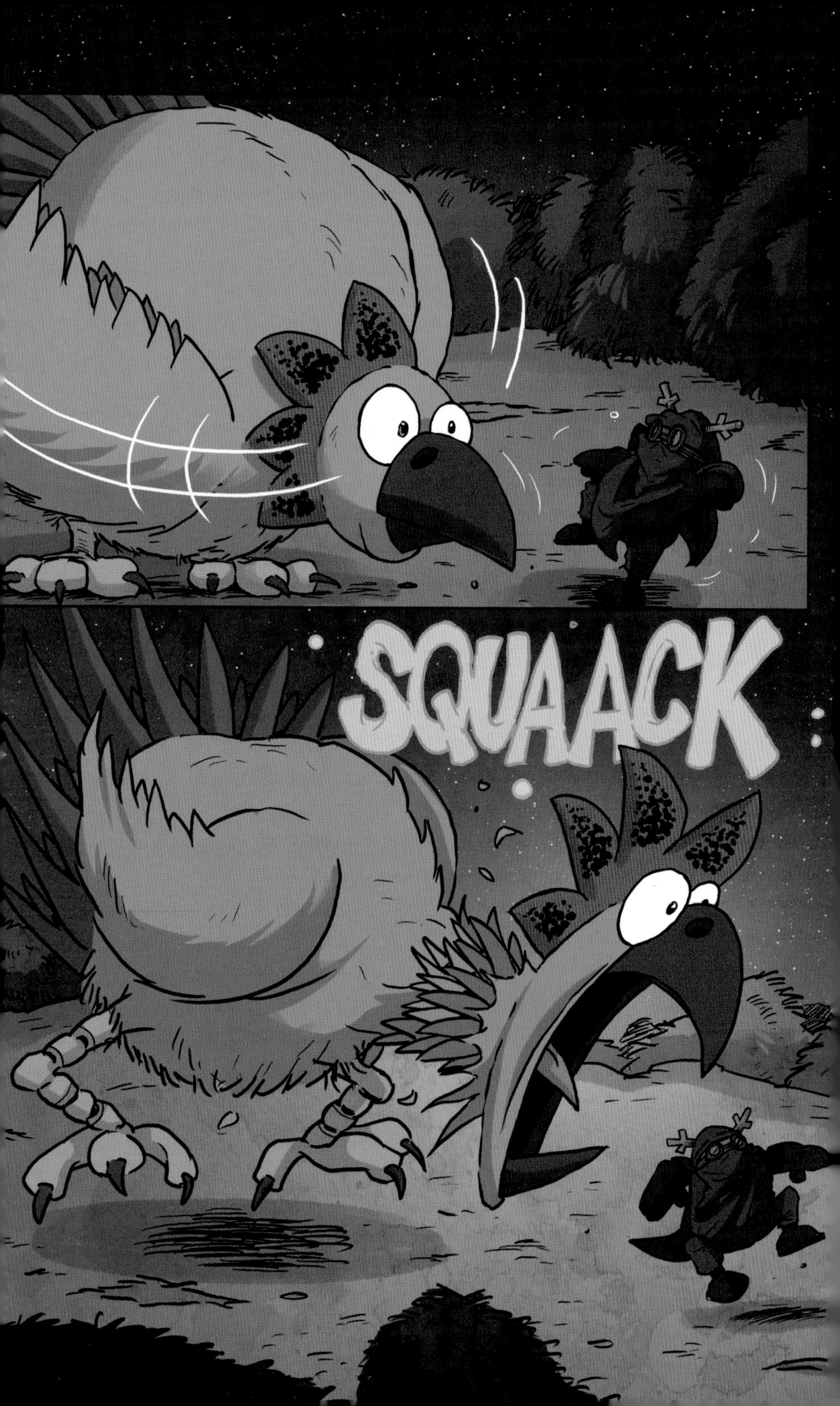
SQUAACK

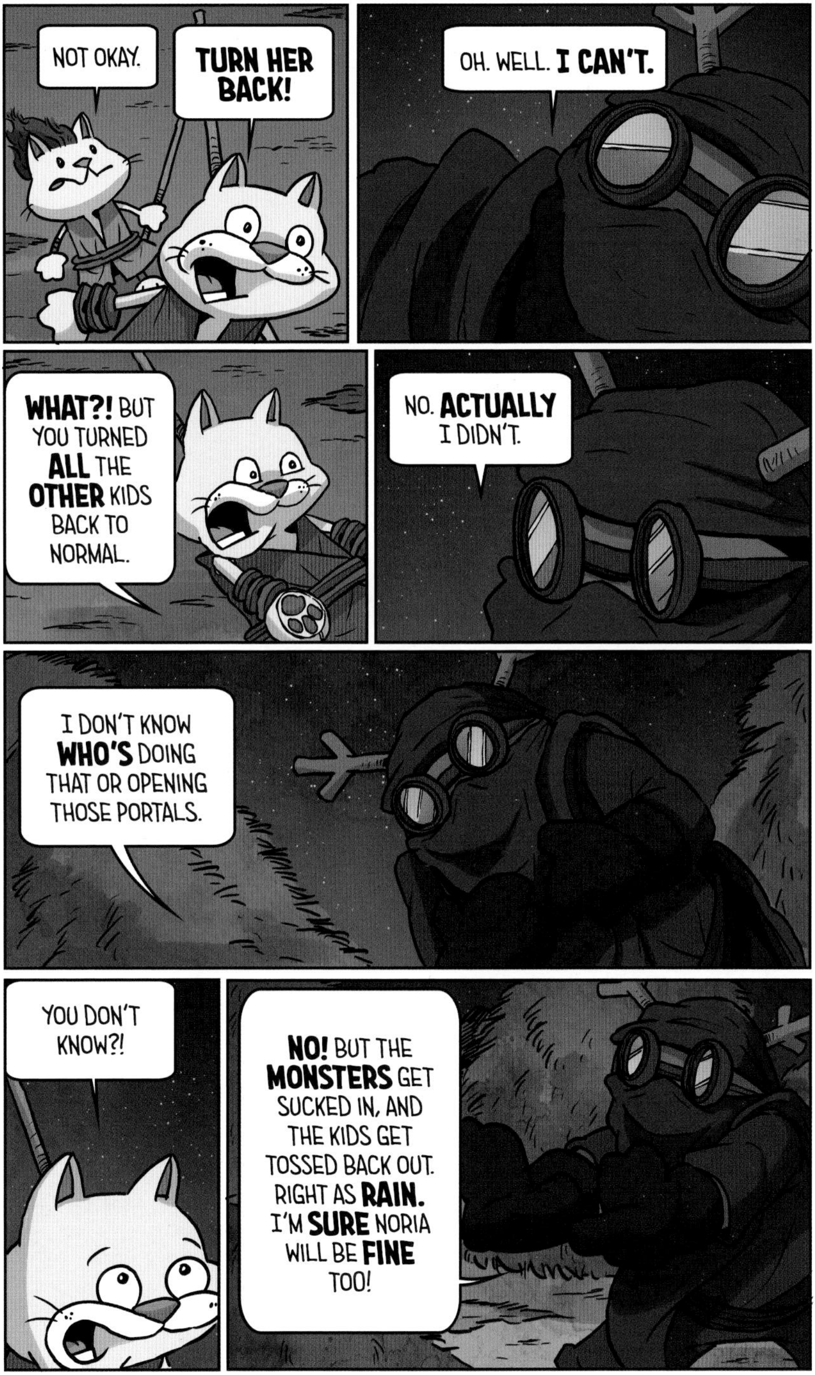
NOT OKAY.
TURN HER BACK!
OH. WELL. I CAN'T.
WHAT?! BUT YOU TURNED ALL THE OTHER KIDS BACK TO NORMAL.
NO. ACTUALLY I DIDN'T.
I DON'T KNOW WHO'S DOING THAT OR OPENING THOSE PORTALS.
YOU DON'T KNOW?!
NO! BUT THE MONSTERS GET SUCKED IN, AND THE KIDS GET TOSSED BACK OUT. RIGHT AS RAIN. I'M SURE NORIA WILL BE FINE TOO!

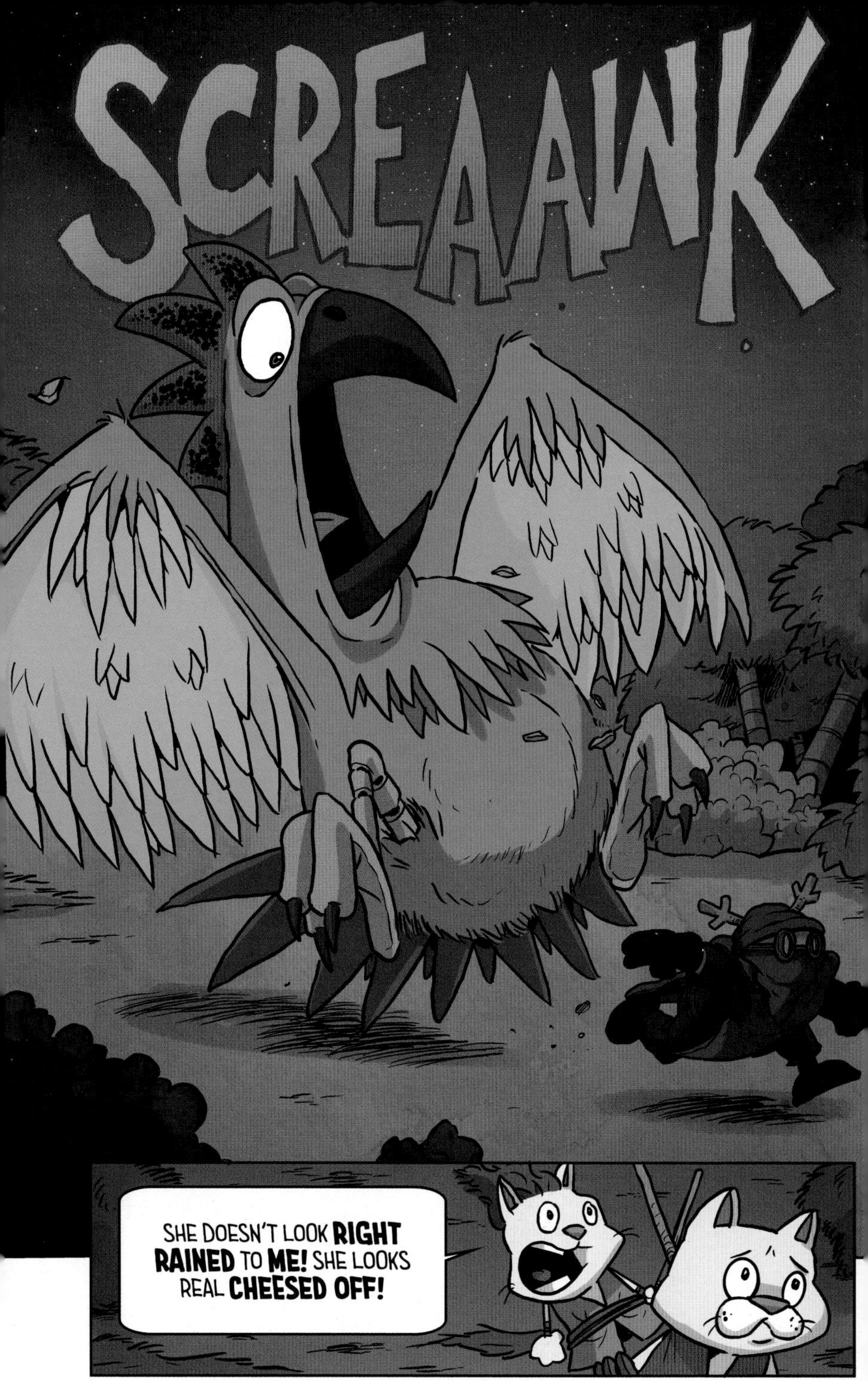
SCREAAWK
SHE DOESN'T LOOK **RIGHT RAINED** TO **ME!** SHE LOOKS REAL **CHEESED OFF!**

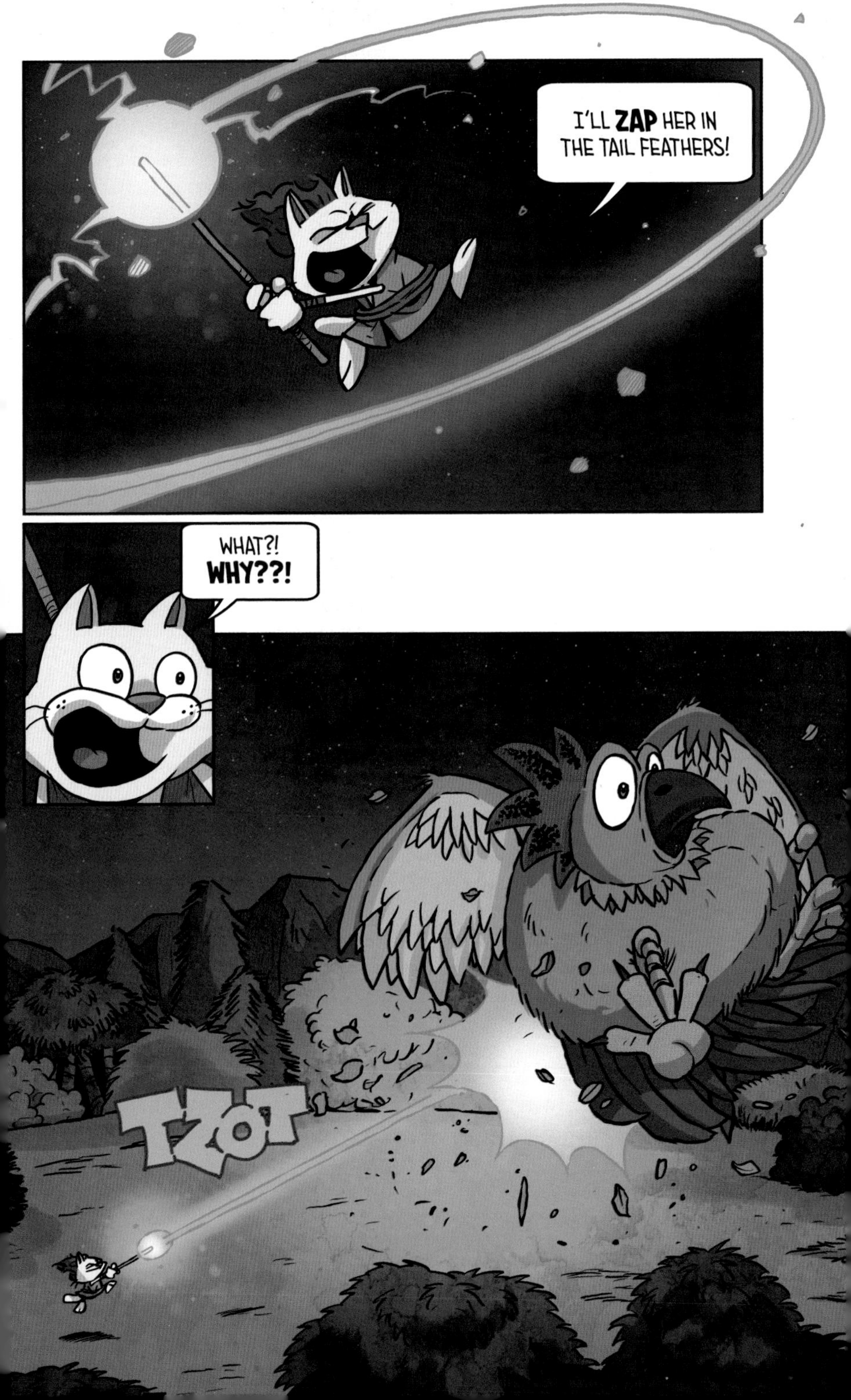
I'LL **ZAP** HER IN THE TAIL FEATHERS!
WHAT?! **WHY??!**
TZOT

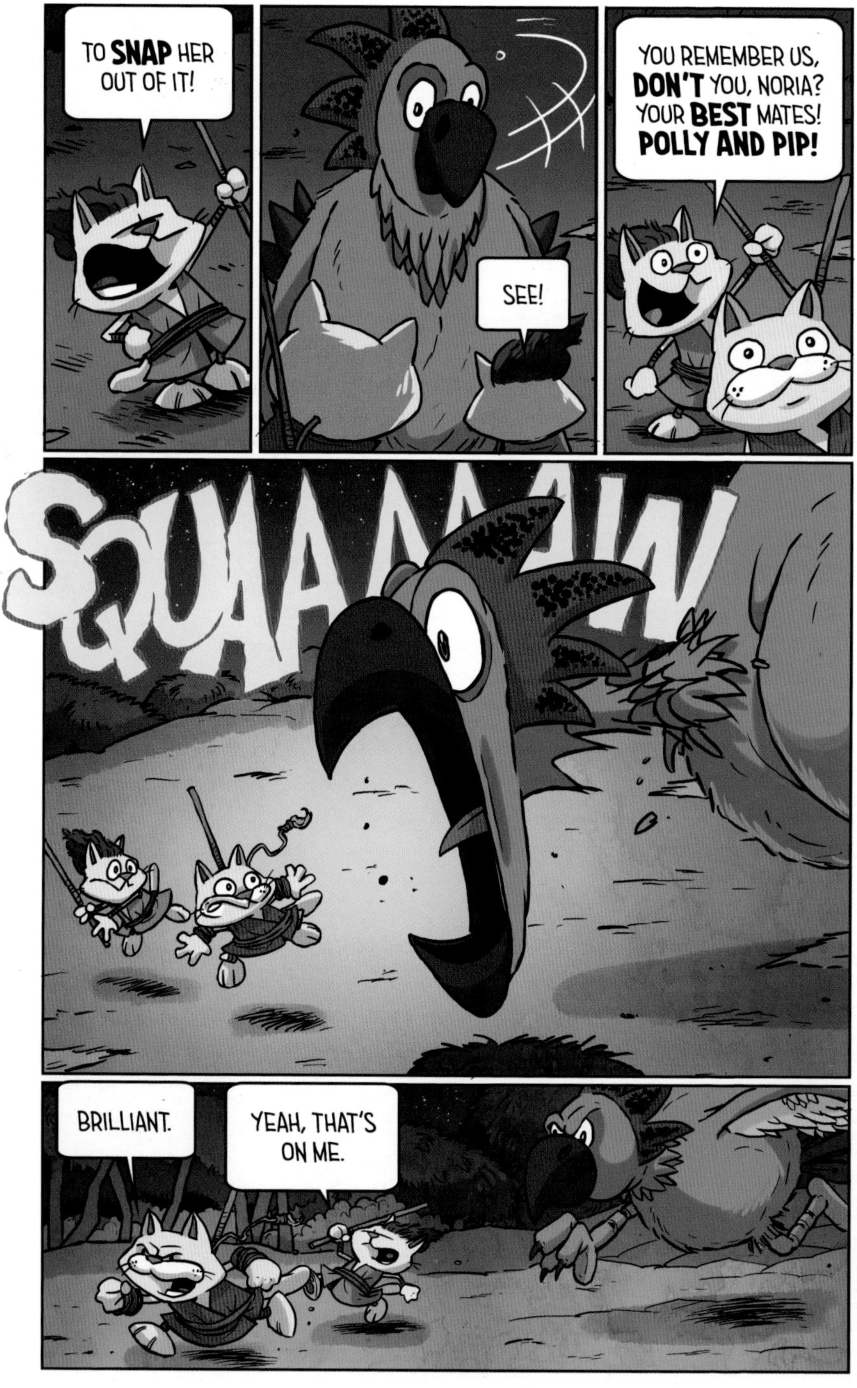
TO SNAP HER OUT OF IT!
SEE!
YOU REMEMBER US, DON'T YOU, NORIA? YOUR BEST MATES! POLLY AND PIP!
SQUAAAAW
BRILLIANT.
YEAH, THAT'S ON ME.

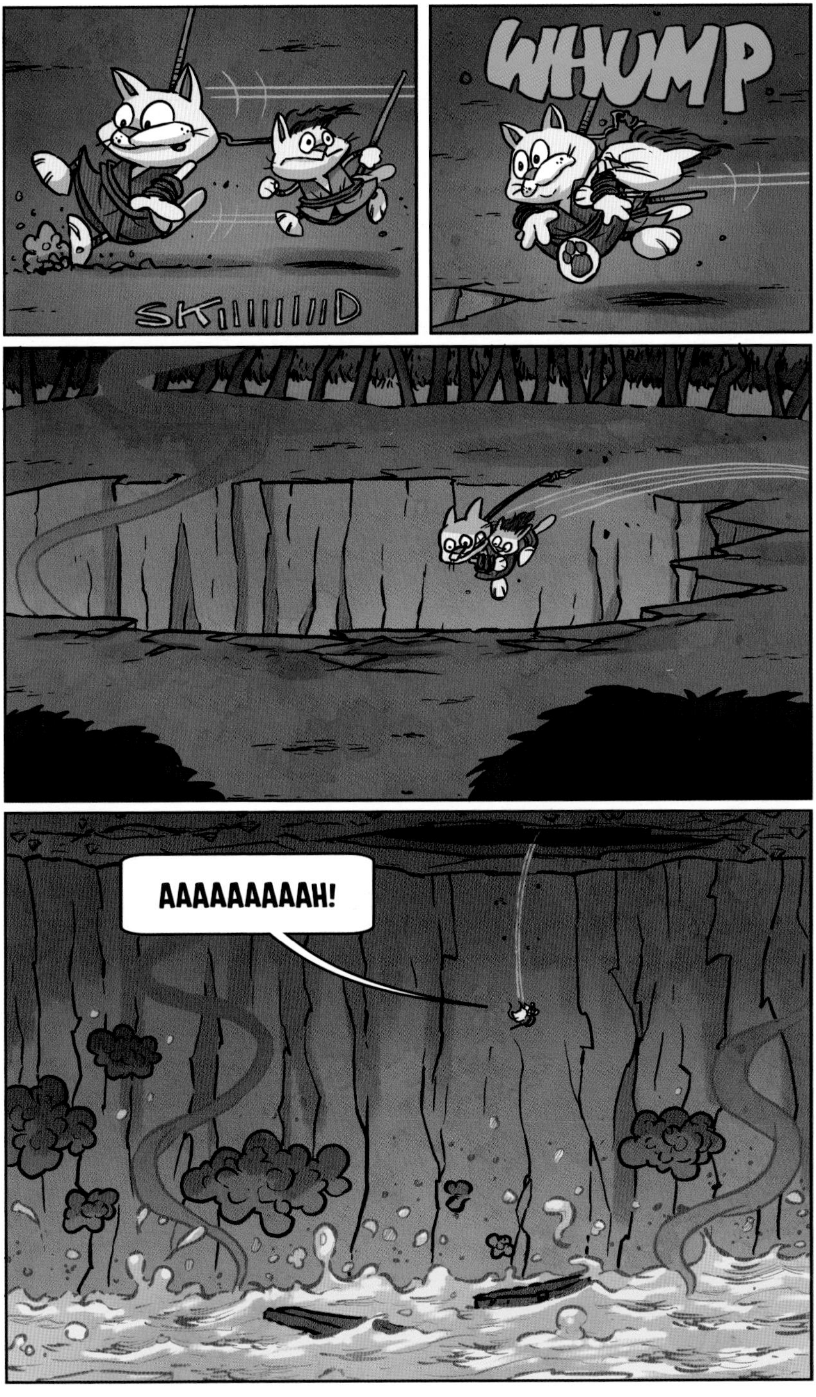
SKIIIIIIID
WHUMP
AAAAAAAAAH!

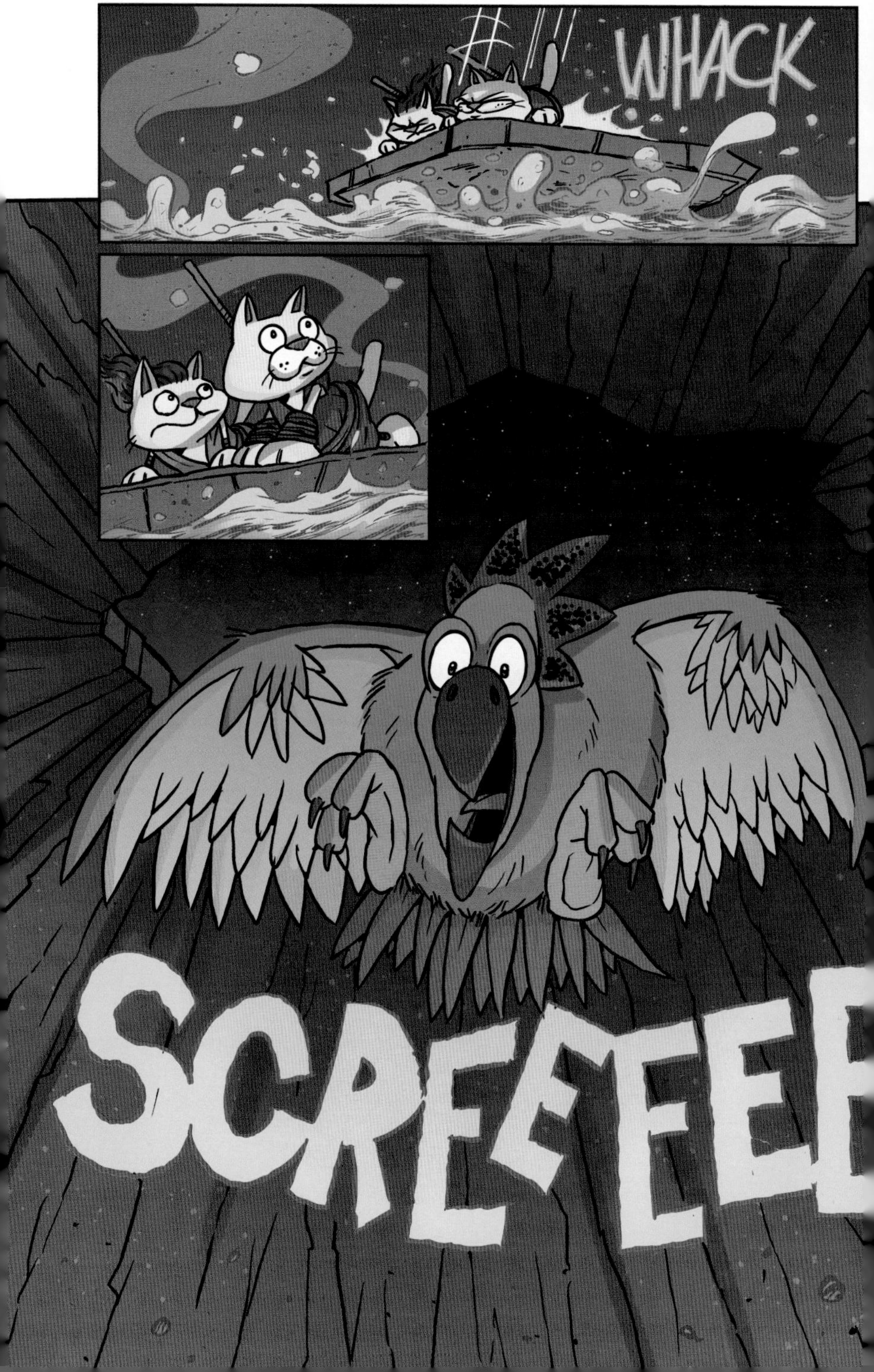
WHACK
SCREEEE

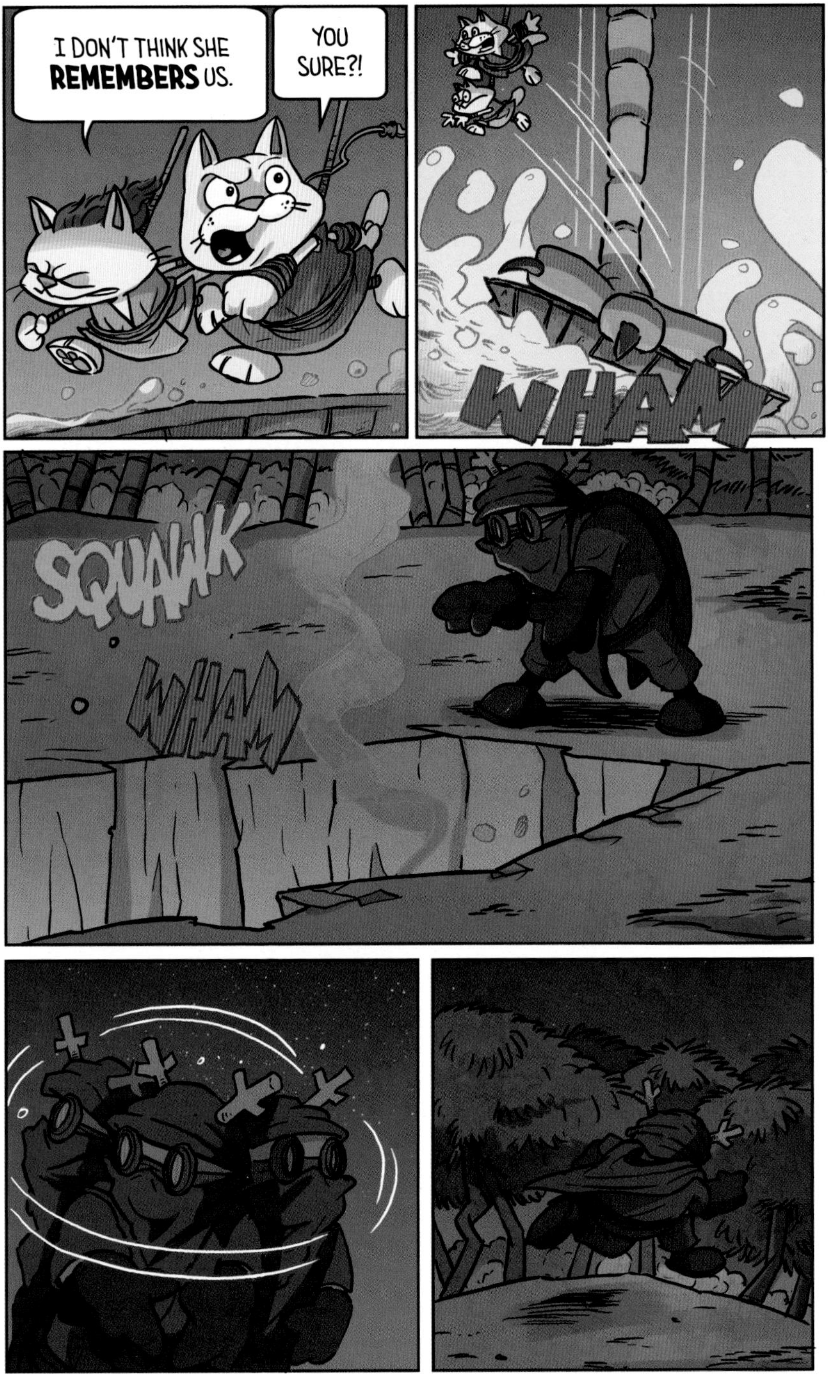
I DON'T THINK SHE **REMEMBERS** US.
YOU SURE?!
WHAM
SQUAWK
WHAM

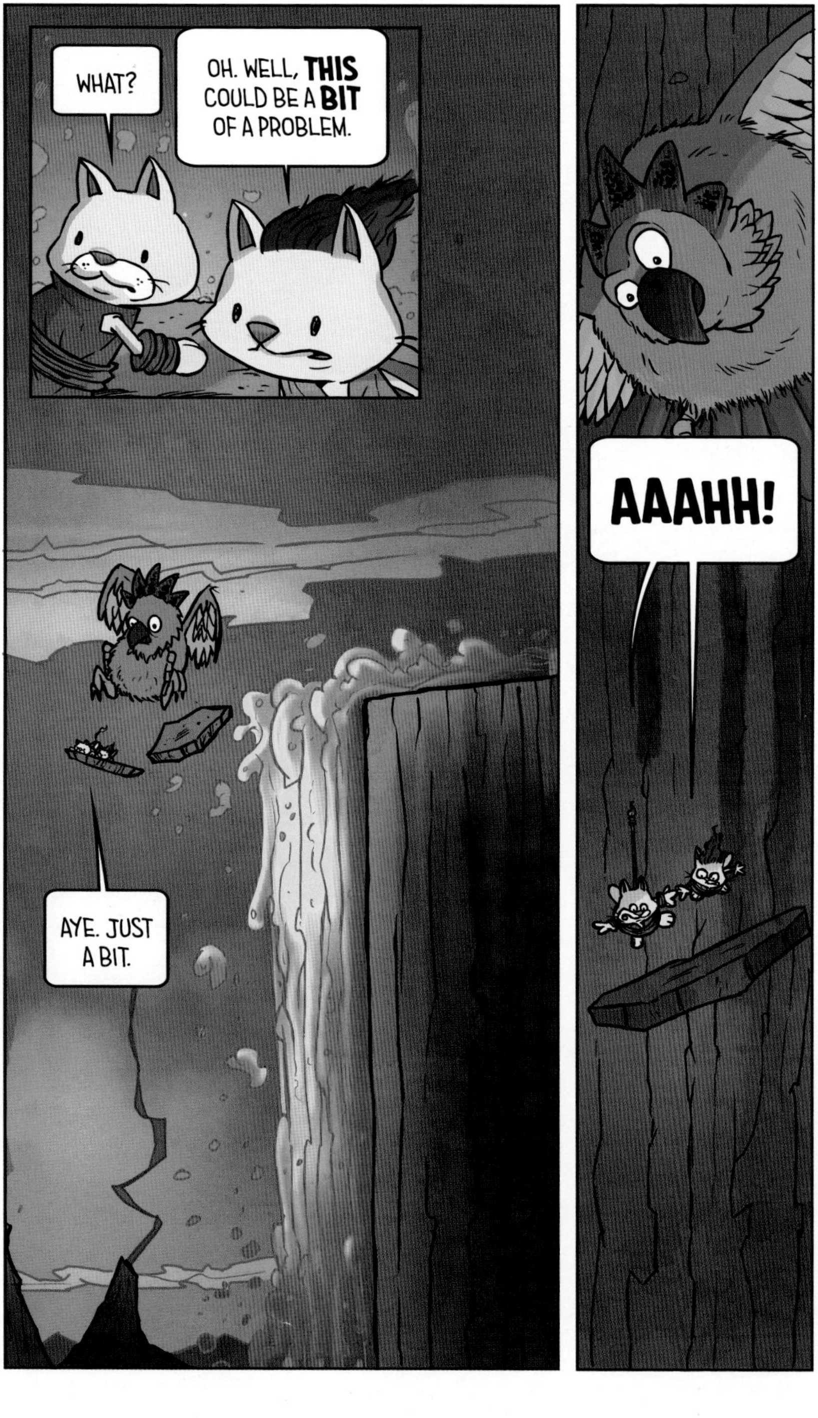
WHAT?
OH. WELL, **THIS** COULD BE A **BIT** OF A PROBLEM.
AYE. JUST A BIT.
AAAHH!

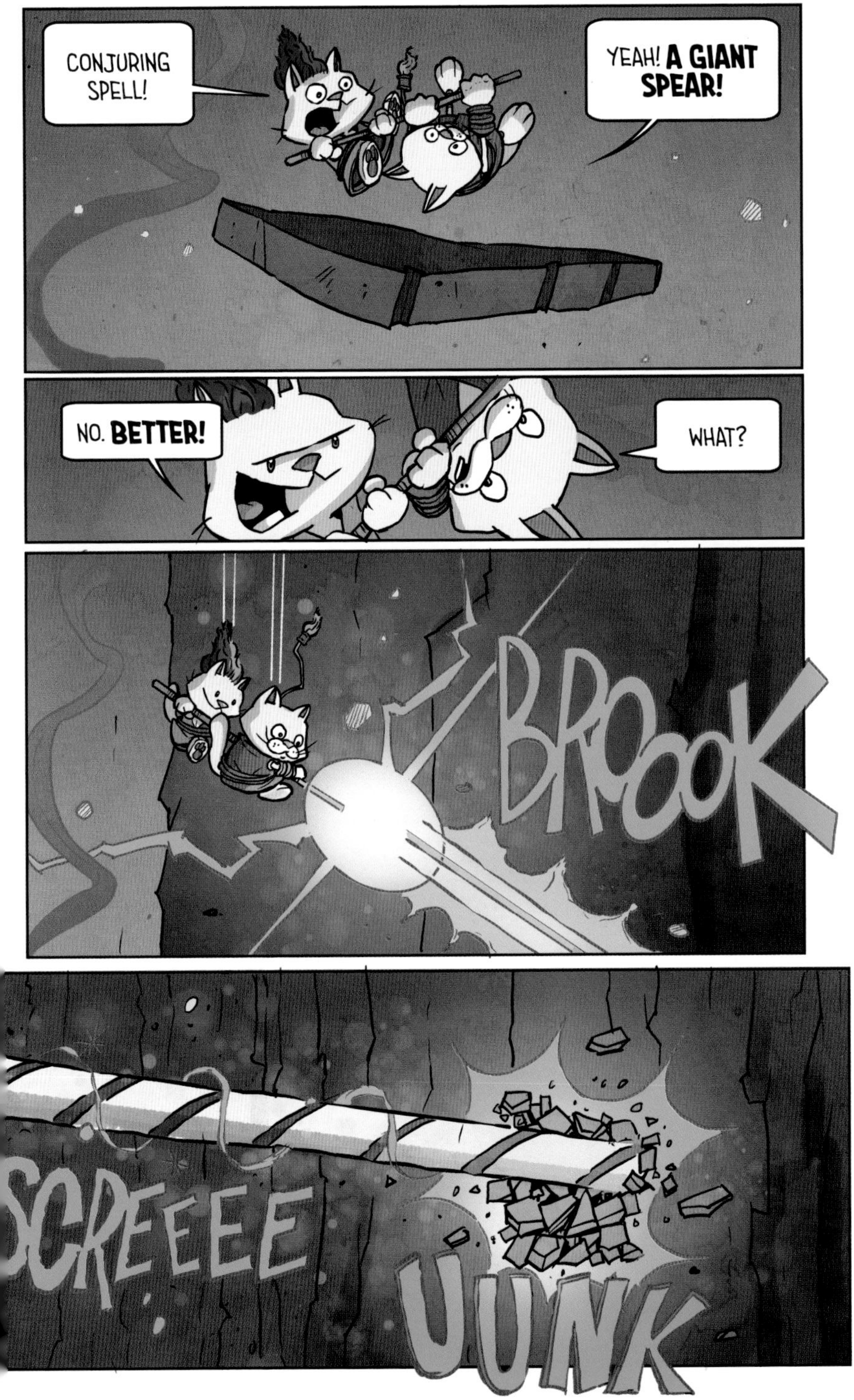
CONJURING SPELL!
YEAH! **A GIANT SPEAR!**
NO. **BETTER!**
WHAT?
BROOOK
SCREEEE
UUNK

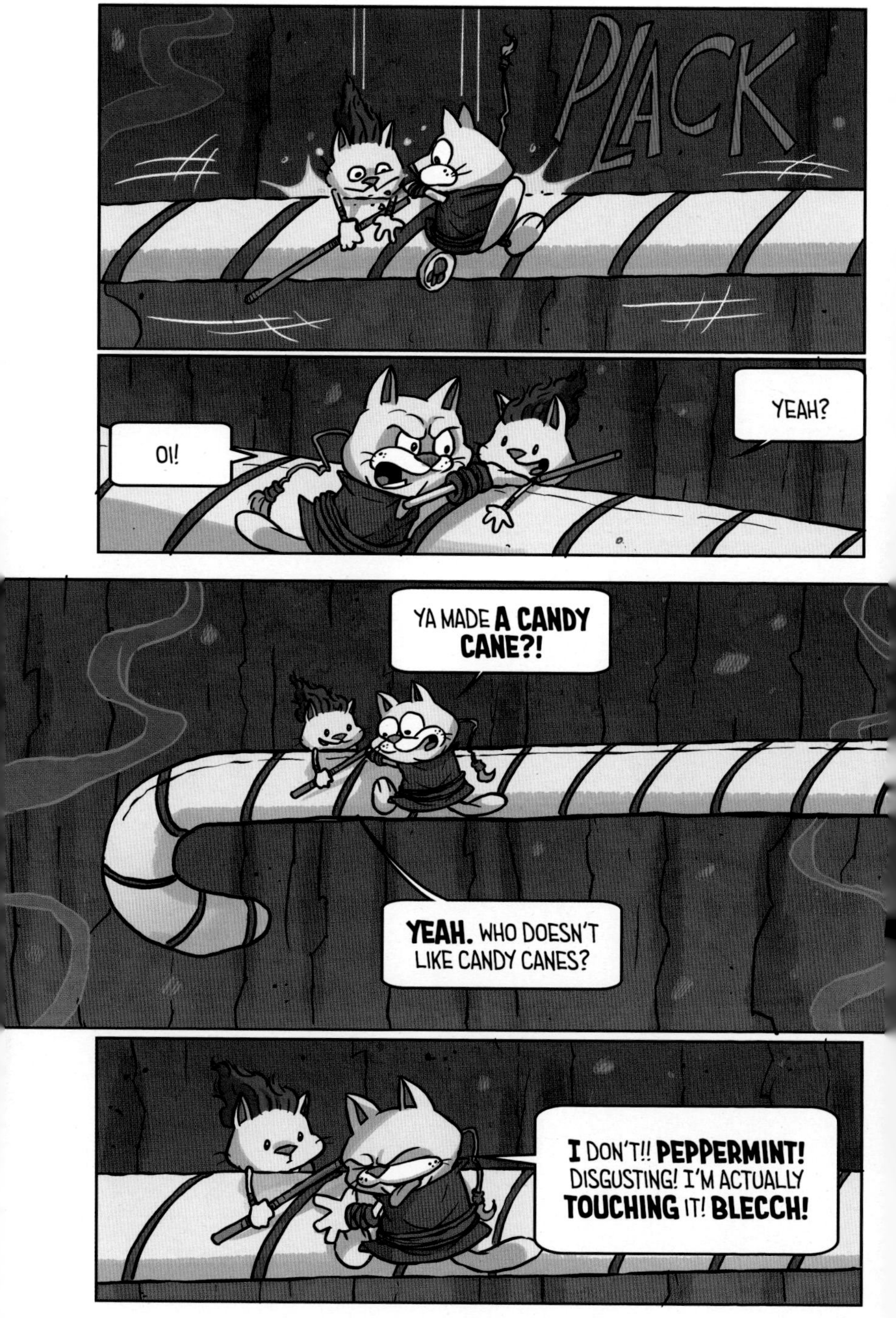
PLACK
OI!
YEAH?
YA MADE **A CANDY CANE?!**
YEAH. WHO DOESN'T LIKE CANDY CANES?
I DON'T!! **PEPPERMINT!** DISGUSTING! I'M ACTUALLY **TOUCHING** IT! **BLECCH!**

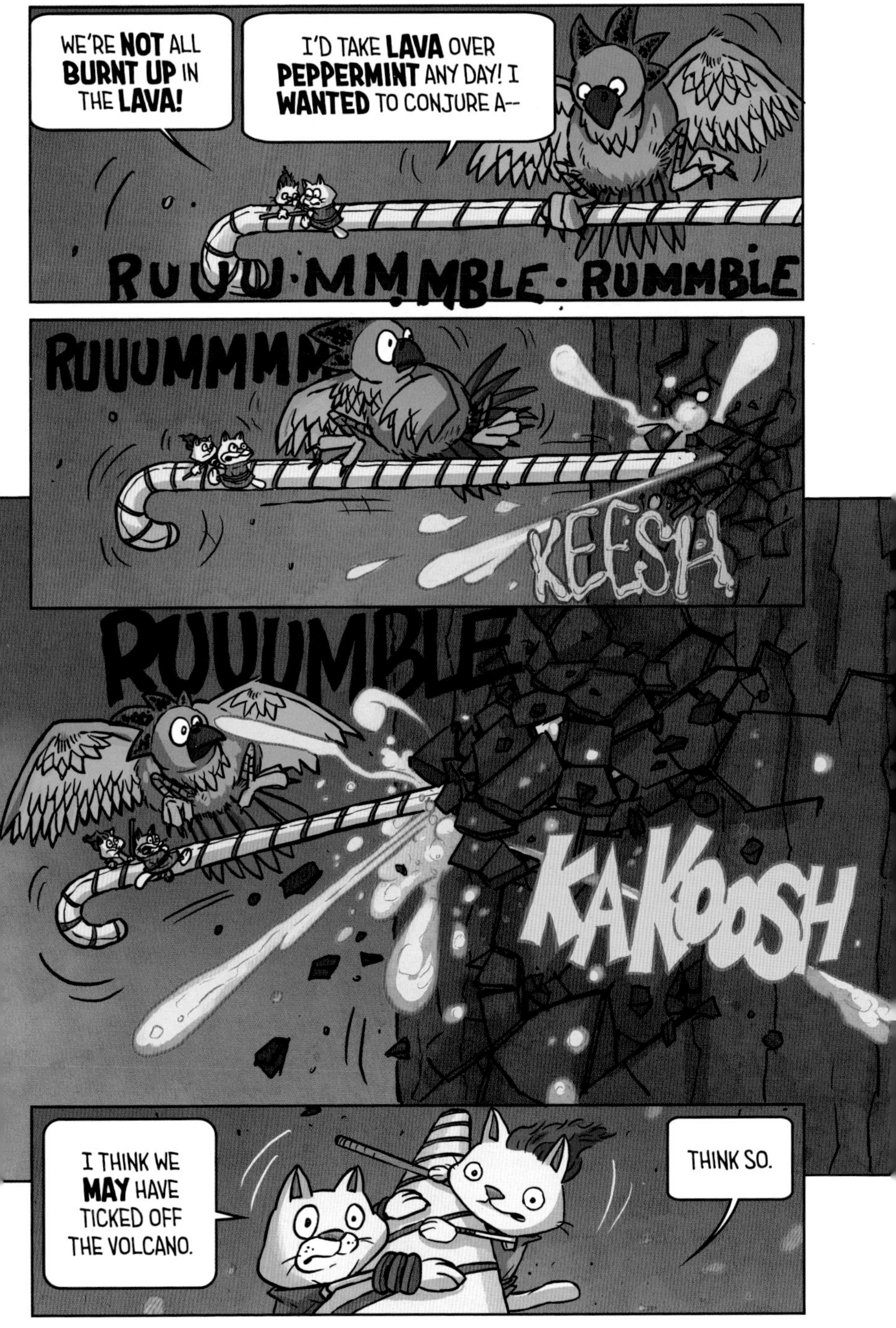
WE'RE NOT ALL BURNT UP IN THE LAVA!
I'D TAKE LAVA OVER PEPPERMINT ANY DAY! I WANTED TO CONJURE A--
RUUU·MMMBLE·RUMMBLE
RUUUMMM
KEESH
RUUUMBLE
KA-KOOSH
I THINK WE MAY HAVE TICKED OFF THE VOLCANO.
THINK SO.

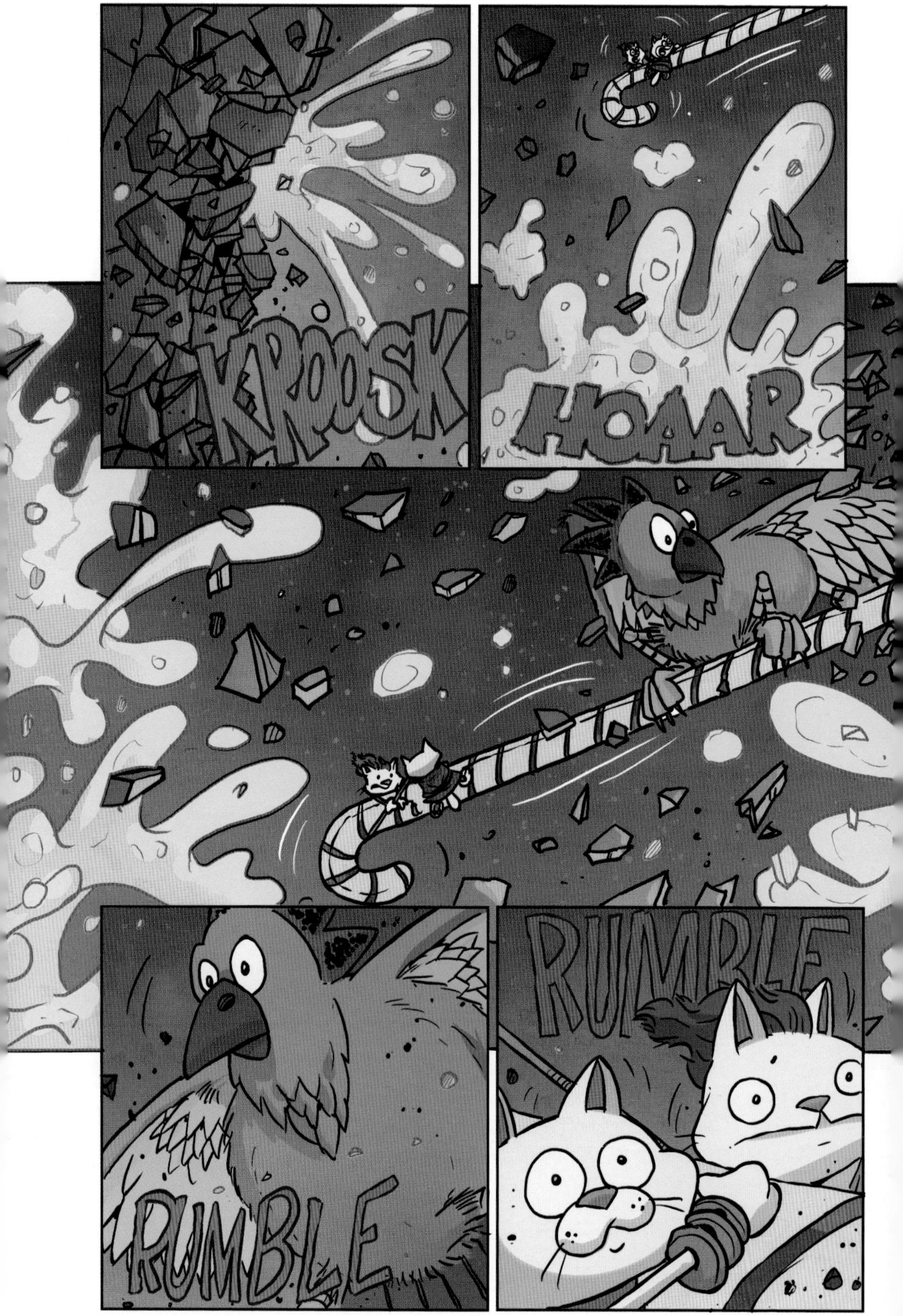
KROOSK
HOAAR
RUMBLE
RUMBLE

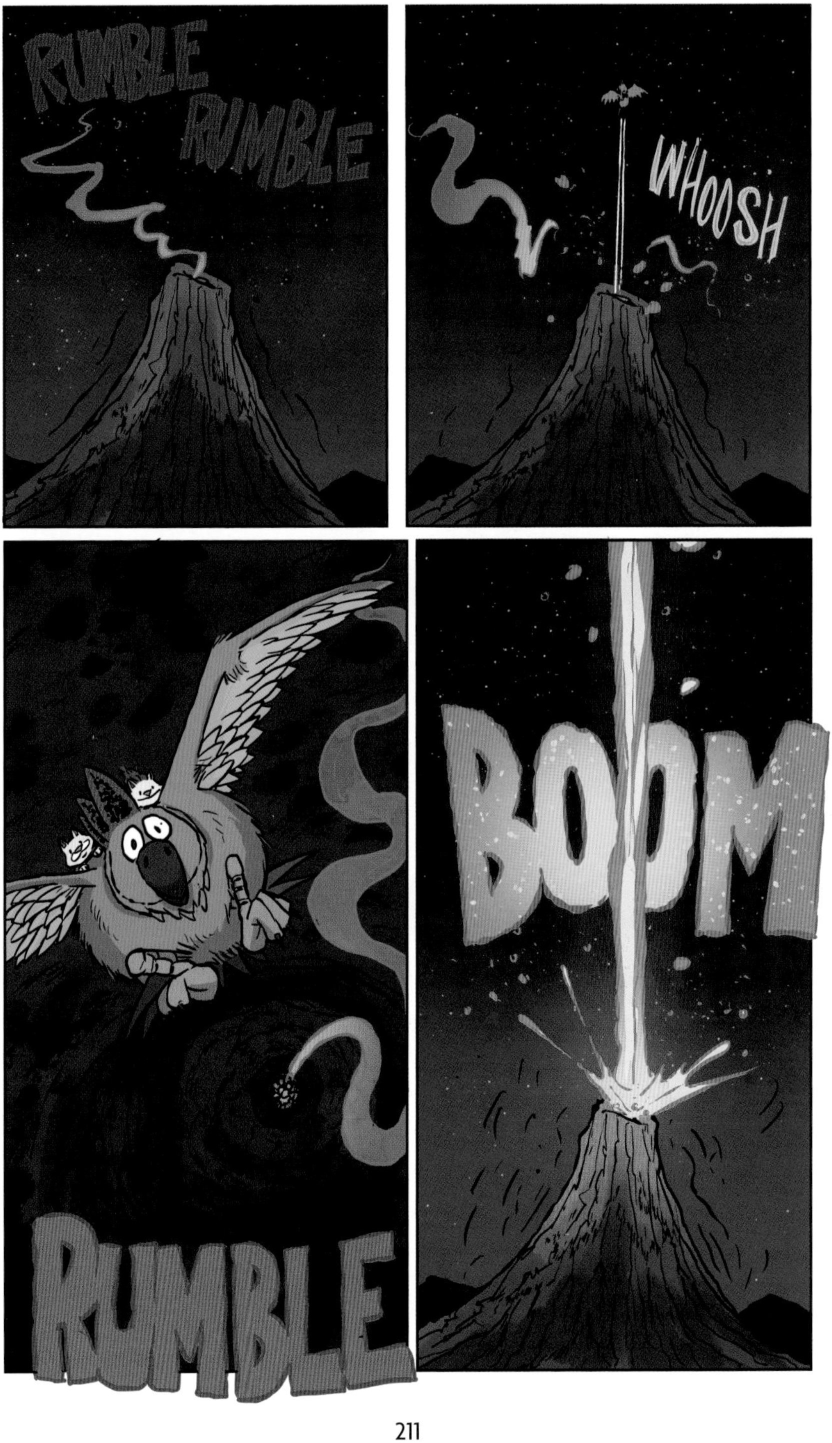
RUMBLE
RUMBLE
WHOOSH
RUMBLE
BOOM

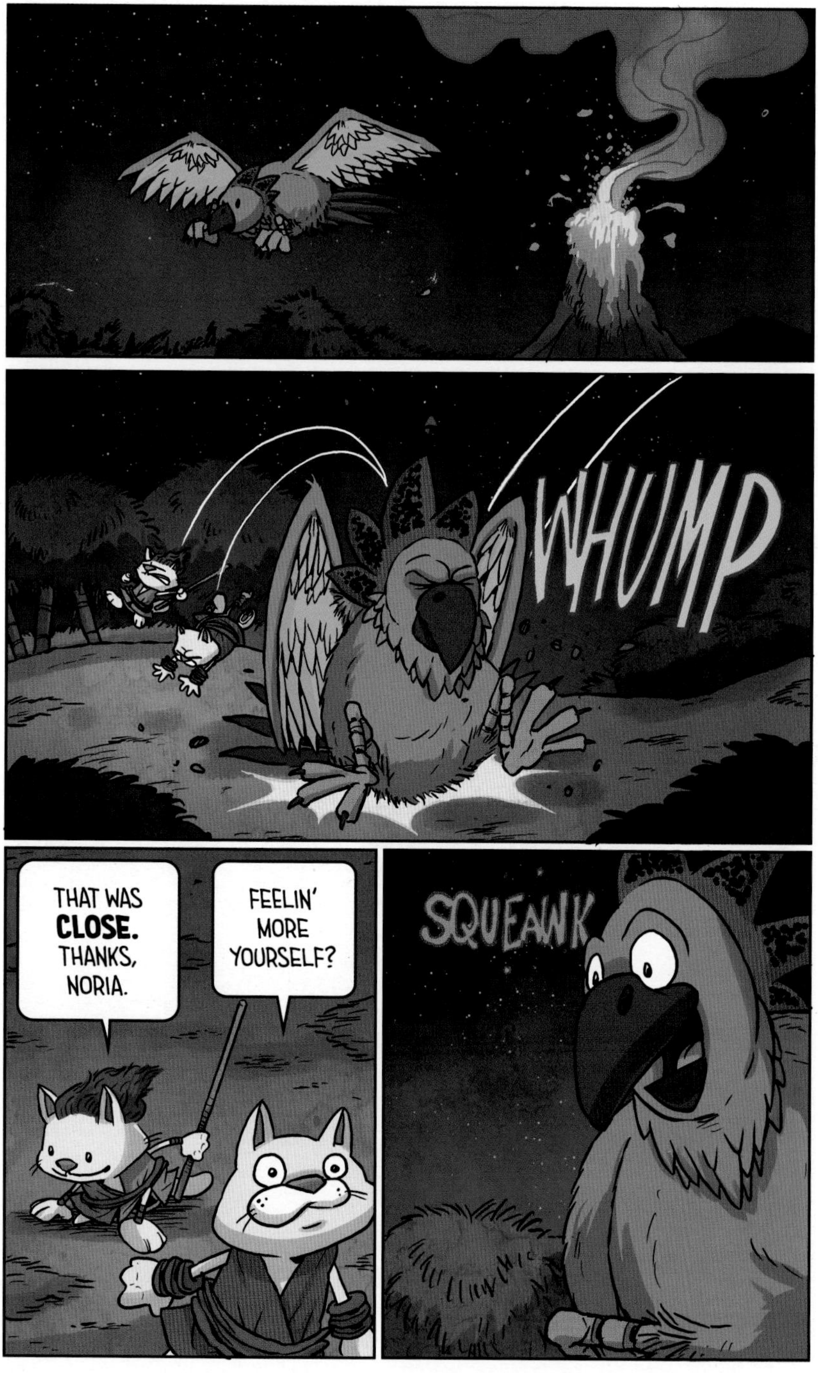
WHUMP
THAT WAS **CLOSE.** THANKS, NORIA.
FEELIN' MORE YOURSELF?
SQUEAWK

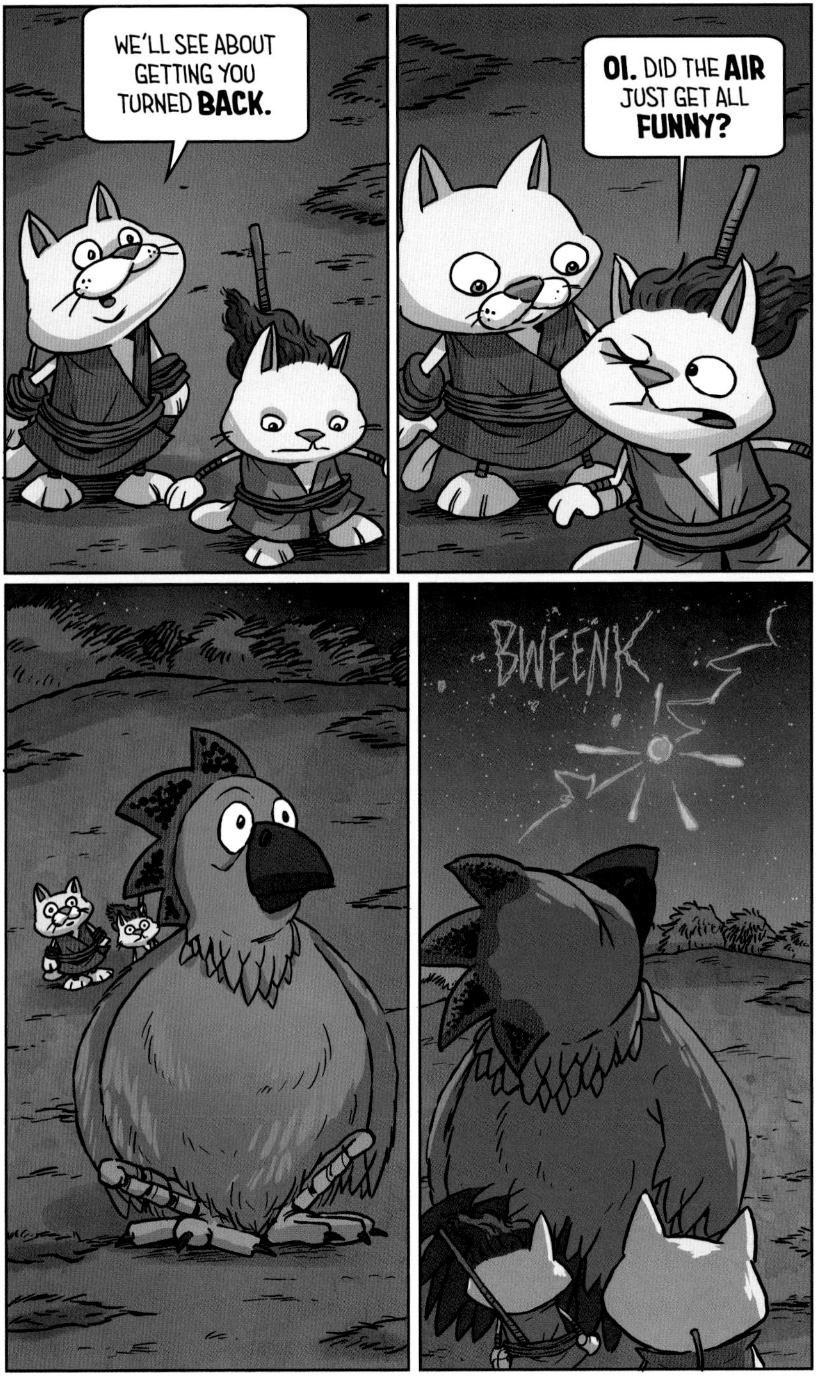
WE'LL SEE ABOUT GETTING YOU TURNED BACK.
OI. DID THE AIR JUST GET ALL FUNNY?
BWEENK

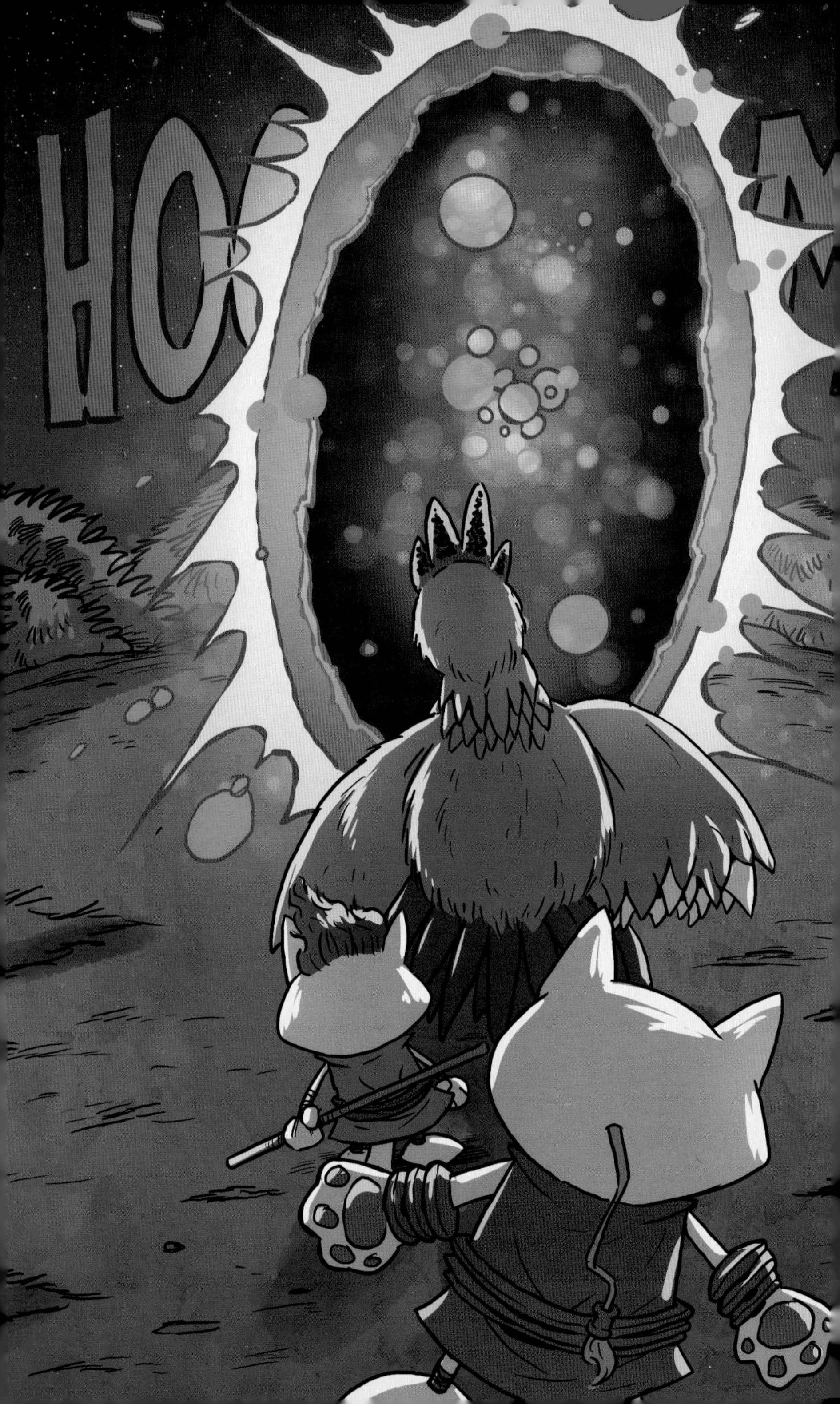

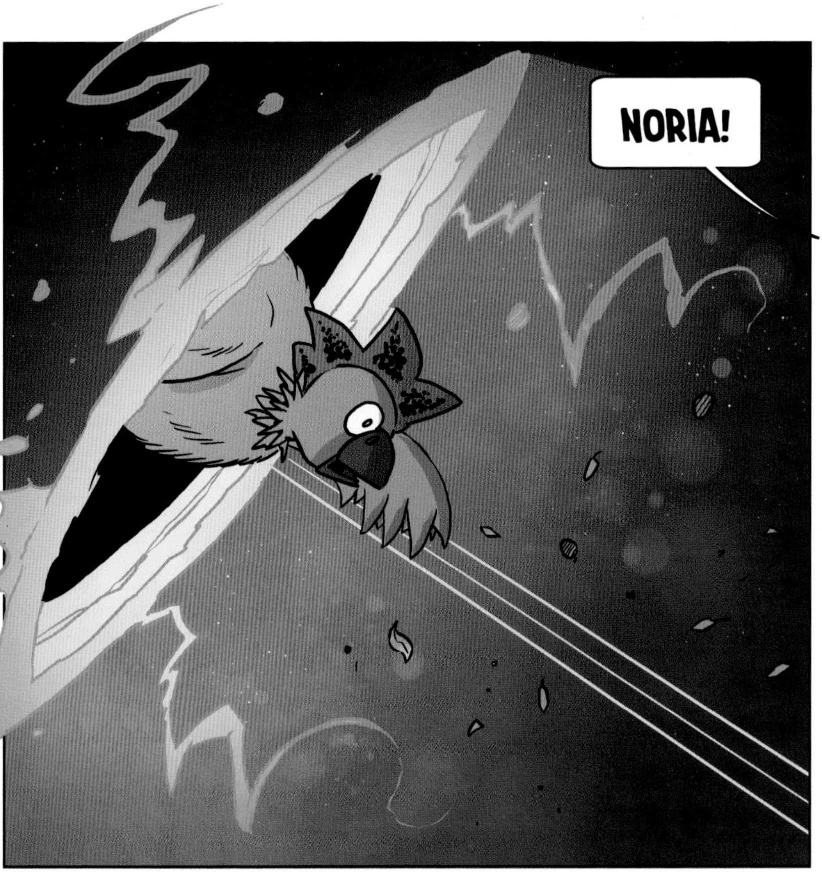
NORIA!

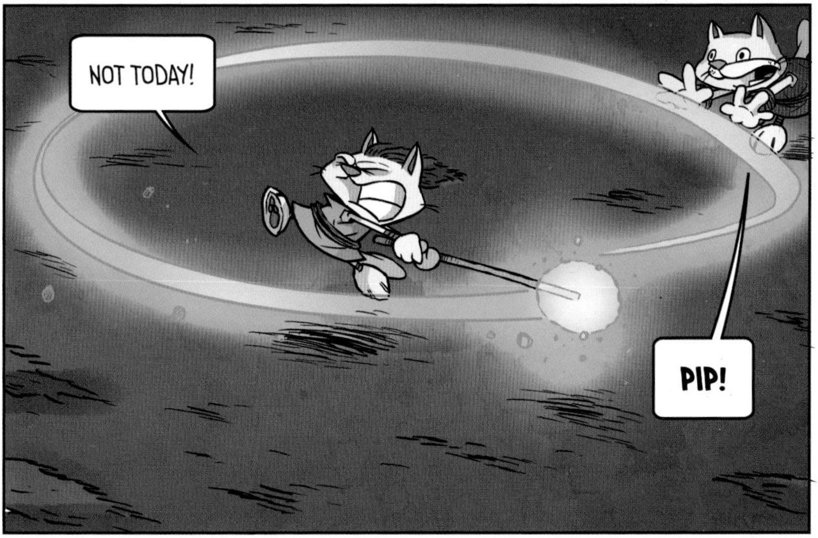
NOT TODAY!
PIP!

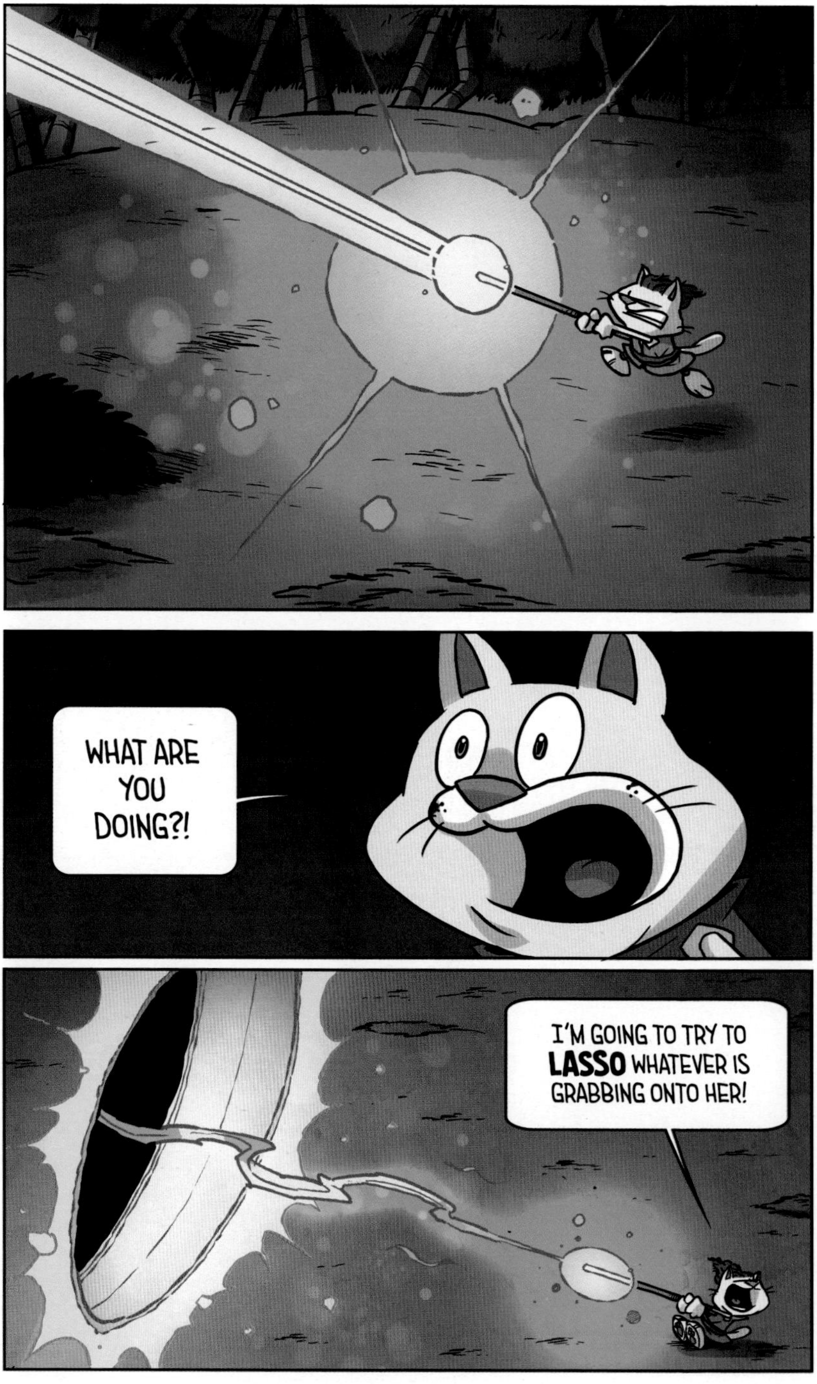
WHAT ARE YOU DOING?!
I'M GOING TO TRY TO **LASSO** WHATEVER IS GRABBING ONTO HER!

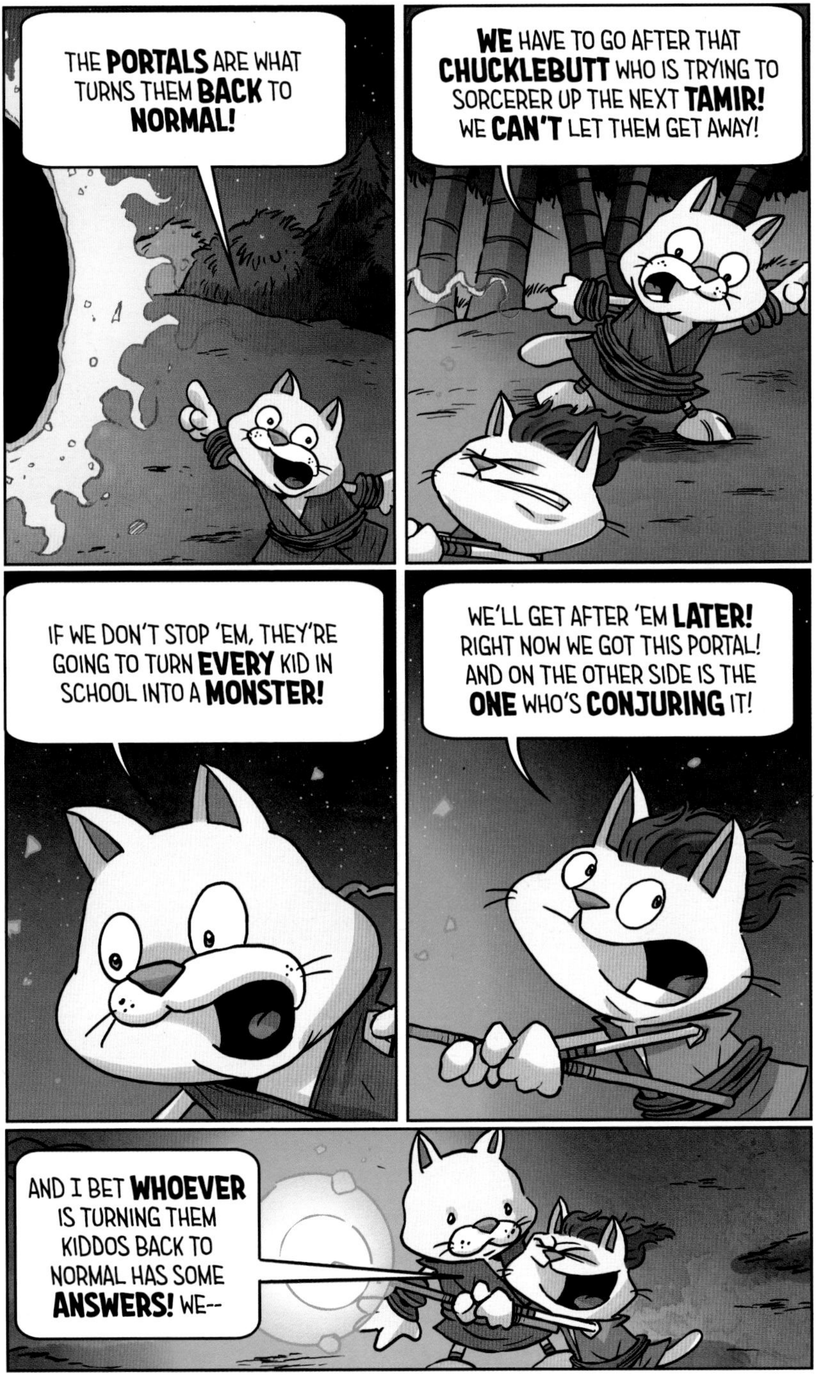
THE PORTALS ARE WHAT TURNS THEM BACK TO NORMAL!
WE HAVE TO GO AFTER THAT CHUCKLEBUTT WHO IS TRYING TO SORCERER UP THE NEXT TAMIR! WE CAN'T LET THEM GET AWAY!
IF WE DON'T STOP 'EM, THEY'RE GOING TO TURN EVERY KID IN SCHOOL INTO A MONSTER!
WE'LL GET AFTER 'EM LATER! RIGHT NOW WE GOT THIS PORTAL! AND ON THE OTHER SIDE IS THE ONE WHO'S CONJURING IT!
AND I BET WHOEVER IS TURNING THEM KIDDOS BACK TO NORMAL HAS SOME ANSWERS! WE--

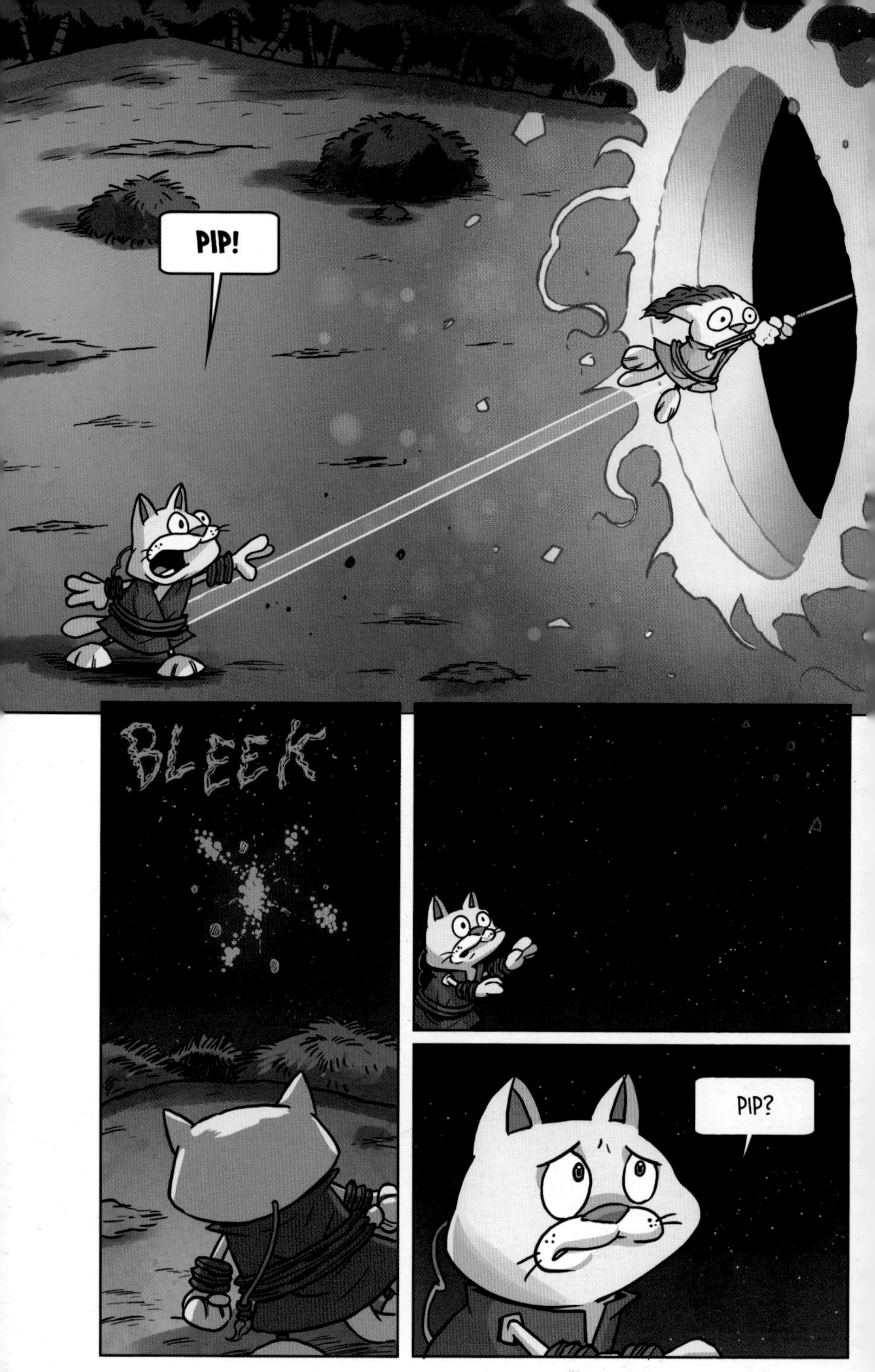
PIP!
BLEEK
PIP?

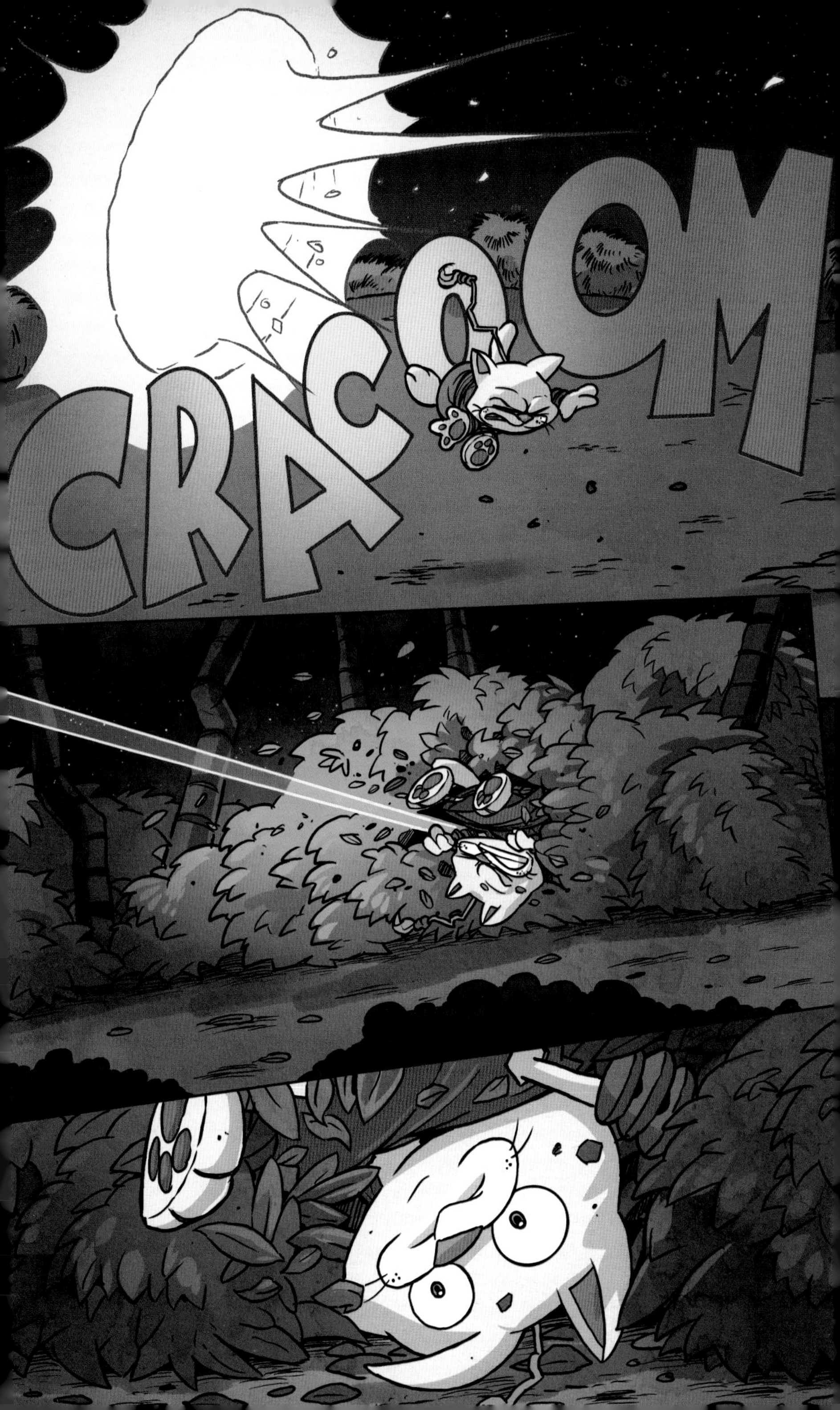
CRACOOM

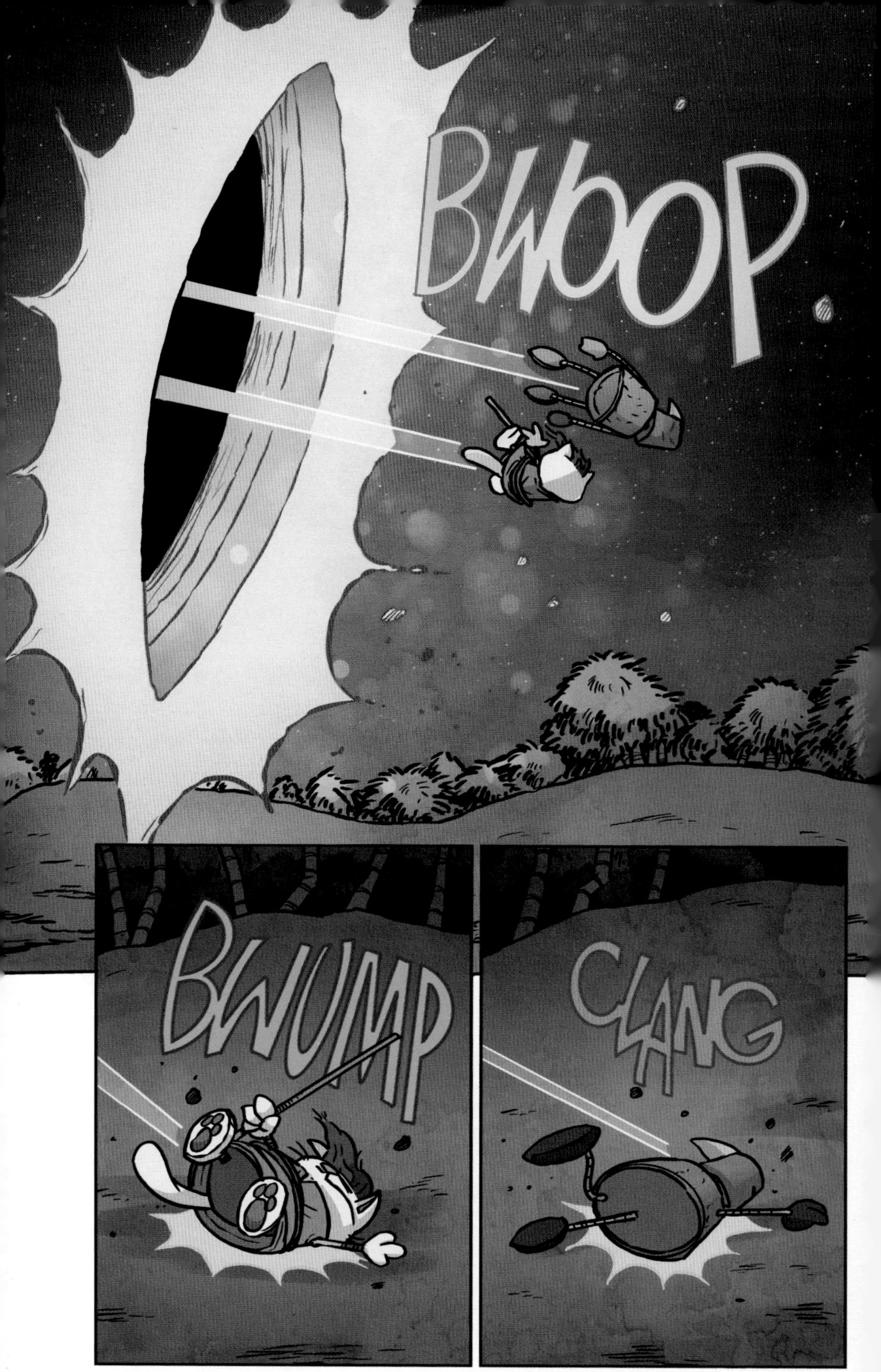
BWOOP
BWUMP
CLANG

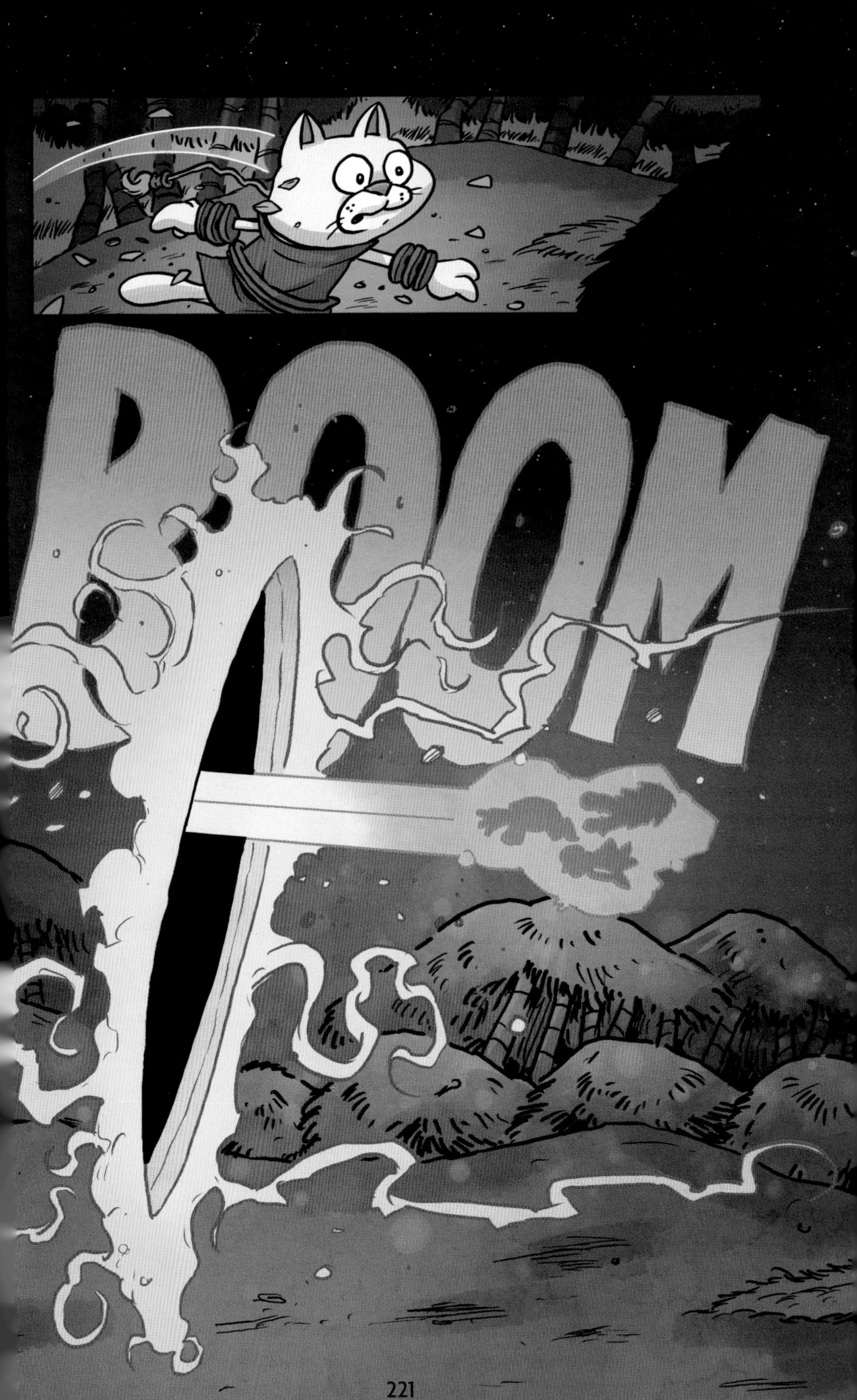
BOOM

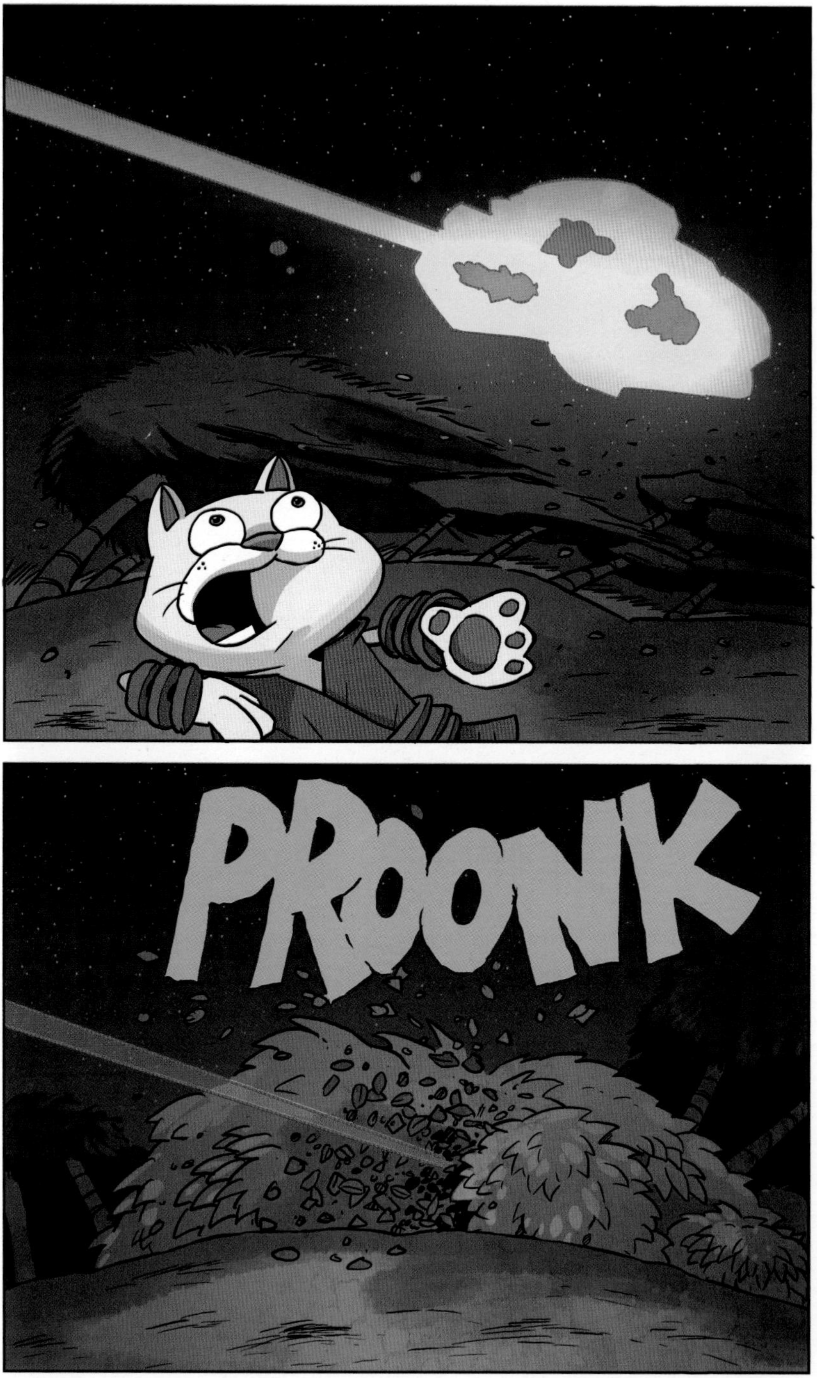
PROONK

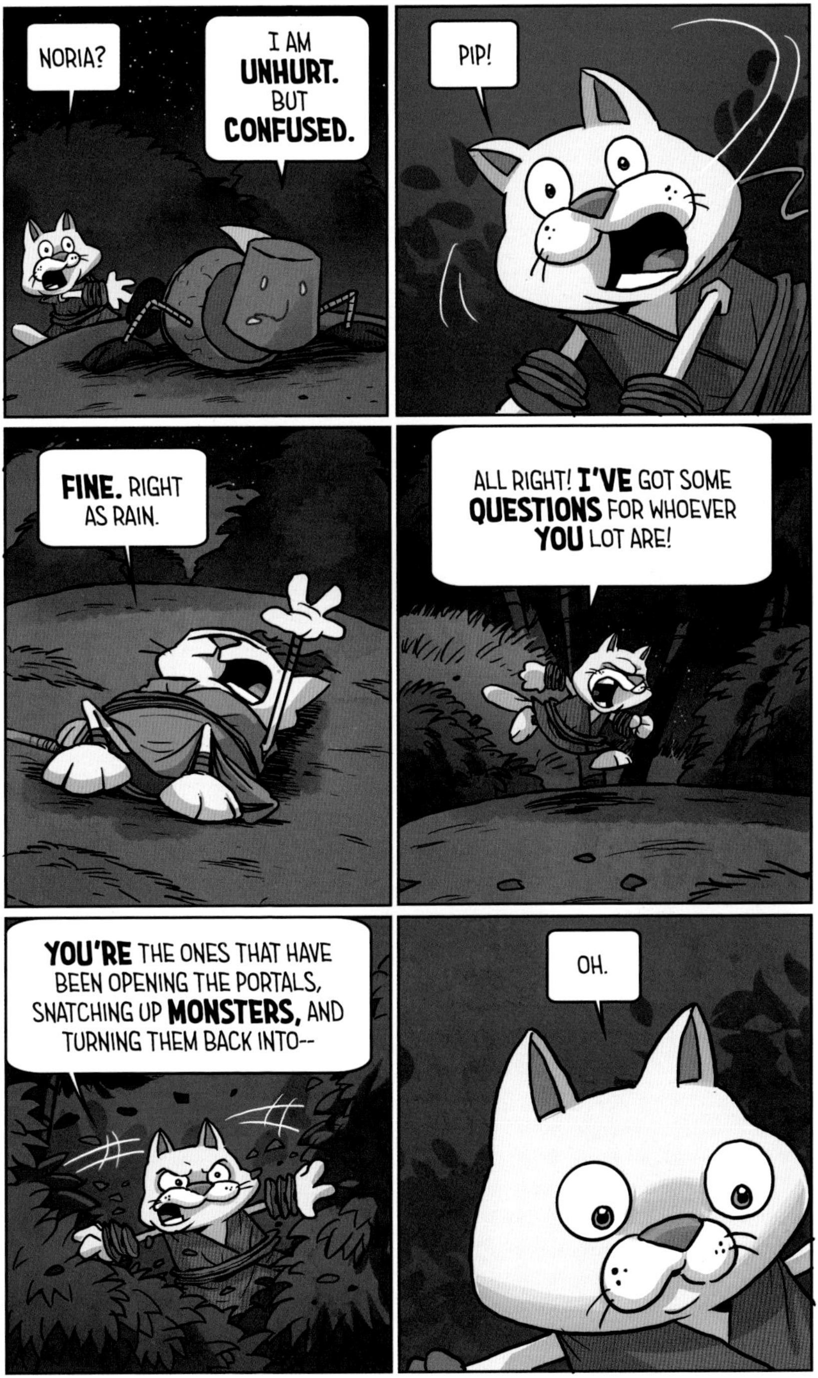
NORIA?
I AM UNHURT. BUT CONFUSED.
PIP!
FINE. RIGHT AS RAIN.
ALL RIGHT! I'VE GOT SOME QUESTIONS FOR WHOEVER YOU LOT ARE!
YOU'RE THE ONES THAT HAVE BEEN OPENING THE PORTALS, SNATCHING UP MONSTERS, AND TURNING THEM BACK INTO--
OH.

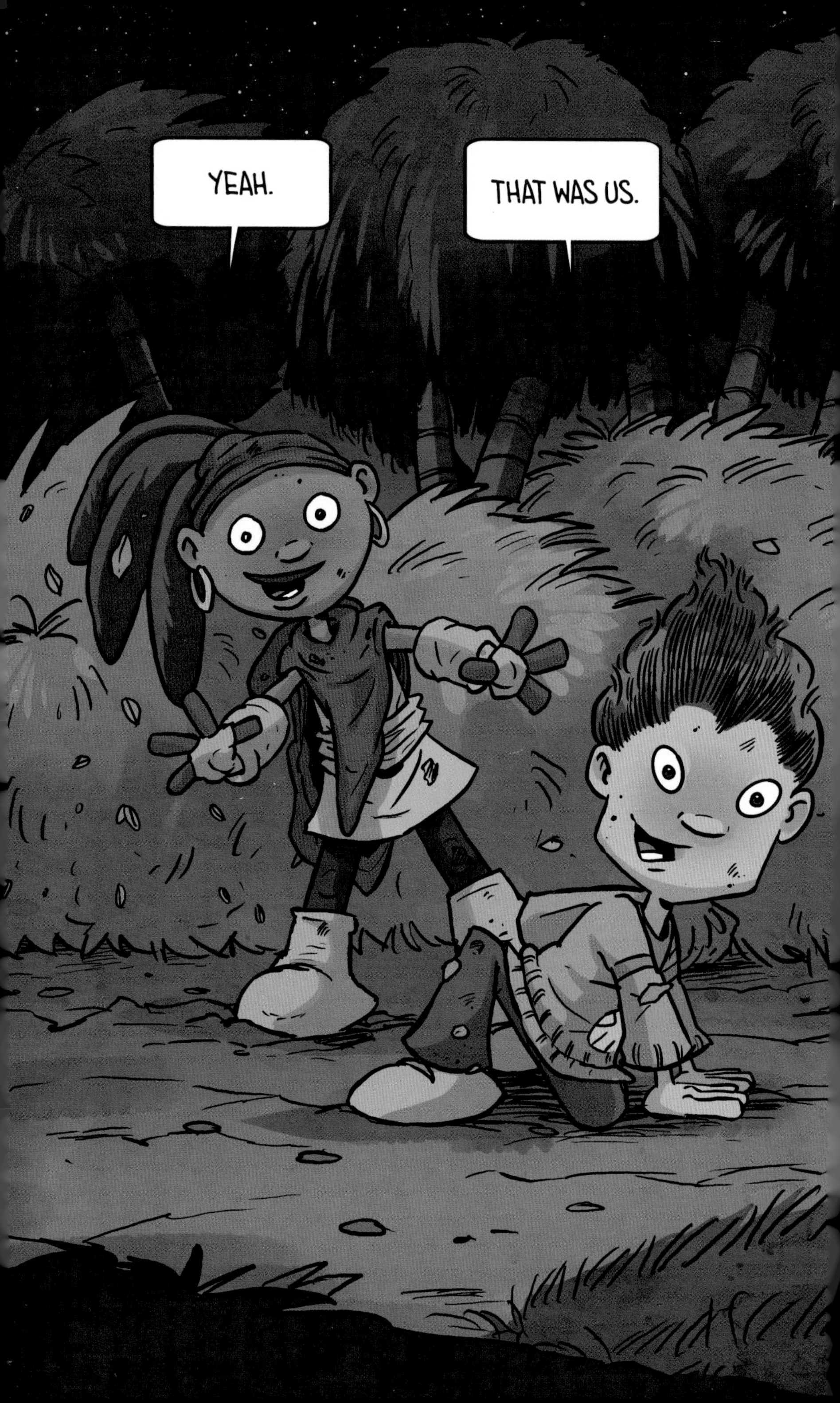
YEAH.
THAT WAS US.

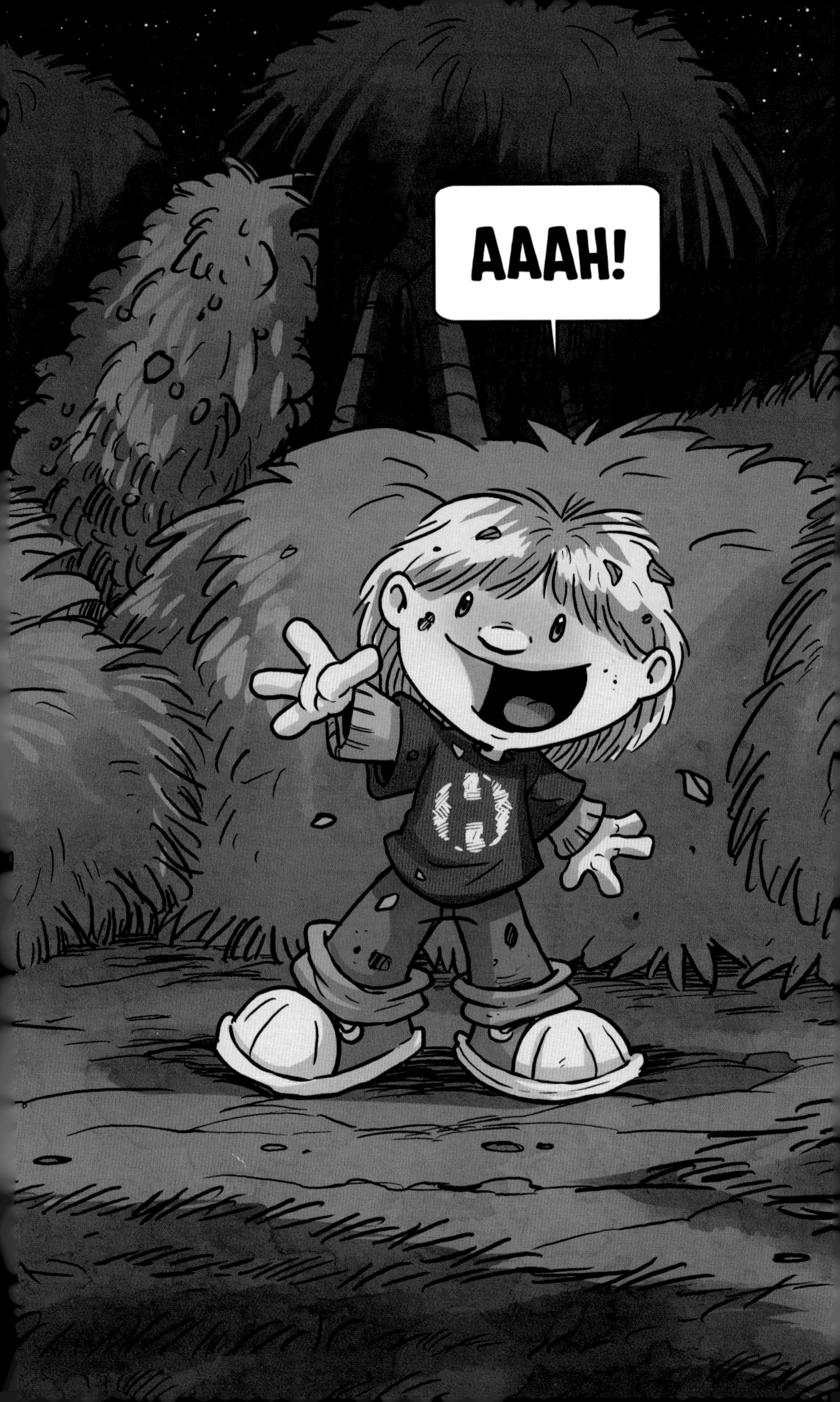
AAAH!

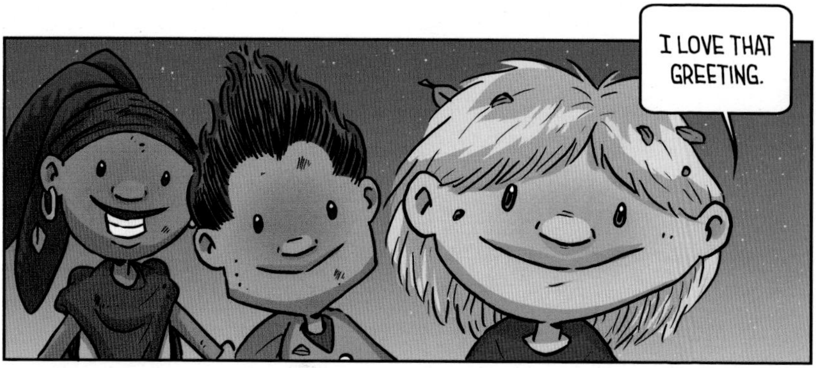
I LOVE THAT GREETING.

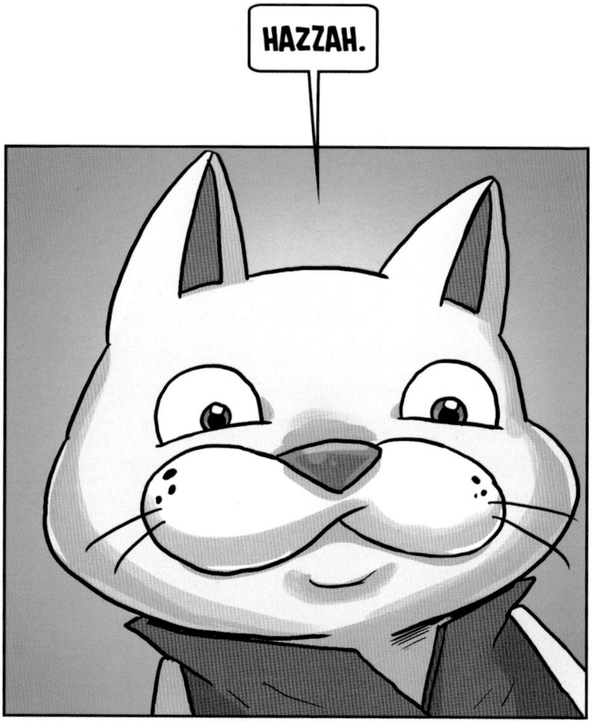
HAZZAH.

END OF BOOK TEN.

Find out what happens next in—

HiLo

THE GREAT SPACE IGUANA

Coming in 2025!

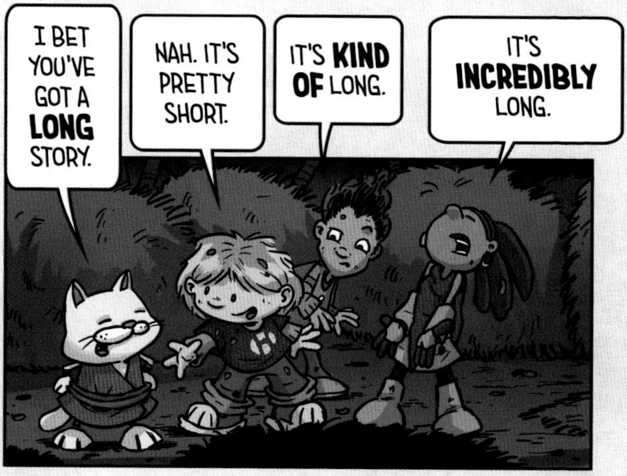
I BET YOU'VE GOT A **LONG** STORY.
NAH. IT'S PRETTY SHORT.
IT'S **KIND OF** LONG.
IT'S **INCREDIBLY** LONG.

The Hilo Bunch

JUDD WINICK is the creator of the award-winning, **New York Times** bestselling Hilo series. Judd grew up on Long Island with a healthy diet of doodling, **X-Men** comics, the newspaper strip **Bloom County,** and **Looney Tunes.** Today, he lives in San Francisco with his wife, Pam Ling; their two kids; their cats, Troy and Abed; and far too many action figures and vinyl toys for a normal adult. Judd created the Cartoon Network series **Juniper Lee;** has written superhero comics, including Batman, Green Lantern, and Green Arrow; and was a cast member of MTV's **The Real World: San Francisco.** Judd is also the author of the highly acclaimed graphic novel **Pedro and Me,** about his **Real World** roommate and friend, AIDS activist Pedro Zamora. Visit Judd and Hilo online at juddspillowfort.com or find him on Twitter at @JuddWinick.

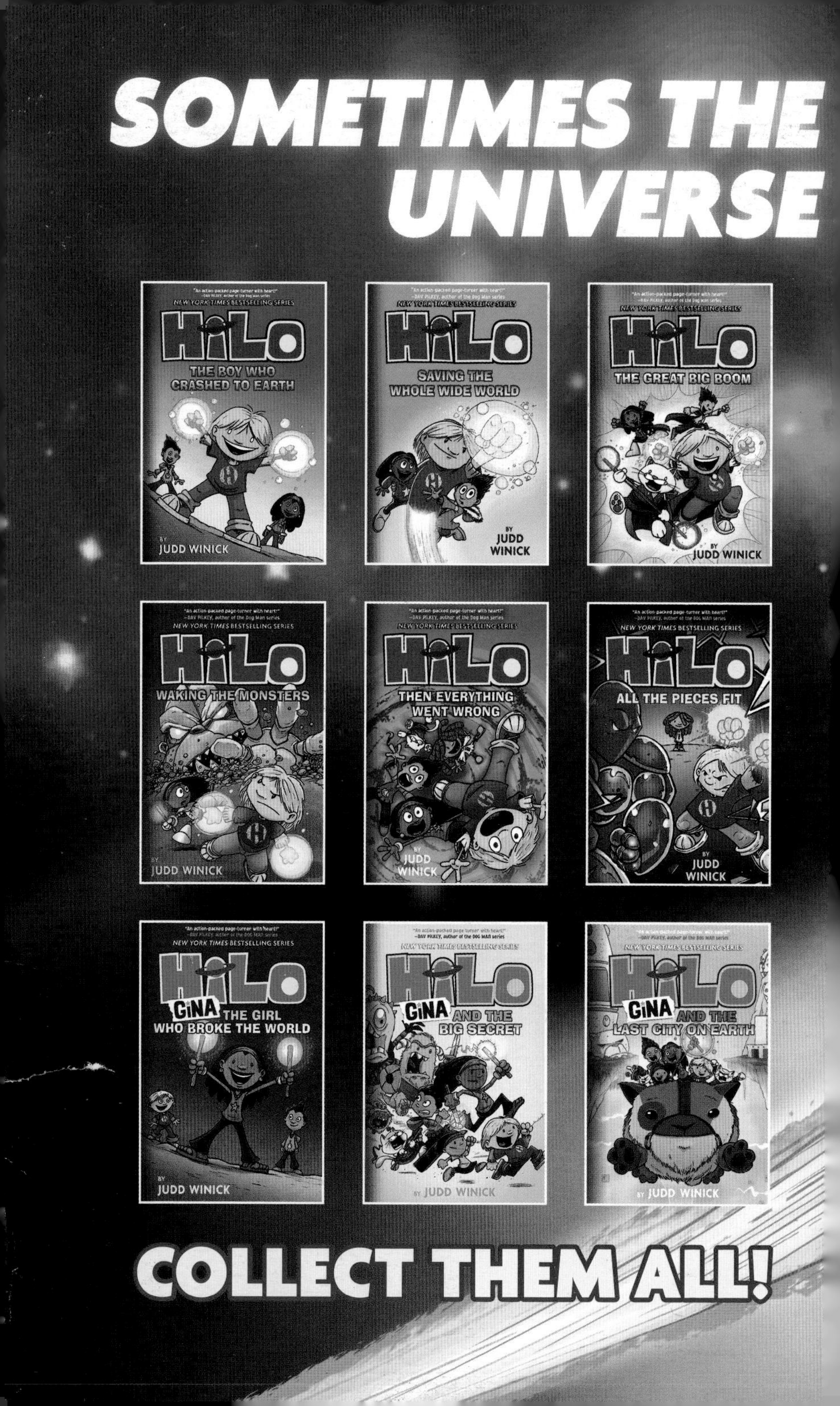
SOMETIMES THE UNIVERSE
HILO THE BOY WHO CRASHED TO EARTH
BY JUDD WINICK
HILO SAVING THE WHOLE WIDE WORLD
BY JUDD WINICK
HILO THE GREAT BIG BOOM
BY JUDD WINICK
HILO WAKING THE MONSTERS
BY JUDD WINICK
HILO THEN EVERYTHING WENT WRONG
BY JUDD WINICK
HILO ALL THE PIECES FIT
BY JUDD WINICK
HILO GINA THE GIRL WHO BROKE THE WORLD
BY JUDD WINICK
HILO GINA AND THE BIG SECRET
BY JUDD WINICK
HILO GINA AND THE LAST CITY ON EARTH
BY JUDD WINICK
COLLECT THEM ALL!